DATE DUE

DEC 7 2009		
DEC 2 2 2009		
JAN 1 1 2010		
APR - 2 2010		

Demco

Mariposa

Mariposa

Greg Bear

Vanguard Press
The Perseus Books Group

Published by Vanguard Press
A Member of the Perseus Books Group

Set in 10.5-point Palatino

Cataloging-in-Publication data for this book is available from the
Library of Congress.
ISBN: 978-1-59315-497-4

Vanguard Press books are available at special discounts for bulk
purchases in the U.S. by corporations, institutions, and other
organizations. For more information, please contact the Special
Markets Department at the Perseus Books Group, 2300 Chestnut
Street, Suite 200, Philadelphia, PA 19103, or call (800) 810-4145,
ext. 5000, or e-mail special.markets@perseusbooks.com.

10 9 8 7 6 5 4 3 2 1

To Diane and David Clark,
profiles in courage

Washington, D.C.
Number One Observatory Circle

Official Residence of the
Vice President of the United States

Edward Benjamin Quinn wiped his hand on a towel and stood back to survey the damage.

The woman on the floor had a slight pulse and was still breathing, but with a slow, jerked rhythm. Soft brown hair fanned in a dark halo around her contorted face.

Irreparable.

He knew a thousand ways he could have killed her outright, and so he must have decided he was going to let her live a little longer. The question was why, of course. He and Beth-Anne hadn't argued. He wasn't drunk, he didn't feel crazy, he wasn't even upset—and he didn't think he had been drugged.

He felt fine, better than fine; he felt strong, justified, square with the big-all world. Without guilt, you learn the quality of your soul. Cross that border and you learn what you are really capable of.

There would be consequences, of course.

Outside, the president was still in the hospital, recovering from three bullets. It had happened in Dallas, of all places. Fortunately she was out of the woods—out of the hospital and out of Dallas—and able to make decisions, but for eight hours Eddie Quinn had been president. Under the circumstances he did not enjoy that honor, but nothing had gone so wrong that he needed to do this.

He couldn't feel the love or the excitement he and Beth-Anne had once known, but that didn't seem reason enough, either.

He walked into the bathroom and inspected the folds of his robe for blood. After washing his hands, he returned to pick up the towel and toss it into the laundry hamper. While he was making this circuit, Beth-Anne stopped breathing. For that he was grateful.

"You're one screwed-up bastard, Eddie," he said.

If this had happened during the eight hours he had been president . . .

"Whoa."

A full-length mirror hung on the back on the bathroom door. He let his robe fall around his broad shoulders and looked at himself as if for the first time. His was still a strong body, with thick, strong arms and short, powerful legs. A paunch had settled over his stomach, from years on the campaign trail and sitting rather than pumping iron and running. Hairs curled around his back, forested his arms, and almost hid the long, coiled scar that stretched from his neck down his right arm. A nice bit of needlework, that. A good stitch. A man's blast-sharpened rib had once stuck out of his chest, just below the clavicle. The hair on his abdomen pointed toward midline and navel, monkey's fur silky and thick. Another scar coiled there, pink and bald, like a burrowing pink centipede. He could almost imagine it creeping under his flesh. It was that vivid, almost pleasant to think about. More pleasant than remembering how the scar got there. The suicide bomber had actually *bitten* him. Fragments of exploded mandible. Hard to forget things like that, very hard: but he had gotten treatment and it had worked, hadn't it?

Then why this?

He tied the robe shut and sat on the edge of the antique maple-frame bed where he and Beth-Anne had made their last child, Jacob, now nine months old, asleep down the hall in the bedroom that he shared with his sister Carina. It was the nanny's night off.

Carina, eight years old, adored her new brother. In a few minutes, Edward would go in and read her a bedtime story.

On the nightstand, his security badge beeped. The house monitored it all. The children's clothing, furniture, and bedding were tagged with small sensors, but he and his wife had chosen to keep their privacy—except when wearing the badges. Still, the house knew something bad had happened. The Secret Service would be here in a few minutes.

One thing at a time.

He walked slowly down the hall to the children's bedroom, arms out like a bird, face creased by a quizzical frown. Pushing open the heavy wooden door, he smiled at Carina where she sat in the outer nimbus of her ceramic moon-glow lamp. He leaned over the crib to check on Jacob—mostly asleep and beautiful—then stooped to pick up *The House on Pooh Corner* and resume where they had left off the night before.

A lovely peace descended upon Eddie Quinn. The promise of Mariposa held true even now—no guilt, no borders, the past wiped away.

It was so rare that he had time to spend with his family.

2

FBI Academy
Quantico, Virginia

William Griffin walked across the concrete to the Jefferson building, footsteps echoing in the eerie morning quiet. The air smelled sweet and cool. A few green-brown leaves whispered past in a gritty swirl between the towers.

The sun cast a long, flicking shadow.

The old FBI Academy in Quantico—the Q—was practically empty. Just a few administrative offices remained, everything else boarded up, mothballed, or on the move to Alameda, where the jewel in Hoover's tarnished tiara was supposedly being reanimated—if congress approved a massive appropriation. Twenty-five billion dollars. But that was looking less and less likely, stalling the Bureau's transfer indefinitely.

For the moment, that was its name—simply the Bureau.

The Academy buildings had suffered neglect: peeling paint and cracked concrete, patchy brown lawns on the surrounding low slopes, varmint mounds and runnels everywhere. Last year, movers had hauled away the monuments to 9/11 and 10/4, the simple black stone replica of New York's twin towers, rising from a Pentagon base, and a donut of twisted steel from the Seattle ferry *Duwamish*. The *Duwamish* had been blown up not by Muslim terrorists but by a demented creep from Missouri, infuriated by gay marriage.

All the old signs had been covered with plastic or pulled out, leaving pits in the walls.

For now, the Bureau was divided like the Roman Empire of old into East and West: two competing directors, two budgets, and next to no money.

Another day older and deeper in debt.

A tall, graying security guard unlocked the heavy glass door as he approached. "You know where to go, Agent Griffin," the guard said. "Don't get lost Mr. Hoover's still spookin' around. I hear he's been getting the goods on a few devils, kicking butt and takin' names."

William chuckled. "What's he got on you, Clarence?"

"The *ladies*, my man." Clarence winked. "Sleek, smart ladies in tight-fittin' power suits. Black or white, Hispanic or Asian, I love 'em all."

"And they love you."

"No time, and still I wish they was more!" Clarence called after him.

While the investigative divisions of other agencies—ATF, Homeland Security, Diplomatic Security, Treasury, even the IRS and the Postal Service—had been happy to suck up some high-profile, high-publicity cases, none had the forensic expertise or the laboratory throughput, and crime never slept.

Nobody knew how that song would end.

Much of top FBI management had evacuated to sunnier positions, leaving behind a few dedicated souls and some spectacular incompetents. William was fortunate that his boss, Alicia Kunsler, fell into the first category.

He hung a left past the broad conversation pit, empty but for two upended couches and rolls of old carpet, and walked along a hallway now bereft of J. Edgar Hoover's favorite pastoral prints. Just a long row of rectangles on a sunned and peeling wall.

Kunsler kept her lonely office at the end of an empty corridor. The overhead lights had been dimmed or removed, but the glow from her half open door guided him around an abandoned desk, a few old gray steel swivel chairs, a tied stack of cardboard, and a bin filled with newspaper clippings someone had deemed unnecessary.

William wondered how much history had already been lost.

Brain transplant. That's what the fetch bloggers called the move to Alameda. *Zombie Bureau. Shoot it in the head and put it out of its misery.*

Serve it right for surveilling Martin Luther King Jr., John Lennon, the Dalai Lama, and, of course—at the request of a former Attorney General, now serving time in Cumberland federal prison—for keeping extensive "Patriot" files on the current president of the United States, the Senate Majority Leader, the Speaker of the House, and six ranking senators.

Burn the old FBI, then jolt it back to life on the operating table of national bankruptcy.

William knocked lightly on the jamb. Kunsler saw his shadow in the doorway, held up a long, thin index finger, then crooked it—come in—and resumed typing in the empty air over her desk. An angular, black-haired woman of forty-one with a hook nose, big hands, and small, dark, intelligent eyes, she sat behind an old avocado-green steel desk, staring through a pair of projector glasses—her spex—and air-typing on a virtual keyboard, fingers jabbing two inches above the antique blotter.

William sat.

Kunsler had proved herself a master at gathering power and influence in a vacuum. After the firing of four directors in the last two years, she had assumed the task of deputy director of the Bureau in Transition East, or BITE, and had moved into this old, stripped-down room in a deserted, musty building filled with unhappy ghosts.

Not the sort of woman—nor the sort of agency, now—that William had thought would have the balls to conduct a months-long, clandestine investigation into the doings of one of the most powerful and secretive men on the planet.

She finished tapping her line, pulled off her spex, and focused full attention on him. "Tell me something cheerful," she said in a small, precise voice.

William sat. "The president has relieved her Secret Service detail."

"Do you blame her?" Kunsler asked.

"She's considering hiring Talos executive security to protect her."

Kunsler sniffed. "I've asked to meet with her twice—and been refused both times."

"Daniel Haze went to congress asking them to override the hire. They can't, of course."

Haze was director of the Secret Service—one of the branches competing with the Bureau for funding and cases.

"The fox will be in the cluck house," Kunsler said. "I'm not feeling the cheer, Agent Griffin. Price's octopus arms are slithering through every branch of government, and I know that bastard is about to make his move. I just wish I knew what it was."

"What about Nabokov?"

This was the code name for an agent who had already spent a year in Lion City, infiltrated into Talos. Kunsler told William what she thought he needed to know, and nothing more.

"On schedule. He's going to have to act fast, though. Someone's spreading manure. Price hires a lot of retired agents."

Kunsler took a zip page out of her desk drawer and passed it across. "I'd like you to look into this personally," she said. "Keep you busy until we know what's up with Nabokov. It's a long shot, but it feels hinky.

"Price put four million dollars into the research of a scientist named Plover—some kind of pharmaceutical wizard. Plover started with cancer drugs, then expanded into a new field called EGCT—epigenetic glial cell therapy. Does that mean Price or someone near him has cancer? If so, they're shit out of luck. Plover's foundation in Baltimore reported he left the premises last week with two and a half million in grant money . . . They have no idea where he absconded to. I like that word, *absconded*, don't you?"

"Fine word," William agreed.

"*We* know where he is, of course—he may be a genius, but he's not used to acting like a bad guy. His wife bought a house in Boise four months ago. She's still using her old credit cards. I'd like you to fly to Idaho and pay them a visit."

"Just me?"

"For now. Maybe Plover's just tired of being a genius. If he can tell us something useful about Price, we can offer immunity and protection. If he's got nothing, take him into custody. Flight at 0600 tomorrow morning from Reagan. Hope this doesn't interfere with your social life."

"Not a problem," William said. "Haven't had a date in two months."

"Some lucky cowgirl will come along and find her buckaroo," Kunsler said, stone-faced.

William broke into laughter. "They pulled down nearly all the posters around here," he said. "But they left the ones on alcohol and domestic abuse. What's that tell you about the private life of an agent?"

Kunsler waved that away and looked unconcerned. "Let me be your matchmaker," she said. "It'll happen."

The secure phone on her desk chimed. She picked it up and listened. Her eyes wandered around the room, met William's.

"Oh my God," she said, then hung up. For a moment, she could not speak. Her eyes welled up with tears. She looked down and rearranged some loose papers. "Does the shit never stop?"

"What is it? The president?"

"She's fine." Kunsler's voice cracked. "It's Beth-Anne Quinn. The vice president just murdered his wife."

3

The Ziggurat
Dubai, United Arab Emirates

Nathaniel Trace walked slowly to the condo window and stared out over Dubai Creek. A few dhows, pleasure boats, and light freighters plied their trade, far below.

From his perspective—six hundred feet up the side of the Ziggurat, a huge steel and glass pyramid—the morning sun burned like a blowtorch on the horizon. The twelve lanes of the Ras al Khor Bridge, mostly empty, cut through the waterway's blinding shimmer.

The strangest feeling pushed through his entire body, as if he were a giant skyscraper and all the light switches were being turned on—or off—in quick succession.

Windows bright, windows dark.

How appropriate, here in Dubai, home of ten thousand audacious, half-empty monuments to the world-class architecture of a failing oil empire.

An incredibly rich city fallen on hard times, where Nathaniel had lived and worked for six months now, interacting with part of the most sophisticated computer system on Earth—and filling his accounts with cash. His work was all but finished. He would be called up if they needed him for a few last details—but that was unlikely.

No, Jones was in control now, buried somewhere in the mountains of Switzerland.

He examined his naked reflection in the glass. Pale, lumpy body. Brush of disheveled ginger hair. Round face with a bump of nose—

thin bridge, bulbous tip, flaring nostrils. Smooth, round cheeks. Generous lips that had once tended to a boyish smile.

Now he looked more like a bewildered Irish car salesman.

Nathaniel shivered and refocused his eyes. He could stare and stare at the sun without blinking and it didn't hurt a bit. If he chose, he could destroy his eyes and not even feel it.

He chose not to.

Something similar had happened a year before. Like the flip of a switch—all the misery, gone. Back then, it had been the pain from a nasty run-in with the wicked old world of the Middle East. Relief from worry and torment might explain his current round of mental pyrotechnics.

But this time, it felt very different.

You will experience liberation.

That's what the doctor had told him. All his old fears and traumas wouldn't just be managed, just painted over—they would be *gone.* He would remember them at any level of detail he willed, like tracing scars with a finger, but the scars would mean *nothing* emotionally.

Freedom from all his blunders, his mistakes . . . freedom from guilt.

That was what Mariposa was supposed to do. Better men, better fighters—everything better. And the doctor's promises had come true.

But now, his recovery and all his personal progress were twisting into something truly weird. Maybe what he was feeling had nothing to do with what had happened in Arabia Deserta, or with Mariposa.

Maybe it was unique to him.

But he didn't think so. His thoughts jumbled, tumbled all over each other like acrobats or hyperactive children. He felt great but he could not *think* straight. The confusion did not cause him actual pain but it scared him.

He felt great but he was scared to death.

He loved being *scared to death.*

Stop it.

The fear went away—but only for a moment.

A bank of dust blowing up from the south obscured the brilliant morning sun. It was going to be a murky day in Dubai. All the glittering steel and glass, and yet the desert still ruled.

Nathaniel felt a sudden urge to test himself, test this new awareness and see how physically in control and adaptable he was.

Get away from the luxury and the air-conditioning. Walk out into the desert. Feel the hot sand on his bare feet. Strip off his clothes and directly face the sun's rays. See if his skin grew a new silvery layer and his nose became broad to radiate heat.

Probably not a good plan, he told himself—the desert would leach him in an hour. He had been incredibly thirsty of late, drinking gallons of Masafi well water and peeing like a race horse.

Yesterday the pee was tinted purple. Then it turned bright yellow and opaque—like paint. Who knew what would happen to him under the pounding glare and the wind-blown grit.

Still . . .

Baby steps.

He let the curtain drop and closed his eyes. Before he lost his last lick of sense—before he decided to actually leave the city and walk out into the desert—he decided he should ride out this part unconscious. This part of whatever was happening to him. But it was all so fascinating. He didn't want to miss a thing.

This new person he was becoming might be human or might not—but he promised more real adventure and change and *fun* than anything Nathaniel had ever experienced.

He consciously willed his heart to speed up—then slowed it down.

Good.

More!

He picked up a long brass bird sculpture from the desktop near the window and, with a slight grunt, bent it double. The effort popped two of his knuckles and strained a ligament in his right arm, but there it was—the sculpture twisted into a pretzel. Something he could never have done before—at least not consciously.

He had read that in an emergency, people can increase their strength tenfold. A frightened mother can lift a car off her injured child. Drugs can have the same effect.

Nathaniel no longer needed the excuse of an emergency—nor drugs.

The needs of the body no longer ruled.

He gripped the two fingers and popped one back into place, then the other. The arm would have to take care of itself—he didn't mind the pain.

I have a cosmic mind, he told himself. He could make himself believe every word—and then smile in perfect awareness that this was crazy. That he was going insane.

But whatever—I am bringing a lot more systems online and under my conscious control than is humanly possible.

He took the sedative with another glass of water—the water tasted like pink platinum, whatever that might be—and lay down on the bed in the condo's coolness, privacy, and extraordinary luxury.

Leased through the efforts of that poor blown-up, beaten-down, guilt-ridden son of a bitch who was being paid, along with the rest of the Turing Seven, to corrupt the world's finances—but couldn't hear a motorbike rip past without breaking into a rank sweat.

His past self.

There was still plenty of money left. The Quiet Man had trained them well. Millions of dollars in hidden bank accounts, just in case. However this turned out, he would soon be leaving it all behind— United Arab Emirates, the Middle East, the desert.

All but the money.

He would make his way back to America. There, with what he knew, and this new sense of *liberation,* maybe he would finally be able to do something different.

Meet important people outside the usual circles.

Spill the beans. Tell the world what he had been up to. Tell them all about the incredible nastiness that was in the works.

Do some good for a change.

Although doing more evil would certainly be exciting.

14 Days

4

Spider/Argus
Tyson's Corner, Virginia

Jane Rowland climbed down from the humming blue-and-green bus and walked with three colleagues, known to her only by their badge numbers, across a walkway through plantings of young trees and turf-squared grass, around a small fountain, to her home away from home.

Under a gray canopy of moody humidity, the new headquarters of Spider/Argus blended with all the other blandly efficient buildings of Tyson's Corner: gray modern architecture both blocky and tidy.

Hotels and malls and restaurants spread throughout the small city catered to some of the most powerful and anonymous people on the planet.

Typically Jane worked the nightshift. Her personal monitor bots were even now preparing reports that only she would see—until she passed them along to her director, who had permanently commissioned her last year to do what she did best.

Spider/Argus had been conceived twenty years ago as a supplement to the National Security Agency, which had proved slow to transition from SigInt—Signals Intelligence: landlines, satellites, cell phones, radio—into the dataflow age of Internet Everywhere.

In the eight years since its creation, S/A had budded off completely from its parent, taking on not just Internet and Web-based research and intelligence, but defensive CPI: counterintelligence, prevention, intervention.

Letting a highly trained watchdog off its leash.

Spider/Argus was not even its official name. Jane knew of just a small fraction of its operations.

Security barricades surrounded all. Nobody approached the building without clearance at the highest levels. Hidden sonic disrupter and microwave heat and pain projectors had been installed at all entrances and in undisclosed locations around the grounds—capable of incapacitating attackers at a distance of several hundred yards.

Lethal force was authorized inside the barbed-wire flanked corridors, patrolled by roller bots and dogs and soldiers. The tunnels of wire that covered nearby freeway overpasses were monitored by thousands of bug-eye cameras.

At regular intervals along all the local freeways and access roads, concrete arches hid .50 caliber, high-speed, radar-guided gun mounts, similar to those used to shoot down missiles and capable of cutting cars and trucks—even armored, military-style trucks—to hamburger-filled scrap within seconds.

Jane passed through the automatic steel and glass doors and submitted her badge and arm chip at the two security gates beyond.

"You'll need a code refresh by tomorrow evening," the female guard told her in a droop-eyed monotone.

For the guards, this had to be one of the most boring jobs in the greater D.C./Maryland/Virginia area. Nobody interesting passed their way. Nobody spoke to them other than brief pleasantries.

Not even sports or weather could be discussed.

But the droop eyes stayed alert and sharp.

Jane waited for her assigned elevator at the automated station, then rose to the third floor. No music and no smell—clean, cool, purified air. Elevators carried singles at all times. Conversation in other than work areas was not just discouraged, it was tracked and fined. Posted lists of recent fines glowed from monitors over the elevator doors—though of course with no names or numbers attached.

There was fun to be had, of course. Floors and divisions with the highest levels of fines had to buy Christmas gifts for charities in the D.C. metro area. Top analysts with the highest fines had to spring for hallway treat tables.

No holiday parties, however.

Those guilty of prohibited violations spent three months in "time-out" at comfortable locations in the Adirondacks, until their cases were processed. Most did not return.

Jane did not find any of this exceptional. Her new office was far more comfortable than the one at the old Naval station on the banks of the Potomac.

The security was no worse, and definitely more effective.

At the end of each work period—usually in the small hours of the morning—she returned to her apartment and her daughter, dismissed the government-provided nanny, a woman with excellent bodyguard credentials, and assumed her favorite role—devoted single mom.

She was very good at everything she did.

Jane approached the door to her office. Beside the door, a black sign with silver letters warned that this was a "Faraday Room."

The room snitch checked her security codes one last time, unlocked the door, and opened access to the banks of office computers, clearing her for work.

Her machines never shut down.

She watched as wide ranks of rectangular displays brightened, switching from low-power mode.

Results of the day's searches started cascading down the line like flipped cards in solitaire. She sat in her special chair—the one item she had brought with her from the old Potomac building—and flexed her fingers before highlighting with airy gestures the top items on her evening work chart.

The room swiftly interpreted her motions either as writing, drawing, or command and control.

On the small bulletin board hung to the left of her monitors, ten months ago—while preparing for her current operation—she had tacked a printout from a Congressional Budget Office report

Many nations, coming out of a long financial downturn, and having acquired assets such as at-risk real estate from beleaguered banks and other institutions, find themselves asset rich but increasingly cash poor. The United States, with debts on the order

of fifty trillion dollars and an unfortunate habit of triggering re-
cessions, is thought by a majority of nations to be the greatest
threat to financial stability in the world.

Investor and debt-holding institutions fear that a disruption
similar to that of 2008–2009 will push the world economy over the
edge, bringing on yet another worldwide crisis, this one of dire
proportions.

Created in 2009, the International Financial Protection Corporation (IFPC) is an international fund that contains and controls
a cumulative 85 percent of U.S. debt through all of its participants
and investors.

The United States has agreed to certain strict conditions, contingent to obtain necessary further loans from IFPC. Those conditions have not been revealed to the public.

Below that, she had pinned a second printout framed top and bottom
with blue scribbles from her boss.

*The following internal warning from the Federal Reserve and the De-
partment of the Treasury has never been released to the public and, God
willing, never will be.*

In order to qualify for all necessary further loans from IFPC, the
United States executive branch, with the agreement of the Federal
Reserve, the Secretary of the Treasury, and three congressional
committees, has agreed to a special troubled nation loan protocol.

Certain national assets are valued and offered up as collateral.
Central authority is ultimately invested in an automated system known as MSARC—Mutual Strategic Asset Recovery and
Control—which can trigger massive reallocations and call in loans,
effectively putting a debtor nation into instant receivership.

Should MSARC decide to act, collateral assets guaranteed under the loan agreements will immediately be transferred to IFPC.

Financial corporations and investment funds around the world
can then call the political shots through a Reallocation Committee.

If MSARC so decides, for the first time in our history, foreigners
will hold almost complete economic and political control of—and
so they will own—the United States of America.

MSARC poses the greatest threat to this nation since the Cold War—maybe greater.

And it's our own damned fault. We do hate paying taxes, and we do love all our precious government services. Squealing piggies at the trough.

Her boss was prone to expressing himself vividly. Nevertheless, she read the posted pages before beginning her work every evening. They neatly bookended the current plight of the United States.

The monitor on her far right—smallest and most antique, losing pixels and fading in the corners to autumn gold—was devoted to displaying a simple digital clock.

The clock counted backward, second by second.

It now read *14 days 13 hours 5 minutes*.

The amount of time left before MSARC began formally judging America.

MSARC was allowed access to information that once would have been considered closely held national secrets. Its central computer banks in Geneva relied on a network surveillance capability that in two years had come to rival many in her own agency.

MSARC also had access to the records of major corporations with government contracts—all but Talos Corporation in Lion City, Texas, one of the biggest holders of U.S. government contracts. That exemption had been passed by congress with hardly a ripple, so many members were beholden to Talos CEO Axel Price. Price had taken a particular interest in MSARC some years back, even serving on a fully briefed government advisory committee.

The first item on Jane's evening agenda was following up on a list of MSARC queries. Stopping or interfering with those queries—or even tracking them—violated the loan agreements, so Jane was discreet, using the full range of search and masking capabilities available to Spider/Argus.

This evening, the list included only thirty queries, concentrating on the Federal Reserve and a number of major software corporations.

The latter might be of interest to other analysts. She copied them to a separate office that evaluated long-term patterns of foreign interest in private business.

More sobering still, MSARC's command center in Geneva was only now ramping up to full capacity—the moment of truth tracked by her backward-counting clock.

No one knew how extensive and powerful those systems were. It was possible Spider/Argus would be completely shut out by a superior program.

Whenever Jane conducted surveys on that particular question, her web "helpers"—thousands of subroutines running in machines everywhere from Cheyenne Conserve to Iron Mountain to right here in Tyson's Corner—came back with results that gave her the spooky feeling she—Jane Rowland herself—was being closely watched by something with almost preternatural instincts.

Human or machine, she could not even begin to guess.

There was evidence this presence was working on behalf of MSARC.

There was also evidence that MSARC was not even aware of its existence.

That contradiction intrigued Jane.

She loved this sort of puzzle.

The second item for this evening was the most important. She was arranging for a brief but powerful ripple of net inactivity—amounting to a thirty-second denial of service—spreading across hundreds of server farms in the northwest and the southeast, with the ultimate goal of helping an agent infiltrated into Talos Corporation in Lion City, Texas.

His code name was Nabokov.

Jane knew almost everything about how the Talos computers accessed the outside world, and how they protected themselves against being accessed. Nabokov was poised to take advantage of a maintenance hole in Talos's infranet to download data crucial to a joint investigation, a rare instance of S/A cooperation with an outside agency—in this case, Alicia Kunsler at Bureau East.

Killing a few minutes' time, Jane pushed her wheeled chair over to her relaxation station—a hot plate, sink, small refrigerator, and rack of cups—and made herself a cup of her favorite, white tea.

Cup in hand, she rolled back.

One-handed, she used a keyboard to type in a warning of the impending system-wide interruption, alerting national security masters throughout Tyson's Corner that this was not the beginning of a foreign assault.

She then paused her finger over the ENTER key, waiting for the precise second . . .

Now or never.

5

Lion City, Texas
Talos Corporate Campus

Footsteps echoed hollowly down the Buckeye main hallway to the central instructor lounge. Fouad Al-Husam was alone. The building seemed deserted.

He had finished his afternoon class teaching regional Farsi and Arabic to a select team of Haitian troops destined to serve as mercenaries in Middle Eastern theaters.

Normally, at the end of each day he returned to his apartment in Lion City and ate dinner alone. His free time he mostly spent reading or watching Islamic history on cable, hungry for another place, another time.

Remembering his strange return to the hot, pure air of the Hejaz—his visit to Mecca.

This evening, he had reserved the central computer annex for half an hour to conduct academic research over the Talos infranet.

The Haitians had surprised Fouad with their intelligence and devotion. Talos was paying for their education. They sent more money home to their families each month than many in Haiti earned in a lifetime.

They reminded Fouad of the Janissaries he had commanded in Turkey, it seemed an age ago—but was just two years.

Two eventful, deceitful years.

It could be said about Axel Price that he was a powerful man, a strange man, even perhaps a corrupt man, but he paid generous wages and maintained strict military discipline in his company and his people.

Fouad was ten times better paid now than he had ever been as an agent.

The Buckeye main lounge surrounding the annex was also empty. Evening classes resumed at eight.

The annex—a smoked glass hexagon on the north side of the lounge—served both faculty and advanced students. It gave access to online instructional materials and teacher/adviser briefings, as well as a host of information services equal or superior to anything available to CEOs of other major American corporations.

Of course, all searches were logged.

The classrooms in Buckeye radiated in eight spokes from a central rotunda, forming a wagon wheel. Three similar wheels in other quarters of the campus were devoted to particular collections of Talos customers.

Each was named after a regional butterfly.

Axel Price loved butterflies. He had the largest collection in the world—hundreds of sealed glass cases, so it was said—but showed it to no one.

Price's other hobby was collecting rare antique cars. They were kept in a huge garage near the Smoky, his ranch and principal residence.

Fouad's fingerprint and arm chip logged him into the annex. The lock took a small DNA sample from his skin oils. Micro-PCR and pore sequencing technology within the lock took less than ten seconds to confirm his genetic identity and compare it with the information on the chip.

The annex's glass and steel door unlocked with a smooth click and slid open. Had he been denied, alarms would have sounded throughout the building.

The chip also enabled Talos to track him anywhere on the ten thousand acre campus. Every few feet, the chip was queried by sensors imbedded in walls and sidewalks, grass, and asphalt. Millions more sensors were scattered over the training fields and surrounding lawns, gardens, and tracks, maintaining a tightly woven net of constant surveillance.

Around Lion City, planes and helicopters had dropped enough sensors to saturate the entire area with the thin disks, two centimeters in diameter—one or two per square yard.

All in the interest, so it was said, of preventing illegal Mexicans from causing trouble.

Fouad carried ice in a cup from the cafeteria to cool his hands. He applied it briefly to his forehead. Within any of the campus buildings, Talos security could record his heart rate, blood pressure, and body temperature for face, hands, and feet. The ice in the cup reduced his blood flow and brought his stress profile more in line with normal activity.

The hexagonal space was equipped with three chairs. There were no tables or monitors. The entire room served as a display. The neutral gray walls were equipped with hundreds of tiny lasers.

Fouad sat in the middle chair.

In a few minutes, a general ripple in the dataflow would pulse through selected servers regularly utilized by the Talos infranet. That would cause no damage, but it might give him a few minutes of deep, unfettered access into the corporate goody bag—without the access being logged.

The ganglion of Talos's network had a specific pattern of behaviors outside of its recorded design specs—what Jane Rowland called "excess personality." During a universal dropout and reacquisition of external servers, the Talos library would likely suffer a "momentary lapse of confidence," as Jane had described it, and—like an infant looking around to see where Momma was—it *might* open a point of entry for a technician to check up on all systems.

This point of entry would be brief, but it would require neither an identifier nor a password other than the original programmer's— which was known to Spider/Argus but not to anyone at Talos.

That password was "Nick72TuringHorta."

The original programmers had created and then concealed such portals, perhaps to allow them to make last-second upgrades and improve their chances of getting the rich Talos contract. Or perhaps because they did not trust Talos any more than the Bureau did.

The blip would be brief and the system would easily recover, so no technician would come calling, but Fouad would be there, ready and equipped with a new way to steal and export data.

He sipped from the melting ice and waited.

6

Spider/Argus
Tyson's Corner, Virginia

Jane pressed ENTER.

The ripple began to run its course. For the next ten seconds, Talos servers would try to access their familiar gateways, and fail.

She sipped her white tea and noted with satisfaction that Nabokov now had an opening—a receptive command node in the Talos infranet, awaiting instructions from a local programmer.

Jane could not get information out of that portal—no one she knew of could breach the Talos firewalls from outside—but if Nabokov was in place, for the next five minutes, the campus servers just might become an open book for him.

The infranet returned a simple bit acknowledgment it was being inspected.

Technician on duty.

Then a little gong went off—a simple oriental *chang.*

Jane sat upright.

That spooky presence again, in a place it definitely did not belong. She swiftly drew a number in the air, then a slash, initiating her visual dialer.

"Give it a miss," she murmured. "Don't go in."

The Spider/Argus call center connected her to Alicia Kunsler in Quantico.

Kunsler picked up on the first droning buzz. "Hey, Jane. He's in?"

"He's in, but here's a hash query search—a patch on the portal. He may be tagged. Something else strange—an analog signal has been

25

laid over the feed, available through the firewall—which would be doubly peculiar, but not really, because it isn't coming from Texas. It's coming from a source I can't trace."

It's coming from that watcher who always knows where I am and what I'm doing.

"Analog? Who in hell sends analog?"

Jane looked over the diagnostics and pathways. Names popped up, hypotheticals:

San Luis Obispo.

San Francisco.

Corpus Christi.

Pendleton Reserve.

"Could be random garbage from a discontinued coastal junction," she said. "A ghost from a TV show or something. It's just odd it popped up now. I don't like it. I think they've made him."

"Recommendations?"

"Yank him, whether he's got what he came for or not."

"Shit. You know there's no way I can reach him. Can you?"

"No," Jane said.

"Then he takes the risk."

Kunsler hung up.

Jane's machines automatically extracted the analog signal, cleaned it up, and played it through her earpiece.

It sounded like a young boy weeping.

Her hands went cold. She cradled the tea mug for warmth.

When she suddenly felt she was about to get dizzy, she let out her breath with a low, agonized whoosh.

7

Talos Campus

Fouad leaned back in the chair.

He had carefully planned his masking search—downloading updates to Yemeni academic and literary e-journals, accessing slow, ancient university servers half a world away.

He had been watching the friendly, scampering images of network busyness flow around him. The incongruity of manic cartoon characters in full battle gear was not lost on him.

The images flickered and froze.

A black rectangle appeared, seeming to hover about a foot from his face. A simple green cursor blinked on its upper left side.

Fouad reached into his shirt pocket and removed the four-pronged connector in its plastic packet. To an untrained eye, it might have looked like a thumbtack.

He stripped off the plastic and shoved the tiny prongs under the cap into his forearm. Then he clamped a digital sensor to the plug, raised his arm to eye level, returned his attention to the screen, and keyed in the six-number technician identifier.

Almost immediately, without knowing whether he was in or not, he ran his true thirty-line search code, memorized months ago under Jane's tutelage.

The figures began to scamper again. They sped up—and then the records he sought floated into view in ranked folios.

The folios opened and pages began to flip. He caught a few frames as they flew past—financial records for accounts in Singapore, United

Arab Emirates, China; transactions with federal employees in Virginia; payments to anonymous vendors in Idaho, California, Iran, Iraq, the new state of Arabia Deserta.

Then, lists of web news organizations and other media, accompanied by figures that seemed to represent the amount of corporate debt owed to offshore institutions.

Fouad could get only a general impression of all the corporate and international connections: banks, holding companies, big investors—many of whom worked for the oil cartels—and several chairmen and CEOs of the International Financial Protection Organization, organized a few years ago to oversee the distribution of the huge U.S. debt.

More lists followed: heads of state and government ministers from the Middle East, Singapore, Jordan, United Arab Emirates, Beijing; lobbyists, lawyers, and licensed foreign representatives working for China and Russia.

They comprised just a few of the hundred or more names that had apparently received a direct invitation from Axel Price himself.

Three retired generals, an admiral, and the new chairman of the Federal Reserve were also invited.

Joining them would be political agents from nearly every nation that used Talos services or held American debt. Conspicuously absent was Israel—which seemed more than odd, given Talos's many past contracts there.

A line of question marks was followed by the designation: "HR undecideds." Fouad could not pause the flow; HR might refer to the House of Representatives, members of congress.

Many of the modern masters of world finance, politicians, world leaders, and even a few prominent military figures were about to come together at Price's call, a gathering of eagles and moles—and weasels.

But where and when?

Fouad tried to pick out the location and date, and then realized he already knew.

Price was sponsoring a big gathering in Lion City in two weeks. Ostensibly he would be showing off the Talos Campus and hawking his wares: reviewing cadres of mercenaries, along with spectacular displays of new security and military equipment in which Price had made substantial investments.

Something else flick-paged by—a cluster of references to MSARC. Mutual Strategic Asset Recovery and Control. The central MSARC computers were supposedly buried deep inside mountains in Switzerland

All part of the new world economic order.

The acronym seemed to him reminiscent of Mutually Assured Destruction, MAD, the working strategy of the decades-long nuclear stalemate during the Cold War.

Perhaps it was meant to be. Just as the split-second decision whether to launch nuclear weapons was once regarded as too important to hand over to mere humans, the challenges of international finance were now too fast, too big, and far too complicated to entrust to flesh-and-blood managers.

The tipping point for another, even deeper decline might occur in hundredths of a second.

More flickering pages, then multiple references to "Jones," either a man or a network possibly linked to MSARC.

All throughout, like obsessive-compulsive little fruit flies, buzzed sections of text from a rambling treatise by Price himself about "fiat" currency and its strategic disadvantages.

Fiat currency—currency defined by a government rather than backed by physical assets—was a pejorative among believers in the gold standard.

The area around his spiky interface began to grow warm. Terabytes of data were now flooding from the open Talos servers into Fouad's arm.

Too long a connection might actually sear a blood vessel, but this was important.

Axel Price was not the man Fouad would ever visualize at the center of a high-powered conference on international finance. He was not trusted in Europe. His connections to Israel had long since grown stale, mirroring the return of a general disenchantment with Jews inside the extreme American right.

Any connection between Price and MSARC would be very interesting in some circles.

The button was causing pain.

The dataflow abruptly ended with a cartoon grunt face—a Talos security guard in full armor and regalia raising night-vision gogs, spinning his assault rifle, and winking.

Done!

The black square of the maintenance window closed.

Records of Fouad's access instantly vanished.

All the data—the reason for his entire mission—now suffused through his blood, downloaded at the source of the plug into thousands of microscopic data stores, amalgams of protein and silicon called *prochines*. The prochines would spend the next hour exchanging data with their blood-borne fellows, performing a kind of bio-backup, until millions of copies spread throughout his body.

Security at Talos was comprehensive and superb, but so far, nobody knew about prochines, nor, had they known, would they have been able to detect them without drawing and analyzing enough blood to kill him.

Fouad needed to get this information out of Lion City quickly. Given the conditions of constant surveillance and the county-wide blanket of sensor chips, and given that his contract did not allow for vacations or travel outside of the campus, the original plan had been for him to be informed of a family emergency within the next few weeks—the timing to be widely separated from this intrusion, in the unlikely event it were ever detected.

But the conference was scheduled to begin in fourteen days. He needed to communicate with his handlers immediately.

And there was only one way he might succeed at doing that, undetected—something almost as antiquated as carrier pigeons, of which he had none.

Fouad left the cage, which locked its door behind him with a confident, steely *chunk*.

8

Dubai

The hours passed. The dust storm blew over and the color outside the window blinds went golden, then dark.

Nathaniel Trace flew in and out of a hypnogogic fantasy . . . Trees and roads all around, wind in his hair, and then a *chingaling* in one ear, like chimes, pretty but not at all soothing.

His phone telling him he had a call.

Interrupting the lazy flow.

He scrunched his lids tight, then opened them wide.

Dark in the room.

Dark outside.

Tree patterns painted on dark walls, windows, furniture. He pushed back against the visuals. He had taken the sedative hours ago. It hadn't knocked him out—not completely.

Now the chemistry was conflicting with whatever else was happening in his body. He was starting to feel really bad. Afraid, and not excited about it. The fear was real. The evil was here, right *beside* him, right here on the bed, a dark, writhing tangle of tree limbs—he could feel them scrape and poke but he couldn't see them, not now.

The room lights came up to dim gold in response to his movement. He rolled over and stared at the empty, creased sheets. Bunched pillows filled with leering ghost faces.

The blinds were drawn. Airplane warning lights on skyscrapers blinked red between the cracks in the blinds.

Chimes again.

He grabbed the phone, an expensive EPR unit. His fingerprint confirmed him and the phone completed the connection. "Yeah," he croaked. "It's me. I think."

The screen demanded another answer code. He fumbled with the keypad projected from the phone's base onto the gray sheets.

Concealed number, but he knew the voice—slightly husked, soft and deep. Despite his discomfort, he sat up in bed and cleared his throat.

This was the boss of the Turing Seven—director of Mind Design and the genius behind Jones. They called him the Quiet Man. His real name was Chan Herbert, but they rarely used it.

Nathaniel had met him in person three times back in La Jolla, California. He was reclusive and cautious to a fault—hence the EPR phones, which could always detect someone unauthorized listening in.

"Where are you?" the Quiet Man asked. "Still in Dubai?"

"Yes sir. Way up in the sky. The Ziggurat."

"You sound drunk."

"I'm trying to get some sleep."

The Quiet Man produced a short, guttural *hm*. "Anybody from Talos call in the last twelve hours? Anybody asking about your health?" He sounded anxious. He did not much like people and rarely betrayed emotion.

"No." Nathaniel tried to keep a drowsy mirth out of his voice.

"Have you heard from Nick?"

"We've closed up shop. I think he's back in Texas."

"He called. He was weeping. Are you *sure* you're okay?"

"I feel great. Better than great."

"Don't bullshit me."

"A little loopy, that's all. Decompression from months of work."

Tell him: I think I'm taking control of my body, all the automatic bits. It sounds crazy but sometimes it feels wonderful. Sometimes . . .

"Nathaniel . . ."

"No, really."

"Talos knows where you are?"

"Probably," Nathaniel admitted, combing his ginger brush of hair with his fingers. "I'm off the clock and off the rez, but they know my habits."

He laid a hand over the bulge of his stomach. *Too much luxury. Good food at the Galaxy Club—served by lovely Indonesian and Thai beauties.*

Maybe I'll straighten out my morals.

Lose weight fast.

"Jones says something bad is heading our way. He's tied into both Talos's and MSARC's secure nets, but he won't tell me what's up until he's sure. That damned truth function—your work, if I remember correctly. I'm ordering everyone back to California."

"What's the hurry?" Nathaniel asked, stretching.

"Pay attention, Nathaniel. Since you're feeling strange—"

"What makes you say that?"

"—and Nick is feeling strange, it's probably something to do with Mariposa."

"Well, we did what we were told. What if it's not bad, but good?"

A pause. Then, with a real edge, "Do you have any idea how deep this is? How important the seven of you are—and how complicit? Price made us wealthy men. If he even suspects we can't be trusted, we're *dead* men. Get out now. Come to LA and call in secure when you arrive."

The connection was cut at the source.

Nathaniel fell back on the bed, tingling throughout his body.

Back to base camp. Back to LA.

He should start packing. He tried with all his might to lift his arms. Nothing.

"I can't," he said to the wall.

A delayed effect. It might last seconds, minutes—or hours. He stared at the long shadows on the ceiling. Started to giggle, then stopped.

"What the hell have you done, you *idiot*?"

How much control did he really have of his formerly autonomous functions? Getting his blood moving faster, for example—as if he were running and not lying down.

Flushing the last of those sedatives through his liver. They should be down to minimum concentrations by now, anyway.

Could he actually *control his liver*?

He lay still for a while.

One of the shadows moved.

Someone was in his room.

He swiveled his eyes until his vision went muzzy.

A short, robed silhouette stood in the lighted doorway. A woman's voice murmured, "Excuse me. For morning house cleaning, *inshallah*—on time, sir? . . . Sir?"

She would probably call for assistance if he didn't answer—the Ziggurat emergency medical team, best in Dubai.

His jaw wouldn't move.

"Are you awake?"

"I'm fine," he finally croaked between clenched teeth. "Just the flu. Leave me alone. Get out."

The silhouette faded into all the other shadows.

The door closed. Maybe he had imagined it, like the trees in his bed. Maybe it had never been there.

Then: a steady inner voice. The same voice he had created soon after the slaughter in Arabia Deserta as a kind of psychic baseline—in remembrance of his former broken self.

Time to get moving, Mr. Trace. They have a lot of influence here. Very long fingers.

He had not heard from that voice in months.

He had presumed Mariposa had killed it off.

If, as the Quiet Man supposes, they want to find you, if they need to find you . . . This is the place. The desert across the water is wide and the sands are deep. They can do whatever they want here and no one would ever know.

His body jerked and then convulsed. He bounced himself off the bed, narrowly avoiding cracking his head on the nightstand.

Slowly twitching on the cold wood floor, he regained control. Finally he could move again, but his fingers felt numb. He got up on wobbly legs and stumbled into the bathroom, into the walk-in shower, where he stared groggily at the water selection nobs.

He chose desalinated, hot—hotter than hell.

Treading on art glass tiles set in the fish mosaic floor, he tolerated the scalding water until he just had to scream—then jumped out and toweled himself down.

Much better. The numbness had faded. Now his skin felt cool and electric.

Still naked, Nathaniel picked up his bag. Hardly anything here was important enough to pack. A few clothes. Toiletries. He could leave the rest without regret, as if it belonged to a different man.

He dressed slowly, luxuriating in the feel of fine linen on his arm hairs.

The fabric brushed his scars.

The condo intercom wheedled. The security system that watched over his class of people in the Ziggurat asked him if he would like to receive visitors—and displayed a picture of three men and a well-dressed, attractive woman.

They were waiting in the spacious lobby, hundreds of feet below.

He did not recognize any of them, and so he did not give permission for them to rise to his unit.

In the lobby, as he watched, the group split up.

Best to find an unobvious way out.

The Ziggurat's security system was accustomed to arranging for exits after dubious late night activities, or drinking in the many bars.

9

Talos Campus

Fouad emerged from the annex, put on his spex, and stood stiffly upright in the lounge—a slight heat pulsing through his torso. The prochines in his blood had never felt like much of anything before. Now, actively bumping up against each other—chock full of distributed data—they seemed to be coming up on the radar of his body's immune system.

A fever at this point might attract attention. Axel Price was almost psychic in his ability to sniff out actions contrary to his plans. Fouad did not want to stay at the building's hub any longer than necessary.

Something was wrong with the building's network; his spex flashed two small yellow antenna symbols, out of range. He walked clockwise around the lounge, glancing north along one of the long Buckeye corridors, lined with classrooms.

Two men in gray shirts and black pants ran in from a garden entrance. Their boots squeaked on the linoleum—armor vests, campus security. For a moment, Fouad thought they were aiming right for him and his stomach muscles tensed.

Armor was unusual on the campus, except in training.

"Need any help?" Fouad called.

"Get the hell out of here!" the larger of the two shouted as the pair aimed for the next radius corridor—one of the spokes—their faces red with adrenaline rush.

Then the big guard slowed, lowered his chin into his bull neck—and spun about. He marched back toward Fouad—crown sporting brown fuzz, broad face, wide rectangular mouth sucking air and showing brownish teeth.

Big Guard. Happy to keep things secure—even happier to be aggressive.

The second guard stopped, shook his head, and reversed to join his partner. This one was slighter and shorter but wiry, with small black eyes, a plump face and butch-cut blond hair.

Little Guard. Happy to follow. He matched his wide stance with Big Guard but curved around to Fouad's left.

"We don't know exactly where the problem is. Network's down, teacher." Big Guard tapped his spex. "Any clues what's going on?"

Big Guard was a bigot. Fouad was being targeted based on skin color and appearance—in his experience, rare at Talos. Bad for discipline.

The pair rushed him in parallel and shoved him against the wall. His back pressed painfully against the corner of a framed poster of one of the nations in which Talos had operations—Nigeria.

Against his first instinct, Fouad let his muscles relax and said nothing. He did not frown, did not smile—did nothing to provoke. Perhaps he had tripped a silent alarm system inside the annex. Perhaps the network had shut down after sensing an unexpected intrusion.

He had to buy time.

"Are *your* spex working?" Big Guard asked, fingers pinching for Fouad's eyes. Another hand came up high and flat to slap him if he resisted.

Little Guard stroked the black knob of his electric baton. The men were starting to grin. Their eyes took on a focused vacancy, getting ready for resistance.

They had found the problem—the problem was a brown man.

Wild, high-pitched shouts echoed from the end of the radius. Big Guard lifted his nose, and Little Guard did likewise—pack dogs scenting other, bigger prey.

Fouad pushed them away—gently.

"Down there, perhaps?" he suggested, eyebrows lifted.

Big Guard and Little Guard smirked, cocked their heads, and again shoved him into the wall—their version of an apology, thanks for wasting our time. They backed off, reversed, and sprinted toward the shouting, louder and more frenetic.

A growing number of men made unhappy.

The pair reached the end of the radius, a hundred feet off, pulled out their electric batons—serious weapons, very painful—and swung left.

Fouad nudged out from the wall. The poster rattled. It was hard to imagine what the difficulty might be. The personnel most likely to engage in fistfights were off at the mess hall—young foreign soldiers and fresh security in training. Perhaps Big Guard and Little Guard belonged to that group. Perhaps a general alarm had brought them over to Buckeye.

He curled his lip in disgust, caught between two impulses.

The only people in Buckeye who stuck around through the dinner hour were software engineers, whose work never seemed to end.

Fouad shrugged to unruck the sleeves and shoulders of his coat. Then he fell back into a crouch at the sound of two rapid pops like champagne corks, followed by staccato slaps, softer echoes, explosive grunts from punches.

More swearing—then sizzling snaps, puppy-like whimpers, sharp cries of pain.

Everyone wore side arms in Talos—Price's mandate—but nobody would be letting off rounds on campus outside of the ranges and training village—nobody who was not in serious trouble. All the side arms were keyed to fingerprints or chips in the gun bearer's hands; shots fired were accounted for at the armory every two days.

Another series of champagne pops. Dust and chips blew out from a wall. Fouad lined up behind the heavy frame of a security door.

Odd that the doors were not closing . . .

Discretion told him to allow the trouble to come to him, but that was not the Talos way. Like dedicated warrior ants, Talos employees were trained to move in fast, whatever the danger. Trouble was to be immediately reported and taken care of—not avoided. Clearing out of the building—even at the forceful suggestion of security—would arouse another set of suspicions.

Good minions—excellent henchmen. All of us expendable.

And of course, as a brown man with an accent, his behavior would be judged by even higher standards.

He loped down the hall, past long windows looking into empty classrooms—flush to the wall, broken-jogging side to side, SIG-Sauer 380 presented at drop angle, finger off trigger . . . He caught himself and raised the barrel, finger back on the trigger—standard Talos training.

Talos operated in parts of the world where accidental shootings were preferable to responding a split-second slow, letting soulless attackers get the drop on you.

It might just be a disgruntled student taking out his anger on a wall or the ceiling. But students were issued weapons that fired *only* in training.

Disgruntled employees were rare in Talos. Most were dedicated, well paid. Price had learned his lesson with out-of-control contract security in Iraq. There, Talos employees had been caught pumping up on steroids, snorting cocaine, even shooting heroin to get through the grueling, dangerous days escorting officials, generals, diplomats, though the hell of Iraqi cities.

Fouad slowed as he came to the end of the hall, the outer circumference of this side of Buckeye. All he heard now was harsh, husky breathing and moaning—four or five men down, wounded or in pain.

A bullet had pocked the cinderblock on his right.

Another had gouged the linoleum floor, interrupting the golden reflection of the outer windows.

He darted a look to the left, around the corner, along the rim of the wagon wheel. In the warm afternoon light, Big Guard and Little Guard were trying to subdue a tall, skinny man and doing a bad job of it. The skinny man wore a green shirt and gray pants—engineering and programming—and jerked this way and that, loose jointed, like a puppet tugged by an idiot. Three other guards had been tossed back like dolls, belts and holsters empty—guns and batons thrown out of reach along the circumference.

Big Guard and Little Guard maneuvered like wrestlers, trying to grab the skinny engineer, but he escaped as if made of smoke.

For an instant, Fouad thought he was witnessing someone out of his head but very strong—on meth or PCP. Clearly the skinny man was not following any formal martial arts training, yet his movements were brilliantly unexpected and effective. He pranced rings around the guards, laughing as if at a dry joke. Big Guard and Little Guard were tiring.

Fouad was sure they were about to make serious mistakes.

He could not make sense out of any of this. Talos tested for drugs a dozen different ways each day. The air was swept regularly for traces and metabolites.

Big Guard had had enough. He gathered up all his remaining energy, yelled, and rushed in with arms spread—while his partner feinted to draw the skinny man his direction.

This time, the maneuver seemed to work. Big Guard took hold of the skinny man's arm, but he reversed and tugged hard—hard enough to pull the arm out of its socket, with an audible pop. Without any sign of distress, the engineer slammed his other fist back, chopping his assailant squarely on the bridge of his nose.

Big Guard fell to his knees like a stunned ox, then toppled, head cracking on the floor.

Fouad trained his SIG but the line was bad—he might hit Little Guard.

"Shoot the bastard!" Little Guard shouted, frantically kicking and sidling away.

The engineer spun like a dancing clown, his injured arm dangling outward, limp. He had to be on drugs, yet his movements had an improvised genius; a wiry, high-speed ballet of showy blows and dodges.

Little Guard was up again, wobbling but still trying to be game. The engineer executed one final move that Fouad could not follow—a backward run, good hand delivering a blind blow from a position of perfect but unlikely balance—force focused all wrong, more self-injury almost certain—but the blow connected.

Little Guard rocked his head back, wobbled, and slumped. The engineer pranced and watched him fall sideways.

He twisted and landed flat on his face.

Another painful crack.

Now the engineer turned on Fouad.

"I heard you coming down the hall!" he shouted. "My God, you're louder than an elephant!"

Fouad could have fired his SIG—certainly preferred that option over trying to physically restrain the man—but there wasn't much more damage that could be done, for the moment, and more guards would be coming.

"You're injured," Fouad said, his voice light, calm, as if speaking to a child.

"I'm not the one shooting up the place. Too freaking fast for bullets. They're trained to kill—I'm just a geek. Where are they? *Send more cops*!" He laughed like a loon. "What's fucking *keeping* them?"

"I am here," Fouad said.

"You're a teacher. Languages, right? Jesus, look at this mess!"

The skinny man was breathing slow and steady, deep, solid. No bullet wounds, only spots of blood on the floor—broken noses, perhaps. Judging by the way the he leaned, he had cracked ribs as well as a dislocated arm. The man was a wreck, but still utterly confident and not in the least concerned by the SIG.

"Doesn't your arm hurt?" Fouad asked.

The engineer stared into Fouad's eyes. "Maybe. I don't know. Trying out new moves, I guess."

There were no audible security alarms in Talos buildings. Guards and other first responders were alerted through earpieces or spex. Strange then that Fouad's own spex still showed no warnings—just two blinking yellow antennas indicating he was still out of range.

"No signal, right? I've cut the network all over the campus," the engineer said. "You look strong. Bring it over here."

"What's your name?" Fouad asked.

"Hey, don't think I'm crazy," the man said. "I'm scared—more scared than you, maybe. But it feels great to be scared! Come on. I don't have a gun."

"It wouldn't be a fair fight," Fouad said, keying in to the engineer's manic rhythm. "I might get hurt."

The man laughed. "You know it, man. You're trained to kill—I can hear it in your voice. All I do is talk to computers. Geek versus killer. You know you can take me."

Fouad stepped to the middle of the hall, gun centered on the programmer's chest.

The five sprawled guards were starting to move. The programmer paid them no obvious attention. One guard had fallen over his Glock—it skittered as he pushed up, a few centimeters from his outstretched hand. His fingers twitched.

Without a backward look, the engineer jumped and horse-kicked the gun down the hall, twisted his foot around, and tapped the guard with his heel.

The guard collapsed with a truncated whimper.

Here was total awareness of environment, more like a martial arts master than a mouse pusher. All judgments off. Nothing could be trusted.

"You know self-defense," Fouad said. "All Talos employees are so trained."

"Yeah, but I flunked." The programmer raised his good arm, the left arm, and waggled his fingers. "Maybe I can deflect bullets with my thoughts. Anything's possible. Let's try it. Use your pop gun. Shoot me."

Fouad lowered the pistol. "No fighting. We should talk. You're more interesting than anything else around here."

The programmer looked disappointed. He shrugged, then put his hand on his limp arm, testing it. Despite what must have been incredible pain, he wobbled and tugged at the joint, trying to reset it, his attention off Fouad . . . and yet, almost certainly not. He seemed to have a greater sensory bubble of awareness, a heightened sense of space and position. Again, like a martial arts master.

"I popped it bad. Bet I could take you with one arm . . ."

"Let's just talk. Tell me what you're feeling."

The engineer laughed. "Ever see combat?"

"Yes," Fouad said.

"Me too. In Arabia. I was never supposed to fight, I'm important, you know—a software designer, a programmer, an essential asset. But the driver screwed up. He took seven of us down Death Alley by mistake and insurgents blew us all to shit. The driver's head ended up in my lap. My *fucking lap*! Dead school kids outside the truck—spread out like raspberry jam. Do you have nightmares, sweats, that sort of thing?"

"Sometimes," Fouad said.

"Interfere with your work?"

"Not much," Fouad said. "I pray. Allah forgives all His children."

"You're a Muslim!"

"Yes," Fouad said.

"A Muslim in Texas. That has *got* to be fun. These bastards—" He swung his good arm at the prone men. "They're hard enough on geeks. Guess I showed them something new, huh?"

"You should come with me. I'll take you to a doctor. Your mind is strong but your body is weak. Have mercy. You can't learn your potential if someone here shoots you."

This finally seemed to make sense. The programmer was pale as a sheet and starting to shiver. He rubbed his temple. "My head *really* hurts. What's your name?"

"Fouad. I'm an instructor . . . in languages, as you guessed. What's yours?"

"Nick. I'm pretty important. Systems about to come online. Back in Texas to check it out, the last details—then, wow! I get my own internal Krell brain boost. Do you know Axel Price? If you see him, tell him the treatment worked—I'm better than ever."

"I will," Fouad said.

A full squad of guards rushed clockwise along the circumference behind Fouad. From the other direction, behind the fallen guards and the programmer, ten more gathered, assault weapons drawn—pointing at Fouad as well as the skinny man.

They were well trained, not trigger-happy—for which he was grateful.

Fouad waved them back. "He's unarmed and he's injured. He's prepared to surrender."

The guards moved in, assault rifles at ready, unconvinced. Three of the five on the floor were again trying to get up.

"Shoot the bastards! Shoot 'em both!" Big Guard shouted, but his hand slipped in his own sweat and he fell and cracked his jaw. That was it for him.

Fouad secretly enjoyed this. For a moment, his sympathies were with the programmer—with Nick.

A short, blocky man in a dark red shirt—senior staff, chief of security—joined the group gathering beside Fouad. "Take him," he ordered.

Three of the guards pulled steel flashlights with big flat heads from their belts. The programmer yelped with delight. "Try it! Try me!"

The three circled at the maximum distance the hall allowed and swept him with super-dazzling flashes of light, brighter than a dozen suns. Nick yelped and covered his face, too late. The brilliance flooded his retinas, stunned the nerves behind his eyes, temporarily locked his brain in something like paralysis.

Helpless, off balance, he stumbled and fell. The guards swarmed him like ants over a grasshopper. In seconds the programmer was strung up like a roped steer.

The chief lifted one gloved hand, game over, then gave Fouad a knowing wink, one warrior to another. "Some show, huh? We'll take care of him from here. Get back to whatever you were doing—and not a word to anybody."

Fouad agreed that would be best.

10

Lion City

Sunset painted the empty land like a sheet of flame, oranges and reds on the horizon, blazing gold overhead. Dusty late summer days in Texas were bookended by wind-blown glimpses of hell. In the morning, the hell began yellow and pink and nearly silent; before nightfall, the sky gates opened, fierce and fiery.

South and east of Lion City, the main campus of Talos Corporation—classrooms, barracks, dining halls, mock towns, firing ranges—sprawled over ten thousand acres, larger than Lion City itself, and prouder, as well. Proud and remote.

The walled, moated, razor-wired campus lay quiet under the hot dusk sky, divided into four compounds like a gigantic cross carved into the west Texas flatland. Each compound was devoted to an aspect of Talos's overall mission: to train the world's police and armies in special tactics.

The gunshots, cannon fire, and explosions of the morning and afternoon had stopped. A couple of helicopters still hovered like lost dragonflies, dropping searchlight beams. The beams danced in the ascending heat. Hours would pass before the Earth cooled enough to kill all the shimmers and dust devils, the djinn of mirages.

Fouad was glad to be driving away from this day. He needed to communicate with his handlers and tell them he had what they wanted.

He pulled up to the lonely blockhouse at the Monarch gate, rolling slowly between three pairs of arched silvery wands, fringed like moth antennae. A guard scanned his iris, then swept batons over his arm chip and the windshield, while another ran mirrors and sensors on low carriages under the frame. Nothing broke this routine, unless they did not want to let you pass.

The guards pulled back the trolleys and mirrors and grimly waved him through. Nobody at the gates ever smiled. Their attitude was always, you made it through this time, but we're waiting for you to *slip up big time*.

Even after years in America, to Fouad, many English phrases still seemed wonderfully colorful, both cryptic and visual.

The chief of security back in Buckeye had not detained him. So perhaps he had not *slipped up big time*, after all.

He drove in sinusoid arcs around the concrete and steel barriers, then down the long, straight black access road that led to Old Tejano Trail, the main north-south artery of Lion County.

Fouad smiled and bared his teeth. Air rushed dry and hot through the open car window. He hung his arm out the door and waved his hand in the oven breeze. In the rearview mirror, his skin glowed and his eyes glittered like a demon's.

Only now did he allow himself to reflect on what had happened back in Buckeye. He had not dared to do so earlier, since one's thoughts were often reflected in one's features, and guards were trained to be alert to such.

As for the programmer, Nick—given his superhuman strength, skill, and startling speed—madness seemed out of the question.

Lion City had received its name from the color of the surrounding land—tawny brown-gold, like a lion's pelt. It was no more than a midsize town, laid out respectably on a square grid, with two big parallel streets lined with shops topped by apartments whose windows looked out over square overhangs and faded awnings.

Nine or ten longer, narrower streets cut crosswise like railroad ties, lined with Chinkapin oaks and modest but neatly kept homes fronted by dying lawns.

Bumped up around them came a scatter of outlying neighborhoods, more industrial, less reputable. People who did not work for Talos

Corporation lived out in those neighborhoods, and for them, these were hard times.

Fouad's stomach growled, but he never stopped at the eateries and truck stops that serviced local traffic and the Talos day and night shifts. All they offered was beef or pork and potatoes. Some had salad bars, but he had become superstitious of late about cross-contamination, perhaps because of long acquaintance with the American manner of fixing and eating food: theirs was a world ingeniously designed to frustrate any Muslim's attempt at keeping to *halal*.

Though no doubt the prochines within him were also *haram*—forbidden.

Still, these were good people, mostly; hard-working and religious, roughly pious, all of the same God, (there is no God but Allah), but Fouad rarely spoke of religion.

For twenty years, Talos's biggest contractor had been the Pentagon, whose officers and troops were trained in the Monarch compound. In the past five years, however, the U.S. military presence at Talos had been reduced to a minimum.

Expansion of the mercenary training program—mostly Haitians—had filled the gap, filling both Buckeye and Monarch.

The second largest bloc of contracts had traditionally come from security agencies of the U.S. government; they had once occupied Swallowtail. Those numbers had been reduced as well of late.

The third largest, considered as a cluster—police from states and municipalities around the United States—took up Birdwing. Several hundred were still in residence, receiving local antiterror (and anti-illegal immigrant) training.

The fourth largest—foreign police and security forces—had expanded in the last two years, and now helped fill the barracks and grounds of Buckeye. Buckeye was also the home of the Talos security and computer system.

Fouad had worked in all four compounds, training forces both foreign and domestic in Islamic languages and culture, with a side emphasis on special tactics in Middle Eastern war zones.

Talos had been pleased with his performance, awarding him two substantial bonuses.

A mile from the campus, Fouad switched on the radio and listened to the news. Food prices were up. They rose each month as more nations cut food exports, preferring to focus on feeding their own.

Bloody civil war finally raged in Burma, as did yet another drug-fueled insurrection in northern Mexico; three assassinations in Russia in the past twenty-four hours; oil prices falling to levels not seen since 2010.

America was finally on a course to energy independence from the Middle East and South America, thereby threatening economic stability in both regions.

As he drove, apartment buildings and condos and gated housing developments popped up like forts on the bare Texas land.

New slender black roads linked them all to Old Tejano.

He switched off the radio, turned west, and swung into the apartment complex that served as home, away from the instructor dorms.

He had spent more time here a few months ago while dating, but that relationship ended and the woman went back to her family, of old Mexican descent; they had not approved of Fouad. No risk—good for his cover. Talos encouraged and expected roots in the community, like Alexander in the east.

Fouad climbed the steps by the enclosed garage and opened the door with a brass key, then stood for a moment on the first floor, in the stuffy, air-conditioned darkness, peering into shadows, checking corners.

The blinds were drawn on the windows and the rear patio door.

He switched on lights in random sequence—never the same. A quick tour showed that nothing had been searched, nothing moved or rearranged except perhaps with micrometer precision.

He assumed the apartment was wired and that sensors were embedded in the paint, the furniture, the carpet. Elsewhere, computers would assemble amorphous streams of visual data into crystal-clear pictures, like so many virtual lenses.

Being watched was a perpetual assumption for anyone who worked for Price. Best not to bet otherwise.

Fouad opened the refrigerator and removed a Coca-Cola. He then climbed the narrow apartment stairs and sat in an armchair by the small den window, sipping with eyes closed, wondering if he should read or watch television. Act as if relaxing.

Settling in from a hard day's work and of course the incident in the circumference hall.

After a few minutes he got up and walked into the bedroom to retrieve from his nightstand a yellow-jacketed university press paperback of Ibn Khaldun. His father had given it to him in Cairo many years ago. He had so few things from his father. It contained a small sample of elegant Arabic script, translated into English with square, precise roman letters:

Allegiance to God above all. But don't tell that to the kings, generals, and tyrants.

He returned to the den to read and think for a few minutes.

He had what he had come here to get. It was time to arrange for his discreet extraction. He could not just drive or walk away. He would likely be intercepted before he reached the county line, either by the Lion City sheriff or by Talos security.

Detectors around Talos used natural dust in the air to reveal and pinpoint laser communications from the ground. Radio and microwave transmissions were detected by other sensors, which quickly triangulated sources.

All unknown transmissions were investigated.

Internet traffic was tightly controlled by Talos as a public service to the Lion County area, to prevent "foreign hackers" from causing trouble and to protect locals from downloading or viewing material of a questionable political nature—or pornography.

Price very likely had access to quantum decrypt, which could crack almost any transmitted cipher in hours.

Talos had once offered a class on breaking foreign encryption, limited to U.S. military and government agents with high security clearances . . . That work had been okayed as a favor to Price back in the days of the Bush administration, when significant aspects of nearly everything about security and defense had been outsourced to corporations like Talos.

In truth, a potentially nasty security breach had spurred the investigation in the first place—the discovery that people beholden to Price
had accessed top secret research documents in the NDI and NSA.

There were still over twenty retired generals—and several former
CIA and NSA officials—on Price's payroll.

With communications in and out of Lion City closely monitored by
people and agencies who either worked for or sympathized with Axel
Price, there was only one channel left open for what Fouad needed to
do: an old method, though not as antiquated as smoke signals and
less traceable.

Somewhere within a ten mile radius of Fouad's apartment complex,
a private home had been rented by the Bureau and equipped with a
hidden earth current transceiver—capable of receiving and transmitting high-voltage, 700-hertz DC signals sent through the dirt itself. An
agent was posted there at all times.

Earth current telephony had a long history but was mostly known
to history buffs and a few ham radio amateurs. Fouad's own unit was
disguised as an antique Grundig radio receiver. Even this had a cover
story. It had originally been purchased by his father in Egypt. He kept
it for sentimental reasons.

Through a hole drilled by hand in the concrete floor of the garage—
where he was relatively certain there was no surveillance—Fouad had
sunk two copper spikes deep into the stony soil, disguising the
arrangement as an ordinary ground wire for a gas pipe. The device's
maximum range was likely less than twelve miles. When atmospherics
were wrong—during the frequent thunderstorms that lashed this
part of the world—sending or receiving a signal would be difficult
or impossible. Lightning surging through the Earth overwhelmed
any other transmission. But the weather today had been calm all
across Texas.

No lightning strikes for hundreds of miles.

Trailing two runs of lamp cord, Fouad descended the steps from the
first floor into the garage. One cord was attached to the radio speaker.
All he needed to do to send a signal was tap the other cord against the
twisted cable. The return signal would come as a series of clicks over
the speaker, above the murmuring crackle of natural noise.

Under clear conditions, voice communication was theoretically possible, and even painfully slow data transmission, but clicks were more difficult to distinguish from background noise: air conditioners and refrigerators switching on and off, motors starting everywhere.

Just in case Talos kept an electronic ear to the dry Texas ground.

Fouad laid a small foam exercise mat on the concrete floor, squatted, and sent his brief message. Within ten seconds, someone at the opposite end began to respond.

He pulled the wires away and coiled them in the cardboard box with the old radio. Then he went upstairs, opened his closet, removed laundry from his small suitcase, took a quick shower, and changed clothes. After, he looked through the almost empty cupboards, contemplating what he might have for supper. Canned fava beans imported from the United Arab Emirates looked likely, mixed with canned chicken and onion and dried vegetable flakes.

This was simmering in a pot on the stove when he heard military vehicles in the parking lot outside. He went to the window and peered down through the open ironwork of the balcony rail. Two armored Torq-Vees—high-riding armored personnel carriers, originally designed for the deep mud roads of Afghanistan—had rumbled into the lot and blocked both exits. The closest Torq-Vee lurched a few yards forward, bumping the garage door, and three helmeted security personnel in black assault gear dropped from the open hatches.

Their boots send heavy thumps and rattles up the stairs and around the apartment.

Frowning, Fouad met them at the open door, bowl of beans steaming in one hand, spoon raised in the other. This was it, he thought. He would be interrogated while still hungry.

"May I help you?" he asked.

The lead, a trim thirtyish man with jet-black hair and pale skin—eyes hidden behind darkened spex—approached the door as his team flanked the steps.

"Mr. Al-Husam, Mr. Price has requested a meeting. We've had communication problems—phones are out. Apologies for the show of force." The guard was smiling but by little movements of his head, Fouad could tell his eyes were scanning Fouad's face and the apartment behind him. "We should get going, sir, if you're going to make your appointment."

"Of course," Fouad said, and replaced his frown with a smile. It was always a privilege to meet with Mr. Price—bragging rights would be his. "Lead on."

II

Dubai

Two hours later, haggard and somber, Nathaniel took a limo to Dubai Airport.

The Quiet Man had always been aware they might face difficulties. As a precaution, Jones had reached out and created false identities for all of the Turing Seven. So many fingers in so many pies around the planet.

Jones was that good.

The people in the Ziggurat lobby . . . He did not know just how they would have disposed of him when they were finished.

The desert, vast and empty.

In the packed airport mall, under the shade of a gigantic hammered-brass palm tree, Nathaniel used one of his assigned IDs to link up with a pilot who flew oil and architecture execs from Jiddah and Dubai back to the states. The pilot arranged for him to hitch an anonymous ride on a MedPetro jet to London.

There, using a new passport—traveling as Robert Sangstrom—he would pay for a ticket to the United States.

He would arrive in Los Angeles just in time to greet the California dawn. Nathaniel had made up his mind. Novelty was the game of the hour.

For now, and just for starters, he would try doing some good, just to see how it felt.

12

Talos Campus

The wide window of the Talos command center looked out over forty acres of calf-high, swaying grass, dazzling green beneath high banks of football lights. The field had been planted at Price's orders to replicate the original Texas tallgrass prairie that had once covered twenty million acres.

Indiangrass and Little Bluestem flowed up to the window, lush and deceptive.

Axel Price was a tough man to see, even when he was doing the summoning. Fouad was increasingly certain his cover was blown. There were many sympathetic to Price even within the Bureau. He wondered which would come first: his meeting or security police dangling handcuffs.

With the slow, painful decline of oil prices in the second decade of the twenty-first century—and the living death of the local cattle industry after three major outbreaks of hoof and mouth disease—Talos Corporation was now the only thing that enabled anyone to make a living in this part of Texas. It supported almost a quarter of the state; it might even elevate Axel Price to governor—*or emperor*, Fouad mused, if the state legislature finished cutting itself away from the feds.

This time, there would be no Abraham Lincoln to stand in their way.

The receptionist—a slender brunette in a tight brown skirt and white blouse, mincing on shiny black high heels—opened the door to his left and tapped across the slate floor. Her glasses were shaped like cat's eyes, with small wings on their outer tips, as if they wanted to fly away.

"I'm sorry, Mr. Al-Husam," she said. "Mr. Price was here a few minutes ago, but a helicopter came and took him out to the Smoky. He told me you should hop a shuttle and meet him there."

"Thank you," Fouad said.

Even more privilege. The Smoky was Price's private ranch, four hundred acres on the northern edge of the Talos Campus. He did not raise cattle or horses but kept antique cars, helicopters, and armored vehicles in hangars and garages nearby—along with a sophisticated fighter jet, a two-seat Sukhoi Su-27 that he sometimes flew out of the Lion City airport, with the help of a professional pilot.

"I've called the van," she continued, "and it'll be here in five minutes. Terribly inconvenient, but he says it's important."

"I will wait out front," Fouad said.

"You do that! It'll be here in a jiff."

He left the reception area and stood on the porch beside the parking lot. Crickets sang in the dark heat. He wondered where they found their moisture. His own lips were dry. Of course, crickets did not have or need lips. Cartoons from television again came to mind: they spat black juice and played guitars.

Or perhaps those were grasshoppers or locusts.

The security team was nowhere in sight.

Other than the timing, there was no good reason to believe he had been discovered. He had been exceptionally careful and Jane Rowland had trained him well.

Still, Talos was a place of unexpected eyes and ears. Price's dictum was that since he trusted everyone, no one should mind being closely watched. *"We're all family here—partners in a big effort. I'm watched, we're all watched. It's no big deal."*

Price had nothing to hide. Of course, reports of his activities ultimately ended up on his own desk.

Fouad did not know what to make of what he had seen of the information that now passed through the tiny machines in his blood. Banks, corporations, international holding companies, names—nations.

He was grateful he was merely a vessel and not an analyst.

Even so, as he waited under the Texas night—the stars bleached from the sky by the banks of lights—he made a few surmises, put together a few educated guesses.

It did not look good.

The Bureau had been right to send him here.

A shuttle pulled up to the curb, a long, broad black van with twelve seats, all empty. The door swung open. The driver was a young, muscular black with short hair. He wore a gray jumpsuit with red stripes on the sleeves and pants legs, as did all support service workers on the campus. He smiled at Fouad as he climbed up the steps and took a front seat, facing the windshield.

"Dry, hot night," the driver said. "Straight to the Smoky, Mr. Al-Husam. Good time to see the ranch. They had choppers up doing practice runs last time I was out there, a couple hours ago. Might still be putting on a show. Real fine."

The shuttle drove through darkness along straight smooth roads, better maintained than the city streets or highways. The headlights painted in brilliant white the occasional jackrabbit, one possum, one *artichoke*—no, *armadillo*. Like little armored rats, armadillos were common around here, unsightly and unclean beasts—or so Fouad surmised. They were frequently seen ruptured and ugly, squashed by passing cars. It was said the treatment for leprosy had been found in the pads of armadillo feet. No Muslim could have made that discovery—nor even come close to touching such a prehistoric curiosity.

Yes, definitely unclean.

The driver delivered him to the gate house for the Smoky, and from there, another driver used an open cart to take Fouad half a mile to the main house, around to a side entrance, and dropped him off at the door.

At no point did this seem to be anything alarming or out of the ordinary.

Yet the network on the campus *had* gone out. Or so they said.

* * *

Price's private office was simple but elegant, the very best money could buy, but without much in the way of ostentation or even artwork, and comparatively small—barely twenty feet on a side.

A modest low bay window looked out over another plot of tall grass and beyond that, a set of gray hangars lined the horizon.

As Fouad watched, the lights surrounding these buildings dimmed, then shut off.

The side windows were open and a clean, grassy night breeze blew into the room, prickling the hairs on his neck.

A curved bank of monitors covered the eastern wall of the office, providing a panoramic view of a broad, distant gray ocean—sunrise or sunset, Fouad could not tell. In the middle monitor, jerky video of a large cargo ship marked "HKA" was apparently being shot from the vantage of a small boat crossing choppy water.

The view swooped to the left to show three other boats bouncing and skimming: trim, fast, purple inflatables known as Starfish.

The CEO of Talos rose from a stool in front of the monitors, took a sharp step forward, and offered his hand to Fouad.

Axel Price would have been difficult to describe to a sketch artist, yet once you saw him, you never forgot him. Beneath neatly trimmed brown hair, his clean, planed face was at once handsome and unmemorable. He had a narrow, knowing smile and observant but not penetrating blue eyes. Very small lines around the corners of his lips could just as easily have been traces of cruelty or humor. Just above his collar line, Fouad saw reddened scars, which he guessed would extend down his back—a case of acne rosacea, perhaps, in Price's impoverished adolescence.

Price stood two inches taller but did not outweigh him. Fouad had put on a little weight in the past year and Price was in top condition though slender, with just the beginning of a stoop.

"I've heard a lot about you," he said as he walked around Fouad to close the door. "You've done a great job for us."

"Always a pleasure serving Talos, sir."

Price returned to the stool and sat with one leg raised, brown Oxford wedged on a cross bar. "I was impressed by how you performed at Buckeye. Sorry you had to be exposed to that silliness. What do you suppose tipped the poor guy?"

"I have no idea," Fouad said. "He is not known to me."

"Not really known to anyone, apparently. Big mistake, hiring those guys. All of them. Scattered all over the planet now, ticking time bombs, waiting to explode." Price waited for a reaction.

Fouad lowered one eyebrow, truly uninformed.

"Well, you handled him better than my guards. A magnificent job of defusing. I'm grateful."

"Is the programmer well?" Fouad asked.

He wondered why programmers as a group would be waiting to explode.

Price lifted one shoulder and grimaced. "No longer your concern."

He pointed to the rightmost monitor. A fast patrol ship in purple and green—Talos colors—was standing off from the cargo vessel.

"Gulf of Aden. You'd think I wanted to be Pompey the Great, with all the pirates my boys discourage and all the ships I recover. Started that business five years ago. When foreign countries want military assistance, they don't go to the U.S. government anymore—they come to me. I sell protective systems to ship owners, but they're slow to spend what they cost—so I charge them for recovery, ten times more expensive. It's hard, dangerous work. Never underestimate what a little boredom and a lot of poverty can do to a bunch of fishermen.

"A few years ago, when our snipers started blowing their brains out, the Somalis acquired a taste for blood as well as treasure." He grinned with a touch of boyish wickedness. "It's an old story—but they're getting tougher and meaner and more desperate every year, poor bastards. So we conduct our raids the same way they do. Surprise, speed, and ass-kicking violence."

Fouad could see no guns on the patrol ship, but recognized a prickly array of LED blinders—bigger versions of the light used on Nick in Buckeye—as well as seizure-inducing strobes, acoustic blasters, and even conical microwave pain projectors, mounted on the bow.

"My team commander has just given the pirates five minutes to abandon the vessel and leave the crew unharmed," Price said. "If they aren't away by then, he'll go in with a pulsed sound and light show—

sends anyone topside into fits, and they don't even have to face the strobes. Backscatter does the trick most of the time. Anybody inside is going to have their sphincters open right up—the crew will be inconvenienced, but Hershey shorts are better than dying. Hell of a sensation. All my guys go through it, though not the strobe fits—too many side effects.

"But we get the ships back, 100 percent, and if the pirates harm anyone—or if any of the crew is severely affected by our recovery operations—then we hunt the pirates down on the open water and blast them to fish food. They never get home to squeeze their kids and kiss the missus."

"And if they depart the vessel as ordered?" Fouad asked.

"We let 'em go. Catch and release. They're one of our biggest centers of profit—fees plus 30 percent of assessed ship and cargo. You trained a few of these Starfish boys in Arabic and Aramaic a few months back. They seem proficient.

"You're very good at what you do, Mr. Al-Husam. *All* that you do."

"Thank you," Fouad said. His neck hairs had not stopped prickling since he entered the office.

The starfish had come within a few hundred yards of the cargo ship, which now switched on its working lights, lighting up like it was in port and waiting to offload.

Men with assault rifles scampered along the gunwales, as seen through a telephoto camera on the lead starfish.

Muzzle flare sparked from several points on the facing port side.

Price humphed. He slid off the stool and approached the monitors. "Getting tired of me, are you, aren't you, you skinny sons of *oola-oola-oola* black bitches?" He glanced at Fouad again, eyes sharp. "Watch this."

The camera lens was blocked by men erecting black foam barriers like curtains around the inflatable.

Bullets splashed in the last visible stretch of water.

"Curtains protect our crew from the worst of it. But all my Starfish team members wear diapers, just in case."

The camera winked out and another view took its place on the central monitor—from the bridge of the patrol ship.

Starfish bobbed like lumps of coal in the water, hundreds of yards from the cargo ship.

"Love this, just *love* this," Price murmured, rapt.

Blinker strobes lit up the ocean. Even through the monitor, Fouad could imagine the dazzle of the rapid-fire flashes of white and blue light, the laser beams drawing red squiggles along the vessel's upper works.

"Here it comes," Price said, folding his arms.

The first big pulse of sound from the bow of the fast patrol ship feathered the ocean like an invisible broom. Fouad could see the hull plates on the cargo ship actually ripple with the impact.

Men flew back like matchsticks.

Their ears would bleed—perforated ear drums, great pain.

Not visible at all were the microwave pain projectors. On deck, the men would feel their skin burn as if bathed in hot oil. The effects were temporary but felt mortal.

Next, through the speakers came a greatly reduced and muffled *thum-thum-thum*, rapid as the flashes of light. Fouad knew the frequencies of both sound and strobes—had witnessed them in training at the Academy, and after, when studying crowd control. Less than lethal, usually, but painful and disturbing.

The deck was soon clear of standing figures.

"That's it," Price said. "They won't abandon ship. We've pushed them too far. Now we board and take them out one by one—lots of skinny black corpses."

Price snapped his fingers and the monitors shut off. "That concludes tonight's show. We'll do the accounting and send off the bills tomorrow."

He focused his attention on Fouad.

"John tells me you're the best we've got with dialects. He's already seeing results with his Haitian boys in the field in Algeria and Libya."

One of Price's three senior partners, a former South African army colonel named John Yardley, was in charge of Talos's Special Forces Training division. The mercenary troops Yardley trained—mostly Haitians—called him "Colonel Sir."

"Your students are highly motivated," Fouad said. "I take pleasure in working with them."

"Good pay, great benefits, terrific prospects," Price said, nodding approval. "Uncle Sam has a moth or two in his pockets and not much more. We're paying our overseas contractors about eight times the average government salary, twelve times the typical military starting pay grade. Causes a bit of a stir."

Price walked to the window. Outside, a very large insect buzzed past. It wasn't an insect, of course.

"I'd like to move you up a notch," he said. "As you know, we've got a big conference in a couple of weeks. I've asked the campus supervisors who's best at translating Arabic dialects—and they all tell me it's you, hands down. You're also well-versed in Texan, I hear." Price chuckled. "Not easy to get a handle on how we talk around here. The food alone . . . well, Muslims aren't big fans of some of our favorite dishes."

Fouad remained smiling.

"We'll be hiding billboards and such that might offend some of our Muslim guests as they limo in from the airport. I've asked restaurant owners to cover up the pink neon pigs, that sort of thing. They're happy to oblige—they know how important this is to Lion City. But once our guests are here, I'd like a fellow I can trust to provide a running commentary, delivered straight to me, on how they're thinking, what they're saying, and maybe pitch in and correct misunderstandings, as need be. I'd like you to be that fellow."

Price gestured to a well-upholstered blue leather chair on one side of the desk, near the window.

"Take a seat, Mr. Al-Husam."

Fouad sat. This was not at all what he had expected. Best to show surprise and quiet pride. "I am honored," he said.

Price beamed. "I pick my people well."

The man could be charming. Many here could be charming and yet hold the most untoward views.

"Tell me what you think that sort of work would require, Fouad . . . if we can go on a first-name basis. And please, call me Axel."

Price's pronunciation was good. He spoke sound but rudimentary Arabic, from the years when he had directed security and other contracts in Iraq, Afghanistan, and Kuwait.

"I could be attached to delegations as a back-up translator," Fouad said. "The guests will rely on their own translators, but they will not be offended if you also position someone with expertise, to listen."

"My thoughts exactly. You can't cover all the conversations—hell, I'll probably only be able to drop by for about a third of the sessions myself. But if I'm there . . . you'll be there. I'd be pleased if we could make that sort of arrangement. Keep you around a while, at a much higher pay grade than a teacher, of course."

"It would be my pleasure, Mr. Price—Axel," Fouad said. "My contract, however, is soon ended, and I have other commitments I would have to adjust."

Price bowed his head and threw up his hand, showing this was not his concern.

"I'm sure you can work it out," he said. "Start now. I might need you in a snap, so we'll put you up in a guest house. Real nice place. Deluxe. You'll sleep out there tonight. My logistics team will move your stuff from Lion City. You'll need a chip upgrade, of course—deep, deep security."

"Thank you," Fouad said, but his heart was not with him. This familiarity felt too convenient. Trust meant nothing to Axel Price—caution was his hallmark.

"The conference is coming up fast," Price said. "Private jets from all over are coming into Lion City airport. About two hundred guests, fifty or sixty from the Emirates, Qatar, Arabia Deserta, Yemen, Jordan—plus retinues. You'll get all the docs and prep you need, plus a finger-key transcriber." He held out his hand and waggled his fingers. "You know how to use it—like a court steno?"

Fouad nodded. It was standard for secure translators.

"Good. FBI trained you well. Any regrets about heading for greener pastures while the Bureau's in limbo?"

"Of course," Fouad said. "But it was inevitable."

"Moving them out of D.C. and Virginia—that's a hoot. Our beltway masters seem to think they need to squeeze everything good out of the South—or squeeze the South out of everything. As if the war never ended."

Price shook his head in wonder at this effrontery. "Be up and dressed by 0700. Prep team will meet you in the cook shack.

"Welcome to the ranch!"

13

Los Angeles, California

The bar was a long, shadowed cave with highlights of blue and gold. The angled glass window beyond the stools and tall tables overlooked a themed restaurant laid out like a 1930s train station. Three dining cars waited beside a wooden platform, sleek roofs lacquered black, sides painted tan and hunter green. Waiters in white jackets and trim black pants and red caps showed customers to their tables while diners watched through half dropped windows.

The restaurant was called The Roundhouse and Rebecca Rose had come here at the invitation of a navy captain. They were in town attending the COPES domestic security conference and had unexpectedly run into each other while registering in the convention center lobby.

His name was Peter Periglas, Captain, USN, retired. It had been two years since they last met—on a ship in the Red Sea.

Two years since Mecca.

She sipped her vodka martini. She didn't like themed restaurants. Worse, the captain was late.

The bartender was a waxen, seen-it-all mannequin with toned shoulders and silicone breasts, eyes dulled by self-doubt and too many boyfriends. She asked Rebecca if she wanted a refill.

"I'm good."

Rebecca was about to get off her stool and return to the hotel when she saw a tall man with black hair enter through heavy glass doors at the far end of the bar.

He caught her eye and waved.

She quirked her lips and waved back.

"Sorry," Periglas said, approaching with a sheepish grin. "My handlers are giving me grief about my speech tomorrow. I seem to be a little stiff."

"I was surprised to see you in the exhibit hall," Rebecca said. "When did you get out of the navy?"

"Last year. Took the rank—they offered it out of rotation—and then retired. Too many secrets, I guess. You?"

"Not really retired—just on extended leave. Furlough."

"So what are you doing?"

"Consulting, traveling. Enjoying life."

"I need a beer," the captain said.

The bartender was occupied by three raucous young men at the far end of the bar.

"How long with the FBI, total?" Periglas asked.

"Eighteen years. And you, the navy?"

"Twenty-three. Enough of the wine-dark sea. Dry land looks good. I'd like to become a private investigator. I could set up a downtown office," Periglas said. "Inland Empire Investigations. Keep a .38 in a drawer. Stare out the window, harass the pigeons, suck on a bottle of hooch and let the California sun bake me through the flyspecked window while I bask in a big oak swivel chair."

"You've given it some thought," Rebecca said. "Sounds pretty good."

She had dealt with navy men before. All the pulling up of roots made them a little too quick, a little too eager, but this time, she didn't mind.

"You could protect all the pretty WAVEs when they come to you with their problems. Sensible shoes, tight skirts, pert little . . . caps."

Even before Periglas had invited her to the bar, Rebecca had checked his left hand. The impressed shadow of a ring.

"My wife—my ex-wife—can't stand me enjoying anything. She was why I knew I would never make admiral. Hates Washington." The captain grinned a what-can-you-do grin. "Do we order bar food or descend to the dining cars?" he asked. "Cost no object. I'm buying."

Rebecca gave a passing thought to dropping her shields. It was about time. He seemed pleasant and smart, a little out-of-breath but not nervous. He might not bite. She might not bite. She felt remarkably strong.

All better now.

"Did you make reservations?" she asked.

"Nope," Periglas said.

"Tail o' the Pup for us, then," Rebecca said, leaning across the bar to get the waxy woman's attention.

No joy.

"That was over on San Vicente," Periglas said. "I'm a native Angeleno. My father might have eaten at the Pup. I never did. It's been gone for years."

He lifted his arm and the bartender gave him a frown and a nod but kept arguing with the young men.

When she finally minced down behind the long bar to their seats, her eyes were like flints and her cheeks flushed cherry.

"We need another war, to filter out pricks like that," she said. "What can I get you?"

Periglas's breath hitched. Sharp lines framed his mouth.

"Nothing," he said. He rose from the stool and leaned toward the bartender, practically in her face. "I've watched young pricks like that get *filtered*," he said. "I'll put up with happy bullshit any day."

He swung around and marched toward the exit.

Rebecca grabbed her purse and followed. She watched him with a fascinated grin, which she tucked away when he looked back at her, replaced with polite interest.

"Apologies, Rebecca. I usually don't show my bitter card until the second date. Let's stalk the evening like wolves," he said, arms swinging. His looseness came from dissipating anger, but also from self-assurance. He was happy to be here, expected nothing in particular, happy to be with her—happy in his own skin.

Not manic, not nervous, not showing off in the least.

He was just that way.

He glanced aside like an embarrassed boy as they came out under the cobalt sky. "So—let's find a little, out-of-the-way bistro and gorge on tiny plates of overpriced food."

Rebecca focused on what she could see of his face and smiled again, this time openly—she smiled a lot around Periglas. This was what she could expect: good talk from a decent man. Some of his stories were doubtless more interesting than hers.

Life at sea, camaraderie and discipline, engines and weather—anything but the creeps and monsters she had had to pursue, capture, help convict—and make miserable—throughout her entire career.

And yet there were always more.

She still kept three pictures in her wallet of a few of the worst that got away. Murderers and rapists—portraits of monsters rather than children.

Perhaps the monsters *were* her children.

"Forget the bistro," she said. "Let's get room service."

Periglas appeared genuinely surprised. For a terrible moment, Rebecca felt like a teenager pushing too far, too fast.

"All right," he said.

"We're civilians, mostly," she said. "They owe us time away from the world."

"No explanation necessary," Periglas said. "Lead on."

Rebecca's phone wheedled. She looked at the number. This was a call she had to take.

"My room," Rebecca said, and passed him a hotel key folder without the key.

Periglas drew his hand over his eyes, fingers spread. "I am beguiled," he said.

"Give me ten minutes," she said.

Rebecca closed the door to the room and set her purse on the nightstand. Biting her lip, more nervous than she had been in months—she returned the call she had been hoping would come.

A recorded voice answered. "Central California Adoption Services. Our offices are closed for the day—"

She punched in the code for Dr. Benvenista. The doctor's high, musical voice came through after the third chime.

"Hello, Rebecca. How's Los Angeles?"

"Nice," Rebecca said, her throat full. She wasn't used to being so scared. "Busy."

"Fresno is scalding. We have great news. You've passed the third round. Though I do wish you had a good man in your life. We could sail you right through."

"I'm working on it," Rebecca said, embarrassed and hopeful enough to stretch the truth.

"Mary is doing quite well. One inspector expressed lingering concern about the race issue, but I think that is not a major objection at this point. You are a stable person and well-motivated, and you are certainly qualified, and I have said so to the committee. Who better to protect a little child than a mommy who's an FBI agent?"

Bureau. On furlough.

"Thank you."

"There will be more news tomorrow, and perhaps the paperwork will clear by the end of the week. Until then, please keep in touch."

Rebecca expressed her thanks and relief, said goodbye, and closed the phone—just as she heard a polite rap on the room door. She opened it, her chest tight, stomach a-flutter. Too much all at once.

Tough to keep up her game face.

Periglas entered as she finished dabbing her eyes with her coat sleeve.

"I don't often have that effect on women," he said, his voice soft, wondering.

"It's not you," Rebecca said, and took his outstretched hand. "Not *just* you, I mean. It's everything. I think I'm becoming a human being again. It's been so goddamned long . . ."

She looked up, across two inches of difference in height, and searched his face.

Her lower lip trembled. She bit it, but did not stop checking out his forehead, his cheeks, his nose, then his eyes.

His eyes were slightly moist, reflecting hers.

"Damn," she whispered.

Periglas put his hands on her shoulders and leaned toward her, as if about to lead her into a dance.

"Dinner first?" he asked.

She wrapped her arms around him and squeezed, frightened and incredibly hungry—ravenous, but not for food.

For a home. A place to rest and arms to rest in.

Hungry for all the glories and sins flesh was heir to.

Maybe you're finally cured.

"Dinner after," she said.

14

Sherman Oaks, California

Nathaniel Trace had arrived in California in a state of rolling nausea and hunger. He could not find the proper foods to eat.

He cabbed from LAX up the 405 to Ventura Boulevard, then checked into a back room in a sprawling old hotel—and locked himself in.

The hotel was seventy-two years old. It had two hundred and fifteen rooms.

He lay down for two hours but could not sleep.

Rising from the rumpled bed, he shook his head to get rid of the dizzies—they came in late morning and sometimes late evening—and drew back the opaque curtains.

There was blood on his hand. It smeared on the rod and a drop or two fell on the carpet. A trail to the bed.

He had bitten his hand.

That made him chuckle.

Extra tip for the maid.

Through the white veil of the inner curtain, glancing at the parking lot, he instantly counted sixty-two cars. Fourteen trees, none of them very tall. Thirteen people walking, four drivers trying to park. Sixty-three buildings visible between nadir and horizon. Five hundred and sixty-four windows. No doors visible from his vantage point, except twenty-four car doors—six opening, one closing.

"Today, in the state where I was born, I am thirty-six years old," Nathaniel said. Numbers were important. If he thought hard enough, counted long enough, they would all add up—like a combination lock.

"I'm turning into fucking Rain Man," he whispered. "Jesus H. Christ. Nobody hires card counters."

He wiped his hand on the curtain, then thought again: time to stop acting like a bloody animal and recharge the old social programming. He went into the bathroom to wash out the bite. Could his own bite be septic? He used soap. There were marks on both hands. He'd have to stop that or wear gloves.

Already today he had cycled through seven different hells and seven different heavens.

When he realized that this was entirely up to him, or some part of him—that some or other will controlled his mood—it scared him. For a few moments there, floating in a disconnected and emotionless void, looking at the wallpaper and feeling like a fish flying through the air, he had for a couple of hours forgotten his real name.

"I should move into a creepy old house," he told the mirror, then looked hard at his reflection and smiled. He had finally found something he could not count: the thick mat of gingery hairs on his head.

Too confused.

My tire chocks have been pulled and I'm rolling free. My emergency brake is busted. It was a lovely feeling for a while.

Now, not so much.

But who the hell am I? If Mariposa is coming undone, then the others must feel the same way—wherever they are.

What if somehow his *fingers* could hold supremacy over his brain? What if central control was now up to his arm, his foot—his liver, his bowels?

He had found several days ago that he could make his vision turn purple, or shade it into the pink—and then push it back to something like normal.

Not even a baby is born this clear.

Everything is possible.

When he believed he was capable of interacting with the public again on some minimal level, Nathaniel dressed, left the room, and forced himself to walk around the hotel grounds, then up and down Ventura Boulevard.

The sun peeking between clouds actually made his skin vibrate. That felt good—good and healthy.

So perhaps this was still just a boost phase and he had not yet achieved a stable orbit, *and what then, old cosmic mind?*

Nathaniel returned to the room and crept into bed. He wiped his hands on the sheets. After a few minutes of studying his palms, frowning deeply, he picked up his disposable cell and slipped in a new quantum card.

Then he typed in a key code and called a dummy transponder in Nicaragua.

The dummy flashed his call to a number none of them knew, which passed it on—again through a quantum EPR cell—to yet another number.

It took several seconds to connect with the Quiet Man.

"Checkpoint Turing." The low voice at the other end sounded calm but exhausted.

"Nathaniel here. I'm in LA."

"You're late. Hugh and Jerry have checked in but nobody's heard from Nick in two days. Have you heard about the vice president?"

"Saw it on a reader headline in the hotel lobby. Wild. What does Jones say?"

"I think he knew about it before the public announcement. He called it a 'potential triggering event.' But he won't say if it was planned."

"So what was it, a coincidence?"

"Unknown."

Nathaniel felt a little sting of mortal practicality—followed by irritation. "We were supposed to be free and clear before the shit hit the fan. Any luck with the new covering IDs?"

"They're in place, twenty-one of them. Better than federal grade. I've kept them away from Jones, so he doesn't feel any conflict. His attitude is fairly even and smooth. I'd like to keep it that way.

"I got a call from Dr. Plover, of all people," the Quiet Man continued. "None of you has had any contact with him for over a year, right?"

"I certainly haven't."

"He sounds unhappy. Says he wants to meet. He asked for you in particular."

"Do we owe him anything?"

"No. But he may have something for us. He's being cagey—seems to be caught between professional responsibility and complete paranoia."

"Maybe he should take some of his own medicine."

"He's staying somewhere in downtown LA, near the convention center—there's a security conference there, COPES, C-O-P-E-S. He was scheduled to give a presentation on Mariposa, but withdrew."

"Was he going to use me as an exhibit?"

"Unknown. I suggest that you meet with him. It's only a suggestion, of course."

Nathaniel thought this over, looked down at his hand. "I'm not all that presentable," he said.

The Quiet Man took one of his long pauses. Nathaniel could hear him breathing—soft, regular. It sounded almost artificial, like a machine.

"He wanted me specifically? Not the others in town?"

"Just you. I shipped him an EPR phone. Here's the number." The Quiet Man read it out to him. It was no problem to memorize the sixty-four digits. And Nathaniel was certain he would not forget.

"Get back to me with whatever you learn."

"What if I don't go?" Nathaniel asked, but the connection had already been cut.

He removed the card from the cell and cracked it in half. Code dust leaked out onto the floor. He scuffed the small mound with his bare foot, grinding the tiny polygons into the carpet.

Now no one could ever trace anything, no matter how hard they tried.

Nathaniel lay back on the bed and stared at the blank ceiling, just to quell his overwhelming urge to count. It didn't work. He started up again with the ghostly floaters drifting through his field of vision.

Closed his eyes.

Counted the speckles in the reddish dark.

Another hour passed.

The voice of interior reason spoke.

Why just you? Better call the others. Besides, don't you want to learn how they're getting along?

Let's surprise the old head poker.

He picked up his cell, inserted another card, and made three calls. The last was to Dr. Plover.

15

Boise, Idaho

William Griffin stood in the middle of the wet street and turned full circle, surrounded by fire trucks, canvas hoses, water streaming into the gutters, backing up behind dams of slushy ash, scraps of black shingle, sopping pink insulation—

And the blackened skeletons of twelve suburban homes.

Everything smelled of deadly sweet smoke. His gray suit would reek on the flight back to Washington.

He walked around the hulk of a compact electric Toyota, formerly cherry red, one side now scorched and melted, the rear end twisted and blown out by exploding batteries. The car was still hooked up by a big yellow cable to the driveway plug stand.

The flames had begun in one house— this one, the residence of Maddy and Howard Plumber, now a low black pile and still smoking. High winds from the west had ignited ten other houses. Then the winds had reversed and thrown burning debris over the rest of the neighborhood on the cul-de-sac, skipping only two homes, which now poked from the ashes like healthy molars in a sick jaw.

In the first house, the firemen had found a charred body—female, identified by the coroner through DNA as Madeline Paris, formerly of Bethesda, Maryland. William knew a little about her: a doctor specializing in hormonal and astrocyte disorders.

Her husband, Dr. Terence Plover, aka Howard Plumber, was missing. He might be buried deeper in the smoldering debris, or he might not have been in the house at all. None of the neighbors seemed to know much about them. They had moved in just a couple of weeks ago and weren't very social.

An unmarked Boise police cruiser drew up beside William. A large, square head with a stub of mustache and short bristly brown hair poked out of the driver's window. One hand flipped open a silver badge. "Boise CID. They told me Griff's pup was out here sniffing around. You don't look like your dad, except maybe the eyes."

William turned to squint through his spex at the driver, a detective old enough to have known William Griffin Sr.—known to his friends and colleagues as Griff—an agent who had always been more popular and more accomplished than his son, back in the FBI's better days.

"I take after my mother's side," William said.

"Sorry to hear about your old man," the detective said. He stopped the car in the middle of the street and got out, then leaned on the car door—a bulky, muscular man with a craggy, critical face.

Sharp eyes, sees everything.

"Back in the day, we'd have welcomed Griff's attention. Can't say we feel the same now. Times change, Agent Griffin. Which is it—FBI, or just the Bureau?"

"Bureau," William said.

"That's right. FBI kaput. Draw the blinds, turn out the lights—make sure to flush before you leave." He turned to take in the destruction. "Fire department has already ruled out arson. Electrical in origin— bad install for a solar power unit. We've got Ada County Crime Analysis, and of course, my people . . . I suppose we'd call ATF if we thought we needed federal help, but we don't. What interests the Bureau? Going after ecoterrorists again?"

William pointed at the white-flagged debris. "I came to interview Howard Plumber."

"What about?"

"Not at liberty."

"Well, either flash your sparks downtown and get a hall pass or move on, Agent Griffin. Feds don't pay their bills. Idaho is happy to take care of its own. Obviously you won't be talking to Plumber today."

William grimaced, half in amusement. "The Ada County coroner's office and fire department have expressed a willingness to share what they know."

"At whose sufferance?"

"Governor Kinchley," William said.

"Fucking dyke," the CID detective said. "Her term's about up. You can tell her I said so."

"I will. Your name, detective?"

"Johnny Carson, Jonathan Bitch-hater Carson. Boise CID. She knows me."

"I'll bet she does."

"I'll be on this street watching until you move along, Agent Griffin." Carson climbed back into the cruiser. "Your dad would have sniffed the wind and left it to the locals."

"I'll tell him you paid your respects," William said.

That dropped Carson's smug grin into blank uncertainty.

"Next time I visit him in Arlington," William added. "He died for his country. A great big country. All you have is Boise—and maybe Green Idaho."

"Fuck you," Carson said.

William stood his ground, shoulders hunched, hands in pockets.

Carson shook his head in disgust and drove down the street a hundred feet or so, then swerved left and parked diagonally, gifting William with a glare.

William ignored him.

The Green Idaho secessionist movement was growing in political power in Ada County and Boise, as well as the rural counties. It freighted a weird mix of ecology, high-tech savvy, rural bigotry, and rugged libertarian individualism. As far as they were concerned, feds, big lumber, big oil and gas, industrialists, and all rich out-of-state landowners could fuck off and vacate, pronto.

Like most secessionists, Green Idaho was comprised mostly of white guys: anti-tax, failed geeks, anarchists—and a fine crop of bigots.

If this was a Green Idaho reprisal, blown out of control by an unexpected wind storm, then it stood to reason that Detective Johnny

Carson would stand guard over the ashes and make excuses until the coast was clear.

A light blinked in the corner of William's spex. He took out his phone and answered the call.

"What's new in Idaho?" Deputy Director Kunsler asked.

Carson watched like a hawk hovering over a mouse.

William turned his back. "Dr. Plover has gone missing. His wife is dead. Looks as if his place was professionally torched—with her in it. But they haven't found his body—so they say."

"Staged?" Kunsler asked.

"Completely," William said. "Green Idaho is all over the scene. They want me out of here—tar and feathers would be too good for me."

"Nabokov sent a short message. He has the goods. But we haven't heard anything more. Get back to the Q."

"I'm on a plane out of Boise at midnight."

"No need. There'll be a jet waiting for you. Something big is in the air, so we're getting an extra drip of cash. Sounds like none of us is going to be getting much sleep. What do you know about Little Jamey?"

"Enough," William said. Everyone in law enforcement knew about Little Jamey. It had been injury on top of insult for the Bureau—and one of several events that had focused attention on Talos. "Is that a leading question?"

"Very. You'll get a full briefing at the Q."

William took a deep breath.

"Ah—my little bitty inbox is filling up with messages," Kunsler said. "Complaints from the locals. Pull out gracefully. Don't ruffle any feathers."

"Too late," William said. "There's one old buzzard I'd love to strangle."

"Tsk. See you bright and early tomorrow—I'll bring coffee. Come home safe, Agent Griffin."

16

Los Angeles

Nathaniel strolled along the indoor length of train track, then stopped and rose up on tiptoes to peer through the windows of a dining car. If he closed his eyes and listened to the recorded sounds, he could almost complete the illusion of a 1930s train station.

Steam puffed from under the sleek silvery locomotive, cut in half and butted up against a mural on the far wall.

He hadn't felt so much pure delight since childhood.

Everything was delightful and vivid. He made it more so, savoring the surreal illusion of a streamliner waiting for passengers, complete with red-capped conductors, leading guests through the waiting area—a Pullman lounge—to three dining cars.

At any moment, Nathaniel could play back something he had just experienced with complete fidelity. His memory was an open book through which he could page at will—making himself his own toy, his own diversion.

At the same time, he heard all the real sounds—people talking, dressed out of character, he thought—cell phones, restaurant pagers dinging, boisterous children talking about the latest games.

Nathaniel was caught between fascination with the children—so like him, unfettered, bold—and the illusion he was finding almost dangerously fascinating.

The colors around the train intensified until he rubbed his eyes and blinked them back. Bee vision, he called that—but he was pretty sure he couldn't actually see UV or infrared. Just a trick of the optical processors, like an LSD trip without the drug. Neon intensity, etched detail, a vibrant fringing around objects of particular interest; followed by sharp disappointment and an acute awareness, almost painful, of the inaccuracies in the restaurant's design.

Gas lanterns, for example. Not at all right.

For a moment, Nathaniel subdued the urge to count everything: people (too late), boards, beams, wheels on the dining car, windows, people again . . . Pushed it back as if swallowing a lump in his brain.

A hand tapped his shoulder. "Hey, Trace."

Pleasant tenor, sweet North Carolina accent—Nathaniel swung around with a toothy smile, looking up to the red, puffy, bristle-beard features of Humphrey Camp. Camp was taller than Nathaniel by four inches and heavier by more than fifty pounds, broad-shouldered and pepper-bearded. He did not look happy or healthy.

Camp coughed into his fist. "This shit seems to be agreeing with you. Not so much for me. Where's Plover?"

"Not here yet," Nathaniel said.

"This place seems a little obvious." Camp scuffed his feet. "Did you look inside? Maybe he's already seated."

"Plover told me to meet him here. That's all I know."

Camp squeezed his nose, then sneezed. "Maybe he can tell me why I feel like shit."

"Do you? I feel excellent." The downturn of the morning seemed less than a dream. Nathaniel didn't actually care how Camp felt, though they had once been good friends—had met at Stanford. He studied the big man closely, as he would an animal in a zoo.

"Fucking hurray," Camp said, then glanced over Nathaniel's shoulder. "Here's Lee."

Jerry Lee was the youngest of the Turing Seven, a dapper-looking man of thirty-one, dressed in his signature black coat, black T-shirt, black jeans. To the other members Lee had always been an enigma. He had come out of the Arabia Deserta attack with the worst physical scars—a divot down the side of his head and his cheek, burns and shrapnel marks down his left torso and rear shoulder.

He had never said much and said even less during their two weeks of treatment in Baltimore.

Lee nodded at Nathaniel but ignored Camp. His coolness and poise contrasted sharply with Camp's bulky fidgets. Lee had been the first to finish his work in Dubai and return to Los Angeles. He was also the only member of the Turing group—besides Nathaniel—who had actually visited the inner recesses of Mind Design in La Jolla and met the Quiet Man in person.

Lee pointed. "Here's our savior," he said.

Carrying a small box, the old head poker himself stepped delicately down the entrance ramp to the siding—Dr. Terence Plover, architect of their exodus from the psychological wounds of war, designer of the Mariposa treatment and now, apparently, a man who did not want to be recognized. He had dyed his hair to silver-gray and looked more like a sixty-something retiree than a well-to-do middle-aged researcher and entrepreneur.

At the sight of three of his former patients—rather than just Nathaniel—Plover looked as if he might turn and flee. But he squared his shoulders, nervously approached, and exchanged quick, formal greetings, looking each in the face with a curt nod, but did not shake—kept his free hand in his pocket.

"Only three?" he asked ironically. He looked up and down the mock station. "Where's Bork? Where's Nick Elder?"

He seemed to assume, as always, that he was in charge, and now behaved as if Nathaniel had violated both his authority and his trust.

Mariposa had been run with a firm hand, Dr. Plover always the sad, gentle tyrant awaiting their arrival to his island of calm and freedom from fear.

"Nick's in Texas," Camp said.

"We don't know that," Lee said.

Plover stroked his chin like a would-be wise man. All he lacked was a goatee and a pipe. Nathaniel subdued an urge to laugh, but a small chuckle escaped.

Plover frowned. "I think we should avoid attracting attention," he said. "Can we *please* do that, gentlemen?"

"This place was your choice," Nathaniel reminded him.

Plover gave him a pained look. "I did not ask *all* of you to come."

"And now we are four," Camp said.

Harry Bork strode onto the platform and joined them, tipping his hand to his forehead. Bork's role in the Turing Seven had always been mediation and negotiation. He had close-set blue eyes and a monkish fringe of blond hair embracing a noble, Nordic square skull, darker brows hovering over a squib of nose and a belligerent jaw.

"Great restaurant," he said. "Best prime rib in LA. Food tastes wonderful, Doc. Better than ever."

"Let's get on with it," Plover said. "We shouldn't be together any longer than necessary."

He unexpectedly leaned into Camp, who held up his arms in support. Plover's eyes fluttered. Catching himself, he straightened and waved them away.

"Apologies. Sleepless for two days," he murmured.

"Let's find our table and order drinks," Bork suggested. "I'm famished."

The waiter—a tall, slouched man with a thick hood of black hair and a long nose, more concerned about their appearance and demeanor than their number—escorted them away from the windows to a room in the back, paneled with dark wood.

A sparkling white cloth lay over a long, narrow table, set with stamped silver and peacock-fold napkins. Above the table hung two antique gas lamps, orange flames surrounded by hot pink auras—at least, in Nathaniel's bee vision.

"We all look daft," Bork said when they had settled in. It was apparent they could feel the awkwardness. They had worked together for months at a time in luxury but also in primitive conditions, had survived hell together—subcontractors for Axel Price and Talos Corporation for six years—yet none of them knew how to react to a reunion, and this caused Camp distress.

"Fuck this shit," he growled.

The four took up their menus and studied them.

Plover sat silent.

"How about the rest of you?" Bork asked. "Don't you feel it? Isn't food terrific?"

"My stomach's killing me," Camp said. "I'm losing weight and I pee purple." He thumped down his menu, winced, and blinked at the lanterns. "Ugly light," he said. "Hurts my eyes."

"Please!" Plover shouted.

Lee scowled.

Camp leaned in. "Quiet, Doc. Like you said, no cops. And no security guards, for Christ's sake."

Plover seemed to shrink in his chair, then rose again to a level of assertion—but kept his voice down. "I invited Mr. Trace to meet with me, exclusively, but now that we're here, I owe all of you an apology. Can you bring yourselves to some place of . . . cooperation, of agreement, so that we can talk sensibly?"

They nodded, all but Camp, and he continued.

"I've canceled my talk at the convention. I'll be leaving Los Angeles this afternoon. Things could hardly get any worse. I've been traveling . . ." He covered his mouth with one hand, cheeks working behind his fingers, as if trying to refit loose dentures.

Then he started to sob.

After a moment, Camp was the first to speak up. "All right. We're your bright boys, Doc, and we've gone wrong," he said. "Why is that?"

Plover managed to recover and straighten as the waiter brought in a tray with their drinks, then took their food orders. That went surprisingly well.

Plover's distress had had an impact. All of them made their choices like properly trained children. Then Bork told the waiter what the final tab would be, to the penny, with a stingy tip.

The waiter gave him a tight look, thanked them all, slouched out, and closed the sliding panel door.

The anachronistic gas lamps flickered and threw long shadows.

"We look like poker playing dogs," Lee said, and touched his forehead as if to adjust a green eyeshade.

"To Mariposa." Nathaniel lifted his red wine in toast. "How many did you cure, Doc? How many are we?" The colors even in this subdued room—even in the flickering, totally wrong gaslight—were amazing.

Plover looked around the table. He dabbed his eyes with his napkin and fixed his gaze on Lee. "You seem the best adapted," he murmured.

Lee lifted the corners of his lips. "I doubt it," he said. "That would be Bork, I think."

"Don't put that load on me," Bork said. "We're all pretty spooky. I hardly recognize some of you. We all *move* different now, did you notice that?"

"I see it," Lee said.

"Finish your drink and tell us something useful, Doc," Camp said.

"None of you should drink," Plover said, his voice shaky.

"Well hell, then, cheers," Camp said, hoisting his mug of Budweiser and swallowing half. He slammed the heavy glass on the table. "I'm a mess. You're a mess. We're all freaks. What the fuck have you done to us, Doc?"

Plover's hand shook as he drank his water. "I've had a terrible week. I left Maryland . . . moved my wife to a secret location. Now I can't reach her. I'm very worried about her."

"Let's be honest," Bork said. "We were a mess when you took us in. We couldn't get our work done. Two weeks later, we went back to work. You cured us."

"Too good to be true," Camp said.

Plover steeled himself. "I would like to know what you gentlemen were doing, to cause me and my wife so many difficulties."

They all sat quiet. Camp fidgeted with a knife, tapping the tablecloth.

"You don't want to know," Bork said.

"I knew you were important," Plover persisted dryly. "I'm just now beginning to understand *how* important."

"What about the Quiet Man?" Camp asked. "What does he know?"

They all looked at Lee.

"A secret international project with a huge bankroll," Lee said. "The Turing Seven were crucial. Then—we were injured. Our wounds healed. Our heads did not. Dr. Plover came to Price with interesting research. He gave you full financing, plus a large bonus, and promised that all his soldiers and personnel who suffered from post-traumatic stress would be funneled through Mariposa. You could have become a rich man."

"What changed that?" Bork asked. "What changed *us*?"

"Not boozing, I'm going to bet," Camp said, and finished his beer.

"You're all reacting differently," Plover said. "There may be similarities . . . I can't know for sure. I could do blood work, but I no longer have a clinic." He swallowed and shook his head, getting the words out with difficulty. "Harvey Belton called my private line last week. I don't know how he got the number . . . it's new. He was hysterical. I heard a shot. The call ended. Stanley Parker called the same number and said he was flying to Fiji, so that he could be in a place where it was quiet. The world was too loud and too bright. Nick Elder . . . I do not know what happened to Nick."

"He's in Texas," Bork said. "At least, he was a few days ago."

The waiter and a busboy brought their food: plates clacking, maneuvering in the narrow space, the waiter's nervous reappraisal of who ordered what.

He backed out and closed the door.

Camp thumped the table once more. "Question not answered!" he said in a harsh voice. "What did you do to us? What the hell is Mariposa?"

Lee frowned and put his hands over his ears.

Plover touched the rim of his water glass with a finger. "I was working with my wife at the National Cancer Institute in Atlanta," he said. "We had what looked like an effective treatment for astrocytomas. Brain tumors. We were in clinical trials—very promising—when I noticed that our test patients often experienced a significant change in affect. In mood.

"One was a veteran from the first Gulf War. He had suffered from PTSD since his late twenties. That suffering stopped. Crime victims, those who had survived rape or domestic abuse—even patients with unrelated psychological disorders—responded positively as well. I altered the focus and expanded the program."

"So you fix cancer and make people happy, at the same time. How?" Bork asked.

"The body—the brain—relies on the genome not only for form but for broad patterns of behavior. But genes are not expressed continually. They are controlled by a marvelous system of checks and balances—including overlays to the actual genetic sequences, epigenetic tags or stops that regulate and even prevent certain genes from being expressed. As in a music box, an activated gene sticks up and plays a note, an inactivated gene falls into a gap and is silent.

"In our childhood and adolescence, tunes emerge and become more or less fixed—the working versions of you and me, better prepared for our environment. However, throughout our lives, our bodies still make changes. As we live, we acquire a few more notes. Our tunes become richer. Little pathways—personality, habits—are worn into our behaviors."

"What's that got to do with cancer?" Lee asked.

"Cells too are educated and trained. If they are continually stressed or traumatized—bathed in toxic chemicals, for example—they reach a crisis and a point of decision. Life isn't good. The bargain they made long ago to be part of a larger body isn't working out. So they may try to become independent, paying no attention to the body's needs. Usually the stubbornly independent cells are killed by the immune system. In some cases, they evade destruction, and tumors grow."

"You're saying we're tumors?" Camp seemed perversely amused.

"No. Perhaps. I don't know . . . These matters are complicated."

"What's Mariposa doing to us now?" Bork asked.

Lee laid his hand on Plover's arm—not in reassurance.

Plover looked down at the tightening fingers. His brow furrowed. "Stress," he said. "Long-term pressure and pain wear deep, dysfunctional ruts, which become fixed by epigenetic tags in our brains—perhaps in astrocytic cells themselves. We respond with heightened sensitivity to less and less stimulus. Brain and body, working in unison, acquire hair triggers. Our behaviors become inappropriate, erratic. Deep down, we think we are still in whatever situation caused our pain to begin with.

"Our tune changes for the worse, sometimes drastically. Sour notes, screeches—anxiety, fear. Panic."

"We weren't in combat for more than a few hours," Nathaniel said.

"A single major traumatic event—pain, destruction, friends killed, imminent threat to life—mere minutes can cause tremendous stress. The persistent drips and trickles of stress that ordinarily shape our lives and thoughts become a sudden flood. Old patterns are swept away. New channels form, deep and devious. Mariposa works by removing the stops we acquire during traumatic events. The genes are set free from the bad habits they acquired under duress. The world seems less threatening. A kind of balance is restored."

Plover's face took on that messianic light Nathaniel remembered from his two weeks in Baltimore, in the clinic—when Plover had been the one who had made them feel human again.

"Balance?" Camp said. "Shit. I'm not in any sort of balance."

"Your pain went away," Plover asserted, defiant. "You all agreed . . . back then."

"Not now," Bork said. "I feel like Proteus in his cave—scary. Maybe we can be *anything*."

"I have no idea what I want to be," Lee said.

"The drug is removing too many controls," Plover said. "We did not see that in animal trials."

"And that means? . . ." Camp asked.

"Our talents and abilities are patterned to fit the needs of a larger group. Best for human society . . . But perhaps more control is now being returned to you as individuals. You have become like newborns, in a way. If too many controls are removed—then you either won't feel the need to serve society at all, or you will do so purely on your own terms."

The table fell quiet. Only Bork and Lee had touched their food. Camp stopped tapping his fork and set it down on his rumpled napkin.

"That's the definition of a sociopath," Bork said thoughtfully.

Lee let go of Plover's arm. "I've started torturing animals," he said. "I'm seriously thinking about hurting people."

"Pleased to meet you, Mr. Hyde," Camp said, tossing Lee a salute.

"Anyone else?" Nathaniel asked, fascinated.

Bork took a bite of rare prime rib and lifted his fork. "Only for a day," he said, chewing. "Then it stopped being fun."

"Did you actually *butcher* someone, you son of a bitch?" Camp asked with a manic grin.

Bork looked back at Camp as if the question were rude—or meaningless.

"Price loves butterflies," Lee said. "Did he suggest you name your program Mariposa? All the soldiers, all his employees, psychologically damaged by combat . . . You said you could restore them, make them bright and shiny again. And we became your test subjects . . . You gave him your guarantee. Didn't you?"

Plover nodded like a bobble-head doll with a stick shoved up one side of its neck. "In a nutshell," he said.

"It's hell to be a baby again, Doc," Camp said.

Plover looked down at his plate.

"The vice president," Nathaniel said. "Was he one of your patients?"

Plover jerked as if stung. "That's privileged," he said, and tried reasserting some last shred of authority. "It's *privileged*—and dangerous!"

"Bingo," Bork said, marking a scored point with his finger in the air. "You're already smarter than you used to be, Nathaniel."

Plover's cell phone buzzed. He fumbled it out of his pocket, dropped it on the table, then retrieved it and answered, "Hello?"

Nathaniel noted this was not an EPR unit; hence, the caller was not the Quiet Man.

"Doc, you shouldn't be talking on those things," Camp said. "Microwaves can ruin your brain."

As Plover listened, his face lost the rest of its color. "Are you sure?"

He shut the phone, closed his eyes. "I have to leave now," he said, struggling to regain whatever was left of his composure. "Mr. Trace, we need to speak in private, as agreed."

"You and the doctor run along," Bork said. "The rest of us will sit here and chitchat."

In the crowded lobby, Nathaniel took Plover's trembling arm and aimed him to the mall restroom. Through the big fire doors, the hall beyond was empty.

Plover handed his package to Nathaniel.

"The Quiet Man mentioned someone named Jones, some sort of expert—you seem to know him. Jones suggested I give this material to you, and that you find a woman named Rebecca Rose. She is in law enforcement, I presume."

Nathaniel listened with interest, enjoying the patterns of blood flow in Plover's face and hands. He could almost feel the heat. Plover was definitely a candidate for a heart attack.

Bee vision.

"Jones might know something," Nathaniel admitted as he opened the package. The doctor watched him closely while he pulled out a reddish-purple dragon about two inches long, printed on a sheet of pliable plastic. The package also contained a badge on a black braided lanyard and a photo of a woman with medium-long hair.

"These are my credentials for the COPES conference, across the street," Plover said. "They'll get you past most of the outer security. The dragon is a skin computer. A dattoo. People put it on their arms and exchange personal data. I've preloaded this one with crucial information. She'll be wearing a dattoo as well. Cross arms, like this." He demonstrated by hooking his arm around Nathaniel's. "It works through clothing."

Nathaniel was amused. He rolled up his sleeve and peeled the dattoo from its plastic sheet. It laid down easily on his inner forearm and conformed to the skin, stretching a little.

"Remember this about Axel Price," Plover said. "He rarely does anything without having two excellent reasons. That's the secret of his success. The seven of you were in a bad way—and there was my research. He needed you healthy, and he saw a way to make huge profits from treating PTSD. Relieving human misery never much concerned him. It's not part of his worldview."

Plover took back the box, threw it into a trash receptacle, and looked around for an exit. "The convention is closed for the day. Try tomorrow morning. Be careful. I've set the dattoo to download only once, and then it will wipe its contents.

"We won't meet again. Good luck, Mr. Trace."

He shuffled toward the exit, clutching one shoulder.

Nathaniel pulled down his sleeve and buttoned it. He wondered who Rebecca Rose was, that she would attract the attention of the Quiet Man—or Plover, or Jones.

And why they chose him as a vector.

All the more interesting.

17

Rebecca shoved the pillow up under her cheek, slowly rising like a swimmer from a dream of birds on a wave-washed beach.

Her body felt relaxed, loose, catlike. She stretched one leg but did not want to open her eyes and come fully awake, the sensation of light and warmth and relaxation was so wonderful—so rare.

Coffee.

She opened one eye.

A black hotel mug floated back and forth in front of her face. Not alone. Her body tensed, then relaxed again.

Captain Peter Periglas took shape beyond the mug.

"Good morning," he said.

The relaxed feeling came from having someone beside her all night. She pushed her mouth off the pillow, then wiped the corner of her lips to make sure it was dry.

"Morning. Late."

"No, we have indulged wonderfully, but we are not teenagers. We got a good night's sleep and it is now seven-thirty."

"I feel too good," Rebecca said, sitting up and taking the mug.

"Blame me," Periglas said. He was wearing a hotel bathrobe, open to reveal his slender chest, not quite Apollonian—a thin patch of graying hair.

"I will," Rebecca promised.

"Fake cream, sugar?"

"No thanks." She looked at him accusingly over the mug. "You got up first to make sure I wasn't drooling."

"I did not, but you certainly were. We are both droolers."

"Oh my."

The first couple of sips of hot black liquid were equally wonderful. She couldn't remember feeling so happy in years—maybe ten years. Since . . .

But no need to let the past cloud things.

Two room service trays still rested on the dresser, stacked steel covers, napkins, water glasses, tilting wine glasses.

Two empty bottles of red wine and she didn't feel even a touch hung over.

"Are you sure we're not teenagers?" she asked, lowering the mug to her naked breasts. She rolled the smooth heat on her skin, holding his gaze as a challenge, *don't look down.*

Periglas failed and let out a long sigh.

"Damn," he said, and untied his robe.

18

The winter sky over downtown Los Angeles had a blued-steel sheen like the glint off an old revolver.

Inside the stark, white western atrium of the convention center, under high panes of bathwater-green glass, all was clearly illuminated as if by a cool, distant star. Nothing and no one cast shadows.

Rebecca ascended a wide flight of steps, counting ten, eleven, twelve. Her thoughts jostled in a caffeinated queue. She was enjoying lovely aches: aches from the night's activities, plus half an hour of exercise at the hotel gym, plus the soft, professional embrace of new pumps.

Twenty-one, twenty-two, twenty-three.

Day two of impressing the troops, promoting her new prospective employer, and hanging with people who understood the life, yet knew nothing of why she was here and not back in Quantico or Washington. That was one story she would not be sharing at the ninth annual Consumer Protection and Education Symposium: COPES.

Four thousand salesmen, entrepreneurs, and professional security and law enforcement types, educated, entertained, fed, and watered each evening while hovered over by honchos from Homeland Security, the Bureau, the FDA, ATF, and a dozen other three-letter acronyms from a government that somehow managed to grow great, bushy branches despite a crushing load of debt and the worst recession in over eighty years.

Which was the same as not calling it a depression.

She glanced up at the snowy horizontal pipes and beams that transported the building's stresses. They made sure the heaviest lifting was handed over to parts that could stand the pressure, a lot like people passing the buck.

At least you've got the prospect of real work, six months out from the rocky coast of the FBI.

Under her breath, forty-one, forty-two . . .

Two years after Mecca. A year after almost going under. Count your blessings. You're alive, you've just met a nice man; maybe you'll even have a daughter.

People to live with and actually love.

As she approached the level of the main exhibition hall, a vague sense of bulk shifted her attention left and she saw a brush of ginger hair, a gray overcoat, a convention badge, and hovering vaguely above them a shy, almost boyish smile in a broad face otherwise made for radio.

Instinct.

Her attention focused. The man stepped forward. She felt her neck muscles tense into cords.

"Ms. Rose. Looking forward to your presentation."

Rebecca paused, refusing to give ground despite the man's odd penetration of her space. Her spex outlined his face with a red circle. In the lower right corner, a cursor blinked: the spex data monkey said he was in her personal facial database. No name came up. She had been getting so many of these notices at the convention she had switched off automatic identification.

She lifted one ankle to adjust her shoe. The face was memorable—small scars around his mouth and under his eyes, a broader beardless pink patch on the left temple from hairline to cheekbone; one eye slightly skewed. Still pleasant enough—but more rugged than she liked. Not actually threatening but not dressed very well—not one of the federal honchos or minions and probably not a cop, with that unkempt hair.

His badge had flipped on its lanyard. She couldn't read his name.

"Do I know you?" she asked.

The man's smile flashed to ten. "Nathaniel Trace. Old FBI, ma'am, seconded to Food and Drug. A great admirer. We were on a panel together in Orlando—International Association of Food Protectors."

Rebecca had indeed served on such a panel, just before her furlough went through. Odd she did not remember. "Good to see you, Agent Trace."

"I've retired," he said. "Actually, they booted me."

"Ah."

"I cooperated. Like you, I assume. The Rout."

She hated that word. "No, Mr. Trace, I did not cooperate and I was not *booted*."

"Well, it's all history. Pardon my intrusion, Ms. Rose, but we should talk, sooner rather than later." He had a look she could not define: not crazy, but not all in one place, like a man divided and then punched back together again. "Sorry to impede the flow. Let's trade."

He pulled back his sleeve and revealed a dattoo.

"You can get back to me if we need to talk."

"Fine," Rebecca said, eager to move on.

Does the word buzz kill mean anything to you, Agent Trace?

She held her arm down but splayed her fingers like knives. No harm—dattoos couldn't mess with each other, simply exchange data. They crossed arms, not actually touching. She felt her skin briefly warm—as if he had just downloaded a lot more than his name and associations.

Trace broke the touch.

Now she was sure he was lying about where they had met, but he did not exhibit the tells of a liar. In that odd mental realm where instinct was indistinguishable from fantasy, where her expertise trapped passing impressions and examined them over and over, before they became actual theories, she wondered if he could convince himself to believe anything he said.

"I've got to be in the hall in twenty seconds," she told him by way of warning. "Four thousand stalwarts to feed and entertain, and we still get to rub elbows with heroes."

The ginger-haired man had the gall to keep pace with her as she moved along. Rebecca felt her neck hairs rise. She did not like this one bit.

"You should be listening closely," he said and put on an intense look, accompanied by a rictus of effort. "You should come away from here . . . with me. I mean it. I don't think it's safe. I've got lots of money stashed away. You're important . . . to somebody who knows. You could be safe—away from here. Let's go outside and get some lunch or dinner and talk about things."

After the night with her captain, and with a busy day coming up, this was the one thing she did not need, would not put up with, here of all places: a crazy former cop or some sadsack salesman, playing the dattoo card and then hitting on her.

Rebecca got up into his face—he was about an inch taller—and tapped his chest firmly with her finger, emphasizing, "Stay . . . the fuck . . . away from me."

"Right," Trace said, and rewarded her with a delighted grin. He backed up and did a swashbuckling sweep with one arm, bowing, clearing her path.

"Thanks." Rebecca stepped away before he could say more and walked swiftly on. Her face was red; she could feel it. She wanted to scratch the dattoo, scrub it off. Creepy.

Screw this. Now I'm down—almost.

She pushed by the signs with arrows that read, *Exhibit Hall. All bags subject to inspection.* One pump already squeaked; the new shoes were a bust.

Damn.

She made sure her badge was face out and veered left by the sparsely populated food court. Lifting her wrist, she brushed the dattoo along an ID post, faced the camera to have her picture taken—

Trace never made it this far. No picture, no record

—then raced past the bored-looking security guards.

The exhibit hall filled an acre under a broad, high roof. On the far side of the hall, windows to the next-level conference rooms looked out over the crowded expanse. Most of the windows were covered by vertical blinds: sessions in progress. But in one, a photographer, tiny at this distance, poked his camera through and was attempting to capture the whole scene from on high.

The scene was worth it. Hundreds of booths lined double-sided aisles, showcasing the latest in professional, business, and home protection. The aisles gradually funneled attendees to open spaces with larger displays.

A family-size bomb shelter offered level-4 filters, whatever that implied. In another open circle, an autonomous DHS/ICE Whisper Bird took center stage, broad, wide rotors folded, guns and rocket pods red-capped and tagged, empty.

Nearby, LAPD Gross Threat Response had brought in two super-sophisticated bomb trucks, brutes big and shiny as city fire trucks but black all over. Each carried, in rear deck and side garages, three mid-size tractor bots and twenty cat-size insect-carriage bots, all black with yellow stripes. Small boxes mounted within the garages were filled with roller bots, like little wheeled dumbbells with video cameras and other sensors, that could be tossed or rolled into almost any situation.

A large group of admiring men and a few women took in a demonstration of small bot prowess.

A public defense tech talking like a circus barker had the city's machines performing Fred Astaire dance routines to music. The midsize bots were light on their feet, but their real talent lay in chemical sensors that could detect any kind of explosive from ten feet away. Pulse-mike sonic arrays could read the internals of a suspect device with a single high-frequency chirp.

Smarter and lighter than ever, the new bots could approach a bomb quiet as a weasel and shut it down with old-fashioned lead shot, a high-powered slug of water, or quick-set polycarbonate.

Techs in bomb suits would soon be ancient history, along with their sniffer dogs.

Rebecca moved on to the crowded aisles.

The Total Team Safety booth boasted a 50K, six-by-three-meter flex display, bright and crisp—though the fabric rippled under a downdraft. The display revealed the schematic of a skyscraper, filled with glowing stars, showing how a tactical security show-runner could monitor up to three thousand personnel in any situation from inside, or from any point on the globe via dedicated satlink.

Much better than the old FBI Lynx system, though that was still in wide use.

Peacock Net Communications offered a whole new lifestyle for both cops and civilians. A skinny young man with a shiny face was extolling the company virtues: "A complete record of your life. Fifteen button cameras, front and rear—full circle, fish-eye if you switch on the shoulder cams. The CPU stitches it all together and stores up to twelve hours of 4K-def video. Best tool law enforcement ever had—but it's also available to citizens, so police departments need to keep their cops cool, well-trained, and polite. No more ticking time bombs on the street. And of course our prowler unit records all the basics, plus video and sound—GPS, speed, nearby vehicles, officer RFID, weather, even vitals if the individual department so desires—heart rate, cortisol, body temp, emotional state. Soon we'll be able to tie in and corroborate our video with brain-scan analysis. No secrets. Foolproof in court—it's all ten-twelve secure-coded to an inviolate chip. Congress is about to set FISA standards for Homeland Security taps into personal networks. It's a new age for law enforcement. Peacock Net. Open society, complete records, total protection."

Rebecca had been linked and recorded many times before, but never so thoroughly.

The Homeland Security Science and Technology booth featured a single-box, universal DNA/RNA identification system, tied in to international criminal and citizen database files. A moist swab of almost any surface within a scene of interest, indoors or outdoors, could yield a comprehensive list of the names and records of individuals who had walked through in the last few years, dropping sweat, skin flakes, fingerprints, whatever—as well as plants, animals, and potential pathogens. The system was known as eDNA, or Edna.

Practically in the shadow of DHS and Edna's bright lights, a tiny startup calling itself DYNA-Forensics was drawing an impressive crowd. Their little gray box promised to provide courtroom-quality certification that DNA evidence was not manufactured, forged, or planted—or, conversely, that it was. With polymerase chain reaction technology capable of creating huge volumes of DNA from even the tiniest source, and several high-profile cases of law enforcement databases being misused to manufacture counterfeit DNA evidence from scratch, this had become a big issue in recent years.

Soon, nobody would be getting away with anything, anywhere. She had to sniff in wonder. Brave new world—lousy old cliché.

Just two booths down, scanners from a company called Rainbow Life Forensics guaranteed to analyze and predict the intent of strangers through their Kirlian Auras.

Something old, something new, something weird.

"Rebecca!"

At the end of the leftmost aisle, Rebecca swiveled and saw Karl Oster leaning from a booth. "How's our favorite Rolodex expert?" he called. A big banner behind him proclaimed NCAP: National Council of Protection Agencies—an NGO trade group.

She swung left and shook his hand.

"Hey, Karl. Most of these youngsters don't even know what a Rolodex is." She pulled back her cuff to reveal the dattoo. "Want to mate?"

Oster smirked, pulled up his sleeve, unbuttoned his cuff, and showed his own dattoo. They crossed arms.

"Don't scratch it," he warned.

"They do itch," Rebecca said. "Congrats."

"Screw that," he said with a grin.

Oster had been portrayed by Johnny Depp in a movie about Waylon Parks, the Karaoke Butcher. Parks had kidnapped twenty-one children in two states, burying them with a backhoe in old shipping containers. Each container had a battery backup unit that powered a small Karaoke machine that ran videos of Parks singing David Bowie songs. Gary Oldman, of course, had portrayed Parks.

"It's bullshit," Oster said. "They should have made a movie about you."

"Fat chance," Rebecca said.

"What irritates the hell out of me is the way these bastards are portrayed by smart, charming actors. We know different. They're broken toys. When you finally catch 'em, they look dead inside."

Karl and Rebecca had gone out for dinner a few times in Washington and stayed friends thereafter, exchanging calls now and then. Karl, a perennial bachelor, had never pushed. She almost wished he had.

But now of course there was her captain. Odd that she was the one feeling fast and possessive.

"Agents love their movies, Karl. Yours wasn't too bad. How's San Francisco?"

"Office is *trés chic*," Oster said, the standing joke.

Rebecca had appointments to keep. She waved and moved on.

19

Nathaniel lingered at the food court for half an hour, uncertain what to do next or where to go. He had run out of instructions, external or internal.

He ordered a tuna sandwich and observed the people coming and going. Mostly reps or salespeople, a few politicians, a fair number of law enforcement officers in plain clothes—and of course security guards.

Watching them all move and mingle was relaxing, like watching an ant farm.

He slowly and meticulously played back Plover's words and actions during and after their dinner the night before. The memory was sharp. With some concentration, he could make it even sharper—until it pushed aside the real world.

It wasn't exactly like living the events again; the replay assumed its own rearranged logic, edited by his brain into a better story, and some parts were already in the process of degradation . . . de-selected, de-rezzed . . .

Interesting to actually watch that happening.

Rebecca Rose had been apprehensive. He thought perhaps she recognized him, but not consciously. Had they met before? His work had absorbed all his attention, even when he was in Baltimore, undergoing Mariposa. He might not have noticed her.

Work—and terror. Terror—and work. All he was, all he had. Back then, if he forgot something, it was likely to stay forgotten. Now . . .

Everybody interested him to some degree. Faces were important. He truly was like a baby—a baby savant.

He had read Rebecca Rose like a book. She had been in a hurry— and not just to get into the hall. She wanted to get away from extraneous thoughts and forces impinging on her life. To move toward pleasant things and away from unpleasant or worrisome things—like him.

Pretty standard palm reader bullshit, so far.

Nathaniel moved forward in memory-time and caught up with the food court, the conference, the amusing ant farm. This was good. This was exhilarating. The old Nathaniel Trace had not liked mysteries.

Now, not having all the answers was like the beginning of an all-absorbing game, a combination of Philip Marlowe and poker. In due time, with patience—something he was trying hard to nurture—facts would come his way. But he could also put himself in the way of facts.

(That patience thing was a work in progress, along with attention span, reining in bee vision, and not biting his hands.)

This convention was turning into a freeway cloverleaf of discovery— a maze of onramps and exits. The longer he stayed, the more he might learn.

He belched tuna sour—food still not agreeing with him—and pushed away the mostly uneaten sandwich. He walked toward the escalators, the high atrium, and the exit, at medium speed, not to attract attention.

Stopped for water at a fountain.

Things playing around in his head. Thoughts seemed to have their own shapes, and now he could see how they might fit together.

Make a picture.

Axel Price's plans involved disruption. Nathaniel had always wondered how it would happen, after the Turing group finished their international wire work. They weren't supposed to know the real purpose of that work, of course. But now it seemed obvious.

He could bring it all up from his subconscious, where it had just fallen into its proper place.

The vice president had put himself in the news. Plover had practically confirmed that Quinn was one of his patients. Plover was beholden to Axel Price.

Something was going wrong with Mariposa.

Because of that, and for other reasons, Price's plans might be in jeopardy. Something in which the vice president was going to play a major role.

The Quiet Man seemed to think so.

Tipping event.

Plover was in danger, trying to hide and not being smart about it. He was a scientist, not a spy. Who would have the strongest reason to want the doctor silenced?

Who would be powerful enough to cause concern for the Quiet Man?

Jerry Lee is torturing animals. Bork . . .

You might all become killers. Get in the news.

Like the vice president.

And then you'd spill the beans. You know you've been thinking about it.

This tickled Nathaniel. He laughed, then covered his mouth like a Japanese girl. His skin flushed—all but the scar.

The Turing Seven had become untrustworthy—Price was upset with *them* as well. All might come unraveled, so Price was angry. Pieces well-shaped, fitting nicely so far. Obvious.

Plover said that Price always had two reasons for doing anything. That was the secret of his success. Here, gathered in the convention center, were two and possibly even *three* reasons. Another tipping event—this one deliberate and planned. Something big, anonymous—destabilizing.

Dress rehearsal.

Prep for the grand finale.

Visions bright and scary flashed in his visual centers, like a waking dream. A whiff of burned metal flitted through his olfactory circuits. Something primal told him to get the hell out of this place. The call in the restaurant had upset the doctor. Perhaps someone had died. Someone he knew and loved and had tried to protect.

His wife.

Nathaniel had warned Rebecca Rose—but why? What was he anticipating?

Once outside the convention center, he considered hiring a taxi, but decided instead to study the nearby construction. He assumed the happiest of attitudes. He felt relaxed and at ease, unlike the day before.

Everything was delightfully potential.

You need to keep a sense of proportion, the wise old voice told him. *What is it you really see—what do you need to see—what is it you* want *to see?*

"I'm just waiting for something to happen," he said.

Passersby didn't look at him funny. He might be talking on a phone . . . but he wasn't. He was a certifiable crazy person.

"Something interesting is coming," he told himself. "Something dangerous."

You can't know that. But how much are you willing to risk by staying here, where it seems to be most dangerous?

"I'll stand over there, then."

Nathaniel crossed three parking lots and stood on Flower Street, where he turned to watch the passing cars, goggle at the buildings, lift squinted eyes to the sapphire sky. He liked making his long coat swirl. Grinning, he felt the scar on his cheek tug. Just walking in the sunshine felt great.

His face warmed everywhere but the scar.

He couldn't get Rebecca Rose out of his thoughts. He did not *want* her out of his thoughts. She was a fascinating part of the puzzle—the next piece to fall into place.

The whole area along Flower Street had undergone a kind of renaissance after years of major down time. A huge new Sofitel was just opening. Workers were pulling away tape and plastic riprap and moving equipment to make way for guests. Too expensive for most of the people at the convention center. That meant the hotel was relatively safe. He should stay here for a while. The hotel lobby looked interesting.

There was a huge crystal chandelier suspended above a beautiful travertine marble floor. Inside, Nathaniel looked up at the chandelier, giggling. A bellman and the concierge behind her desk watched him. Nathaniel dropped his shoulders.

His sense of time slowed. *Safe.*

The next thing that happened was intense.

The crystal chandelier jumped and sang with a thousand brilliant high notes. He felt it, saw it—

The puzzle *came alive.*

"That's an explosion," he whispered.

Glass was breaking and falling everywhere—behind him, a shower of prisms pinged and exploded against the marble floor. Eruptions of diamond pebbles water falled out of the tall front windows, exposing the interior to a shockwave of warm air.

He was visualizing a distant explosion in clinical detail—analyzing the frequencies of the vibrations, the directions in which the walls of the hotel would move—periodicity, amplitude, the layout of the building and the surrounding streets, the way taller buildings would absorb the shock.

As he walked out of the hotel, the walls still seemed to shake. Staying on his feet as the ground heaved was easy enough—like dancing to a syncopated, swaying tune.

The convention center puffed huge white and gray clouds.

Enough.

He thwacked himself on the temple with the palm of his hand.

Nathaniel stood trembling outside, away from the Sofitel lobby, across the street and back in sunshine. The hotel's windows were intact, the chandelier—visible through the windows—still suspended above the marble floor.

He let out a half-frightened, entirely delighted whistle. This was utterly cool. The cloverleaf of discovery had just changed in a most intriguing way. The whole world had become his chess board. He could see millions of moves in advance . . . keyed in, of course, to the kings and queens, the power players.

His head hurt so bad his entire body was throbbing. But he felt no sense of danger, only a deep conviction that he was *not wrong.*

His metabolism had become that of a hummingbird. Time for a sugary drink.

Time to return to the convention center.

20

Walking through the exhibit hall, Rebecca felt like Alice down the high-tech rabbit hole. The moral equivalent of Hitler under the old lady's bed had become huge business since 9/11 and 10/4.

COPES cut right through the body politic and revealed a cross-section of American nightmares. The long aisles were lined with pipe-and-curtain booths promoting aids to justice and anodynes to fear, from the specific and timely to the shapeless and eternal, all put together with businesslike style and just enough color.

Men in dark suits and women in gray or pastel suits casually conversed with retailers and cops about public protection, crime and detection, less-than-lethal takedown, and the tools they all needed to buy that elusive sense of security from, and justice for, all the bad guys.

Some tools could be lethal by happenstance, of course. A mock-up cutaway of an armored Ford Crown Victoria revealed dark layers of "C-ERA," electromagnetic reactive armor packed with carbon fiber nanotubes—good protection for you, inside, not so good for the crowds around you, sprayed with pulverized shrapnel. A sign over the somber, gray vehicle proclaimed: "This is one ERA you'll ratify!"

"Har," Rebecca said softly.

By and large, male cops were still chauvinists—and probably always would be. Gather male and female law enforcement together—especially the young—and a few of the males always felt it necessary to challenge the females as to credentials, fitness, their place in the cruel masculine world—which was properly staying home and making babies. With their willing assistance, of course.

The captain had exhibited none of that. That could mean he was simply more experienced with women.

Stop it. Enjoy the moment.

D&P—Detection and Protection—systems abounded for radiation and bio-attacks of any kind, personal or large-scale. D&P came in the form of networked phones, bracelets, even radio-alerted chips under the skin.

Be the first on your block to get the hell away from your block . . . when the bad guys spray it with nerve gas or anthrax.

Rebecca made a face and let out a small puff of breath. She lingered for a few seconds at the FreezeCrime forensics display, a ring in the middle of two aisles, revealing all the latest in sealing and preserving crime scenes: room-size cooling units and rail-mounted bots designed to pick up samples without leaving "cop residue." The bar was being raised on crime scenes. She had often wondered why human techs were allowed to stomp and shed their way through those delicate, information-rich landscapes. And if human investigators had to be there—a case could still be made for that—there were plastic suits designed to protect cops from contamination, and protect the evidence from the dusty, hairy, sweaty presence of cops.

The food square at the back of the hall was fenced by black ropes and guarded by another phalanx of security, perhaps the most impressive and vigilant. Their job was to wave off conventioneers without food privileges: press, day-trippers, salespeople.

She wove through clusters of diners grazing off the buffet—chatting, balancing glasses and plastic plates—then proceeded to the end of the C aisle, where she was scheduled to be a star speaker. Her future boss, Stan Philips, stood under a simple black banner with a company logo printed in silver-gray: BLUE EYES EXECUTIVE SERVICES.

A little platform had been set up to one side of the booth. Within sight of the food. Terrific. She would be competing with steam tables and salad bars.

Stan was with a tall fellow in a dark gray suit. This made Stan look shorter than his five feet eight inches. The tall fellow had thick brown hair; Stan's hair was sallow and wispy. The tall fellow's voice deep and hard to make out over the noise in the hall. Stan, as usual, was mostly listening. Stan seldom expressed his opinions unless pressed. That was one reason he liked Rebecca and she got along with him. She was taciturn but not silent. Stan was often too quiet, and that confused their clients, who seemed to think they were paying for words, not results.

Stan introduced Rebecca to the tall fellow. He was some official or another from some agency or another and he was here at the show hoping to find better employment.

"I'm interested in art security," the man said. "I hear you guys are pretty good at protection and provenance. I did undergrad work in art history at Long Beach State."

Rebecca shut off her ears and locked in her smile. Nodding to the conversational beats, she turned her sharp green eyes to a small group gathered in front of the lectern. Four guys in suits. Small groups made her more nervous than large ones.

She wished she were somewhere else—maybe over by the steam table, picking through the General Tso's chicken, pepper beef and broccoli, green onion pancakes and mu shu sauce. Or sitting in the audience across the exhibit floor, listening to Captain Pcriglas's presentation.

She sucked in her breath, wanting simply to be with her captain, with her prospective daughter, to be far, far away—in a small house, mortgage paid off, easy to clean, a simple garden.

Maybe the young male agents were right about women after all. It was a lovely vision.

Stan handed the tall man a card and suggested he join the audience. "Rebecca's got a great take on high-tech security," he said. "Worth hearing."

Rebecca clutched her hands in front of her, waiting for the clock to tick over. In the corner of her eye, she noticed a knot of activity around the no-host bar on the northern side of the catering square. Three young men and two women in black-and-white uniforms were talking and pointing to something behind the bar.

One young man knelt out of sight and then stood, frowning and holding out his hand.

She tried to read his lips.

He might have been saying, *It's cold.*

She tuned into the louder voice of the female bartender. "It's just Coke. Maybe it's fizzing."

They seemed more puzzled than worried. But a long line of customers was getting impatient.

Something was not right.

She turned from the tall man, muttered something to Stan, and pushed under the rope to walk toward the bar. One of the security guards arrived three steps ahead of her: short, middle-aged, Hispanic, with a round face and smart black eyes that probably missed nothing.

"Is there a problem?" he asked.

Rebecca stood back respectfully.

"Something weird with our syrup canisters," the male bartender said.

"It's just Coke!" the female bartender insisted.

"It's cycling hot and cold," the male said. "I've *never* seen it do that." His voice squeaked, and somehow that made it real.

Rebecca met the eyes of the guard and they exchanged a look. The guard knelt behind the bar. He touched stainless steel canister and jerked back his hand.

"Hot," he said.

Six other canisters waited their turn, lined up to the left side of the black-draped bar.

"It's just Coke," the female bartender insisted once more, face pinched. So many tips just lined up and waiting.

The catering supervisor ran with short, quick steps from the rear of the hall—like a small, unhappy dog—and stood aside, chin in hand, as the male bartender filled him in.

The supervisor looked provoked. "There can't possibly be a problem," he announced. "All our supplies go through half a dozen security checkpoints. This is the most secure place in Los Angeles."

The canisters had frosted over—all seven of them.

Rebecca saw it happen.

Cycling.

Had she been a spaniel, she would have gone on point. The guard had the same reaction—not ESP, just a prickle of cop sense.

She stood beside the guard and said in a low voice, "Let's clear the hall."

The catering supervisor listened in dismay and was about to pitch a fit, but the guard nodded agreement with Rebecca and held up a thick strong brown hand—right in the supervisor's face.

Then he pressed a red button on his old-fashioned lapel mike.

"Shit!" the supervisor shouted, throwing up his arms.

An alarm sounded throughout the building.

A loud, female robo-voice echoed under the steel beam roof. "This is an emergency. Leave all personal belongings and evacuate the convention center immediately. Proceed to any exit marked by a flashing green light. Gather at staging areas designated by mall security and await—"

"Get out of here," the guard said to the bartenders and wait staff. Looking pointedly at Rebecca, he added, "You too. *Everybody.*"

The female bartender squeaked "What the fuck?" and then broke into a run. The catering supervisor held his ground, his jaw muscles practically convulsing.

Rebecca swiveled to face the booth and Stan and the five men waiting for her talk. She gestured to Stan—an emphatic, double-handed wave.

"Clear out!" she called, then ran for the far exit.

Her left pump wobbled and the heel snapped.

She kept running.

Something intense going on in those cylinders. Probably nothing. Just Coke. But endothermic, exothermic.

Her broken heel and something like instinct jigged her left and she got the black LAPD bomb truck between her and the bar.

She remembered a cat she had seen as a child, hunkering wide-eyed in the middle of a dirt road just before it was run over by a taxi. Not enough time. A kind of curious, helpless calm.

Rebecca got down on her knees and then fell on the shiny concrete floor, the edge of red carpet.

She drew her arm over her face.

Sound.

No other word for it.

It came as a rocky wall, bigger and hotter than she could have imagined. The windows and meeting rooms and the roof above them lifted and vanished in a gray pall of smoke pierced by white flame.

The big black truck parted the blast wave.

The searing hand of a very bad thing scooped her up and flipped her over like a burger. People, tables, booths to either side simply whisked away.

The last thing Rebecca Rose remembered, before the man with the ginger hair came back to find her, was that huge truck and three or four men in black uniforms flying and twisting over her head.

The truck bent in the middle and fell on her.

Ribs snapped like sticks under a boot.

The pain was unbelievable.

21

Nathaniel felt the concrete dust sift and settle on his head and shoulders, cake around his eyes. This time he imagined nothing. It had happened for real, almost exactly as he had pictured it—including the puffs from the shattered atrium windows.

Gray and black people rushed past, trying to escape the falling chunks, the wailing sirens and automatic alarm voices.

Nathaniel's senses jammed with observations, like a flood under a bridge carrying sharp, spiky logs. The flood keyed into his innate sense of self-preservation—so many fright bells ringing.

As he walked under the twisted beams, feet crunching through diamonds of glass—and as he climbed the groaning, shuddering escalator and the cracked concrete steps, counting each step, he again felt a surge of deep somatic fear—this time warning against the sharp draining of his physical and mental energy, like a dying battery—as well as the noise and the darkness.

All that imagining had worn him down and might have cost him what needed to stay alive.

I can't stop thinking. There won't be enough blood sugar left to keep my heart pumping.

The roof over the main exhibit hall had collapsed. Fire and rescue teams pushed through the fog of smoke and dust. Nobody was interested in keeping people out. Cordons had not yet been established.

Nathaniel walked steadily toward the center of the chaos. He could see the causal knots loosen, then tighten again. All of it made weird sense. His body screamed outrage that he would have to experience everything awful *twice* from now on.

But he knew who had done this. He knew who was ultimately responsible.

The Quiet Man—or Jones, if that was possible—had anticipated problems and assigned Nathaniel a task: to pass along something important. He had done so.

But all of it would be futile unless Rebecca Rose was still alive.

22

Rebecca couldn't take a deep breath without something driving into her chest, like a belt of nails cinched tight.

Water underneath.

Dark behind, light in front.

She had somehow crawled into a cave and got stuck.

Awful noisy, for a cave. Too confused.

She tried to open her eyes but got grit in them, and then keeping them shut hurt as well.

People were banging and turning on big motors and there was lots of yelling and even screaming.

At first, she could not bring her hands up to her face to rub her eyes. She kept wriggling. The scariest noise of all was the sound of metal above groaning like a huge dog.

The belt cinched tighter and she gasped.

All right. She was not getting out of this place—cave or whatever—without assistance. She needed to pull her arm around and push it forward. Someone at the mouth of the cave might see her fingers twitching—they must be close, she could see light.

More motors, engines, very big, and a banshee screech of cut metal. She imagined circular saw blades and sparks flying and then it struck her this couldn't be a cave. Her mind just couldn't fix on where she was, where she had been before, how she had gotten into this fix.

The water was warming. She smelled smoke. A lot of smoke and heat. Okay, definitely not a cave—a roof had collapsed. She had been in her office or maybe her hotel room. She had been in the gym, strapping on her new pumps, the ones that had been comfortable at first, but then the soles had squeaked and the heel had come loose and she had walked in circles to the left . . .

Los Angeles. She was on the West Coast.

Earthquake seemed likely. The floor was still trembling. Big earthquake and a collapsed building. Concrete dust. Heat from a fire.

Periglas. The executive officer of the *Robert Heinlein*. He had looked nervous, seeing her. *Maybe we shouldn't all be in the same place.*

Why had he said that? *Had* he said that?

They had been in the food court of the convention center. She had seen him there for just a few minutes, touched his hand, moved on . . .

Ended up here.

Flat as a bug.

No. They had got together for dinner. A late dinner. She had placed a call to the adoption center. Everything was on track. She had told Periglas about her wish to adopt—she had spoken of it while they were in bed.

He had looked at her and smiled.

Ah, Christ, she thought. *Stupid, stupid!*

A hideous noise very close vibrated everything and made her teeth hurt.

BLAM—and then the sound of a saw cutting through rebar. Somewhere, they were using a CIRT pounder to blast a hole through concrete with shotgun shells for hammers. What did CIRT mean?

She couldn't remember.

Controller Impact Rescue Tool.

"Atta girl," she whispered. "Nine thousand acronyms in the naked city. This is just one."

Someone was in worse trouble than she was.

The mass above her lifted a few fractions of an inch, and she could push her arm around and touch her nose, pressed into the concrete, water up one nostril.

She managed to pry open one eye and wipe it with a finger, enough to get the big chunks of grit off her lower lid. Somehow she dipped a finger in the flowing water and washed that eye, not much improvement, but now she could look out to the light and see smoke-hazy shapes moving.

All right.

What next?

Voices over the noise. Someone calling, "Anybody down there? If you can't talk, try to cough. We know it's tough. We're working."

Mary, I know you're out there waiting for me to come and help make a home.

God, I hate bombs.

Okay then. It *had* been a bomb—a big one. A gigantic Coke bomb, seven cans full, maybe more, first hot, then cold, whatever that meant. She had never heard of anything like it. Maybe she was still squashing memories and images together. A visit to the no-host bar, a peek behind: frost and fire.

"Give us a sign!"

"I'm down here!" she moaned. "Get this shit off of me."

The weight lifted another inch and she turned her head to look straight out at the triangle of light. Where she could manage to focus, she saw a mound of white girders, parts burned gray, and chunks of stuff all different colors.

Red.

Lots of red.

Maybe she had wiped blood and not water on her eye.

Then a different shade of red, blurry and smaller, and below it, a face.

"I know you," said a man's voice, and she saw a well-meaning smile. "You're Rebecca. Say something, Rebecca."

"Ten, nine, eight, seven . . . " She imagined herself walking backward down the steps, counting, on her way out of the Los Angeles Convention Center, about to go home.

"That's it. Keep talking. We're going to get this whopping big truck off of you."

"Truck?"

She remembered more. Flying truck.

The face went away and came back.

Ginger hair, tan coat.

"I know you," she said. "Your name is Trace. Nathaniel Trace."

"Sorry to have frightened you earlier. I'd like to have another word with you, Rebecca. If that's all right. Not right now, but when . . . you're free."

"Very funny."

Trace's smile was brilliant. He was not an ugly man, even with those scars.

"They're going to get you out," he said. "I see it happening. We'll talk soon."

The scarred face under the ginger hair pulled back and away. The giant blades of a fork lift moved slowly to within six or eight inches of her head. The blades lifted. Someone kicked a wooden block into the growing gap. The blades lifted again. Stuff shifted. The whole thing on top of her screamed and groaned, as if the big old black truck was still alive but trying to die.

Bomb truck.

Another groan, another wooden block, and then scraping cinder blocks. A fireman in a bright yellow rubber coat, face coated with soot, pushed between the blocks and got right up next to her.

They could have kissed.

"I hate bombs," she said.

"Me too, beautiful," he said. "Can you move your legs? Move your legs for me, honey."

She wanted to cry, that sounded so wonderful. Someone still cared. "I'll try."

"There's a lot of blood down here. Are you bleeding?"

"I don't know. I think I busted some ribs."

"You sound strong. Couple of more heaves, then we'll get it stable and I'll come back for you."

"Don't leave!"

The fireman winked and pulled out. Her foot felt like it was on fire. She tried to move her legs and could not. Other firemen moved in and more blocks were positioned.

In a compartment directly over her head, something big and hard fell with a nauseating clang followed by a prolonged, metallic fingernail screech. Rebecca tried not to think how many tons, where it might be balanced, how a robot in its lair—or a bomb tech's broken body— could suddenly lurch and upset the entire balance.

There was commotion beyond the triangle of light. Boots thumped past, raising puffs of acrid gray dust. She blinked rapidly, trying to focus. The bottom curve of a huge tire rolled by, followed by another, and another.

Big truck. Big crane. That made her feel better. How in hell could they get it in through all the debris?

Let them do their work.

She realized she had tensed all over, trying to keep the weight from closing in. That wasn't helpful. The tension of a tiny, trapped blob of protoplasm wasn't going to make any difference.

She relaxed, closed her eyes, let out her breath in a jagged sigh.

It was going to be a long night.

23

Washington, D.C.

Alicia Kunsler's armored limo pulled away from Reagan National and took an unexpected direction—to Dulles.

William sat beside her in the backseat, watching the Beltway give way to fields and forest land. He knew she had other things on her mind and had met him at the airport to save time.

The news from Spider/Argus had cast a pall. Kunsler had filled him in a little—just enough to both depress him and pique curiosity.

"I had a call yesterday from deputy director Scholes, West Coast," she said. "He tells me they have reliable intel that Nabokov is in bed with the enemy. He's playing us. They're working under the assumption that the mission is compromised."

William half closed his eyes and both snorted and shivered. His shoulders seemed to shrug this off, and then he straightened in the seat and stared out the window.

"Credible?" he asked.

"No. Hell, I don't know—we haven't heard anything since Thursday. But the Bureau has two heads, and right now, Alameda is feeling threatened—low men on the funding pole. Scholes is working hard to squash me. This could be his best hammer yet."

"Maybe you should let me know who it is we're trying to save," William said.

"Not relevant."

"If I know him—"

"Not relevant, Agent Griffin. The less you know, the safer your career. If I go down, I can cut you loose with minimal damage."

"After all of this, why would Nabokov give in to Price?" William asked. "What's their theory?"

"They feel the Saudis are working hard to reverse the Arabian revolution—and they're looking for a U.S. connection. A point of leverage. Bureau East has been working on that assumption for a year, against Alameda's steadfast resistance—but now they've flipped. They agree, but they're playing it against us. Price has a long relationship with the royal family. Nabokov is a Muslim."

"Which is how he got into Talos in the first place."

"Yeah. Scholes thinks they've turned him," Kunsler said. "His thinking is clouded, to say the least—Muslim equals traitor. Unfortunately, Scholes has political cover with a senior senator who went to Harvard with the AG, who gets along very well with the Israeli lobby and who, incidentally, hates Muslims—in private, of course. Fortunately, Spider/Argus is still on our side, and they have a lot of influence. We need Nabokov's information—now. We're trying to figure a workaround. Maybe two."

Rain dotted the thick glass. The limo rumbled and hissed over the wet roadway.

Kunsler broke the quiet. "Now listen close. There's something else bad—but also good. You worked with Rebecca Rose, right?"

"I did," William said. "What about her?"

"She survived the convention center bombing."

"Jesus!" William said, with a blunt nerve buzz of genuine shock.

"Two hundred others didn't. I'll be meeting her tomorrow in LA."

William remembered his last days at the FBI Academy in Quantico, coming into the trainee lounge and watching on TV the Washington State blast that had mortally wounded his father. Rebecca Rose had been there, as well, and survived.

He had met her on that case—and they had joined the group that had traveled to Mecca. Everything seemed to be orbiting around the Middle East yet again.

He didn't like that one bit.

He kept his voice flat. "How is she?"

His tone didn't fool Kunsler. "Light concussion. Cracked ribs. Sprained ankle. I'm delivering her new orders—straight from the president. And not without qualms, even though that will chap Scholes's ass—which is always fun. This mess is getting thick as pea soup. But there's nothing we can do until we retrieve Nabokov."

"Give her my regards," William said.

"Don't be stupid," Kunsler said. "Why should I know you from Adam? You're just a lowly agent slogging along with a losing team. The team that's close to being out of a job."

William looked chagrined.

"What do you know about Little Jamey?" she asked.

"Only what was in the news," he said.

Little Jamey Trues was the son of Reggie Trues, Special Agent in Charge of the El Paso Division of the FBI. He had been arrested and charged with first degree murder in Lion City, Texas. He had shot his best friend, the son of Lion City's mayor, with a small pistol, in the friend's bedroom. Both boys had been thirteen at the time.

The mayor was a good friend of Axel Price.

The shooting had been ruled an accident by both the Texas Rangers and the FBI, but the Lion County coroner's office had declared it premeditated homicide.

A Lion City jury of twelve older white men had convicted Little Jamey and sentenced him to death at the Walls Unit in Huntsville. Everybody in the agency had been shocked by the blatant miscarriage of justice—but were powerless to act. The federal government was on borrowed time in that part of Texas, many said. The U.S. of A. couldn't pay its bills.

Alaska, California, and Idaho were already talking seriously about breaking up into separate economic units—New Republics, they hoped to call themselves. The fate of an agent's adolescent son seemed a trivial lump in the awful stew.

"Bad times in a bad town," William said.

Kunsler jammed her eyebrows together. "Well, some in the Bureau haven't been so philosophical. A few agents and former agents in Washington have unofficially arranged for a cockamamie rescue. A real tour de forcemeat. But bold, I'll say that. If it's carried out, I suspect everyone on the ground will end up dead or paraded around in cages down the streets of Lion City.

"I've sequestered the agent who was planning and directing the rescue. I know most of the others, where they're stationed and what stage they're at—just a couple of days from carrying out the plan. I was on the brink of hauling them in and stripping their credentials too, but now . . ."

She looked up. "I think we might have a use for Little Jamey Trues. Like to hear more?"

William's heart sank. He had suspected for several months now that Nabokov was actually Fouad Al-Husam. Jane Rowland was part of this investigation—he had known that for some time. And now it seemed Kunsler was about to expand William's role in the operation.

They made up three out of the four agents who had taken part in the Mecca operation.

The fourth was Rebecca Rose.

He did not like revisiting the past. Taking a second look at FBI history had ended up killing his father. And of course it was history that had dragged them to Mecca in the first place.

"Okay," he said. "Where do I fit in?"

24

Long Beach, California

Nathaniel Trace waited inside his childhood home for the next prostitute to show.

He wanted to learn what level of self-control he possessed at this point in his unfolding. That was how he thought of it now; unfolding, pushing through the pupa case and spreading his wings, pumping them until they were broad and stiff, letting them set in the dry air, ready for flight.

Plain to see, the first prostitute—a skinny brunette with a wide, pretty smile and haunted eyes—had been abused since childhood. Nathaniel found he could not engage the proper responses with someone who had such a history. The hooker's counter to his lack of enthusiasm was sadly professional. She suggested an interesting catalog of circumstances and techniques, but Nathaniel had fixated on the fact that she could not—or deliberately *would* not—share pleasure. Working in the sex trade had made her numb.

It wasn't that professionals rarely enjoyed their work. He recognized her symptoms. She had PTSD.

He tipped her a thousand dollars and she left the house without a backward glance.

Nathaniel would not allow himself to fly if he thought he didn't have the necessary control. Was he like a child, working to acquire new instincts and training—or a passionless demon waiting to explode?

As far as he was concerned, that first encounter had taught him only part of what he needed to know. It was not that he cared about those around him. He did not even much care what happened to himself. But he had set his own ground rules early on, when he realized what he was becoming:

A building without walls. A mountain without rocks. A storm without winds. A drunkboat without a compass.

So far he had not exhibited the psychopathic tendencies Jerry Lee had spoken of, but that did not mean they weren't there. The difficult thing about his present situation was he could not predict his own behavior.

And so he would try one more time.

The house stood on a quiet street in a century-old neighborhood in Long Beach, California. There had been a few changes since his boyhood, but the lineaments were the same. His parents had died in a car crash on their way to ski at Big Bear. The house had been sold and he had moved to Costa Mesa to live with his aunt in a dingy, cramped apartment.

A year ago, while recovering in Baltimore, he had purchased the house outright from its then-owner, without knowing why. The house's history carried no sentiment for him but now that he was here he could, if he wished, unroll his childhood like a spool of film, shining on each frame a precision torch that had little to do with real human needs . . . See it all in full motion and vivid color, but spotty sound.

The house was teaching him how to access his past more efficiently.

Late last night, he had replayed the convention center blast and tried to rewind his emotions. That triggered another change. Deep ennui rolled in. He cared about nothing. This was probably a delayed effect of smoke and fire and bodies—so much larger than the atrocity in Arabia Deserta, though this time he had not been badly hurt—just a few scratches.

Even so, he could almost feel Mariposa working to separate his echoing emotions into manageable chunks.

Though wide awake, he had hardly moved for several hours. Somewhere in that void was when the Quiet Man called and left a message on his EPR cell.

Coming out of fugue just before dawn, he idly keyed in his ID and
retrieved the message. The Quiet Man's voice was steady. "Dr. Plover
says he gave you the materials. You invited the others, and that upset
the doctor—but it's probably for the best. Be careful with those aliases.
They may be using parts of Jones to track us. We have nine days before
MSARC kicks in. They already know where I am, of course. Jones will
not tell me who was responsible for the convention center bombs, but I
suspect he knows—and that means *we* know. I believe Nick is dead.
This is the last time I will call. Good luck, Nathaniel."

Nathaniel shut off the phone and stared through the front window,
between the gauze curtains, at the growing light on the quiet street.

Low on cash after his exorbitant tip, he had paid the second escort
service in advance—three hundred dollars—using one of three credit
cards registered to Robert Sangstrom.

Robert Sangstrom had recently flown from Dubai to Los Angeles—
just after Nathaniel Trace skipped out of the unscheduled meeting at
the Ziggurat.

Nathaniel could see everything so clearly now.

The next stage of the game was inevitable, and there was scant time
to prepare.

Late in the morning, while waiting for the second prostitute to show,
he used an old computer in the attic apartment, once rented to students attending Long Beach State. Routing through a skeleton server
in Bangladesh, he employed a former Talos student's log-in code for
the Survival Education Group—not a heavily secured site—to study
online manuals on self-defense and close-in combat. The manuals
were part of a mandatory Talos training program.

In the army, he had not done well in martial arts. Talos had tried
again to persuade him—and the rest of the Turing group—that everyone must know how to fight hand-to-hand in several different ways.
All seven had flunked, but the manuals were clearly illustrated and
quite good.

His entire body began to imagine the situations described and de-
picted. His head hurt again, and then his arms, his legs, his back.

Muscles tensed and relaxed.

He stood and lifted his arms. He could feel the burn—and a weird sense of *anger* directed at his faltering will. Physical training was a lengthy, focused process involving coordination between brain, nerves, muscles. But Nathaniel was now aware that learning also sacrificed conservative elements—parts of his body that did not wish to learn, that actively *objected* to learning; perhaps because the learning process would lead to these habits, tissues, neural partnerships and accommodations, being *phased out*.

Learning was like revolution, and the body hated change.

Aches, throbs, twinges, sharp jabs—all became a sign of success, as long as he didn't get lost in the cycle of regrowth, retraining. Like a horse spurred by its rider until it joyously ran itself to death—or leaped over a cliff.

He closed his eyes and controlled the endorphin rush; otherwise it would wash over him and leave him groggy.

Still, the prostitute did not show.

Lunch consisted of a half cup of shortening, a bowl of pasta without sauce, two candy bars, and a long slug of Gatorade. On that diet he did not piss purple, but for half an hour, he smelled terrible.

Something like ketosis, he suspected.

After thirty minutes and what passed for digestion, he tried out some basic physical moves—bracing, angling, kicking, striking. He would have to be careful not to injure himself. The body already felt too confident.

Mistakenly judging that weeks of intense training had passed, it *knew* it was ready. In reality, his body learned different things at different rates. The connection between sight-learning, text-learning, and actual physical action was unpredictable. He would not know how much he had absorbed, or how effectively, until the kick-in moment, triggered by real physical stress.

Danger to life and limb.

The prostitute was now two hours late. That was interesting, but not irritating. He could completely control his sense of passing time.

He had put on an exercise suit, black with red trim. Tight clothing bothered him. He preferred going naked, though for some reason did not like looking in mirrors. What he saw seemed inadequate compared to how he felt. His body had too much shape, its proportions were too fixed.

Intellect—the rules of the game—would have to make up for what he now lacked: social instinct, behavioral boundaries. A couple of days ago, he had been worried that everything he had ever been— all his memories, possibly even his physical form—would be erased and his life would become a blank tablet in the hands of an idiot with a big piece of chalk.

But the memories remained. He did not turn into a pile of mush. He just lacked perspective on what to do with what he had, and certainly how to feel about it.

Take Rebecca Rose, for example.

He had risked his life to find her in the collapsed convention center—and not just to make sure Plover's information reached its intended destination.

He had anonymously checked on her in the hospital.

Why?

Three hours late.

More than interesting; intriguing. The first woman had been spot on time.

He sat on the back porch, face bathed in sunny warmth, eyes closed, muscles twitching.

When dog legs twitch, we think they're dreaming of chasing rabbits. What if they're actually dreaming of being in a big number in a Busby Berkley musical?

Who would ever know?

The doorbell rang.

Nathaniel opened his eyes, got up from the chair, returned to the kitchen, pushed through the swinging door into the dining room, and crossed the maple floor around the heavy oak table. He smiled at the shushing sound his slippered feet made on the wood, and how that was silenced by the oriental carpet in the entry, behind the old Craftsman front door with the three crackle-glaze windows.

He unlatched the brass viewport. A woman in her early thirties stood outside, squinting at the afternoon glow over the surrounding houses, filtered through the trees: the famous golden hour.

She was attractive enough, with regular features—but other than that, nothing like the first.

He closed the viewport and took a deep breath.

All wrong.

Looking back at prostitutes he had been with in his youthful Army days and in France, Russia, and in Dubai—again, in full color and full motion, like playing back a video—he saw them frayed like tattered velveteen rabbits, hard-used, eyes haunted, subjected to the worst that men had to offer and too often left out, left behind. They had made themselves into closeted sweatshops of poorly manufactured lust, painted over, shaved, and discouraged. Some had decent acting skills, but the bloom was off their rose and they knew it; they knew their clocks were running out.

The woman waiting on the other side of the door dressed the part but had clear, sure eyes and a quality of skin—pellucid freshness rather than powdered pallor.

More than likely, Nathaniel guessed—though he would not call it guessing—she was ex-military, sleek and confident and fit. He compared her with the woman who had been part of the group in the Ziggurat—on the security camera, requesting entrance to his condo. Likely the same. Talos was expending huge resources to find him.

Nathaniel's next test would be to stay alive for more than a few more minutes.

The day before, he had walked around the yard visually mapping the neighboring houses, counting the windows, the doors—and now they lit up in his mind's eye. He saw the house and its environs as if in an isometric projection.

He shaped avenues of escape.

In the ten seconds since ringing the doorbell, the woman had grown restless. He could see her by listening to her movements.

With a rueful smile, he suggested to the new masters of his body that superpowers would be cool—true X-ray vision, the ears of a bat, the nose of a dog. But nothing against the laws of physics had arrived with the relaxing of his prior limitations.

No avoiding a fight. Here it was.

Nathaniel opened the door. The woman swung her head to look at him but held her body sideways like a fencer—keeping a line of fire open.

Someone was drawing a bead from across the street.

"Mr. Sangstrom?" she asked.

She had killed before. She was used to killing.

"That's me," he said, and opened the screen door.

They were roughly of a height to his advantage. He kept his center axis aligned with hers to discourage an easy shot.

"I've never done this sort of thing," he said.

"Of course not." She smiled brightly, eyes measuring relevant distances with saccadic micro-movements. "May I come in?"

She wore a coat over a short red dress. Sensible walking shoes, no high heels or pumps. "I took a bus and then walked," she said. "Good for the legs." She lifted her bag, catching the hem of the coat and revealing fit calves. "I brought high heels. If you want, I can put them on."

"I am putty in your hands," Nathaniel said.

Her eyes turned sharp, like a cat about to leap.

Crazy confidence flooded him. At the last instant, he decided nobody would die. He would escape, they would have no idea where he had gone, and the team they had assigned to catch or kill him would survive—mostly intact. He could see it, almost experience it—run it through on a loop.

Edit the mistakes.

Just for fun. But there's something else, isn't there? You're free of every human emotion but two: pride—and curiosity.

The woman stepped around the screen door with the quick grace of a dancer—or a trained Navy Seal.

"Hold on a moment," he said. "That's my phone."

He let the screen door go and it started to swing shut.

She dropped her bag, blocking it. Her left hand flew toward the bridge of his nose. He feinted. Her right hand, edge on, came around to wedge him in the throat or fist him behind his jaw—or failing that, drop and hit him just below the sternum.

She missed.

Time slowed—nothing new. He had seen it before in Iraq and Arabia Deserta. What astonished him was how much *slower* time seemed *now*, slower even than it had been at the LA Convention Center—and how much more it hurt at a deep level as he almost instantly burned through the ATP in his brain, the energy in his nerves.

He increased his heart rate to replenish blood flow.

The woman avoided his first rounding kick, which would easily have knocked her legs out from under her—but not the higher, faster second. His slippered foot took her under her raised arm, emptying her lungs with a whoosh and slamming her into the left doorframe.

She slumped like a sack.

His groin muscles wanted to spasm. He didn't allow it.

He was now exposed to the street, but jumped back and to his right. A bullet *shnizzed* just under his extended arm and blew a tan puff of splinters from a beam.

He kept going.

The white curtains drawn across the front windows covered his movement, but the sniper followed a probable trajectory and sent three more shots through the glass.

Close, very close. But seeing it all as if in film previews, Nathaniel had dropped to the floor—so fast he almost dislocated his hip.

He could feel his arm muscles start to rip.

No brakes.

His internal narration—the amused, wise old professional voice said, *He lands in a crouch, drops, and slithers into the dining room, away from the backdoor, where others now enter.*

The large bay window in the dining room reached over the walkway on the left side of the house. He lifted aside a chair, silent as a snake, and crawled under the heavy table.

One man's denim-clad legs appeared in the swinging door to the kitchen. The man pushed the door wide with one hand. The other hand no doubt held a gun—a pistol.

Nathaniel heard quiet movement down the middle hall—coming in on another route from the back porch. Heavier footsteps sent quivers along the wooden floor boards.

These two would form a pincer.

He squatted, braced, and shouldered the entire table like Atlas, tilting and shoving it into six rapid pistol shots from the man in the kitchen door—one of which penetrated the table's dense wood and grazed his shoulder.

The table pressed the shooter's arm against the door frame, bending it until it snapped it like a tree branch. Pinned, the man would not move—certainly not for the next few seconds.

Nathaniel was now exposed from the rear, but the man in the hall had not yet reached the living room—no doubt taking a couple of crucial seconds to assess the condition of his female colleague outside.

Nathaniel moved flat along the wall that paralleled the middle hall and retrieved an iron elephant bookend from the top of the built-in cupboard. With a bent grin, he watched the assailant's hand come into view, guessed the height of his head, and round-housed the bookend not into the man's face—*no fatalities*—but level with the jaw and the neck.

The man was fast but the elephant dropped him like a brick.

By now, the sniper and other team members would be up on the front porch.

Nathaniel returned to the dining room, lifted the oak table by its central pillar—ignoring another blaze of pain—rotated the three hundred pounds, easy-peasy, and heaved it through the bay window.

Broken arm released, the pinned man fell with a scream. The kitchen door swished back and hit his head.

He grunted and stopped screaming.

Nathaniel jumped after the table, through the shattered panes of glass. Table and body landed in the side oleanders in a painful tangle. He extricated himself and lurched to the right, around the back—behind other houses, through other yards.

One last bullet cracked, a wild shot inside the house.

Some blocks away, limping toward Long Beach Boulevard and a city bus or taxi, Nathaniel assessed the damage.

Not good.

He was thirty-seven years old, not in prime condition, and this was going to hurt like hell for days, maybe weeks. Nothing broken, however, and no bullet holes—just a few cuts in his forehead and arms and a graze that had already caked over.

He stopped by a curb and leaned on a signpost and started to laugh. The laugh sounded like a leopard's cough in a bad jungle night.

No ordinary humor—not even satisfaction at having survived an attempt on his life. A man who took no heed of pain or fear was in real danger.

He had to find a place to lie low and recuperate.

25

Los Angeles

"Rebecca!"

Rebecca swung into her hospital room on new crutches.

Two men and two women stood by her empty bed. She knew Hiram Newsome, former director of the FBI and her onetime rabbi and mentor in the Bureau.

His friends had always called him News, even during his tenure as director.

She recognized Deputy Director Alicia Kunsler from their earlier days in the FBI, when they had worked together several times. Kunsler looked mannish and frumpy—short-cut dark hair, pale skin, small, discerning eyes, square in all her angles.

The short, long-armed and short-legged forty-something male was Ruben Scholes, Deputy Director of the Bureau in Transition West. His friends reportedly called him Monk, but a slippery grasp on power was losing him most of those friends.

The true-blue grapevine—backed by an extensive series of articles in *NYT Online*—told of bad blood between Scholes and Kunsler, not surprising, since they were jockeying for ultimate control of the Bureau.

The second woman, a thin-faced, aquiline blond in her early thirties, wore a green pantsuit and pale gray shoes. Behind her thin and impressive nose followed a sharply attractive face.

They had never met and Rebecca did not recognize her.

News stepped forward and hugged Rebecca gingerly. She pulled in her crutches, looking in puzzlement over his shoulder at Kunsler.

"You're on God's payroll now, Rebecca," News said. "I hear a truck flipped over on you."

"And part of a roof," the blond said.

"I'm okay," Rebecca said. "Just a few cracked ribs and a sprained ankle."

News pulled back. "I don't believe you've met Shawna Prouse, JTTF Los Angeles, SAC of the convention center bombing investigation." SAC—he pronounced it letter by letter—meant Special Agent in Charge. "Agent Prouse, Rebecca Rose. You know our East and West Coast directors."

"Pleasure," Rebecca said. "I wasn't expecting a reception committee. They serve Jell-O in fifteen minutes."

"Not much in the way of visible damage," Scholes said, touching his own left cheek.

Rebecca started to lift a hand, then stopped herself. "They're removing the specks this afternoon," she said. "The burn marks should fade."

"Can't imagine," Scholes said. "I'd need counseling, at the very least."

Rebecca swallowed and looked plaintively at News. His hound-jowled expression told him he could not save her.

"News has been kind enough to fly in from Virginia for this meeting," Kunsler said.

"At Deputy Director Kunsler's request," Scholes added as if that were important.

"This is a meeting?" Rebecca asked, little-girl innocent. She crutched past them and sat on the bed, propping her braced and bandaged leg on a plastic stool. "It's great to see News again, but I've been debriefed half a dozen times—at least four times by your own people, Agent Prouse. I'm squeezed dry."

"This time, I'm here to give *you* information," Prouse said. "Let's start with the bombs." She laid her slate on the bed. "We've got an early report. What took the roof off the Los Angeles Convention Center was a device made of sugar, nitrogen, and a load of phosphate."

"Coke syrup?" Rebecca asked.

"With something new mixed in," Prouse said. "It's called a *synthobe*. A small, minimum-genome synthetic microbe tailored to carry out specific chemical reactions. Used for industrial applications, mostly.

Not really alive—can't reproduce. The synthobe kills itself, or deactivates, after getting the job done."

Rebecca felt an angry flush creep up her face. The burned patch on her jaw and cheek started to throb. "Some job," she said.

"Turns out twenty-eight of the canisters brought in for the convention by the catering company were inoculated with synthobes. The sealed canisters compounded the effect. Pressurized with nitrogen. The synthobes converted nitrogen, sugar, a trace of phosphate, and certain additives into a highly explosive gel. Security didn't detect any of this because this kind of bomb doesn't contain an explosive until all the ingredients are combined.

"The gel is heavier than water and it sinks to the bottom of the canister. It rises in temperature just before the explosion. Becomes as sensitive as old nitro. When it goes off, it instantly superheats the water to steam and compounds the force.

"We don't have a chain of possession established, but we're working on it," Prouse finished.

Rebecca looked out the window. "Any idea who's that clever?"

"Half a dozen going concerns, most of them in Belarus or North Korea," Prouse said. "A few more in Russia. One, very likely, in Haiti or the Dominican Republic."

Scholes looked concerned, as he would be expected to.

News and Kunsler were stone-faced.

Scholes said, "You mentioned before the blast, a self-proclaimed former agent met you outside the exhibition hall, and that he helped rescue you after."

"Ginger-haired fellow," Newsome said. He was obviously here as her advocate. That meant she was either in trouble or something strange was in the wind. "Dumpy, disheveled. You didn't think he looked FBI."

"Bureau," Scholes corrected.

"I only remember a little," Rebecca said, massaging her upper calf. "What about him?"

"You said he called himself Trace. Nathaniel Trace. There's never been an agent with that name," Scholes said. "And he wasn't registered at the convention. He must have been using someone else's badge."

News was getting irritated. "This is all well away from our mission."

"You were at COPES about to give a presentation, when the bombs went off," Prouse said. "You had clearance from the Bureau."

"Yes."

"From Deputy Director Kunsler?"

"From the former director, actually—before he resigned," Rebecca said.

"What's your current status, Ms. Rose?" Scholes asked.

"She's on indefinite furlough," Kunsler said. "Rebecca checked into the Los Angeles office before attending COPES and cleared her speech with your people. You have that on record, I'm sure."

"You've been out of action for eleven months," Scholes said. "What was your speech about, Ms. Rose?"

"Surveillance technologies."

Scholes took Prouse's notes and looked them over with pursed lips, then passed the slate to Kunsler. Rebecca saw she was being tag-teamed, almost—but not quite—as if she were a suspect.

"You met up with Captain Peter Periglas the night before. Drinks and dinner?" Scholes asked.

"We met up," Rebecca said.

"And he accompanied you to your room."

Rebecca did not blink. "He did," she said.

"You were involved in the clandestine Mecca operation. Both of you."

"I can only—"

Scholes's dark eyes flashed. "I am here to background an executive request. Did you and Periglas publicly discuss your work in Mecca?"

"Just by allusion," Rebecca said.

"What's that mean?" Scholes asked.

"We alluded to it indirectly. Peter—Captain Periglas—said that maybe we shouldn't be seen together." Rebecca bit the inside of her cheek. The "executive request" remark puzzled her. They were saving something for last.

Kunsler might be sympathetic, but Rebecca had never felt comfortable with FBI management—except News. "Did Captain Periglas say he had been approached by anyone regarding Mecca?" Kunsler asked.

"No."

"Why was he at COPES?"

"Representing a security consulting firm with navy contracts."

"Building better brigs?" Scholes said.

"Goddammit," News said. "Agent Rose has been through hell."

Scholes glared. "Everybody wants to protect everybody else. I'm here to protect the Bureau."

"I appreciate that," Kunsler said. "But the executive request went through Bureau East. We're not here to grill Agent Rose about her personal contacts. In light of—"

Scholes held up his hand. "Agent Rose, you're on high-level furlough, but nobody told Bureau West until last week, and I've yet to figure out what all that means."

"Extended leave without pay, with the option to return to active duty," Newsome said.

Kunsler held up her own hand and waggled her fingers until Scholes looked her way. "Agent Rose is looking at early retirement. She has interviewed with other government agencies as well as private security firms."

"That seems unusual," Scholes said.

"Half the FBI has been furloughed or let go," News said. "Something of a stampede."

"Agent Rose, what about your contacts in the private sector? Tell us about the last six months."

"I've talked with half a dozen companies that offer executive protection, forensic accounting—art investigation for rich collectors," Rebecca said. "I also interviewed for permanent positions with Diplomatic Security, EPA, Border Security, IRS. They turned me down."

"And who's most likely to utilize your expertise, do you think?"

"Blue Eyes Executive Services."

"Sounds like a call girl ring," Scholes said.

Newsome's cheeks pinked, but Rebecca ignored that. "Private investigations," she said. "Courtroom rehearsal and prep for law enforcement. Art forgery investigations as a sideline."

Stan had survived—barely. He was down the hall, fresh out of intensive care and looking like a Borg nightmare—but all in white, not black.

"They have any advantages over other outfits?" Kunsler asked.

"Keeps me local."

"You suffered from PTSD—post-traumatic stress disorder. Was that behind your rejection by the other agencies?"

The change of atmosphere was electric—and so sudden that Rebecca felt another barb of apprehension.

"Not your concern, Ruben," Kunsler said.

"It seems particularly relevant to the executive request," Scholes said.

"We're aware of it," Kunsler said. "It isn't relevant to Bureau East."

"Upon diagnosis, I volunteered for treatment," Rebecca said. "A clinic came recommended by folks at the marine base in Quantico."

Scholes gave News the kind of look you might expect from a prosecuting attorney about to nail a conviction. "Hiram, did you arrange for that recommendation? Upon your own evaluation of Ms. Rose?"

"I haven't heard about this until now," Newsome said.

Rebecca had told no one other than her FBI-appointed psychiatrist and personal physician. It didn't seem to be anybody's business but hers. At the time, she had already been furloughed.

For her, Mecca had screwed up everything royally, within the agency and personally.

"I feel fine, if that's your question," Rebecca said.

Scholes shrugged. "No judgment, no onus. But I suspect that might have played a role in your being refused by so many agencies."

"It was supposed to be confidential."

Newsome shook his head with a look that Rebecca new well—dismay at the ways of this silly, wicked world.

Now Kunsler sprang the reason for all of them being here. "President Larsen has asked for you to lead a White House investigation."

"The Bureau needs to be sure that won't backfire on all of us," Scholes added.

Rebecca was taken aback. She glanced at Prouse. "To work with you?"

Prouse shook her head. "I'd be proud to have you on our team—but, no."

"The Quinn homicide," Kunsler said. "The president seems to trust you. She enjoyed working with you—the last time."

Rebecca was suddenly tired and irritated and nervous, all at once. Her ribs ached abominably, as they always did around this time of day.

"The president has requested a personal meeting," Kunsler said. "She isn't asking for anyone's approval. You're being vetted by people outside the Bureau. You extend us a courtesy by answering our questions."

"Terrific." Rebecca looked aside at News, crinkling one eye.

Scholes sighed, petulant. "It should be said, despite my concerns, that I do believe you were one of our finest assets, Ms. Rose. I'm sincerely sorry about Captain Periglas."

News cringed. Kunsler looked hard at Scholes.

"I haven't had a chance to talk to Peter," Rebecca said. "If you debriefed him—"

"You haven't heard?" Scholes asked.

Prouse looked away and said, "Everyone wanted to make sure she was physically strong."

Rebecca sucked in her breath, like a half sob or hiccup, before she could catch herself.

"He was in an elevator in the parking garage," Prouse said. "He never made it down to the convention floor. The whole structure collapsed."

"It goes a lot deeper than that," Scholes said, trying to recover lost ground. "Informants in Arabia Deserta tell us there's a connection with your operation in Mecca. We think you and Captain Periglas may have been targeted."

"Someone blew up the entire building—to kill two people?"

"Under those circumstances," Scholes said, despite a warning glance from Prouse and News, and a wide roll of Kunsler's eyes, "I would assume your time with the president is going to be brief, tightly controlled—and secret."

"They're drawing a connection with the assassination attempt?" Rebecca asked. She turned to Kunsler. "Is this legit?"

"So far, it's pure speculation," Kunsler said, but Scholes would not be deterred.

"Solid intel," he insisted. "Probably financed by the same group. If they are who we think they are, they've been kicked out of Arabia Deserta, but they have plenty of money and international connections—

and they still think it's their mission to protect Mecca from infidels. President Larsen gave the orders authorizing your incursion. She would be an obvious target."

Rebecca looked out the window. There it went—not that she had ever had much hope. No normal life, ever again; no child, no man, no escape.

No waking up from the nightmare.

"When does the president want to see me?" she asked, voice barely a whisper.

"Tomorrow," Kunsler said. "You're under the executive branch from this point on. White House chief of staff is making the arrangements. One more thing . . . we need to download your dattoo. We think we might be able to recover the data."

Rebecca lifted her sleeve and looked down at the cracked and smeared dragon that had been the conference symbol.

"Indeed," Scholes said, though it was obvious this was the first he had heard about it.

Kunsler waved and a technician with a briefcase entered the room.

Rebecca lifted her arm as the technician unrolled a cuff. He wrapped the cuff around the dattoo. A few minutes later, he looked up with a frown. "Has anyone else accessed this? It's blank."

Rebecca looked back at him, guileless. She had already called upon a talented colleague to perform this task, but did not feel any need to reveal that fact. She was no longer an agent.

They didn't tell me about Peter until now.

"I was unconscious for several hours," she said. "It's pretty badly scuffed."

The technician packed up his equipment and left the room.

Kunsler nodded to Prouse and News—and then, with a small sound in her throat, as if clearing some phlegm, to Scholes. "My game from here, thank you," she said.

News gave her a backward glance of sympathy and warning as he followed Prouse and Scholes out of the room.

Rebecca offered the single chair. Kunsler seated herself with a heavy sigh. "I'm sitting here with a tough lady who represents everything I admire about the old Bureau . . . and it's my duty to tell her I can't protect her. Not that I was ever that effective in that regard . . . She needs to watch her ass like a hawk."

Rebecca snorted. "Third-person hawk," she said.

"No kidding," Kunsler said. "The president is in the middle of the biggest mess of her administration. Her approval ratings are in the single digits. She got a bump from the assassination attempt . . . the public always tips a hat to a politico who's just been shot. Up to 20 percent approval. But it doesn't last. Not in times like this. The vice president's insanity is probably the least of her worries. Fourteen counties in three states are setting up free economic zones—that means they're going to garnish all federal tax revenues. That might once have been called secession.

"The whole country is hurting."

Rebecca rearranged herself on the bed and looked through the room's east-facing window at a row of brown and gray buildings. "If I report to the president, I report only to her. I can't serve two mistresses."

"Understood," Kunsler said. "I'm making your furlough permanent. You're officially out of the Bureau. The president doesn't trust anyone right now—least of all us."

Kunsler got up from the chair. "To keep lines open, we're working the White House through contacts in the attorney general's office. When you're settled in D.C., I'm going to have someone I know look in on you—with the president's permission, of course. I hope we'll stay in touch. Get stronger, Rebecca. I mean it. We all think the world's a better place with you in it."

7 Days

26

Costa Mesa, California

The nursery was quiet this time of the afternoon. Rebecca took a straight-backed chair and set it aside from the sunlight, then settled into it with a sigh, arranging her left leg so that the foot did not hurt so much. Her lip quivered.

She wiped her eyes quickly with a handkerchief from her small black purse.

Sun cut a warm golden square on the blue and red flower carpet. The air held the faintest dodge of disinfectant and baby powder.

Throughout the morning, prospective parents auditioned for the privilege of taking home little Latin babies orphaned by the ten-year southern drought: Mexicans, Central Americans, Peruvians. From noon to three, more couples came to see if Miss Wickham (she of the upswept blaze of curly brown hair) would approve them for a fine crop of Burmese infants, or Filipinos, or Ethiopians, orphaned by war and politics.

At three, the nursery closed until after dinner, and then more couples, more interviews, more babies on parade; more babies almost than anyone could imagine, brought to the United States not because it was the richest nation on Earth, which it wasn't—not anymore, not after decades of economic waste and political stubbornness—but because it was the last major power that accepted orphans of any color, any heritage, and almost any health issue.

The nursery walls were pasted with colorful posters and stickers of balloons and farm animals and giraffes, big silver airplanes, and along the north wall, a hand-painted mural of a fairy tale castle, done by a volunteer with some talent.

The square of sun moved to a worn green couch.

Miss Wickham had approved the adoption last week, despite the news of the Los Angeles bomb attack; Miss Wickham was tough as nails and hard to sway once her mind was settled, and she had settled on Rebecca as being a decent parent for little Mary, whatever the world delivered along the way.

Rebecca had spent six months in interviews and record searches and corralling testimonials to get to this point, and yesterday, her request over the phone from the hospital had been met with several seconds of stony silence; Rebecca could easily imagine the extra width and extension of Wickham's pop eyes, the tap of her pencil on the steel top of the office desk.

"You'll have to tell her in person, Ms. Rose," Miss Wickham had said. "She's got her own set of hopes. She already knows you. You'll have to explain this yourself."

"She's two years old," Rebecca whispered to herself in the silent nursery. "She'll get over it."

But Rebecca never would. This was her last chance.

The door opened on the far side of the nursery and Miss Wickham's young assistant entered. Rebecca tried to remember her name; a faded slip of a girl in her late twenties, with large eyes, gentle hands, and a gently anemic smile. The sort of girl who took care of damaged animals and lost children and dreamed at night of de-balling the cruel bastards who caused all this loss and pain. Not that she would ever reveal that to anyone, certainly not to Miss Wickham.

The girl sidestepped the square of sun and stood before Rebecca, carrying a wireless freepad in one hand. "Mary's just finished her nap. She'll be here in a moment."

Rebecca nodded.

"It's not good to wait this far into the process," the girl said.

Rebecca nodded again, and for no good reason stared intently at her until the girl turned away with lips set in irritation, even anger; who could tell the difference?

Sometimes the saints of the world . . .

Miss Wickham entered, holding little Mary's hand. Mary saw Rebecca and her round face and beautiful black eyes all came together in the sweetest, shyest smile.

I am not going to blubber. I'll cry in front of Miss Wickham if I have to, but not this bleached-out killer saint.

"We'll leave you two to talk," Miss Wickham said, and let go of Mary's hand just in front of Rebecca

She and the killer saint left the nursery.

Five minutes. That was all they had left. No lifetime of love and watching this tiny, silky creature grow into young womanhood. Just a few words and a few minutes, all because Rebecca's life had come to a brick wall she had to climb alone.

Mary walked to Rebecca and Rebecca picked her up and hugged her. She was beginning to speak a few words of English. She came from Hong Kong, Miss Wickham said, or perhaps from Shanghai; there was no way of knowing. She had been found on a small island where the female infants of the daughters of wealthy, politically connected Chinese were often left to the care of patient, inured villagers.

Fishermen a hungry civilization had left with nothing to catch but abandoned children.

"I see you," Mary said.

She stood on Rebecca's lap and wrapped her skinny arms around Rebecca's neck. Rebecca let her cling for a few minutes, then gently pulled her back and sat her down.

Smoothed her hair, soft and fine.

What could they say to each other?

"I've been away in a hospital," Rebecca began her rehearsed speech.

Mary looked up and interpreted her expression, then imitated it, eyes narrow, lips sad. "Why?"

"I'm going to have to go away. I love you more than anything, but we can't live together like I planned. I still want to, it's nothing you've done . . ."

Some people want me dead. I won't put you in danger. No way to explain. Mary could not understand.

"You're the loveliest, sweetest little girl in the world, but we can't live together. I have to go away."

Mary's face froze, but she was no longer looking directly at Rebecca. Her gaze wandered to the window.

She played with Rebecca's sleeve. "No more," she said.

"Someone wonderful will love you just as much as I do, I know that."

"So sorry," Mary said.

Rebecca touched Mary's arm and stroked the smooth skin.

Miss Wickham returned.

"Mary, we have to go back. Say goodbye to Ms. Rose."

Mary just let go and slid off her lap. She did not look at Rebecca. Only at the window.

"We'll sign your release in the office," Miss Wickham told Rebecca, and hoisted Mary to her shoulder.

Rebecca watched Mary's little face withdraw down the long, bright hallway.

In the office, Miss Wickham settled back in her desk chair with a sigh. "I think I'm a good enough judge of people to know you have your reasons. Care to share?"

Rebecca shook her head. It would sound crazy.

"But you have a *very* good reason."

"I do."

"You're ill, something like that. Something I can put down on the forms, other than . . ."

"That'll work," Rebecca said.

Miss Wickham wrote for a minute, then passed a photo across the desk to Rebecca.

"We usually try to place our children with someone of their own heritage, but I believed this was a good match. I stuck my neck out and overruled procedure. Luckily, I've got another couple lined up. They're older, they're Asian—Chinese, in fact. Los Angeles couple, not wealthy, but solid family. No children. Their name is Choy. Her name will be Mary Choy—pretty, don't you think?"

Rebecca did not believe it was policy to reveal the names of adoptive parents. This was either Miss Wickham's special gift, to allay her fears that Mary would never find a home—or a kind of revenge.

She looked down at the man and woman in the photo. They looked bland and serious.

"Lovely name," she said.

"Sign here and we're done."

Back in her rental car, Rebecca looked through her spex at a list of messages. There was one she needed to return right away. She double-blinked to connect.

"Tom here," came the answer.

"Rebecca. Anything interesting?"

"Probably. It's a proprietary encryption, but I think I know where the PAR numbers are, and I think there's enough so I can reconstruct the rest of the memory."

"Great," Rebecca said. "Get it to me quick. No other copy. And bill my personal account."

"No cost," Tom said, his voice far away. "This one's for Captain Periglas."

Part Two
6 Days

27

The White House

"We're getting too old for this."

President Eve Carol Larsen arranged pillows in the corners of a large leather chair, then sat with a groan and propped her leg up on a bolster. "News tells me you're going to stop in at Bethesda while you're here."

"I have an appointment with the gimp squad," Rebecca said, arranging her crutches, then settling into the seat across from the Commander in Chief. Still gave her goose bumps. "It's good to see you up and about, Madam President."

"My trauma surgeon said I was like the lunch special at KFC. Breast, wing, and thigh." Larsen leaned to one side and tapped her polished fingernail on the chair arm. "Funny, huh? Laughing makes my chest hurt. You're an ex-smoker, right?"

"Yes," Rebecca said.

"Me too. I need a cigarette just to talk about it. The projectiles came from four miles away. I saw ruby-red spots of light—lasers doing speckle interferometry. The laser goes out through the air, gets refracted by temperature, wind, the way the ground or the building shivers—whatever.

"The sniper has a tiny scope-mounted computer that tracks the laser and also refines my image, then calculates the odds of a shot getting through. The shooter squeezes the trigger to begin the sequence—but the bullets don't fire right away. The imager and the interferometer work with the firing mechanism. The shots are let loose at the best, most opportune intervals—ten of them.

"Four go through the window. Three hit me."

Rebecca watched the woman's eyes soften with puzzled wonder, like a little girl looking at a dying pet.

The president sat up and hardened her features. "They tell me the shooter was using the same algorithms and technology that astronomers use at the Keck Observatory in Hawaii. That's what the Secret Service says. They couldn't stop me from getting shot, and they couldn't save Beth-Anne from that . . . bastard. Screw all the ingenious bastards and all their high-tech devices. But enough about *that*. Someone told me a good story about *you*."

"Uh-oh," Rebecca said.

"Eighteen months ago, just after you returned from Mecca, you were asked to help investigate a case involving a young woman kidnapped and transported across state lines, then murdered."

"Fort Lewis," Rebecca said.

"Tell me more."

"Not much to tell."

"Believe it or not, I've cleared two solid hours for this meeting." The president settled back with a sigh, as if getting comfortable at story time.

Rebecca leaned forward, dubious. "It's an old case, Madam President. I'm not sure what it has to do with anything here."

"Hiram Newsome says it highlights the way your mind works. He says you can be spooky. Spooky might be useful to us now."

"News thinks of me as his daughter, ma'am. He's not objective."

The president pushed her lips together in her trademark, sharp-eyed smile. "Please."

Rebecca hated going down memory lane, but this had the air of an executive order. "She was found in the base apartment of a soldier just returned from Arabia Deserta. She had been traded to the soldier by her kidnapper. She was only fourteen."

She looked through the ripple glass toward the south lawn. "Madigan Army Medical Center at Fort Lewis was handling a lot of troubled vets. Counselors, psychiatrists, researchers—the northwest center for treating post-traumatic stress disorder, PTSD. More than 350,000 cases. But this sort of violence was rare. Family troubles—abuse by young soldiers hooking up with girlfriends who had babies by another father—that sort of thing is much more common, planned for by the commanders, almost expected. The criminal mistakes of marginal recruits forced through tough times, suffering back-to-back stop-losses. But true psychopathic behaviors catch everyone's attention, because some experts are worried our Gen-Z boys might react to PTSD differently than past generations. So the authorities, both military and civilian, wanted to nail this suspect and work up the chain to the kidnapper, find out how they had hooked up and why. They had a second suspect, but the girl was dead, and the soldier was pretty much out of it. So the Bureau came in to examine the evidence.

"I asked to see the girl in the morgue at Fort Lewis."

The president looked away. "Fourteen," she said.

"Thin, just a wisp," Rebecca continued, "and young. Hair cut short, pert little nose—pretty before they got hold of her. The kidnapper used her for two or three weeks, until he got tired of her, then opened an anonymous Flickface account and offered to trade the girl for drugs. The Fort Lewis soldier took him up on his offer. I examined the body."

"Tweezers," Larsen said, sitting up. "Sorry. Go on."

"The kidnapper apparently wanted to keep her face intact. The rest was a mess. When the kidnapper delivered her to the soldier, outside Fort Lewis, in a van, he had cleaned her up and scrubbed out his DNA. The younger man objected to her condition. Still, they reached an agreement and smuggled her onto the base.

"After a while, the soldier killed her with an overdose of morphine. Their only mercy. The kidnapper took his drugs and left while the soldier was busy. A roommate found the soldier in a stupor—along with the girl's body, a few hours later."

"Unbelievably cruel and stupid," Larsen said.

"The case against the soldier was solid. He raped her before he killed her. But even when he plea-bargained to avoid the death penalty, he couldn't provide enough of a description for us to ID the kidnapper."

Rebecca had seen enough mutilated bodies in her career, but her response never changed. She hated being reminded that flesh was like pudding: soft and easily smashed.

She swallowed. Other violent memories accompanied this one, having nothing to do with the dead girl. Not long ago, those memories would have made her break out in a cold sweat.

"In the morgue, I pulled back the sheet. The girl had been autopsied, fumed for fingerprints, pretty much desecrated every which way you could think of. But she looked peaceful enough if you ignored the scars and sutures. I touched her cheek. Took off the glove and just smoothed her skin with a bare finger. Something like the tiniest splinter poked up—a bristle. I asked for a pair of fine tweezers, sterile.

"Once I pinched a boyfriend's beard to get his attention. I found hair tips stuck in my finger pads. When men use electric shavers, the blades do a rough job. The ends look like porcupine quills, with a sharp pointy tip and little barbs.

"This bristle wasn't from the soldier. He had hardly any beard and didn't shave. We bagged it and sent it off to Quantico for keratin extraction. They got enough DNA to locate the perp in CODIS. We got a warrant and apprehended him within two days.

"He was forty-two, a white male transient with a long sheet, nearly all violent felonies. Washington State convicted him, life without parole in Walla Walla. Hard time.

"That was all I had to do with it," Rebecca finished. "Nothing spectacular."

Larsen murmured polite disagreement. "Now tell me what you know about Edward."

"The vice president hit his wife on the neck and back of her skull with a lamp, crushed her windpipe with his hands, and left her to suffocate. When the Secret Service entered the house, Quinn was reading to his daughter in an upstairs bedroom. His infant son was asleep. No motive, no disputes, no history."

"The last guy anyone would suspect," the president said. "War hero, family man, best damned governor Ohio has had in decades . . . A good campaigner and a shrewd but honest advisor. My husband thought of him as his best friend. Now he's locked up in a special compound at Fort McNair while everyone figures out what to do— where and how to indict and try him, whether to go for the death penalty . . . all that dreadful crap. I'll announce a new veep in the next few days. Then—we'll do our damnedest to act as if it never happened. We have to move on.

"But the bottom line: we almost had a psychopath become president of the United States, Rebecca. I wonder how long before anyone would have noticed."

Rebecca looked down at her hands.

"You've gone over our early briefing," Larsen said, shifting her hips to get more comfortable. "Thoughts?"

Rebecca took a moment before answering. "He revealed a history of drug use during the campaign. Has he indulged in the last three years, to your knowledge?"

"To anybody's knowledge, he has not."

"There are drugs that can slip by even the best tox screens. Designer metaboloids like tart or syncrom." Rebecca looked squarely at the president.

Larsen did not blink. "Believe me, if we could use that as an excuse, we would."

"Nobody in your administration has been implicated in any sort of drug activity?"

The president shook her head.

"Because this does look like a doped horse."

"It does," Larsen admitted. "A thoroughbred."

"Food testing—here and abroad—all secure?"

"The best."

"No secret snacks, nipping out to the ice cream parlor at midnight in Istanbul with the kids or the mistress?"

"Edward was lactose intolerant—strictly soy. No mistress. You know this already."

Rebecca nodded. "I like to hear it from someone close. Better than a briefing from someone who's never met the man."

The president took on a distant look, like trying to see a lighthouse through thick fog. "Something smeared on his skin, the bloggers say . . . could have delivered it from a couch or even the inner sleeve of his coat. A psychotropic contact drug, maybe in two or three parts—combine them and you set him off."

"Possibly." Rebecca opened to that page in the printout. "No evidence, however. And I know a lot of these investigators and analysts—they're the best."

Rebecca knew that a major reason some former agents were talking with the White House, and joining the investigation, was the whiff of payback. Vice president Quinn had stood just behind the head of the Senate task force that had recommended dismantling the FBI and moving it west.

"So I keep being told," Larsen said. "But the bomb that almost got you—nobody ever heard of that before, either. I'd like to take all the pinhead bastards who spend their time thinking up this stuff and line them up . . ." She formed her hand into a gun, then caught herself and relaxed her finger with a tight wriggle. "What the hell is *wrong* with them?"

Rebecca nodded. "You wouldn't have called me here unless you thought I had some sort of useful expertise. Other than the wit to use tweezers."

"Being shot hurts, but this hurts more. Edward was a brave man and a friend. This administration—my administration—is going to do everything it can to get beyond this and get his story off the front pages. But I want to make sure we know the *whole* story. If we missed something awful during the vetting process, I need to know. News tells me you're the best agent he ever worked with. I've read the reports on Mecca. As much as I can trust anyone, Rebecca, I'm going to trust you."

The sun cut through the ripple glass, lovely shades on the room's custom red and gray and beige carpet.

They sat for a few seconds, like two cats across a room.

"I'll need everything, Madam President."

"Thank you," Larsen said in some relief, but under her breath.

"I'd like to start with the internal White House research—the VP vetting papers—then the DOJ and FBI reports and whatever the beltway sleuths dug up for your election team."

"They're setting up a secure room in the Eisenhower building, an executive assistant, however many gofers you want—plus a security detail. White House counsel will escort the drives and files."

"I want security under my control."

"They've heard you might be a special target," Larsen said. "The Saudi exiles."

"Doesn't make sense. I was a much easier target before I went to COPES," Rebecca said. "I'll need to talk to Quinn's staff—and his daughter."

"The children have their own attorney, of course. She might not let that happen."

"Most important, I need to talk to Quinn."

"Difficult. No one is allowed to see him now except DOJ people and his attorney. Separation of powers is really mucking things up."

"I need to hear him answer my questions in person, Madam President."

"We'll do our best. Time's short, Rebecca. We're turning on a spit. We have less than a week before we cook through."

28

FBI Academy
Quantico, Virginia

"I don't like it down here," Alicia Kunsler said. William walked beside her down the long hallway that had once led to the old forensic training lab. The lights had been removed from every other fixture, creating a faster, rhythmic shadow vs. brightness as Kunsler increased her pace. "This is where I saw my first dead crime victim. They used to do that—until it became politically incorrect to make agent trainees puke."

"I didn't know."

"Nobody will admit to it. One particular instructor seemed to really enjoy it—a total hard ass. Best instructor I ever had. He's no longer with us. He'd bring in unclaimed corpses—indigents, drug smugglers, prostitutes. They'd lay out on a steel autopsy table, meat under a sheet—of course they'd been autopsied and cleaned up a little—and the instructor would pull back the sheet and give the agent trainees the person's stats, where he or she or he/she was found, the circumstances of death, and the one central truth of the entire day—that the killer or killers would never be identified or prosecuted. The resources did not exist. Back then, Mexico was having a pretty fierce drug war—worse than now, even. Thousands were being killed. Mules and dealers in the U.S. were being taken down.

"Our special corpse had been photographed crossing the border into El Paso in the company of a trucker who claimed she was his daughter. She was sixteen, a U.S. citizen—born in Los Angeles—and so on. The details don't matter."

"They're always interesting," William said.

"Do you dream of crime scenes, Agent Griffin?"

"Of course."

"Last night?"

"Yeah. I can never get the evidence to stay in one place, or collect it fast enough—it evaporates or someone walks out with it and I can't stop them. It never comes together, even if the clues are laid out like a board game. They keep skittering away. I wake up feeling groggy and stupid."

Kunsler smiled and pointed. "Left up ahead, through the double glass doors."

"What about the girl?"

"The trucker had beaten her to death, snipped off her fingers with garden shears, and cut off her head with a hacksaw. He was never seen again. Maybe he's down in the bone desert south of Juarez somewhere—the least he deserved."

"How'd you identify her?"

"Tattoo on her left shoulder. Eagle holding a snake." She snapped her fingers and looked relieved. "That's the connection. It's been bothering me. El Paso and snakes."

They passed left through the doors and found three men in blue windbreakers and khaki pants standing in front of a steel autopsy table, blocking most of the view.

Kunsler introduced them quickly. "Agent William Griffin, this is Johnny Walker."

The man on the left smiled and held out his hand. He had a high narrow brow, a long jaw, a trim young head of brown hair.

"The rest will please introduce themselves," Kunsler said. "I'm not a drinking woman. I get you confused."

"I am Wild Turkey," said the second man, shorter, balding, plumper. "My friends call me Turk."

The third—slight and skinny, long-nosed, with thick glasses, not spex—stepped up to shake hands.

"I am usually Captain Morgan. But today, you can call me Q."

William caught a glimpse of something small and tan, coiled in the middle of the steel table like a rope or a whip. "*Star Trek* Q, or Bond Q?" he asked.

The others chuckled.

"Take your choice," Q said. "What we do *is* weirdly godlike."

"These gentlemen do not wish to be remembered," Kunsler said. "Their services are on loan, along with their equipment. Mr. Q, proceed."

William knew better than to blurt out some smart-ass guess as to where the three were from. Spider/Argus had over the years partnered regularly with DARPA—the Defense Advance Research Projects Agency. And DARPA had funded quite a few projects involving robotics.

"We assume you both signed our NDA," Q said.

Kunsler passed them the sealed envelope.

The men parted like a human curtain.

The coil on the table appeared to be a snake—tan and brown with black specks and a spade-shaped head. It did not look alive and it did not look dead.

"This is not a toy," Q said. "It's not exactly top secret, but close. We're still working on a clever acronym. Agent Griffin, you'll take away our lovely sidewinder and three of its brothers in a custom-made suitcase. Use as instructed—they'll be preprogrammed and ready to go. We would like them back. They're rare and they cost about a million dollars apiece."

Q bent to remove the black plastic case from under the table. He opened the case and took out a small cardboard box, from which he withdrew a plastic tube about half an inch wide and two inches long, with a screw top. The tube had a small reservoir at one end.

Within the tube was a small steel lancet.

"We were not informed what *that* is for," he said. "But it all fits in *here*." He reached down and partially uncoiled the snake, then squeezed its middle. A small hatch popped open, giving a glimpse of gleaming steel ribs and wires. He placed the tube inside the snake, then closed the hatch.

"The snake has hi-res terrain mapping tied in with augmented GPS, and in this model, face and voice recognition. Pretty good software, if I say so," Q boasted.

"We all say so," Johnny Walker affirmed.

"Within sight of a targeted individual—I mean, the intended individual—it will make an audible announcement and open its hatch. There is no self-destruct mechanism—we're delivering on short notice. If its mission is not completed, there's a risk that some one smarter than us will draw some or other conclusion by examining its payload—though we ourselves have yet to come up with a believable hypothesis."

"Thank you," Kunsler said. "Tell your secret masters we're appreciative, and will provide all the relevant details, should our mission prove a success."

"One more thing," Johnny Walker said. He pulled a cable from the box. "Keep this plugged into a cigarette lighter for half an hour before you release."

"The fuel cell option has been delayed," Wild Turkey said, with a hangdog expression. "My bad. It turns on like this . . ."

He demonstrated. The snake twitched and coiled, then raised its head with a hiss and shake of its tail. Kunsler leaped back about a foot and gave a convulsive shudder.

"Very convincing," she said as the snake performed an S-curve crawl around the table. "But sidewinders are Sonoran desert, not west Texas."

"As I said, short notice," Q said.

29

Washington, D.C.

The Eisenhower Executive Office Building was by any definition a
stately pile, a great angular staggered front rising to an elaborate
Mansard roof. With marble floors, cast-iron columns, and brass details, the EEOB looked Baroque to Rebecca, who knew from the architecture, but the Marine guard—a short, muscular woman with
the most beautiful, sympathetic eyes—proudly told her it was actually French Second Empire. Whatever, it was crammed with over
five hundred and fifty rooms and two miles of hallways—a warren
of office spaces woven around restored ceremonial rooms and spacious executive suites.

The EEOB housed the solar plexus of executive government and its
proximity to the White House had made it a desirable stack of real estate for almost a hundred and forty years. It also housed the vice president's offices, and a weary-looking quartet of two marines and two
Diplomatic Security agents stood guard by the tape-sealed doors.

All four sets of eyes, sharp as hawks, locked on Rebecca as she
walked by.

Tours had been stopped right after the Quinn murders. Nobody
wanted to deal with large and curious crowds or the extra publicity of
ghoulish souvenir hounds removing chunks of historical ornament.
More than twenty such had already been arrested trying to breach the
grounds of the Naval Observatory.

Rebecca's escort steered her through the quiet, echoing sadness to
a small waiting room furnished with ornate wooden benches and a

magazine table. The escort sat across from her, biting her thumb and providing more architectural details

A tall, straight woman with short gray hair and a neat gray pantsuit opened the door, then looked down at her notebook. "You're Rebecca Rose?"

"Yes, ma'am," Rebecca said.

"I'm Thalia Ripper. I used to be the president's campaign manager. Now I help with legal and other matters—call it damage control. We have a desk and secure terminal for you in an annex near the vice president's office. The office has been processed and will be made available to you. A lot of boxes are being delivered, more boxes every hour. I have a staff of three waiting to assist, all of the highest integrity and loyalty. If they seem stiff and unhappy, well . . . you understand. Let's start on a first name basis."

"I understand . . . Thalia."

"Ripper." Half lidded eyes. "Like a Bond girl."

Rebecca grinned.

Ripper cocked her head and threw back her shoulders. "Used to look like one, too."

Rebecca had no difficulty believing that.

Ripper took Rebecca through nearly empty hallways and down a flight of stairs. They peered into the Indian Treaty Room, fancy digs indeed, one corner stacked six feet high with neat, white file boxes on carts with soft rubber wheels, not to mar the flooring.

Rebecca's space took up a back room beside the deserted vice president's office.

"This used to be occupied by Quinn's staff," Ripper said. "They handed in their resignations as fast as they could. We all loved Beth-Anne."

The walls were draped with pale gray fabric. The ceiling was hung with similar fabric. Surrounded by this canopy, a small desk supported a flat screen with a virtual keyboard.

"I'll need a big, flat worktable," Rebecca said.

"I'll get one, but I recommend against spreading out documents," Ripper said. "We haven't had time to blind the room. There was a restoration project in the EEOB three years ago. Little things in the paint, you know. A constant problem. Hence the drapes. They're presumed to be effective, but presumption doesn't cut it."

Rebecca leafed through a small pile of papers sitting under an orange cover on the desk: lists of documents denied to the White House by various agencies and departments. "The Bureau won't give us the FBI's vetting docs for Quinn," she noted.

"That was Bureau West's call," Ripper said. "You having issues with the deputy director in Alameda?"

Rebecca shook her head. "No way of knowing."

"We may have copies," Ripper said. "We're still looking."

Rebecca set her teeth and pulled out the barely padded, decades-old visitor's chair, then sat and stretched her leg. "I worked with the AG on a political background check eight years ago," she said.

"The same one who's serving time in Cumberland?"

Rebecca nodded. "With politically sensitive subjects, Office of Intelligence usually got involved. Back then, the info went straight back to the White House. Not anymore, I assume."

"Not anymore," Ripper confirmed.

"OI also exchanged data with CIA. To cover their asses after the torture trials, the CIA liaisons trucked paper dupes of their findings over the river to a warehouse in McLean. They didn't trust the White House not to erase them."

Ripper smiled. "I'll make an inquiry."

Another trolley of boxes arrived as Rebecca continued to run down the list. At least 90 percent of the blocked documents, she was sure, would be available somewhere in a cached blog or government web page.

Within a couple of hours, the small room was half filled with boxes, each packed tight with thousands of sheets of paper: folders, binders, briefing booklets.

Some dated back to 1979.

"The vice president went into the army in 2004," Ripper said, tapping a flat gray box. "These are his official records—fitness reports, Silver Star and Bronze Star commissions, medical and Purple Heart documentation—that sort of thing. I'll leave you to it."

Two staffers showed up on the first day, with another promised soon. Rebecca asked these serious young workers to bring her the first three boxes, by date, from the larger room.

Together, they began working through Quinn's life. Document search and analysis was the sort of labor Rebecca knew was essential, and hated. Worm days, she had called it at the Academy. Bookworm.

At five, before dawn, she was escorted by her assigned Secret Service agent, Roger Baumann—tall, balding, with an oft-broken nose and calm, brown, spaniel eyes—from the rear of her hotel, a small, comfortable old establishment, empty but for her. Baumann drove her a block and a half to the EEOB in a massive armored Cadillac, to be set loose in the former office of the vice president, rapidly filling with millions of cold, impenetrable words and images describing a life effectively over.

She now had four assistants, each with Hill staff or Library of Congress experience. This morning, they were guided through metal detectors and whiffers and inspected by a row of small but intrusive imaging machines. One staffer—Judith, the oldest at thirty-four—bragged she now knew more about her intestinal tract than she ever wanted to.

Rebecca put Judith in charge of the team. She did this despite her instinct that Judith was a spy for Thalia Ripper. Ripper was providing cover for Rebecca's work. It was only natural for her to want to know the details, day by day.

Each staffer was accompanied into a small restroom and provided with special clothing. Rebecca was allowed to wear her own clothes.

To put a cap on the strangeness, at the end of the day, they all submitted to blood tests. No one explained why.

Rebecca joked that someone must have found a new way to smuggle information. "I've got a copy machine in my tummy."

The doctor drawing her sample avoided her eyes and did not smile.

So far, the research was routine. Quinn had been vetted by the FBI before being chosen as running mate, and by the CIA before the election—the latter investigation conducted in strict secrecy and without the campaign's knowledge. Other divisions—the far-flung branches of Homeland Security and the Department of Defense—had conducted their own investigations, in greater or lesser degrees of internal secrecy, just to know what to expect if these folks ever happened to move into the White House.

This morning, Rebecca's entourage passed a group of trim men and women in black suits, escorting a man she recognized from online photos and videos: William Raphkind, the solemn young governor of New Jersey. Raphkind was on the short list to be appointed vice president once Quinn was formally removed, which would be any day. No doubt he was being vetted even more thoroughly than Quinn.

There was a lot about candidate vetting that the public was ignorant of. Bureaucrats—the behind-the-scenes power brokers in Washington—looked on elected and appointed officials much as the servants of a castle looked on newly resident royalty, but with considerably less respect. Jobs were at stake, but also legacies. Quinn had probably been investigated on the sly a dozen times by private beltway security firms. Most of those documents had been deep-sixed on the night of the election. No one knew if any still existed, because they had never existed in the first place.

For all of that, nobody had found much in Quinn's life beyond the usual youthful embarrassments and middle-aged fluctuations of emotion. A good husband and father. Quick temper, some said; others, a strong command presence that brooked no nonsense. The usual executive-level male forcefulness, which Rebecca, personally, could take or leave. She had known worse offenders in that regard who had also been excellent agents.

For a man severely wounded, Quinn had glided back into civilian life in a relatively smooth slope and with a soft landing—welcome return to loving family, wife pregnant with their first child—and then selection, nomination, election, and transition into major public office.

Party recruiters had apparently been grooming Quinn's image even while he was in Iraq, and there was considerable press coverage of his exploits—but less information about the violent 2007 incident in Fallujah that had left him with scars and medals.

Rebecca kept the gray military box and its records on that incident beside her at all times. It radiated political and tactical self-protection.

Investigations of "encounters" involving civilian deaths had become routine, almost cookie-cutter by that chaotic stage of the war. No one in the Bush administration or in the Pentagon had wanted anything to obscure the success of the Surge, which after four years of trial and error, had finally been appreciable, then considerable—until the final combat draw-down, followed within two years by civil war and the end of all hope for sustained political influence in that part of the Middle East.

Rebecca sat before the small desk and arranged five manila folders in a tall rectangle. Three flat displays relayed the morning's news and interdepartmental text feeds. She looked them over with a pruned-up face, then glanced down at the folders.

Laid her hands beside them.

Something had been left out or trimmed away; she knew it instinctively. But she wasn't sure she actually trusted that instinct. One of the first lessons drummed into those who would be law enforcement professionals, who *must* for the sake of public safety study the behavior and misbehavior of others, is the Prime Error: projecting one's own biography and experience over another's.

She rearranged the folders as if searching for a perfect combination.

I am not Quinn. But a career in the FBI, one big bomb in Washington State—one extraordinary day in Mecca. I've lived through a lot of violence and I've seen a lot of death. Didn't exactly leave me ready to smoothly transition back into the peacetime world. Messed with my head; I folded.

I sought treatment.

Quinn had lived on the outskirts of hell for over a year and a half. Twenty-three civilians killed in the middle of a fierce firefight, a convoy pinned down for two hours. And yet . . . no emotional scars. No recurring nightmares, no long hours of lying in bed sweating in a freezing room, jumping or shrieking at loud noises, seeing the faces of the dead come back like a string of ghosts hanging off the tail of a Chinese junk

For Quinn, apparently, nothing like the awfulness that had pushed Rebecca into special therapy.

Another big bomb . . . Maybe I'll fold again, who knows?

She tapped her stylus at the bottom left folder, rearranged them one more time.

Lieutenant Colonel Edward Quinn had reacted to combat and injury like a hero, a true candidate for public office. Nothing could be allowed to get in the way of those goals. People did not like weaklings
in the White House.

Judith rolled in another cart.

"Hey," Rebecca said, and raised her hand like a girl in class.

"Yes, ma'am." Judith stood quietly beside the cart.

"Where would an important, well-connected politician go in this
town to solve a personal problem?"

"What sort of problem?"

"Psychological. Potential for political fallout. The Betty Ford clinic?"

"Quinn no longer drinks, stopped taking drugs back when he was a
soldier—ma'am. You know that." Judith frowned and thought this
through. "Are you asking about combat-related problems?"

Rebecca shook her head. No sense playing her hand just yet. "I'm
fishing. I'd like a list of all the treatment centers for embarrassing
disorders of any sort . . . to be made available, by major donors or par-
tisan groups, to a man being groomed for high office. Expensive, discreet. When am I scheduled to meet with Quinn?"

"Tomorrow morning, 10:30 A.M., at Cumberland, ma'am."

"Cumberland?" Rebecca swung around in her chair. "I thought he
was at Fort McNair."

Judith looked at her slate of appointments. "He was transferred yesterday to a terrorist compound at Cumberland. No explanation." She
pressed her lips into an incurious line.

30

Rebecca walked around the mall in the lengthening shadows. Baumann usually managed to stay out of her line of sight when she jogged, but this evening, she said she needed complete privacy to meet with a reluctant informant. A half hour of hot debate and Rebecca had threatened to call the president. Baumann had turned red, made his own call—and relented.

She had snuck out at 5:00 P.M. and now, half an hour later, was thoroughly enjoying the lovely feel of no bandage or ankle brace, and both of her feet shod in the latest high-tech sneakers, one luxury she could never cure herself of—the cop's best friend, great shoes.

The new programmable protein drugs were remarkable. The doctors had told her she should walk only a hundred feet or so per day, nothing more strenuous; so she jogged a few dozen yards, then dropped back with a slight limp and a wry expression.

The sky over the Capitol dome was a shade of pure enameled blue. The sun dropped with steadfast serenity behind a gray wall, a hovering front stalled to the west. The air had turned crisp and cool. Body heat puffed rhythmically from the collar of her sweatshirt.

Stages were being set up at the north end for a concert. Joggers and pedestrians and tourists had worn the grass down to dirt; gardeners tried to stake out territories for new grass, but hardly anyone paid the ribbons much attention, and soon, fifty or sixty thousand people would gather and stamp their feet in time with the latest bluegrass sensation. Rebecca didn't mind; she liked bluegrass. Her momma had liked bluegrass. Her daddy had liked bluegrass, and their mommies and daddies before them. Bluegrass never went away. It might even outlast the sun. Billions of years in the future, there might be concerts playing bluegrass to people made of beautiful walls of light, jiggling with the rhythm as it was broadcast out to new stars in a thin black sky.

She shook her head as she tried not to limp. Jogging didn't help her think. It helped her get away from thinking. She had been thinking too much the last few days and sleeping too little. Tomorrow she would talk with Edward Quinn. That meeting had taken two difficult days to arrange. Her ankle suddenly shot a bolt up her leg and she lurched toward a bench. Nothing big; the pain was already trailing off to a dull throb.

She grimaced and sat, waiting.

Tom Cantor appeared a few minutes later, also jogging. He wore jeans and a black sweatshirt with a transparent hoodie—D.C. regulations forbade opaque hoodies—that barely veiled his balding head and fringe of long straggly hair. Thin as a rail, he carried a slim backpack and nothing else. With a whuff, he sat beside her and leaned back, slung his arms over the bench, and regarded her with large brown eyes.

He flashed a generously kooky grin. "Come here often?"

"I'd like to," she said. "Ankle gives me grief."

"Better soon, I pray. Well, this one's pretty interesting. More so every hour."

"Interesting, how?"

"I recovered a spreadsheet file—mostly a list of names. Put it on zip paper for you. Fingerprint the upper corner and all will be revealed. Pull back the plastic tab and bend the corner—all gone."

"I know how to use zip paper. Thanks, Tom."

"The biggest parcel looks like a digital sound file. It's desperately fragmented. I'll need another day. Any reason it's important?"

"Fate of the planet," Rebecca said.

Tom shook his head and pushed up with another whuff. "Hate to do all this work just to nail some boring old white slavery ring. So—one more day?"

"Do I have a choice?"

"Nope. Sorry." And he jogged off, waving his hand without looking back.

Tom Cantor had never failed her—or anyone else who relied on his services. And many very important people did.

Until now, no problem she had passed along to his expert hands had taken him more than a few hours to solve.

4 Days

31

Cumberland Federal Prison

"We're breaking new ground here, no doubt about it."

Lionel Blake walked beside Rebecca down the long corridor, lined with white tile and precisely laid ochre brick. Quinn's attorney nodded to three Secret Service agents, arrayed in a blocking triangle across the hall; the agents squinted and parted to let them pass. One tracked Rebecca's rear. The other two, more professional, studied her face, her briefcase, and her purse—before glancing at her rear.

Lionel Blake's representation of the former vice president of the United States could have cost at least a thousand dollars an hour. Quinn's family was not wealthy and the White House legal defense fund was not paying; perhaps Blake was doing it pro bono, for the considerable publicity. None of these motives endeared Blake to Rebecca, who as a rule was not fond of lawyers, less fond still of defense attorneys.

"Your visit is the first real sign of attention from the White House since my client's arrest," Blake said. "I don't know whether to be encouraged or just accept it as another layer of ass armor."

Two correctional officers sat outside the heavy, inset steel doorway. They rose and folded their arms like genies. Their faces—one black, one white, both beaded with sweat in the corridor's steam heat—were perfect blanks.

Blake paused. "Nobody goes in without four guards present. He's no Hannibal Lecter but he's no fun, either. Strong and unpredictable. Make up your own mind. He's more dangerous to himself . . . well,

I won't go so far as to say that. But he hasn't hurt anybody since he killed Beth-Anne."

Rebecca glanced at the door—semi-gloss black enamel, featureless except for a small viewport at eye level and a pass-through near the base—and looked back down the corridor, then up at the steel plate ceiling. She hated prisons. Coming back here was no treat—the last time, she had been lightly worked over by a couple of beefy matrons, overseen by a super-zealous Diplomatic Security agent. They thought she might have information about a terrorist incident.

She sincerely hoped they were all out on their asses now, slopped away in the departing flood of medieval thinkers.

"I insisted you be allowed to interview him," Blake said. "Anything you learn can only support our case."

"How much has he said?" Rebecca asked.

Blake shrugged. "I can't stop him from saying whatever he wants. He's his own man, no doubt about it." Blake seemed cheerful, considering the atmosphere.

Easy case, she thought. *Open and shut. Edward Quinn is innocent by reason of stark, raving, hoo-ha insanity.*

Four more Cumberland officers came through the opposite door, one at a time to avoid knocking elbows—huge guys in padded suits with thick arms and thicker gloves, more suited to training guard dogs. The two officers at the desk had Blake and Rebecca sign in and finish the last round of waivers. One used a walkie-talkie to have the cell door remotely disarmed, like an airplane hatch. Small electric whirring and three clunks followed. Nothing was done hastily in this wing. The other guard peered through the viewport, then plugged a small mike into the door.

"Mr. Quinn, stand back to receive visitors—your attorney and a guest."

Quinn's voice sounded from a speaker in the wall to the right of the door, clear and pleasant. "Happy to have visitors. I'm feeling safe today."

Blake cast a doubtful look at Rebecca. "Here we come, Edward," he said into the microphone.

The correctional officers stood by for another ten seconds. Two of the guys in padded suits moved in like mirror images to flank the door. The door clicked again and opened a few inches with an oily piston sound. The third padded officer—the senior lead—pushed between Rebecca and Blake, as a shield, and pulled the door open the rest of the way.

It was a very heavy door. The cells had been built to hold former Gitmo detainees. Quinn stood at the back. He had a cast on his left arm, covered with tough-looking black mesh. The mesh extended over his hand.

"That arm's broken," the senior lead said in an undertone. "He's ripped the cast off twice. It's a bitch to replace. Takes five of us plus the doc. Anyway, he says he doesn't need it."

"How did he break his arm?" Rebecca asked.

"Exercising," the senior lead said, and entered the cell with a slight waddle, facing Quinn all the while. "McNair couldn't handle him. We're sort of used to tough guys—terror detainees were hard cases, you know. The shit they went through . . ." He shook his head.

The men in padded suits surrounded Quinn where he had backed himself up against the bare wall. Quinn looked them over with little head jerks, like a cartoon fly.

Then he fastened his eyes on Rebecca. They were sharp as needles. Another flick of his head, and he looked askance, as if staring at her was like staring at the sun.

"If you're here to listen, that's terrific," he said. "Find out what went wrong. Because before all this happened, it worked. It really worked great."

One of the guards carried in a folding plastic chair and stood beside it as Rebecca sat. She took out her notepad and switched on the record function in her new spex.

"Cute glasses," Quinn said. "Never got used to them. Beth-Anne was going to buy a pair, for travel."

"My name is Rebecca Rose," she began.

"Son and daughter—okay?" Quinn asked.

"They're fine," Rebecca said. "I'm here on behalf of the president. I'd like to ask some questions."

"Wish her all the best," Quinn said. "Everything smoothes over. The past can be made to go away. Or at least you don't feel it."

"We'd all like to finish this sooner rather than later, ma'am," the senior lead said. "He'll talk and talk if you let him."

"Ask away," Quinn said.

"The president has instructed me to investigate the circumstances leading up to—"

"Beth-Anne." Quinn frowned until his eyebrows met and looked earnestly at her.

"You remember everything?" she asked.

"Yes. A mistake."

"Why did you do it?"

"Testing. Tried other things first. Experiments."

"What sort of experiments?"

Quinn continued in a light, conversational tone. "Hid things. Re-arranged desk drawers after the staff had gone home for the evening. Pulled pranks. Put a pin—P-I-N, sharp—on a seat. Heard the office secretary Francine yelp when she sat on it. Didn't laugh—nothing."

"What did you learn from your experiments?"

"Could do anything without guilt or even embarrassment."

"What else?"

"Told lies during hearings. Aides to senators caught them, then the press. Got concerned reports from staff. Politicians always misspeak. A true Washington animal. At night, when everyone was asleep, sat in the office chair in the observatory. Went exploring through the past—very clear. Could remember events but they all seemed out of context, like someone else had lived them. Realized there was no need to worry. The worries went away. Erased them. But it's not disease that kills a leper, it's because he keeps hurting himself but feels no pain—no consequences. Losing a conscience, that's like having leprosy. Conscience gone—how much damage?"

"Hurry it up," the senior lead said. "He'll go on and on. Ask him what you need to know. We all have other duties."

The fact that she had gotten into Cumberland at all gave Rebecca confidence that she could take her own sweet time. "How did you compensate for having no conscience?"

Quinn smiled. "Each morning, with coffee, read from a handwritten list of things to feel guilty about, just to stay human, you know, for the day's events. Didn't want to act like an arrogant prick. And then . . . different handwriting."

"How?"

"Looked at the old signature from signed documents. New signature, different. Caused concern intellectually. But it didn't frighten. Becoming fearless is even more dangerous than not feeling guilt."

"Nothing frightened you?"

"Could imitate fear for a little while, thinking of really bad things that might happen. But then . . ." He shrugged.

"Is it possible this condition began when you were in Iraq?"

"Felt fear in Iraq, just like everybody else," Quinn said. "Normal."

"After you got home, did the fear return unexpectedly?"

Quinn focused. "Afraid all the time."

"Flashbacks?"

"Worse. Dreamed things that never happened. Very bad things."

Rebecca relaxed her jaw. She had been clamping her teeth as Quinn answered. "Were you suffering from post-traumatic stress disorder?"

Quinn shrugged.

"You knew there were treatment programs, didn't you?"

Quinn's voice turned rough. He sounded as if he were quoting: "'Cowards and fools don't get elected.' Saw how officers looked at the broken soldiers. Disgusted. Wanted them out of the barrel before they contaminated the others."

"I can't find any record of your being treated," Rebecca said. "Yet you admit that you experienced classic symptoms of PTSD."

"Right," Quinn said. "Pure Terror, Surely Damned."

"You must have found some way to control it, like you do now. Taking charge of your life."

Quinn shrugged again.

"Did you seek advice?"

He looked away.

"Are you feeling guilty now?" Rebecca asked.

"Yeah," Quinn said. "Maybe. Damn." He grinned like a boy caught stealing cookies.

"You say you can control all of your emotional reactions."

"Sometimes it takes a day or two."

"If I come back later, will you answer my question?"

"Which question?"

"About seeking help for your illness."

Quinn looked down, shrugged.

"This is a sham." Rebecca folded her notebook and removed her spex. "No personal pronouns. That's pretty on the nose, don't you think? Your attorney coached you."

Blake started to protest.

Quinn lifted his broken arm. "Bullshit. Better, quicker, stronger. If I . . . *there*! If I had felt this way when I was in Iraq, would have been a better soldier—an excellent soldier. Would have come home ready to be with the family—no nightmares, no flashbacks. Look at . . . *me*." He tapped his chest with his cast. "Training so hard now," *thump*, "snapped this arm. Does that sound like something a lawyer would tell . . . *me* to say? Lawyers aren't that creative."

"I don't believe you could accomplish all that on your own."

"Well, score one for you."

"Then you sought treatment. Discreet treatment."

"If you say so."

"Where?"

"Cowards don't get elected."

Blake folded his arms, more confident than ever.

"You've always wanted to serve in public office," Rebecca said. "That's over. There's nothing left to lose."

Quinn lifted his eyes to the grill-covered light.

"Did you practice before you killed your wife?"

Quinn's smile was more of a spasm. "Score two. Birds, squirrels, cats," he said. "Couldn't feel it. The ultimate test had to be someone . . . *I* thought I loved . . . once." Quinn leaned his head to one side.

Rebecca stood and moved behind the plastic chair. "Tell me where you went for treatment."

Quinn lost himself. His lips turned up at the corners and his eyes half closed, as if he were having an orgasm. "Guilt! So little goes such a long way. Almost make believe . . . *I* did something wrong. But now *I'm* doing something right."

Rebecca touched her spex. "We're done," she said to the guards.

"It'll all be over as soon as the Secret Service withdraws," Quinn said. "That's why they moved . . . me to Cumberland. Guards here under contract . . . outside. Best to hurry."

"Why bother?" Rebecca said, flashing him a look. "You're hiding something, but you'll never give it up."

"Doing it right."

"Doing what?"

"Not talking."

"Right for *who*?"

"For my son and daughter," Quinn said.

"Fat good that does Beth-Anne."

Blake's face worked. As if he could think of nothing better, he smiled.

"You're useless," Rebecca said to Quinn. "Useless to the president— useless to everybody."

She turned to leave.

"Now *that's* freedom!" Quinn shouted as the guards withdrew, carrying away the chair.

The door to Quinn's cell closed with a heavy gasp.

Down the long hall, Blake accelerated to keep up with Rebecca. She was walking quickly, ignoring her ankle's protests.

Blake watched with concern. "Quinn's certifiable, but he isn't paranoid," he said. "I didn't coach him. I hope you think I have a modicum of smarts. The pronoun bit—that showed up yesterday."

Rebecca stopped in front of the glassed-in inspection station to retrieve her purse. Just for good measure, she was subjected to another pat down and sent through the imaging gates. Blake looked away while she went through, but she saw herself in the station monitor: gray, ghostly naked, and awful, like a lumpy corpse.

"You're an unexpected gentleman, Mr. Blake," Rebecca said as they returned to the parking lot. "Quinn's under suicide watch. He's surrounded by guards. What could happen to him?"

"Someone in the federal system pulled a chain and flushed him out of McNair," Blake said. "There was nothing wrong with security there. He's not afraid, but I am. Neither of us knows how it will happen. But it's going to happen. The Secret Service detail is perfunctory, at best, and even that will be withdrawn in a few days."

"Where's the threat to his family?" Rebecca asked.

Blake shook his head. "The president gets shot. You and everyone else in the Los Angeles Convention Center get hit with some clever new type of bomb, targeting—maybe—an undersecretary of Homeland Security and forty or more active and retired federal agents. Someone seems to want to destabilize what little government we have left—which teeters on insolvency. The Secret Service is in disarray. Morale is shot. The FBI is in transit—or limbo. Half the remaining security in Washington has ties to private contractor firms. Based on past performance, whoever writes the biggest checks has the most say. Quinn's onto something. He won't tell me, either. But my firm did our own research before we took on his case. He had interesting contacts, and apparently he utilized their services."

Having accompanied her across the parking lot, Blake stood beside Rebecca with hands folded as Baumann opened the limo door.

Rebecca paused by the open door. The defense attorney's close presence made her uncomfortable. "So?"

Baumann focused on Blake's shoulders, his arms—what he could see of them.

Blake looked around, then leaned in to speak softly. "Someone's working down a list. I have absolutely no idea why."

"But you know *who*, don't you?"

Blake pulled back. "It's going to come out. It has to."

When Baumann looked away, distracted by a passing car, Blake pressed a folded piece of paper into her hand.

"Do what you can to get Quinn moved back to McNair. He has useful information, it'll just take time. Don't call me or my firm. When it all comes out, this is going to be pure poison and we do a lot of business around here."

Rebecca sat in the limo, lifting her leg and swinging it into the car. She watched Blake return to the visitor's center entrance.

"Anything interesting, Ms. Rose?" Baumann asked as he prepared to close her door.

"I don't know, Roger. Not yet."

"Was that crack he made supposed to be some kind of a threat?"

"Good ears, Roger. I don't know that, either."

"I can have him hauled in," Baumann said, looking back at her in the rearview mirror, eyes narrowed.

"Don't bullshit yourself. You'd be yanked faster than a pit bull in a chicken yard."

"I was on Quinn's detail," he said a few minutes later. "Jesus. A veteran and war hero—a real family man. No marital problems I ever saw. Ms. Rose?"

"Yes, Roger?"

"No more going out on your own."

"I'll let you know, Roger."

She opened the folded piece of paper. All it said was "*Talos.*"

The rest of the day seemed routine but Rebecca was looking for any and all connections between the former vice president and Talos Corporation—or CEO Axel Price. She used tailored searches to process millions of archived White House emails, sent over from the National Archives.

Nothing of interest. White bread politics, not even whole wheat.

And nothing about Talos.

32
Washington, D.C.

Rebecca unlocked the door to her hotel room. The clock on the wall glowed 1707.

She took the pot from the hotel coffeemaker and poured a cup before sitting at the desk, leg stretched out to ease the ache. She opened Tom's manila envelope and laid its contents on the desk. One sheet of zip paper.

She thumbed the tab.

The first entries from the dattoo, arranged in indexed pages, were people she had met at the COPES conference. Next, Tom had arranged fragments of degraded files, a mess of keyboard symbols that meant nothing to her. He had annotated some of the lines of code, suggesting, in parentheses, what they might mean. Most were names—again, people she had met at the conference.

But Tom had also written, on the third page, "Sound file encoded and fragmented. Can't reconstruct yet. Still working. But name is recoverable: 'Confession of VP.'"

Rebecca finished her coffee, then touched the zip paper's right arrow to access the fourth page. Tom had prefaced this new list of names, marked off in a matrix of lines, with "Not dattoo files. Separate single Excel formatted file, recovered complete. Analysis of this file gives a machine ID, Microsoft license and serial number, location of store where software was purchased eight years ago—Trig Medical Office Outfitters, Bethesda, Maryland. Name of installer or licensee— Madeline Paris, doctor. Simple hacker shit. You're welcome. Sorry about the delay on the sound file."

Rebecca looked over the names. Tom had underlined two without comment: Edward Quinn, listed on the entry as "Primary, First Patient List, Mariposa 01"; and near the bottom, third from the last, "Rebecca Rose, Fourth Patient List (outlier), Mariposa 03."

She frowned, moved her finger down, scrolling the zip page, and read the thirteenth name: "Nathaniel Trace, Second Patient List, Mariposa 02."

Mariposa was butterfly in Spanish. By itself, that meant nothing to her. But Nathaniel Trace, Edward Quinn, and Rebecca Rose all had something in common. That something was in—or had been in—Bethesda, Maryland.

Rebecca had only one connection to anything in Bethesda. She had gone to a clinic there to undergo treatment for delayed PTSD.

The same PTSD that had gotten her indefinitely furloughed from the FBI—not retired, not shitcanned, but furloughed, because she knew too much, and keeping 'em on the payroll was standard practice at the time for alcoholic, drug-addled, or otherwise defective agents who knew embarrassing things.

Or who broke into a raging, paper-tossing fury in a case meeting at a simple challenge from the then-director.

She took a deep breath. The meeting with Nathaniel Trace meant that someone had known even before she did that the president was going to ask her to investigate the VP.

The White House had a leak.

Nathaniel Trace was connected with that someone—friend or foe, who could tell? As for the list of names . . .

Quinn had secretly gone for treatment at the same clinic—hush-hush in the extreme. Mariposa. Quinn. Trace.

Rebecca Rose.

Quinn had gone off his nut and killed his wife. Not drugs in his doughnuts, not a surreptitious injection or contact poison. Side effects of Mariposa, perhaps. Very possibly.

Likely.

Rebecca closed her eyes and sat for a long, long cascade of steady breaths, against the sincere wishes of her ribs.

I'm part of the problem.

This information had to go to the president, delivered personally. But the president was in the Catoctins, at Camp David. She had been there for three days and no one could reach her—not even Rebecca.

The room's old landline phone rang. She never used it. She picked up the wireless handset and searched for the talk button.

"You don't know me, Mrs. Rose," said the voice on the other end— masculine, soft and steady. Her brow furrowed. No one was supposed to know she was staying here. Despite the voice's mildness, something was wrong—and not just because he called her *missus*.

"No, I don't," she said. "Who are you?"

"I hope you've had time to read the documents your young man recovered for you."

"Who is this?"

"Someone is coming to visit, Mrs. Rose." The voice repeated her name as it had the first time—*exactly* as it had the first time. "Please don't get alarmed. He's behaving erratically, which is understandable, under the circumstances. But he means well. Please be careful."

"You can't—"

The connection ended with a swift growl-rising-to musical tone that indicated somewhere along the path, an EPR phone was involved— very expensive, limited to big corporations and just a few government agencies.

She replaced the handset in its charging cradle.

The doorbell rang. She jumped.

Nobody was supposed to be able to do *that* without warning, either.

She slipped the zip pages into a drawer, then thought for a moment, brow still furrowed. Waited to see how long it took whoever was there to ring for a second time.

Ten seconds.

Drawing herself straight, she went to answer.

A gray-haired man in a tweed coat stood in the hall, stooped from worry and exhaustion. He tried to smile, then twitched a look over his shoulder. Baumann usually kept watch this time of the evening at the end of the hall, near the elevator.

He wasn't there.

The gray-haired man withdrew a 9 mm Luger from an inside pocket and pointed it in her general direction, with his finger on the trigger.

The safety catch on the left was off. He wobbled the barrel, uncertain what to do next.

Amateurs with guns scared the hell out of her.

"My name is Dr. Terence Plover," he said.

Rebecca had to reassure him before he fired a round out of panic—or several rounds. She stood back, smiled, and said, "Come on in, Dr. Plover. I've been told to expect you. The place is a bit of a mess."

33

Plover sat in the corner chair beside the counter of the kitchenette, the single pole lamp behind him and his face in shadow.

The barrel of the Luger poked into the cone of light.

He sounded asthmatic. He might be ill. Or just scared out of his wits. "Thank you for meeting with me," he said. "I've been told you have useful connections."

"Blake set this up?" Rebecca asked.

"Who is that?" Plover asked.

"Quinn's attorney."

"He had nothing to do with this."

The silence lengthened.

"My wife has been murdered," Plover said, eyes wandering. "She was very dear to me, and very important. A brilliant woman, too humble . . . but brilliant. I hope you understand my precautions." He tapped the Luger with one finger. "This belonged to my grandfather. He took it from a German soldier who no longer needed it. It was the only gun I had access to when I left Bethesda."

"I've read some of your wife's documents," Rebecca said. "Quinn came to your clinic for treatment. Nathaniel Trace was one of your patients after that. And then—me."

"I don't remember your face, but I remember your name. I didn't meet with you personally. Sorry. I hope we were able to give you some relief."

"It was a short visit. But yes, it helped. So far."

"I have since given up my practice, my clinic, my companies. My wife and I moved . . . After I learned what Quinn was involved in."

"Murder?"

"No, before."

"And that was? . . ."

Plover looked dismayed. "You were given his confession!"

"The sound file?"

"I thought you'd have delivered it to the president by now."

"It's corrupted. I have someone working to recover it."

Plover looked even more distressed. "This is awful," he said. "I wanted it to be over. He found *our home*. And he killed my wife, I'm sure of it. He would have killed me . . . had I been there."

"Who?"

"I made a financial bargain. A devil's bargain," Plover said, and leaned back, pointing the Luger on a wavering line through her chest, her pelvis, her arm. "A bargain with a man who has no mercy, if you cause him trouble—or put his plans in jeopardy."

"I'm listening," Rebecca said.

Plover shook his head, not yet. "As one of my patients, I also came here to warn you. I'd like to warn all my patients, but that isn't going to be possible. Someone arranged this for me. The Quiet Man."

"The voice on the phone."

"Yes."

"Go on."

"Seroprixoline. Madeline first learned about it in *JAMA, Journal of the American Medical Association*. It was being used in an experimental program to treat cancer. It's a tightly bound complex of small proteins—no need to bore you with the structural details. It helps reprogram targeted cells. Removes defects caused by environmental conditioning." He swallowed. "Crucial for bringing a cancer under control."

"And what was your contribution?"

"I theorized that seroprixoline might be useful to reverse psychological conditions induced by constant or catastrophic stress. Inappropriate response leads a traumatized patient down a rutted path of behaviors. Conditioned traits sum to many varieties of what we call post-traumatic stress disorder. PTSD. But you know that—personally."

"And you thought you could use this drug right away—on patients?"

"No. I searched for corporate sponsors. Hundreds of thousands of our soldiers have returned from combat situations with PTSD. Treating their symptoms effectively would be a godsend to those soldiers and their families."

"So you approached Axel Price."

That wasn't much of a leap at this point, but just mentioning the name gave Rebecca chills.

A list.

No mercy.

Plover lowered the gun and dropped his gaze as if resigned. "He has money, his corporation has divisions around the world. He supplies universal logistics for our troops. He sells his services to nearly every branch of our government, federal and state. Tens of thousands of his employees work not just overseas, but throughout the government—from the White House to the Pentagon . . . He misses no tricks—leases out a network of funeral facilities that process soldiers when they're shipped home . . . in boxes, under flags, as heroes. Boot camp to grave.

"In the beginning, I thought it was a perfect match. Not only a humanitarian result, but a gold-plated investment model. Great sums of money to be made. I showed Price the results in our animal studies—very impressive. He saw I was given more than sufficient research funds. The program was accelerated.

"Then . . . Price brought me the vice president. He told me the animal results were so good that human trials were in order. And this was an emergency. People were willing to pay very well, and as it would be done in complete secrecy, there would be no risk to me, professionally.

"The results for the vice president were excellent, a great relief to both Madeline and to me. Price was pleased. Using Quinn's results, I made adjustments in dosage. We continued animal trials, and I even believed we might begin human trials soon."

He looked at her as if beseeching her understanding.

"But just weeks after that, before I was ready, Price brought in seven more men—computer programmers who worked for him. Subcontractors. They had suffered through a horrible incident in Arabia . . . Arabia Deserta. He wouldn't take no for an answer, said they were absolutely essential to him.

"I treated them, as well—using the reduced dosage. They all experienced complete elimination of symptoms. Price then suggested that we open our doors to a larger group of clients—mostly rich families whose sons had gone to war. He was eager to start making this project earn money. I could hardly refuse him. We treated dozens. I don't know how, but you became part of that larger group.

"Later, after the vice president killed his wife—when it was obvious Price was going to clean up the mess any way he could—a courier came to me, recommended by the Quiet Man. Somehow, the Quiet Man knew about the president's request for your help."

"Even before I did," Rebecca said.

"During treatment . . . the vice president became briefly vulnerable. He told me things. Awful things. I regret ever hearing those words. The Quiet Man thought you would inform the president. That hasn't happened yet, has it?"

"No. Who's the Quiet Man? What's his real name?"

"I don't know. He worked for Price, too. But he stayed in California—in La Jolla, I believe—and sent his workers overseas. I was scheduled months ago to give a presentation at the COPES conference in Los Angeles—but bowed out the day before the bombing. I was still on the schedule."

"The bomb was meant for you?" Rebecca asked.

"For anyone Price no longer trusts. Or perhaps just as a warning, or a disruption. I don't know."

"You're still pointing the gun at me."

"I am," Plover said, and looked down with wide eyes, flexing its grayish shine in the single light.

"What did Quinn say, when he was vulnerable?"

Plover shook his head. "This room could be bugged."

"It isn't," Rebecca said, but sensed Plover wasn't going to say anymore on that topic.

"What's your connection with the courier, Nathaniel Trace?"

"One of the seven programmers. They've also experienced side effects. Your group received an even smaller dose."

"Are we all going to turn into homicidal maniacs?"

"I want to doubt it, I *need* to doubt it," Plover said. "It would take years to know. Epigenetic testing . . . learning which genes are clamped in which individuals, and how that affects their behavior . . . still at an early stage. I'm tired. I've told you all I know."

"Has anyone in the third group experienced problems?" Rebecca asked.

Plover became even more agitated. Rebecca considered a feint and an attempt to take away the gun.

"I don't know. I don't know! It's like an ocean of sewage, spreading out in a huge wave. And for Price, Mariposa is an atomic bomb smack in the middle of that ocean. *Pwoosh.*"

Plover threw out his free hand and flicked his fingers, spattering metaphoric shit.

Startled, she missed her chance to go for the gun. "Someone called to say you'd be coming. The Quiet Man?"

"I don't know who else it could be. He protected me, found me a place to hide and offered me advice I thought was sound. I trusted him. Because of him, I am still alive."

"He didn't protect your wife."

"That was before I trusted him. But I don't trust anyone now. I even regret giving you those files . . ."

He pointed the Luger squarely at her chest. "If you die, now . . . Price . . ."

"You did it to avenge Madeline's murder."

Plover tried to pull himself together. "I wanted to inform you, as one of my patients . . . It's all so tangled. When this is over, if I can continue my research—if the good guys win," and he afforded Rebecca a small, shy smile, "Mariposa will be the greatest boon to humanity since fire. Think of it. Sanity for all. But first . . . we have to climb over this wall and get to the other side. I'm glad I did it. I had to. The Quiet Man was right, bomb or no bomb. You're the one with the connections to stop Axel Price. Please do it. For Madeline."

Plover got to his feet, then backed across the room and opened the door.

He closed the door behind him.

She heard his footsteps going down the hall. After that, silence. She opened the door and looked out. Baumann was still away from his post.

Nobody had replaced him.

She closed the door and sat in the half dark, blinking, bringing her breath under control. She could end up like the broken man she had interviewed this morning. She could end up like the programmers, wherever they were, whatever their symptoms might be—and the odd Mr. Trace, who at least had shown some sort of courage and even, possibly, compassion.

It all sounded incredibly nasty and unpredictable.

How would she feel when . . . if, it began to happen?

36 Hours

34

Lion City, Texas

A light breeze blew grit and silt from Mexico, leaving brown streaks across the Texas sky—the ragged hem of famine's cloak.

William Griffin parked the old Chevette at the dry grassy margin in front of a small bungalow and kicked down the emergency brake, then sat for a moment, head bowed, steadying his nerves.

His next action would be the first bead on a bone rosary of sacred violations. He—a special agent—was going to assault a sworn peace officer. After this, he could never again hold himself above the criminal; he was part of that world, one of them . . .

Undercover and way outside his known universe.

He peered through the rivulets of dust on the windshield, sweeping up the shadowy details of the sleeping neighborhood on the eastern outskirts of Lion City: a loose scatter of dusty yards and screen porch houses, oaks and dogwood, boarded-up auto shops, a shuttered feed store, a recycled tire store—hard times.

On a dirt lot across from the house, idle truck trailers and big rigs stretched out silver gray in the promise of dawn, surprisingly pretty, though covered with dew and a film of mud.

A rooster strutted across the dusty patched asphalt of Farm to Market Road.

Nothing but the rooster and William.

William had met his new partners two days ago and explained the switch-out. The agent formerly in charge of the Little Jamey operation, codenamed Vanilla Extract, had been unexpectedly reassigned to Alameda.

William had been in on the secret planning of this whole operation and was in cahoots with agents in D.C.

He was immediately accepted. Some of the agents had heard vague rumors about Mecca and admired that kind of rogue reputation.

He seemed to fit right in.

A heavy-duty Econoline van, gray and green, windows thick-meshed and interior customized for prisoner transport, had been parked under a dying oak tree far down the driveway. Block letters on its rear doors read "PerpTrans."

He touched the temple piece of his MacArthur-style spex and murmured, "Let's wake him up."

William rolled down his window. He heard a phone jangle. After four rings, someone picked up. William caught a bit of the dialog through his earpiece.

The man in the house was half asleep.

Wrong number.

William heard the heavy clack-ka-ching from inside the house even before the grid passed along the angry words: "Well, goddammit, it's 5:00 A.M.!"

A message tickered in the corner of William's lightly tinted spex:

Time. Bring leash.

William gritted his teeth and got out. A bit of sand had lodged under one eyelid but there was nothing he could do; seconds counted. He walked up to the porch and sliced through the screen with his pocket knife, flicked up the hook, then swung open the screen door with a ghostly creak.

The brass monkey knocker was mounted on the inside door. Red glass eyes glowed in the leering face. The banner over the knocker read, "Welcome to the Monkey House."

He lifted the monkey's paw and rapped.

"Who's there?" a grating voice asked.

"Travis Coolidge, Lion County jail. I'm to ride in with you. I have the itinerary for this morning's transfer."

"Well, hell. Something's changed?"

The door opened and William faced Eddie Mallom. Mallom blearily eyed William, recognized a cop when he saw one, and swung the front door wide. "Anything different from what we got faxed last night?"

"Just me."

The brass paw rattled. "Jesus. We're not due for another hour and a half. You coulda let me sleep in."

Mallom was in his mid-thirties, a bachelor, about William's height but skinnier, slope-shouldered but not a weakling judging by the rope-knot muscles that poked from the sleeves of his T-shirt. His face was lean and grizzled with a thick morning beard.

William and his new partners had closely watched their respective clients all last evening. There had been an employee toot at the local BBQ. The PerpTrans boys had left around two in the morning, barely three hours ago.

Mallom turned his back. "Hell with it, come on in. I'll get coffee."

William reached into his windbreaker and removed a small cylinder of Spray-Cuff.

Mallom was not completely oblivious. He looked over his shoulder just as the quick-setting gray cord crazy-tangled his upper body. The strands instantly tightened and bound his arms to his torso. William pointed the nozzle down and webbed the man's legs as he hopped around, then muffled his last few grunts with another discharge around the face and eyes.

Trussed like a fly, Mallom toppled. William caught him and eased his fall, then made sure the man could breathe by spreading two air holes in the nylon-tough strands around the man's nose and mouth. Mallom couldn't see much and could do little more than squirm and make strangled complaints, not very loud, since he couldn't draw a really deep breath.

"Relax," William said. "Just go limp."

Mallom's single visible eye was puffy and glaring, but he stopped struggling.

"Ooo hhuck aw ya? Cri own kimee."

William dragged him into the short middle hall and then into a bachelor-filthy bathroom: pee stains around the toilet, greasy hair tangles in the corners, underwear poking from the ratty laundry hamper.

He made sure the narrow window over the shower stall was latched shut. A quick search in the kitchen turned up a plastic drink jug from the local Cactus Stop. He filled it with water. The wide green flex-straw went into Mallom's mouth.

"Don't let yourself dry out. Pee if you have to. It might be a day or two before someone comes to look for you. Sorry about that."

Mallom now suspected he wasn't going to be murdered, so he grunted an expletive.

William found the man's employee uniform, cap, and equipment hanging on a valet and the bedroom dresser, put them on—not a great fit, but good enough—and stuffed his own clothes into a plastic bag. The house was a mess but not Mallom's uniform; shirt and pants had been neatly pressed, the shoes polished to a high sheen.

William made sure to lock the front door behind him, and returned to the car to get the black case.

The dawn was brighter now and the rooster was starting to prance before belting out a cockcrow. Across the street, a portly truck driver in a red jacket walked around his rig with a step a little like the rooster's. He cleared his nose into a kerchief and waved at William.

At this distance, he was reacting to the uniform. The gray early light obscured features.

"Going to haul Little Jamey's ass down to Huntsville?" the trucker asked.

William nodded under his cap.

"Screw Washington," the trucker said, and spat. "Screw the FBI. Screw Larsen and all the tax-hiking sons of bitches. Screw the New York press. Serves the bastards right."

Lion City and the Texas Department of Corrections, headquartered in Huntsville, in recent years had become a law unto themselves and so, as the trucker said, screw the FBI and screw New York.

William shrugged, lifted one hand, and climbed into Mallom's transport van. He slipped the black case between the van's seat and the engine cover.

The van recognized the recently implanted chip in his arm, a duplicate of the one issued to Mallom—good beginning. Everyone in Lion City was chipped. One big, happy family, almost all of them eager to execute Little Jamey. He started the motor, let it idle for a minute, backed it out of the driveway, and drove along Farm to Market Road, then swung east, toward the Lion County Correction Center.

Right on schedule.

The clandestine grid had been silent for a while.

No doubt Kapp and Curteze had been as busy as William.

Then, in his ear, a calm voice from Washington, D.C.—Jane Rowland, as he had suspected all along. She had taken over this part of the operation and was running it for Alicia Kunsler.

"Old Pap is frantic for news. What'll I tell him?"

"Tell him Jim's got his raft," William said. "We're heading for the river."

Shortly, he would have to ditch his spex. Talos tracked nearly all communications around Lion City and the campus—and if they couldn't ID any particular signal, they sent out employees or sheriff's deputies to locate the source—just to make sure.

35

Pendelton Reserve, California

The morning trip south from Los Angeles was swift, peaceful, without incident. Nathaniel Trace was glad he could drive like a normal human being and not draw attention.

The Quiet Man had left a message—a series of numbers. The Mind Design circuit was still working. The original Turing Seven still had their EPR phone accounts, and the Quiet Man had one as well, but the display showed only three phones logged on.

The phones would not work for anyone but their assigned owners. While it was conceivable that their codes could be cracked—Nathaniel had a number of ideas how that might be done—the circuits would tell them if someone unauthorized was listening in.

So far, nobody was.

The Quiet Man was very fond of EPR technology.

Nathaniel drove down Camino Del Mar, then stopped at a coffee shop to pick up Humphrey Camp. He was alone. The right side of his face was paler than the left, and his left hand showed an intermittent tremor.

Driving south in light fog, Camp opened the window and waved his fingers in the cool, moist slipstream. "I can't think straight for more than five minutes," he complained. "My stomach is ruined. I still don't know what to eat—I'm starving to death and I don't even care." He touched the pale side of his face, then pinched it hard. "Feeling comes and goes. It's like someone's put a voodoo doll up to a mirror. Bork's gone into hiding—won't say where. Jerry Lee seems happy. He's stalking women in Santa Monica. I don't feel guilty knowing that, either. But look at you—you're driving a Hyundai, Mr. Sober and Responsible, for Christ's sake."

Nathaniel had bought a nice, safe car, unlikely to encourage him to explore the wild limits of his new abilities—and had paid cash. That evening he had filled the tank, stopped over for a few hours at a beach motel, then driven in the dark to downtown Laguna Beach, where he had received his last call from the Quiet Man, telling him where to pick up Camp.

Camp rambled on. "You think Talos blew up the LA Convention Center to kill Plover, right?"

"I don't know," Nathaniel said. "Seems a bit extreme, if you ask me."

"But you stuck around. You did what Plover asked. Why?"

"He seemed sincere."

Camp pulled in his hand and scratched his nose. "Okay. You hung around for no good reason. Why?"

"Checking out the weather. A hunch, call it."

"Hunches seem different. You know why Jerry Lee is stalking women?"

"No idea," Nathaniel said.

"Maybe it's a hunch. After the blast, the Quiet Man told me you went right back inside, to check up on a woman you just met."

"Seemed the thing to do," Nathaniel said.

"Maybe *you* were stalking *her*," Camp said.

The Quiet Man's numbers needed to be broken down into groups of seven. In his head, Nathaniel stacked them and ran them through the most likely coding algorithm—one with seven steps—and recovered what appeared to be a set of coordinates. There was one last step, known only to the Turing Seven—what the Quiet Man called an "acciditional" twist or renormalizing of the results.

Without looking at a map or engaging the nav system, Nathaniel visualized where the first set of numbers would take them: out to Mind Design, near the beach in La Jolla.

That was too obvious, too dangerous—why even bother with encoding? If the Turing Seven were a threat to Price, wasn't Mind Design one of the first places they would look?

Seven numbers. Seven programmers.
Seven stations of the crossed.

Then he renormalized, using the "accidional" twist.

"If you ask me," Camp said, "you might go all psycho on my ass any minute."

"I'm okay with women," Nathaniel said, and grinned at Camp, showing his teeth.

"How about male colleagues?"

Nathaniel pirate-squinched his face, then let it relax. "Sorry. Nothing."

"*Fuck* you," Camp said.

The new coordinates would take them out of La Jolla entirely, up into the hills overlooking Camp Pendleton.

Camp chuffed. "The Doc thought Lee was the most stable—but then, he's always looked cool and collected. In Arabia, Lee was cooler than the Talos goon squad—even with his arm in shreds. But right now, it's you, isn't it?"

"I go day to day. I want to know what's happening. Don't you?"

"Curiosity worth dying for?"

"Life is discovery. The Quiet Man wants us to follow a trail. Maybe he wants us to put a stop to what we've started."

"Never met him," Camp said. "Just took orders from the rest of you and did my work. But it takes a strange man to work a thirty million dollar contract for three years and then get all moral and weepy."

"Then maybe he just wants revenge."

"That I can get behind," Camp said.

The drive was going to take longer than Nathaniel expected. He turned east on 76 and headed toward Vista. Camp's hand had stopped its periodic tremor and his face was regaining its color, but his head nodded to some internal, irregular beat.

"It changes all the time," he said. "If we're coming unglued, if our genes are getting shut off in weird sequences . . . who knows what that could do, medically? Maybe it'll end up killing us."

"They tested it on animals," Nathaniel said.

"That's *so* reassuring," Camp said. "Maybe it's like a way to make assassins better killers, easier to brainwash. Wouldn't Price want something like that?"

Nathaniel thought that over as he turned off 76 and headed north. The country here was gray and dry, the trees by the side of the black-top roads mostly dead. This area used to be covered with groves and farms. Now it looked blasted. This wasn't drought caused by global warming, however; this was the way California always looked when the money and the water went away.

It looked like much of Mexico.

"I don't feel easy to indoctrinate, and I don't like taking orders any more than I did before, maybe less," Nathaniel finally said. "How about you?"

"No," Camp admitted. "I'm like a cranky baby. But I *am* more coordinated, in a weird way—better at physical stuff. And quicker at learning some things. You?"

Nathaniel nodded. "Up to a point." His shoulder and wrists were still sore.

"I wouldn't much care if I actually did kill somebody, though. Guilt tank running on empty. Feels good—liberation plus. About this little trip—you're taking us someplace you've never been, without a map, just some coordinates. How?"

Nathaniel tapped the rearview mirror, which displayed a compass rose and *NNE*. "The compass, the speedometer, and the clock."

"In your head? Were you always that good?" Camp asked.

"No," Nathaniel said. "Runs down the blood sugar. Sometimes it hurts. There's energy bars in the glove box. Hand me one and help yourself."

The Hyundai did well enough on the next part of the journey, a rutted dirt road across a low plateau of scrub. At the end of the road, still within sight of the ocean—perhaps three miles down the gentle west-facing slope and surrounded by a chain-link fence topped with razor wire—they spotted a square concrete blockhouse and a smaller shack, separated by about a hundred feet.

No visible power lines stretched this far, and no evidence of any sort of receiver dish or telecom setup, either.

"The middle of nowhere," Camp said.

Nathaniel pulled the car up to a gate. A weather-beaten keypad-speaker combo and video camera mounted on a pole poked up from the dirt to the left.

Several old metal signs lay face down inside the fence perimeter.

The keypad was new and looked more than interesting. It provoked another variety of bee vision: brilliant warm colors for objects of particular significance, other areas cool and subdued or totally grayed—a way for his mind to leap-frog the old lines between conscious and subconscious reasoning.

It might take him months to harness this talent—or he'd never get the trick of it.

For now, Nathaniel suspected both he and Camp shared the same opinion. If this property had ever belonged to the Quiet Man, none of the Turing Seven had been informed. And likely the Quiet Man had kept it secret from Price as well.

The speaker crackled and the camera angled to take them in. Then the Quiet Man's voice—unmistakable—said, "Nathaniel! Come on in. Is that Camp sitting beside you?"

"Yes, sir," Camp said with a toothy grin.

"The gate's open. See you at the first stop—the tumbledown place. Glad you could both make it."

36

Lion City

For many years, Texas had been touchy about the death chamber in Huntsville. Texas still led the world in per capita executions, and also in DNA exonerations, but that did not stop the fatally grinding wheels of state justice. Lion City alone had sent fifteen of its former citizens to the Walls Unit in the ten years since the town's incorporation, so many that both the Bureau of Prisons and JPATS—the Justice Prisoner and Alien Transportation system, a decades old mash-up of the U.S. Marshals and Border Security—had refused to transport their prisoners, leaving it to the Department of Corrections to "haul their own garbage," as the local fetch bloggers put it.

JPATS was having a tough enough job dealing with hundreds of thousands of Mexicans eager to get north, get work, get food; away from death squads, cartels, and paramilitary reprisals. In the drought, Mexico was coming apart like a piñata in a major league batting cage.

Add in the U.S. near-bankruptcy and the efforts by twenty Texas counties to go their own way and not pay taxes . . .

Tacitly supported by the governor . . .

Border Security, the Department of Justice, and Texas state law enforcement had long since put up brick walls between their operations. No federal agency wanted to be tarred by Texas justice.

The Tunnel began a third of a mile from the Lion City Correctional Center, a spare, sandstone-faced building with tiny narrow windows adjacent to the historic county courthouse. The Tunnel had been expensive but it kept out reporters—though lately very few reporters had been covering the case of Little Jamey Trues.

Too dangerous.

This was where Talos Corporation got its justice served out to Axel Price's secret orders, and there was no reason to let the outside world know every little detail, including who was being sent where.

The dwindling national press—those journalists who still had a travel budget, who still worked for networks or newspapers or the five prime news sites and could afford to travel rather than just sit in front of a screen and suck back coffee and pontificate on what others saw and wrote—was as worn out and discouraged as the rest of the nation.

Screw the bastards.

He touched the temple piece on his spex and went off grid, then removed the glasses, folded them in a leather case, and stuffed the case into his shirt pocket.

Most federal agencies had been quietly but steadily releasing private companies from their sensitive law enforcement activities. Texas, however, had dug in. Working through Talos, the state DOC relied on Midland-based PerpTrans Inc. to transport its prisoners.

PerpTrans drivers were allowed to park their prisoner transport vans at home. Some used them to haul kids to birthday parties and carry college students back and forth to binges.

And that was one gap in Price's steel gauntlet.

The Tunnel scanned William's new chip and the truck's serial number and accepted the Econoline through its automated steel doors. The Vanilla Extract team had been told that people (and only people) monitored the security cameras that sprouted like shiny black mushrooms around the concrete entrance. No automated face recognition.

Even so, William wore his hat low over his face.

Jesus, it's working.

The correction center was not Lion City's highest tech enterprise— surprising, considering how much Talos had invested in securing the rest of the county.

"Hey, Mallom," came a twangy female voice over the van radio: the transfer dispatcher. William imagined her in her mid-forties, a heavy smoker with pruny skin and hennaed hair. "Hustle it, young man. Prisoner is at the gate."

"Down the chute," William said.

The DOC folks here were relying entirely on steely eyes and strong iron. Human judgment all the way.

The transfer station was an underground concrete cavern backed by a loading dock, the dock flanked by five parking spaces on each side, reserved for prison brass and visitors. This wide, cool box was dimly illuminated by a red bulb on the right and the greenish glow from an observation window about six feet wide and three feet high, made of inch-thick bulletproof plastic.

As William drove the PerpTrans van through the steel security gate, lights came on over the dock. A guard poked out from the access door and waved in the van.

William joggled the van around in the narrow space and backed it up to the loading dock. Two men emerged from an old Toyota Corolla in a visitor space—no longer the original DOC prisoner escorts, Sanchez and Markette, but Bureau replacements, Special Agents Glenn Curteze and Jonathan Kapp.

Someone had slipped a powder into a few beers at the PerpTrans BBQ toot.

The agents would soon join Little Jamey in the back of the van. No doubt by the end of the day, heads would roll at Texas DOC. That did not concern William. He was sweating profusely. The uniform's inseam pinched his crotch. The sleeves rode up and his socks showed.

Two more guards came through the door and stood on the dock. They looked glumly serious. The guards disliked this ritual, the darkest part of their duty. There would be no joking and little conversation, nothing to relieve the tension.

Dead man walking.

William remotely unlocked the van's rear doors. The guards opened them and Kapp and Curteze climbed in first, then prepared the chains and locking cross-bars.

William acknowledged their presence through the viewport behind the driver. They passed him their papers—Curteze offered up a shit-eating smile—and he stuck them in his folder.

A female guard approached the driver side door and William slid open a conversation port.

"New directions," she said, and handed him another slip of paper. "You choose the third segment, the third leg. Off the beaten path, if possible. Tracking isn't fully operational. They promise to have it fixed in twenty or thirty minutes. You can stay here until they confirm, if you want."

William frowned. "We're supposed to be in Huntsville this evening. We could bill you and wait until tomorrow . . . That's what our contract stipulates if you cancel and it's not our fault."

"Not an option," the guard said.

"They should have flown this one," William said.

"Do you have a plane? Because we don't."

"I hear you," William said.

"Maybe Mr. Price should loan us a private jet," the guard said.

All of Price's jets were in the air, winging executives and politicians from around the world to the Talos corporate shindig. That could explain the jam-up in tracking—the roads around Lion City were already crowded with unfamiliar vehicles.

Another point in their favor.

William brushed his lip with a finger. "We'll get him where he belongs. Just hand him over."

The guard nodded and returned to the dock.

Kapp and Curteze prepared for the transfer. The door at the back of the loading dock opened and they lifted Little Jamey along in his orange prison jumper. The boy looked sleepy. The prison medicos had sedated him for the transfer. His heels floated and his chains clanked.

Kapp and Curteze took charge of the prisoner, ran his arm chip under their scanners, then signed multiple documents formally transferring custody.

The van's rear doors closed. William sealed them. Ominous clunks and chunks sounded. An obnoxious little horn beeped until he entered the code on the prisoner's transport slip. The horn stopped with a happy chirp. The van was now authorized to proceed up the Tunnel to its last security checkpoint before Huntsville.

William could hardly believe they had made it this far.

The indictment, trial, and conviction of Little Jamey had ignited a firestorm among law enforcement agencies around the nation. Most of them, anyway.

He didn't know how many courageous people in Washington and Texas—or inside the Texas DOC itself—had cooperated to make this rescue possible, at risk to career and personal freedom.

None were known to William, nor he to them.

And they in turn would learn nothing about their new partners, Bureau East and Spider/Argus, each with their own ulterior motives.

37

Pendleton Reserve, California

The shack supported a small cistern that collected rainwater and delivered it through plastic pipes to a small flower garden. The garden was a prickle patch of desiccated stems and the last dried buds from the summer before—all gray. The cistern had sprung a leak—a bullet hole.

The hole showed up intensely purple in Nathaniel's bee vision.

"Someone's been shooting here," he said.

"Kids or dumb hunters," Camp said, gesturing over his shoulder. "Up by the road, too—road signs and mailboxes."

Nathaniel paced before the path that led to the shack, head down. His whole body ached with the intensity of his thought. Finally he paused and flung his hands up in the air. "Goddamn it," he said. "There's no way in hell I can see what's happening. This place used to be important—but why? Nobody's taken care of it for a long time."

Camp assumed a farmer's slouch with hands deep in pockets. He shrugged. "The Quiet Man isn't here?" he asked doubtfully.

"I don't think so," Nathaniel said.

"We heard his voice. He recognized us."

"He's probably watching from someplace remote—maybe the main building in La Jolla." Though that seemed unlikely, as well.

"Then why guide us all the way out here? We should leave. Let's just chuck it."

"He must have a good reason."

"Lady or the tiger," Camp said, pointing to the shack, then to the blockhouse.

Nathaniel realized he was going to have to follow his instructions or abandon the scene completely and start over again—without guidance. That made his head hurt more.

"Stay here," he said.

"Give me the car keys," Camp suggested, snapping his fingers, and Nathaniel tossed him the ring. Then he started down the path to the shack—slow, cautious steps, eyes on the ground searching for disturbed earth, triggers, trip wires. The ground all around looked gray, uninteresting. Rain had washed away any evidence of foot traffic, but the grass near the trail had been trampled in a few spots. Four sad little eucalyptus trees leaned away from the shack, their largest branches broken off and littering the ground—also gray. Everything was gray except for the bullet holes.

He climbed the single step and paused on the porch, then looked back over his shoulder. Camp stood slouched as before, key ring dangling from one hand.

Nathaniel squinted and rubbed his temples.

The sun-warped wooden door made a click and opened. The whole front of the cabin seemed to explode with sudden color. Nathaniel averted his eyes until he could regain visual control. Some part of him was still capable of expressing fear, or at least caution—but from way down deep. Lizard brain stuff.

"All *right*," he said under his breath. "I get it."

He nudged the door with one foot. It opened stiffly. Watery daylight spilled into the interior, revealing nothing but a crumpled paper airplane on the dirty floorboards.

Someone had picked it up and scrunched it in a fist, then tossed it down again.

Mind Design's logo was a paper airplane with its nose pointed skyward—merging with an illuminati pyramid and all-seeing eye.

Nathaniel picked up the airplane, shook it free of dust, and unfolded it. One wing's inner surface was covered with scribbles—penciled rows of numbers.

Seven groups of seven.

"Hell," he murmured, but more out of concern at the fascination that now flooded through him. He was being jerked around like a bloodhound pushed down a trail of funky rags—but this bloodhound was a number geek from way back, and the Quiet Man, or somebody, was perfectly happy to play with his oh-so-genius-class head.

The numbers presented little difficulty. In essence, the relation between the first three sets solved most efficiently to a half circle, or 180 degrees. The next two solved to any rectangle wider than it was tall, and the last two strings easily converted from ASCII to a word: DEADMAN.

Seven letters.

The Quiet Man had probably spent years of his youth playing video games. So had Nathaniel, of course, and most of the Turing Seven. He looked around the cabin. Nothing else of interest; heightened edge perception made sure of that, even in the shack's semidarkness.

His eyes burned as if they were on fire, so he shut them for a few seconds.

"You okay?" Camp called.

"Fine," Nathaniel said.

Nathaniel stepped back into the cloudy sunshine. The air was still cool, still moist. He had always liked Southern California autumn weather, particularly near the coast. Fog might roll in from the ocean soon, as high or higher than this small plateau, about four hundred feet above sea level. It would leave everything moist and dripping through the night.

He waved for Camp to join him. "We're supposed to go to the blockhouse."

"He could have told us that right off," Camp suggested.

The breeze shifted and wafted a mild stench—stale but still foul—from behind the shack. Nathaniel's body stiffened. He had smelled death before—in Iraq and in Jordan and of course in Arabia Deserta.

Day-old death in dry, dusty air.

This was death many days old, in moist, cool air.

Nathaniel stepped gingerly through the yellow, dew-moist grass to the rear of the shack, again on alert for tripwires.

Three bodies had been laid out in a row in the grass. The bee vision outlines of shocking red and electric blue were totally unnecessary.

"What is it?" Camp called.

He was slunching through the grass to join Nathaniel.

"Watch your feet," Nathaniel said. "Three dead people. All men, I think."

Camp stood beside him. "Holy crap. Who are they?"

The bodies had lain out in the open for at least a week and a half. The clothing was stained with bloat and bursting. Maggots still wriggled in a desultory fashion around a series of small thoracic holes gnawed by some animal through the clothing. Raccoons, maybe.

Raccoons might not like the taste of human flesh, but they knew how to farm a corpse: they chewed holes in a body and waited for maggots to cluster, then ate the tasty, high-protein morsels on a steady basis for several days, until the maggot food and thus the maggot supply chain gave out. Nathaniel had read about that in a crime novel years ago.

He recognized an MIT class ring on one brown, leathery finger. "That's Harvey Belton," he said.

Harvey "Bourbaki" Belton had been the eldest of the Turing Seven, a world expert in nested and recursively competitive algorithms. He had practically invented acciditional functions, finding a use for so-called accidental numbers—until then considered one of the most useless ideas in math. He could have won a Nobel, but went for the money instead.

They hadn't spoken in months.

"Three of us?" Camp asked in a plaintive voice. "Just dumped out here?"

Nathaniel stooped down and tried to guess the corpses' statures: five–four, six–one, five–ten respectively. Their weight and build were more difficult to judge.

He had a bad feeling about one of them. The face, though crusted and shrunken, still looked familiar. Wispy grayish hair was slicked down by blood and dew. A sheen of something gray and cheesy coated the cheeks and nose—what was it called?

Adipocere.

He had read that in a crime novel, too.

Strange. Bee vision gone. The colors had dropped right back into normal. His subconscious was as stunned as the rest of his brain.

"We should check out the blockhouse," Nathaniel said, rising.

"What can we learn that we don't already know?" Camp asked. "Someone's killing us. I knew that already."

Nathaniel looked again at the middle of the three bodies. A ruck of checked wool poked through a gap in the muddy leather jacket. "I think that's Stan Parker," he said. "Fits his taste in shirts."

"All right," Camp said. "Seven little Indians. How many does that leave?"

"You, me . . ." He looked again at the third body and felt sweat break out. He did not want to say who this was, because it was impossible. He had heard the voice. The voice had been giving him instructions for days.

"You. Me. Jerry Lee. Bork," he finished. "Maybe that's it."

38

Lion City

William drove the PerpTrans van off the road and behind a deserted, boarded-up gas station garage. To Little Jamey's slack-jawed astonishment, the two DOC officers riding with him in the back pulled jeans and sweatshirts from a knapsack and started to peel off their uniforms.

William unlocked the driver side door and Kapp came around to insert his plug into the van's security port, just below the dashboard.

Kapp was short and stocky, with thinning brown hair and a fine, patrician nose. "Four minutes, then we smash the GPS tracking unit. That'll take the van off any grid."

Curteze unlocked and pulled open the garage door and stood before a rancher's old Tahoe—stashed here three weeks ago under a tarp. Curteze was tallest, rangy, with thick, black hair slicked back from his forehead.

He pulled away the tarp. The Tahoe was still equipped with the rancher's radio frequency ID transponder. Texans were serious about immigration reform. Unchipped vehicles were pulled over and searched by all local police agencies.

As well, Talos security birds flew over most of west Texas and could also ping vehicles.

This part of the plan had been particularly difficult to carry out. The RFID chips were custom programmed in Midland and shipped around the state. In the end, someone in the Bureau had purchased the SUV at a farm auction from the owner's widow and paid her extra not to report her husband's demise to DMV or the local police.

The widow had assumed the purchasers were going to ship Mexicans north. No skin off her nose—she was getting the hell out of Texas and moving to Florida. An extra five thousand dollars would spend just fine.

Curteze unlocked the driver's door and got in. The engine started quickly enough but idled rough for a few seconds. When it settled down, all three agents broke out of their frozen postures and returned to the tasks at hand.

"Good to go," Curteze called to Kapp and William.

Jamey Trues watched with goggle eyes through the open rear doors.

Kapp took a hammer, bent down, slid under the transport van, and slammed the tracking transmitter until pieces clattered on the ground.

"How's that for finesse?" he asked.

They took out their keys and approached Jamey. The boy was starting to come around.

"Who are you?" he asked.

"Friends." William did not want to provide any more hope or encouragement than he felt was deserved, since for now he thought their chances of getting away were slim to nonexistent. He removed the cuffs and bars and helped the boy down from the back of the Perp-Trans van.

"Let's boogie," Kapp said.

"You going to lynch me?" the boy asked. He was only fifteen but had been through a lot in the last year.

Before William could answer, the boy slumped and almost fell. The jailers in Lion City had given him a time-release sedative for the duration of the trip, to keep him quiet right up until they strapped him to the gurney in the Walls Unit.

The second round was kicking in.

"We're not going to lynch you," William murmured as Curteze helped slide the boy into the rear seat of the Tahoe. "We're going to drive you out of state."

"He can't hear you," Kapp said.

They strapped him in—seatbelt only, no cuffs.

They had nothing to fear from Little Jamey.

Nobody did, actually.

"We won't get far unless we cut that chip out of him," Curteze said.

"There's an abandoned field just outside of town," William said. "We'll do it there."

That field was the closest they were likely to get to the Smoky, Price's ranch—a mile and a half. Satellites had located Fouad. He was being kept in a bungalow a hundred yards behind the main complex.

The snake bots had an operational round-trip range of no more than seven miles.

39

Pendleton

They walked around the shack, then cut across to the blockhouse, avoiding the scrub. The blockhouse's southern wall had a narrow in-set door accessed by a short flight of steps sunk a couple of feet into the earth.

"Maybe this was some sort of communication station," Camp said. "Loran or Alcan or something."

"Alcan's a highway."

"They'd have buried the power lines, right?"

"Maybe."

"Could still have juice."

A small black camera eye poked from the concrete over the steel door. Someone had tried to hammer their way through the door and failed—it still looked strong and secure.

But as they approached, this door also clicked open, just like the gate and the door to the shack.

"Maybe he's here after all," Camp said.

The interior was simple, old—dusty. A dark brown couch, uphol-stered in worn velour, had been planted in the middle of the floor.

More interesting, a low, putty-colored box about the size of an early-model Jones 1.0 sat on a wooden bench. Behind the table, a metal con-nection box had been set flush with the wall. A thick pipe dropped from the box through the concrete floor.

Competors like Jones were the next step up from computers. They used competitive algorithms to solve problems—some called them evolution engines. The Turing Seven were probably the best in the world at thinking up such algorithms, a very specialized mathematical discipline.

The Quiet Man had once said that the next step up from competors would be called "thinkers."

"Is that what it looks like?" Camp asked.

"Don't go near the table. It's probably rigged to explode."

"Right. Game logic," Camp said. "But there *is* a couch. Unfair to blow up a couch. Gamers like to sit. We should sit."

They inspected the couch, lifting the cushions—nothing suspicious—then sat, slowly.

A sensor under the couch clicked, making them both jump up, cursing—but a voice spoke from a small speaker mounted in the wall directly ahead.

"Gentlemen, I regret to inform you that I am no longer able to guide your quest," the voice said. "If everything here still works, you will soon learn why."

It was the Quiet Man—unmistakable.

At the tap of a tiny solenoid, a small piece of plaster fell from the wall. Four shiny, black lenses pushed through the hole, angling with tiny whirring noises to find faces, focus on eyes.

"Please sit."

Again, they settled in.

The projectors painted beams of laser light directly onto their retinas, reproducing an image for both of them—a live image, Nathaniel guessed.

The projected point of view was of someone about six feet tall standing in the lobby of Mind Design, facing panoramic picture windows. Mind Design's main building sat on a bluff overlooking the ocean, southwest of their present location—in La Jolla.

"Wow," Camp said. "How old is all this shit? Why not just hand us spex?"

He had a point—the blockhouse interior had been designed and built at least a decade ago. It definitely smacked of spare time, paranoia—and some sort of outmoded cool factor.

Which fit well with what Nathaniel knew about the Quiet Man.

"You seeing what I'm seeing?" Camp asked in an undertone. "Mind Design. Great view."

"Yeah. Shh," Nathaniel said.

"I was there once, four years ago," Camp said. "So is the Quiet Man here—I mean, there—or hiding nearby—or somewhere even safer?"

Camp's caviling about POV was disorienting Nathaniel. *Here, there . . . past, future, present.* Numbers and coordinates.

The lasers were forcing him to see and thus think a certain way. He was having real problems controlling memories evoked by the remote images.

"I'm getting a nasty premonition," Camp said. "That sucks. I don't know how to react."

For Nathaniel, the image suddenly tangled up with memory, imagination, suspended fear.

He tried to turn away but could not.

Mind Design was a sixties-style suspended rectangle of white and stainless steel, hanging out over a bluff above the brilliant blue ocean.

Every wave . . .

Nathaniel knew their numbers. He knew these buildings inside and out, backwards and forwards; he could visualize every room just by closing his eyes.

Stop that. Keep it together.

For a few seconds, he relived parking in the shadow of a grove of tall eucalyptus—maybe two years ago. The Mind Design parking lot held no more than twenty cars, and at least ten spaces had been roped off after a storm had brought down big branches. Folks liked their legacy trees. Southern California—and in particular La Jolla—was nothing without eucalyptus.

Nathaniel got out of the car and leaned against the door. The purple of the ice plant on the slope in front of the car was so intense he had to avert his eyes.

Keep your mind on the couch. You are here. You are not in the lobby.

But his mind was fanatically searching for significant patterns, numbers, novelty—and so the memory rolled on. He could make out every single purple flower, every fleshy green blade. If he wanted, he could know their numbers and what those numbers would mean for thousands of years to come.

He had worked at Mind Design four years before the company had sent him to Talos in Lion City, and then to Jordan, and then to Arabia Deserta, and after a few months' hiatus, finally to Dubai, to create a backdoor into MSARC.

On the couch, Nathaniel's muscles twitched as if they were moving, carrying him forward. Walking. Every twitch was like a little orgasm. The muscles reveled in their new multidimensional freedom from time, space, reality.

His body felt younger, unconstrained.

My flesh and blood and bone before the firefight. Before the scars and the pain—physical and mental.

My brain before Mariposa.

He looked with longing at the fast, sleek hybrids parked in the lot, including his: red and silver. Hooked up and plugged in, charged and ready to race down Torrey Pines Road at a hundred and forty miles an hour: just as green for Gaia as for the well-paid programmers and designers.

He walked up the sidewalk to the half-hidden glass door, punched in his old security code, added a suffix that the Quiet Man had not mentioned, but that he knew would work.

Mind Design was open to him once more. He would know its numbers.

The building welcomed him as an old, secret friend.

"Nathaniel? We should get going. This is starting to feel like a trap."

He ignored Camp. Camp's mind wasn't yet wrapped around the impossibility of that body laid out behind the tumbledown shack.

Back at Mind Design: deep in the subbasement, around the corner from the freight elevator, through a door in a half-height wall topped with panes of thick glass, an early version of Jones lay spread out on the concrete floor like an art installation: oddly patterned and spaced cubes of plastic and steel hooked up with thick fiber optic cables and pipes carrying nutrient fluids.

Jones Zero had taken five years to build and two to charge up; they had learned a lot from simply getting him to turn on and give simple responses to basic neurologic queries, Gödel number key code strings—lifeboat backups, net housekeeping.

Like HAL, Jones Zero had learned a birthday diagnostic song: not "Daisy" but "Sgt. Pepper's." That was how much artificial thinking had advanced in fifty years.

Of course, even the later versions of Jones were not real minds, not yet true thinkers—more like idiot savants. But after the launch, it soon became obvious that this was the best pattern recognition tool anyone had yet devised.

Jones Zero could not only comprehend any natural language and find matches in even highly degraded databases, but he could deliver highly reliable analytics as to dialect, accent, even birthplace and level of education.

He—they always referred to a Jones as if it were human—could tell whether a voice came from a native who had learned the language as a child, or from a highly educated person who had learned it in school—and even the age at which the language training had begun.

What was more, Jones could penetrate any false accent and pick up the underlying native tongue.

The Quiet Man and the Turing Seven had soon moved Jones Zero up to weather. He had learned quickly. In six months, the distributed competer in its liquid-filled boxes—made up of borax, glass, and gel-suspended rods of PNA and DNA—had quickly proved itself to be a master of winds.

Jones 1.0—smaller, faster, better—beat the best automated and human long-range forecasters.

The Quiet Man decided that Jones 1.0 could be duplicated and shipped to key positions around the planet, standing in for the next step, Jones 2.0, already in development. Jones 1.0 would act as the trigger for his successor, as an atom bomb is used to trigger a hydrogen bomb.

There was to be only one Jones 2.0, and his work was destined to be very important indeed: supervising the world's first nanosecond-updated, worldwide financial data network, collected by over five thousand mainframes controlling server farms throughout Asia, Europe, and the Middle East.

Jones 2.0 was about to become the quiet, humming heart of MSARC. Mind Design's connection with Talos Corporation was the biggest secret of all.

The Quiet Man kept Jones Zero in the basement of Mind Design as a kind of museum piece. Nathaniel Trace seemed to be alone with the machine in its concrete chamber. He felt almost shy in its quiet presence.

The Quiet Man—Chan Herbert—emerged from a rear cold chamber, where volatile Jones components were stored.

He pulled off a watch cap and unzipped his black windbreaker.

"Hello," he said.

Nathaniel bit his lip. Back on the couch, no longer traveling through memory's vivid album.

Seemingly live, in real time, Chan Herbert was being projected into their eyes.

"Hello, Mr. Herbert," Camp said.

Herbert looked up at a corner, eyes hunting, like a blind man. "Hello, Mr. Camp. I thought that was you. Hello, Nathaniel. How's the viewing?"

"It's fine," Nathaniel said. "Why the spy stuff?"

"Backdoor precautions. Always good when working with certain business types. I'm a little paranoid, naturally, and right now that's useful. Jones 2.0 has come online in Switzerland. They've run all their tests. He passed with flying colors. MSARC is going operational in fourteen days."

Actually, less than thirty hours. The Quiet Man was relaying old information.

"So?" Camp said, not reassured. "Off the hook. That's a good thing. Our work is done."

"Not yet. Something's gone wrong."

Nathaniel felt a weird twinge. "A programming glitch?"

"No. Besides, Jones 2.0 is well beyond our programming at this point. He's harder to get hold of than a venture capital broker. What can you tell me about Mariposa?"

"It works," Camp said. "But it adds stuff. Weird shit."

"You were test monkeys," Herbert said. "As always, Price thought he should kill two birds with one stone—repair the Turing Seven to finish their job, and at the same time, get positive test results for Mariposa. Now Dr. Plover has revealed who the first monkey actually was: the vice president. And he's not the only one who's flipped. Nick Elder. When I heard from Nick is when I called you and told you to get out of Dubai."

"Old news," Camp murmured.

"Jerry Lee is feeling odd, too. He's in Arabia Deserta, and he seems to be making a fuss—killing animals, I hear."

Jerry Lee hadn't been in Arabia in weeks, perhaps months. Nathaniel felt feverish. "Why are we here?" he asked.

The Quiet Man gave a little jerk before responding. "After 9/11, the telecommunications industry duplicated the fiber optic point of entry for Asia and the Middle East to a centralized commercial facility in San Francisco. Somehow, they forgot to deactivate the old junction stations—which make excellent listening posts. Three of them serve me as personal tin cans strung on all the world's data traffic. Every blockhouse has a Jones 1.0 analyzing traffic.

"Jones 2.0 has the option to tie in with one or more of his siblings. Sometimes I ask an older Jones—the one right next to you, for example—to pull up anomalies in government traffic. He knows how to behave like a blank pipe or a legitimate client. He's still pretty sharp, even though most people think he's past his operational prime.

"In fact, both Talos and the regulators at MSARC believe all of the earlier versions have been shut down. Tell me how you feel, Nathaniel."

"Different," Nathaniel said.

"Like you want to kill somebody?"

Nathaniel twitched his folded hands. "Mostly, I just feel free to choose."

"You're unpredictable. You can't be trusted. You need a fallback."

"Why tell us to come *here*, then?" Nathaniel looked askance at the Quiet Man. The projected image skewed. He looked back, and there it was again, but seeming less and less real.

Low-res.

Of course, his eyes might still be playing tricks.

"Because that's the only place you can still see me," Herbert said.

"You reluctant to leave Mind Design?" Camp asked.

"No," Herbert said. "Not reluctant. I'm dead, Mr. Camp. They killed me fourteen days ago."

Camp started to chuckle, a grim exhibition of bitter humor, but his chuckle gurgled out when Herbert faded from the distant basement laboratory.

"What the hell?" Camp blurted.

Herbert's image slowly returned. "I often use Jones as a kind of answering machine," the voice said. "I recorded phrases, then trained him to select and modify and assemble them. Images, too.

"I like being two places at once. Now I'm nowhere at all. Jones can still answer questions, give out my messages, but only for a while. Pretty soon, Jones will run out of my words. He's sophisticated enough to make up new phrases—but I don't know whether he wants to.

"If he doesn't—I'm afraid you're completely on your own."

Nathaniel blinked rapidly, blurring the image of the Mind Design lab—not at all sure *any* of it was real.

The Quiet Man looked around as if sharing Nathaniel's confusion, then continued. "Dr. Plover passed along the name of a woman from the FBI who was in the Mariposa program. She was one of the third stage patients. The Turing Seven were all second stage. Jones snooped and told me the president would chose this agent to investigate the vice president's little incident. If she now has the information Dr. Plover gave to you to deliver—then there may still be a chance to derail Price's plan. She may or may not be feeling similar side effects. It's a risk we have to take."

"Been there," Nathaniel muttered.

"I wonder how Jones will react to all this," Herbert mused. He looked thoughtful. "I mean, he isn't a sophisticated personality. But there's as much of me in him as any of you. If Jones learns that I have been hurt or killed, what will he do? What will that knowledge do to him?"

More men appeared in the chamber, flickering around Herbert, brutally knocking him around. His mouth hung open in terror.

"Christ," Camp said.

One very solid-looking arm reached out and delivered an electric baton to the back of Herbert's leg. The arm withdrew and Herbert folded like a sack of rocks.

The disembodied arms and legs moved in and beat him over and over. Blood spray shot up.

The image flickered and then returned, sharp but quiet—the chamber empty but for a smashed, pitiful body.

Then the body was dragged away.

Jones knew. He had seen it all.

Herbert's uninjured form returned and again looked at the high corner. "If we accomplish the task that Talos set for us, then Axel Price will be in charge of much of our nation, perhaps much of the world. It will be a nasty place to live for everyone.

"A poet once said, 'You won't like what comes after America.'"

Herbert's image froze and faded and did not return.

The projectors shut down with a tiny snap.

Camp pushed up from the couch, face white like bread dough. "Out behind the shack—that's the Quiet Man, isn't it? Fuck this, Nathaniel. We got to leave—now."

Nathaniel remained on the couch, a weird numbness spreading through his chest and neck, up to his head.

The last living message Nathaniel received from Herbert had probably been back in Dubai. The communications since had been from one or more of the linked versions of Jones, recreating Herbert's voice—and now his image, leading them and others, including Plover, down a track of correction and discovery.

They could try to set Jones straight—or deactivate him. But surely it was too late for that. Jones 2.0 was locked in a vault in the mountains of Switzerland, access tightly controlled. Nathaniel was pretty sure the safeguards would keep out even him.

Unless, of course, Jones *wanted* Nathaniel to get in.

Unless Jones had become the Quiet Man once and for all.

Chan Herbert—the ghost in the machine.

40

Lion County, West Texas

William leveled the candle-sterile knife blade above the boy's sweaty, white forearm. The shadowy interior of the pump house fell quiet. The air smelled hot and damp and muddy. From somewhere nearby drifted the punk of an old pile of manure.

The boy was nervous, but after all he had been through, that was to be expected. William squatted in front of him and looked into his face, beaded with sweat and pale from a year in custody. Fifteen: large brown eyes, soft mousy hair, handsome enough but pudgy.

They were all sweating. It was ninety degrees outside even at nine o'clock, and inside the shed was hotter.

Glenn Curteze sat on the gray pump housing and held up the boy's arm. Jonathan Kapp stood on his right, one deeply tanned hand on the boy's shoulder.

The boy swallowed hard. "You're going to cut it out."

William nodded.

"If you leave it in, it'll set off alarms," the boy said, eyes moving between the agents.

"It's got your life history," Kapp said with a narrow smile, hand on the boy's shoulder. "Wouldn't want that to get out, would we?"

"It's down deep," the boy said. "It really hurt when they put it in."

"It's wrapped in a sanitary sleeve," William explained. "Intramuscular injection, state prison issue. At least it's not very big. I see the scar—that pink spot. It's about half an inch below that. I've got some spray that will dull the skin, but we couldn't get anything else on short notice."

The boy locked William's eyes. "Will you guys hold me down . . . please?"

"Of course," Curteze said, shifting left to grip the boy's shoulders. "He'll have it out in a jiffy."

"Then . . . we're leaving? I won't be brought back?"

"That's our plan," William said. "We don't think anyone will extradite, under the circumstances." There was a possibility they'd have to avoid Oklahoma and Green Idaho, but every state west of Texas would offer sanctuary.

"My lawyer told me they were going to transport me down to Huntsville. They didn't even care my dad's with the FBI. I didn't mean to shoot Daryl. We were looking at the guns in the study. His father had a really great collection. Somehow, he found one that was loaded."

"Right," William said. "We've seen the video."

"Please," the boy said. "Do it now."

William applied the numbing spray from a drugstore can. Kapp and Curteze held the boy down. Curteze had a twist of keychain leather in one pocket and he offered it to the boy, who opened his mouth and bit down.

Classic Texas moment, William thought, and pushed the blade down deep and distal.

The boy gave a shriek around the leather.

William plunged in the tweezers, heard the small *tink* of contact with the chip sheath, and pinched it tight on the first try. Blood welled up from the incision. He used toilet paper to mop up the drops, then dribbled antiseptic powder over the wound and closed it with a Band-aid. No time for stitches.

"All done," William said, and held up the chip.

"Just like *The Matrix*," the boy said, and then fainted.

William wiped the blade and heated it in the candle flame. "Now me."

All three of the agents had chips.

When the cutting was done, William returned to the van and out of sight of the others, retrieved the case.

He unplugged the case from a rear outlet and poured the snakes onto the edge of the field. They immediately wriggled away, maybe too convincing.

Out here, people liked to shoot snakes.

41

California

Nathaniel drove Camp to the Oceanside commuter train station—a midsize steel and glass vault, like a big Quonset hut cut in half—and dropped him off in the parking lot.

Camp took his travel bag with him and didn't look back or wave as he walked through the doors to the passenger waiting area.

With Camp sent on his way, Nathaniel drove back up the broken paved road in the misty dusk, returned to the blockhouse, and sat on the old couch, staring at the blank wall. He tried to feel sadness—no go. Something else undefined had replaced grief, as with fear.

No visuals. No grays highlighted with brilliant colors. His subconscious was utterly clueless about what would happen next.

Outside, fog rolled in. The old fiber optic cable that crossed the ocean and came ashore and snaked its way right up to this blockhouse was no doubt filled with Eastern traffic—a spillover from half the world's billion trillion messages, all the buzz and hype and music and shows and movies and love and hate and codes and schemes, all the essential financial traffic, government traffic, all passing through the small box in the corner, the next-to-greatest pattern recognizer and language analyzer and voice identifier in human history—the elder cousin of Jones 2.0, who might or might not be the true god of this new economic age.

Nathaniel was willing to stay here all night if need be. Sleep had to come. He nodded off for a few hours, and awoke slumped on the couch and cold.

It was early morning.

Sometime while he slept, a single lens reappeared from behind the hole in the wall.

It seemed to be watching him.

"Hello, Jones," Nathaniel said. "No more games. No more hiding. We're sad—or we should be, both of us. I'd like to be more help. You've been pointing me in the right direction, haven't you?"

The lens did not move. There was no way of knowing if the ghost was still listening.

After a while, Nathaniel left the blockhouse, closing and locking the battered steel door behind him.

Near the shack, he placed a sprig of dried sage over the shrunken face of the Quiet Man and said his farewells. Then he stared up at the hills to the east, outlined by sky glow from suburban tracts.

He squinted to pick out snipers, killers, other deadly hired hands— hoping for bee vision.

Nothing popped—nothing visible.

Back to the fog creeping in from the ocean, dark and wet and black.

Now for the dangerous part.

42

Washington, D.C.

Neither the president's chief of staff nor Thalia Ripper was returning Rebecca's calls or emails. She had been working in a near-vacuum of authority for almost four days; there wasn't much she felt she could do until the president heard the full story of what she had learned so far—along with her own personal revelation or confession.

None of it looked good. Rebecca suspected the president would ask her to remove herself from the investigation.

Roger Baumann met her outside the hotel door and escorted her under the front awning to the armored limo.

"My room was unguarded for a time last night," Rebecca said.

Baumann winced. "We hoped you wouldn't notice."

"I noticed."

"Any problems, ma'am?" Baumann asked.

"No."

Baumann seemed preoccupied—unhappy and unwilling to say more. Rebecca decided not to push it.

The limo took an unusual turn on the short trip, not toward the EEOB but right on H Avenue Northwest. Rebecca leaned forward.

"What's up now?" she asked.

"You've got an appointment."

"With the president?"

"No, ma'am. My boss."

The limo came to a stop in front of Secret Service headquarters. Baumann got out and opened the door. She sat back and braced herself for a moment, never happy with obscurities, then emerged with her usual swivel and push up, and some courteous help from the agent.

"An apology for the lapse?" she asked.

"No, ma'am. My boss would like to spend a few minutes with you before I drop you off at the EEOB."

"Does the president know?"

Baumann shook his head.

"Relevant to my investigation? And in no way compromising the president's trust in me?"

"Yes, ma'am, and yes again, ma'am."

Rebecca lifted her hand, lead on.

They took an elevator to the basement. He led her down a corridor lined with closed doors to a corner office marked with a temporary standee sign: "Incident Investigation. No Admittance."

Baumann brushed past the sign and opened the door. He held out his arm and a low, clear voice inside welcomed her into the cramped room.

Stacks of media—discs and portable drives—filled open cabinets on one side. Three humming servers sat in a corner on a square metal table, looking small and lonely.

Sitting on a tall-back chair before a small desk, a short, muscular, very bald man turned to face her as she walked in. She recognized the shining dome. She had seen him once before, in a hallway in the West Wing: Daniel Haze, director of the Secret Service.

Haze stood and welcomed her with a tight smile and a handshake. "Glad to finally meet you, Ms. Rose," Haze said.

"Let's be quick," Rebecca said.

"Yes, ma'am." Haze pulled out a folding chair and offered her the tall-backed chair.

Rebecca demurred.

They both sat. "I hear you did a pretty good number on Quinn."

"I tried."

Haze's eyes were light gray and his face was chiseled and square, a prominent chin giving him the look of an actor destined always to portray Nazi generals. He lifted a piece of paper covered with hand-written notes. "But he didn't give you what you wanted."

"You listened in?" Rebecca said.

Haze shrugged. "This is the first time anyone I've protected has been shot—and it is sure as hell the first time for something like Quinn."

Rebecca made a sympathetic "Hmm."

"It's still possible we can help each other."

Rebecca looked into his gray eyes. "I'm happy to cooperate—if the president agrees."

"Have you spoken with the president in the last four days?"

"No," Rebecca said.

"Nobody I know has spoken with her. I hate being out of the loop. Something's wrong, and nobody tells me anything now." Haze leaned his chair back. "She's going outside for her security. Private executive protection services. A really terrible idea. We're still the best in the world at what we do."

"Hmm," Rebecca said again.

Haze lifted a bag and pulled out a broken pair of spex—the same color as the pair Rebecca had been wearing in the Los Angeles convention center. "The EMS folks tossed these into a recycle bin at the hospital where you were treated. My agents retrieved them."

"I'm impressed," Rebecca said as Haze dangled the glasses by a temple piece. "You were already vetting me—before the explosion. Must have been awkward—the convention center bombing wasn't your turf."

Haze nodded. "You'd had these for a few months before the bombing. You downloaded personal data from an older set of FBI gogs a year ago."

"Did you retrieve those, too?" Rebecca felt her face heating.

Haze wrinkled his forehead. "You told investigators someone came up to you at COPES before the blast and introduced himself. Used the name Nathaniel Trace."

"That's right." Rebecca met Haze's gray look. "He wanted to talk— I brushed him off."

"What you didn't tell us was that your spex tagged him as someone you'd met before."

Rebecca looked puzzled. "I was getting a lot of that at the convention. Is he someone of interest?"

"Not to the bombing investigation—not yet, at any rate. But we've done our duty and passed this material on to ATF. May I tell you a little about Mr. Trace?"

Rebecca nodded.

"We ID'd him based on fingerprints from the business card he gave you—"

"You went through my personal effects?"

"It was in the trash, in a bin right next to the spex—along with your ruined clothing. Using that, we confirmed the ID using facial tags from our Homeland Security airport database. He last entered the country under the name of Robert Sangstrom—a very ornate cover identity. Deep detail throughout our system. But that's not your problem, not yet, at any rate. He's a software engineer—something of a pudgy bright boy, according to his employment record. He enlisted in the National Guard, was called up to serve in Iraq—Signal Corps, no combat action—between 2006 and 2008. After that, he returned to the Middle East as a subcontractor for Talos Corporation. He spent a few years working for them in California, then in Jordan and Arabia Deserta. May have been injured in a rebel event in Arabia or Jordan—private evac and medical treatment. Here the trail goes blurry—we can't get into Talos, and nobody's talking. He could have had a legitimate reason for being at COPES, under his own name—but he wasn't registered either as Sangstrom or as Trace. None of the survivors we've interviewed knows anything about him."

"Sounds pretty conspiratorial," Rebecca said.

Haze nodded. "Talos was represented at COPES by three salesmen, but not by Trace. All three of the Talos reps departed the convention center just before the blast. Lucky for them. Has Trace tried to contact you since?"

"No. Do my spex tell you where I met him before?"

"That's lost. Can you remember?"

"I draw a blank." That much was true. This meeting was both unexpected and dangerous. Haze certainly had the power to arrest her, for any number of reasons, and hold her indefinitely—with or without the president's approval.

"Why would Trace want to talk with you? Did he already know about Quinn? Was he trying to warn you?"

"Warn me about what?"

"We got DNA from the business card. We spectro-analyzed Trace's skin oils for chemicals—drugs. Yours, too. Interesting results." Haze held out his hand, dangling the cracked, broken spex. "We're finished with these."

Rebecca took the spex and slipped them into her pocket. "That's it?"

"Both you and Trace tested positive for residues of a metabolite known to be associated with an experimental cancer drug called Seraprixoline. If you have cancer, that would show up in other traces . . . you don't. There's another use, off label, so to speak. It's been used on a limited basis to treat PTSD. Quinn has the same residues, by the way. I'm tracking down information that Talos might have funded this research."

"Oh," Rebecca said.

"Last night, there was a glitch on our Lynx network. Our agent was called away by a false emergency message. We lost track of you for ninety minutes. Then our system crashed. That whole ninety minutes is a void for us. When the system came back online, we heard something unusual. A little boy weeping. Weird, huh?"

"Very," Rebecca said.

Haze gave her a moment to say more, but she just watched him, as interested in his reaction as he was in hers.

"I'm hearing a lot about Talos these days," he said. "Their executive security division is a top contender for the president's private contract. I'm concerned your connections to Trace, and presumably to Talos, might compromise any service you perform for the president. I'm concerned you might be tainted, Ms. Rose."

"I appreciate your concern," Rebecca said. "Are you going to hold me or let me go? I need to make my report to the president whenever she becomes available."

Haze shrugged. "Just a professional courtesy, actually, at this stage," he said. "Good luck getting through to her."

* * *

Baumann dropped her off at the EEOB. She was met by two Marine guards who escorted her in precise silence to her offices, opened the door, and let her in, to meet the startled faces of her assistants, lined up as if for formal inspection.

Judith stepped forward to meet Rebecca's onslaught—to defend the others.

The door closed behind Rebecca with a large, soft thump and a resonant click. For a moment, she wondered if they were all being held prisoner, but she could hear one of the guards marching off down the hall.

When she opened the door and peered out, like a little girl at school, only one Marine remained—and Baumann, who had come up from parking the limo.

He seemed very unhappy, listening to his earpiece, and wouldn't meet her eyes.

Rebecca shut the door and leaned back against it.

"What is going on?" Judith asked. "Everyone's jumpy as grasshoppers on a griddle."

"I wish I knew," Rebecca said. "It's like the whole town is getting ready for a punch in the gut. We've got work to do. Let's do it."

For the next few hours, she returned to the documents, struggling to put all she knew, or thought she knew, into context. She closed the door to her small office and leaned back in the chair, stretching her ankle . . . but waiting for a clear picture to emerge was like waiting for a lightning strike. The air was thick with potential.

She would not have taken this job had she known how utterly powerless she would be, just when things were coming to a head.

At four-thirty, Rebecca opened her door.

"You got a delivery," Judith said, stepping forward to give her a small disc in a gray plastic sleeve. "From an arrogant young man I've never met. He seems to have credentials to go anywhere he wants."

"Tom," Rebecca said.

"He said he was an assistant to somebody named Tom, who was elsewhere on important business," Judith said disapprovingly. "He did not follow protocol."

Tom, his assistants, and their solutions had been welcomed in places far more secure than the EEOB. "He doesn't have to—so he doesn't know how."

Rebecca took the disc back to her desk, closed the door again, and plugged it into a player, then slipped on headphones.

Tom had fully restored Quinn's digital voice file—less than five minutes.

As she listened, she felt her stomach knot, then threaten to turn. No wonder Plover had left Baltimore and tried to hide. She returned the disk to its sleeve and slipped it into her pocket. She hoped Tom had not listened to it. If he had, he might be in danger as well.

Plover's information had become absolutely toxic.

Rebecca emerged again and took Judith aside. "Call Thalia Ripper. You two know each other—she put you in my service to report on me, didn't she?"

Judith stared up in owlish resentment, then nodded.

"Call her at home if necessary. Tell her, if I don't have an appointment in an hour, directly with the president, I'm going to the Bureau with what I've learned. Or to Haze. Or both. Tell her I mean business. Tell her I've gone off my nut, if you have to—but get me that appointment."

"You can't breach the president's trust!" Judith said, appalled.

"Call."

Judith left wringing her hands—literally—and Rebecca used her cell to call Quinn's attorney. The secretary who took her call was already in shock, barely audible. "Mr. Blake is not available. I'll let him know you called," she said.

Rebecca listened to the secretary's quavering tone. "Something's wrong," she said. "What is it?"

The secretary abruptly hung up. Rebecca put her coat on and was almost out the door—causing Baumann to stir into action—when Judith shouted across the room, from her desk: "The vice president is dead! It's on the web! Quinn is dead!"

The Marine looked left out, young, confused.

"Jesus," Rebecca murmured. She turned to Baumann.

He tapped his earpiece and nodded. "It's true," he said, pale spots around his lips and the corners of his jaw. "Suicide."

A whirring sounded over Rebecca's head. She looked up and saw a security camera tracking someone at the end of the long hall.

Without thinking, she glanced in that direction.

A man in a tan raincoat stood there, hands thrust deep in outer pockets. Even from this distance, she could see that he had a scar on his right cheek—and a tousled head of gingery hair.

He nodded to her, then turned and stepped around the corner.

Baumann was still listening, waiting for instructions.

"I've got to visit the ladies room," she told him, one eyebrow raised, feeling like a little girl about to play hooky. He grimaced and reached out but she was quick—amazingly quick, running down the hall.

After a couple of devious turns, she left the rear of the building and stood for a moment, watching cars hum past.

No sign of Baumann, poor man. There would no doubt be a swarm of agents out looking for her any minute, but she knew from long undercover and tracking experience how to evade, hide, blend in.

What now?

Go for a walk, she decided.

43

The Smoky

Two shining black Torq-Vees exited the Monarch Gate, trailing a tail of dust as they veered south along the direct road to the Smoky.

Fouad rode left middle passenger in the second vehicle as they ferried him back to his temporary quarters on Price's ranch. His driver was a silent Haitian, one of Colonel Sir's mercenaries, and behind him sat three escorts, all beefy Anglos with shaved heads and black T-shirts, their left arms sporting tats: grinning death's-heads wreathed by laurels over the words "Fallujah 2004."

The Anglos were soft-spoken, tightly controlled—supremely fit middle-aged men who had survived many bad times.

Fouad could not help but respect their demeanor, their polite say-nothing-but-say-it-pleasant banter. They were much too good at their jobs to talk sports scores. Instead, without seeming to pry into his prior life, they discussed geography.

They even played a game of Muslim surnames, at which they were experts.

They were excellent company.

Halfway to the compound—surrounded by acres of scrub—Fouad looked left through the thick armored glass and saw another blazing Texas sunset, the beginning of another protected, isolated night.

The prelude to another day of being briefed for his new role as translator to the Saudi royal family—another long day of meetings, protocol, and cultural prep, where everyone behaved as if he were Axel Price's new favorite, his most recent handpicked protégé.

It was too polite, all dumb show. Fouad suspected no one believed he was fooled by this ruse.

Thirteen agonizing days after his intrusion into the Talos infranet.

The great gathering on the Talos Campus would begin in less than twenty hours. Already, support and cargo planes were landing at Lion City's Judah P. Benjamin International Airport—delivering armored luxury vehicles for a few of the guests, and also, perhaps, more logistical support for whatever grand dance Price was choreographing. The world's deepest, most powerful shadow bankers, international hedge fund managers . . . the richest oleocrats from Russia, South America, Canada (no surprise—and perhaps without the knowledge of the Canadian government), and of course the Middle East.

And to top it off, a select list of congressional representatives and perhaps a couple of senators.

It would have been perfect if he could access the information he carried, but of course it was coded deep in his bloodstream, and thus far, no one had given any hint that Price suspected as much.

They would have killed him then and there—and then cremated him.

The lead Torq-Vee stopped outside the main ranch house. The second vehicle paused for a quick inspection, then proceeded to the outlying bungalow. There, under the fiery sky, they dropped him at his front porch.

"I have tea and coffee, if you would like to join me," Fouad offered, smiling broadly, unctuously happy to be so respected, so highly elevated—as he knew these strong, experienced men would both appreciate and expect. Like him, they were far travelers in a dangerous and diverse world, but their prejudices lay even deeper—injected long ago by parents, grandparents, aunts, and uncles.

Generations of ideas about the true rulers of Earth, the true favored of God.

The most affable of these tattooed men—Captain Rick Schmitz, U.S. Army, Ret.—thanked him for his offer. Quick, pleasant grin, hard yet friendly eyes.

"No thank you, Mr. Al-Husam. We've got more folks to escort, and we're told Mr. Price wants you up early tomorrow, refreshed and ready to go. The prince himself might be coming in early. Have a nice night."

The Torq-Vee rumbled off, its thick, armored tires shivering the sandy ground. Of course it could engage a sound suppression system that would almost magically control the tire angle and pitch and reduce that distinctive, warlike noise to a whisper. But that ate up fuel and reduced travel time, and why bother in this part of the world?

This was the heart of Price's empire. And perhaps the starting point for something new and unexpected.

Fouad had been thinking a great deal of history and economics and had put together several scenarios that were making more and more sense. He was mostly ignorant of what he carried, but that did not make him helpless.

His father, who had died in Egypt the year before, had a confessed habit of thinking "far too large for my pay grade. I hope you are smart enough to stay humble." Fouad of course would never be that smart—and his father had smiled as he spoke those words, more than dispensation to disobey—a sly suggestion that it might be essential.

His father had known too well that the USA was a fickle fatherland.

Fouad climbed the board steps to the screened porch, pushed his boots through the bristle brush mounted on the right—as he might have in many parts of the Middle East, also plagued by dust and on occasion mud—and ran his arm past the security sensor. The door lock snicked open.

He reached for the handle and then froze, hearing a noise that separated itself from the light chorus of alternating crickets that accompanied the growing shadows.

A distinctive slithering, *gravelly* sound.

He turned and looked down.

Two snakes—sidewinders, he thought—S-curled slowly along the pebbly margin of the path to the porch.

He had seen perhaps a dozen snakes since arriving in Texas, of course—mostly rattlesnakes, never sidewinders. That two might make their way into this compound was not surprising—perhaps they were shy natives. Price did not encourage the killing of Texas wildlife, but the locals outside often did target practice on hapless reptiles.

Heads raised, the two reptiles stared up at him with shining black eyes. The slithering stopped, the heads swayed in unison, and then a small musical tone sounded.

The heads dropped.

The bodies straightened.

They were not real.

Despite himself, Fouad smiled in boyish delight. Clever toys! Perhaps Price was paying for Disney-like robots to repopulate his prairies—an expensive hobby.

Just in case, he remained on the top step.

The snakes emitted two more tones, followed by a tinny voice. "Confirm ID by speaking your name," the voice instructed.

He bent on one knee, fascinated. "Al Smith," he said.

"No match. Confirm ID by speaking your name."

"Fouad Al-Husam," he said.

"Match. Repeat your name."

He repeated.

The snakes rolled over and two rectangular hatches, covered with scaled skin, popped open to reveal transparent tubes and a watchmaker's hint of automated innards.

"Thank you," the voice said. "Please remove our contents and perform the instructed functions, then replace the contents, close both hatches manually, and we will be on our way."

Still hunched, ready to spring back at a false move, Fouad stepped down and pinched out one of the tubes. It was a simple mechanism for drawing blood—hidden needle, ampoule.

He stared in astonishment at the implications of such a thing, such a wonder—and felt a chill, as if staring into his own grave.

They badly wanted his blood and the prochine memory it contained. They did not think he would live to escape Lion City.

44

Washington, D.C.
The Mall

Supernatural.

Fairy-tale pretty.

Golden sheets of drizzle fell away over the capital like a lady's discarded shawl. A rainbow drew a vivid crayon bridge above and to the north of the Washington Monument. The monument itself stuck up from beyond the solemn, graceless stone blocks of the World War Two memorial like a needle waiting for the thumb of a careless giant.

Rebecca walked the path along the reflecting pool, sick to her stomach—and not with worry. Worry did not seem to be a problem.

Starting just this morning, food wasn't sitting well.

But colors were amazing. Smells overwhelmed. The sound of traffic from Constitution Avenue was almost painfully rich and detailed—extended in both high and low frequency. She could make out cars, buses, trucks, and with her ears alone, follow them down the street as individual vehicles . . .

She had easily lost Baumann, getting lost in the tourist crowds. But after just a few minutes, she felt a desperate kind of exhaustion, all her senses overloaded.

And here came a motorcade, sirens blowing aside traffic. Not the president. Rebecca covered her ears and closed her eyes. She had to stay alert.

It seemed to be starting, just as Plover had warned.

A hand touched her shoulder and made her jump like a startled cat.

She turned full circle, hands out in claws, hunched over, and stared at the blur of colors, no outlines, no sense, until something popped—his face.

Faces were important.

A man's face. Blocky, late thirties, ginger hair, startling green eyes. She saw it wrapped in a red circle and laughed at the visual joke. Her new brain had a sense of humor.

"I know you," she said, straightening. "How did you get into the Eisenhower building?"

Nathaniel held his finger to his lips. "We don't want to be conspicuous."

They drew cautious, sidewise inspection from several men and women and one escorted child, people out walking after the storm. Rebecca stared after the departing child, who stuck out her tongue.

"I'm a kid again, is that it?" Rebecca asked.

Nathaniel took her arm. "Laugh like we're old friends."

Rebecca laughed. "Aren't we? Old friends?"

"I'm flying level, but you're a kite," he observed. "Keep it tight. We've got things to discuss. Things you need to take back to your boss lady. And we don't have much time."

"Christ, I *am* a kite. I don't care. Even though Quinn's dead," Rebecca said. "He hanged himself."

"No, he didn't," Nathaniel said. "We don't get suicidal. Homicidal, maybe."

"Quinn said he was . . . His attorney . . . I didn't want to believe it. Things can't be that far gone."

"They've been going south for a long time now. We're right on the edge of losing it all—this country, our freedom, and for you and me—anybody who went through Mariposa—our lives."

"First, our sanity," Rebecca said.

"Dispensable," Trace said. "Across that border lies a whole new country. Believe me."

"Tell me—does it get better—more stable?"

"Yes and no. You're third stage. You and a few hundred others. You may not go through any of the big swings—I hope. Did Plover talk to you?"

"Yes."

"He's screwed things up royally for Axel Price."

"The vice president was key," Rebecca said.

Rebecca felt the loop start to coil and the knot to shrink. The visuals faded to a normal range of colors—not at all fairy-tale, just D.C. after an autumn shower. The sun was going down, she was cold, and she was walking beside a man who scared her.

"I'm still capable of being frightened," she said. "Quinn was beyond that. But he must have started out as a real a piece of work. I listened to his—"

"What do you know about Jones?"

She looked over Trace sharply, judging his facial muscles, his hands. "Nothing. Is Jones someone you worked with?"

"Jones is very close to our problem—perhaps he *is* our problem, but he could also be our ace in the hole."

"Is Jones a code name for a human?"

"No. A machine personality."

"You built it . . . him for Talos? Axel Price?"

"I worked for Mind Design. We helped program a key part of MSARC. And for a lot of money, we built in a couple of nasty backdoors. One for Price . . . and several that none of us knew about, devised by our owner and CEO, who did not trust Price. The extra entry points were supposed to shut down once the system went online . . . three weeks ago. They didn't. Jones controls all of them. Maybe he's one, maybe he's many, but the way MSARC works, he has access to nearly everything in the world hooked up to a computer."

"Jones is like a hydra. Many heads."

"Good enough," Nathaniel said. They strolled along the damp path. "But he's not just a computer. He's a self-initiated, evolutionary problem solver. A competer."

"Ah," Rebecca said. "It all makes sense."

"Does it?" Nathaniel asked.

"No."

Two joggers in their twenties—long white legs, pumping arms, hair pasted to their heads, damp and smiling—broke to pass around them. Rebecca smelled the female's spoor, rich as cinnamon. She looked at Trace, who sternly faced forward.

"Right," he said. "She's pregnant. Beautiful scent."

"Oh, my lord," Rebecca said.

Nathaniel looked up at the sky and took a deep, nasal breath. "Jones has had a nasty shock. If I could take a guess, he's very disturbed. He doesn't know what he's going to do next."

"He feels emotions?"

"Not like ordinary people. But he has attachments and a weird something like loyalty."

"Maybe we're turning into Jones," Rebecca said.

"Believe me, at our most variant, we're nothing like him—his emotions might be more those of an insect, or a lizard at the most complicated. But that seems to be changing."

"What's changed—changing, for you?"

"You've had self-defense training."

She watched him closely, as she would an unpredictable animal. "So?"

"You'll soon be ten times better—but you'll have to relearn how and when to move; otherwise you'll end up breaking every bone in your body. We lose some level of autonomic control, down to the cellular level—not all of it, just the nervous system, and only parts of that. Key parts. But let's get back to Jones. There's not much time."

"Okay. A hydra, right?"

"So you say."

"Right now, at least one of his heads is very upset—even angry. How odd," Rebecca said. "What does an angry computer . . . competer do to get even?" Then she thought of the obvious question, which had not occurred to her at first. Logic seemed to be working backwards. "What made Jones angry?"

"Murder," Nathaniel said. "Jones had seven programmers, including me. We called ourselves the Turing Seven. It was our job to help design him, build him, teach him, and debug him—that is, understand him. At least four of the Turing Seven are dead. Jones also had a master designer—our boss. We called him the Quiet Man. His real name was Chan Herbert. He's dead, too. Axel Price killed Jones's father."

45

Lion County

The boy was still asleep in the backseat. The long twilight had dwindled to a blue and gold haze on the straight horizon. Black, low mountains to their right. Twilight the most dangerous time of day: eyes still adjusted for bright but dark settling in.

William wondered what Kapp and Curteze might have thought if they had seen him releasing the snakes into the scrub. Just ordinary agents—honorable young men caught up by the thrill of what they thought was a simple rescue, and a chance for a little payback. Payback played a big role in cop psychology.

Strangely, for William, sitting in the driver's seat both figuratively and literally, it mattered not at all. He was at the point in his career where simply having a career—and surviving the twists and turns of that career—meant a hell of a lot more than showing the world's tricky players who was really kicking butt and taking names.

Curteze, riding shotgun, was passing the time by engaging in showbiz trivia.

"All right, then. Where's the big guy in *Lifeboat*?"

William frowned, pretending to take his time. Then: "Newspaper ad. Fat guy in a suit—before and after."

Curteze murmured his irritation.

"Well?" William asked.

"Yeah, that's it. What about *Psycho*?"

"Through the window after Janet Leigh comes back to the real estate office. He's wearing a cowboy hat."

"Everyone knows that one. *Rear Window*?"

"Winding a clock in the songwriter's apartment."

"Have you seen them all?"

"Every single film, including the silents," William said. "He shows up twice in *The Lodger*."

"Fuck you," Curteze murmured, shrinking down in the seat. "Bet is off."

"We weren't betting," William reminded him.

"I saw *Vertigo*," Kapp said. "Hated it when the cop slid off the roof. Gave me nightmares as a kid."

"What about Jimmy Stewart?" Curteze asked. "Didn't you worry about him?"

"I knew *he* was going to make it. The movie wasn't even started yet."

"When I was a kid, I always told people I was born in Texas," William said. "Sounded braver than being born in California. Alamo and all that."

"John Wayne as Davy Crockett, Richard Widmark as Travis," Curteze said.

"Billy Bob Thornton as Crockett," William said. "Screaming out his lungs when the Mexicans kill him."

"I didn't understand that part," Kapp said.

They switched positions and Kapp swiftly ground the Yukon over the rough ranch road, swerving to avoid huge potholes that loomed at the last second.

Curteze took out a Thermos of coffee and tried to pour William a cup. Most of it slopped.

"U.S. 62 in a couple of miles," Curteze said, consulting his pocket GPS. "We're west of the Guadalupe Mountains. They got lots of tanks out here, it says—Army tanks?"

"Cattle tanks. Ponds, lakes," Kapp explained. "Give me some of that."

"Drive better and maybe I will."

They had to cross twenty miles north over the old grazing acreage, now left dry and dusty in the drought.

"Texas feels like a foreign country," William said.

"Might as well *be* a foreign country," Curteze said.

"It's what some of these folks have always wanted," Kapp said as he swung the wheel left. They lurched around a hole big enough to hide a cow. This road had seen better days. Still, there was enough traffic out here that a Yukon—especially a Yukon equipped with a citizen transponder—might not seem out of place.

Already, they could see the lights of El Paso on their left. They'd meet 62 and drive west. Their next obstacle might come at a Texas Ranger checkpoint this side of the New Mexico border. There had been some incidents between New Mexico state troopers and Texas Rangers in the last few months. Shots fired, patrolmen and troopers down. First shots of the new civil war, some called it. New Mexico was staying loyal to the federal government.

Large parts of Texas were on their own track, and nobody in Washington had the guts or the money to stop them.

Kapp pointed out the driver's side window and let out a chirpy whistle. "Got a bird," he said. "Flying low and matching speed. About the size of a crow."

William saw it and shook his head.

"Mexican standoff," Curteze said. "We don't have brown faces, and besides, the border boys don't report to the Rangers anymore."

"If it *is* a Border Security bird," William said. "Talos flies a lot of its own surveillance."

After five years of extreme drought, illegal immigration from Mexico had reached catastrophic proportions. South of the Rio Grande, two million people were starving and the U.S. could not afford much in the way of relief aid. The Chinese and Europeans were helping but it was not nearly enough. Under this pressure, Texas went its own way, but mostly tolerated Border Security and ICE.

Even so, the feds did not report to the state and certainly not to Talos's auxiliaries.

"We'll probably end up with bullets in the backs of our pointy little heads," Curteze said.

"Shh," William said, and nodded at the sleeping boy.

Kapp drove on into the darkness. The crow-size drone kept up with them until a mile before the highway, then buzzed off into the night.

Ahead, headlights flashed in pairs—straight on, not the distant lights of traffic. There were at least a dozen vehicles—most the size of pickup trucks—lined up between them and 62.

"We're going to have to park," William said. "Looks like they've laid down a blockade."

"How would they know where we are?" Curteze asked, keeping his voice low. "The birds can't tell us from a rancher—right?"

"This whole thing's a crapshoot," William said. "Half of our plan is they don't want to start a war. Maybe they do. Feds are certainly distracted right now—it might not even hit the national news."

Kapp lurched the truck left, away from the highway, off the ranch road and into the scrub.

The ride got rougher.

46

El Paso, Texas

Joe Mason shook hands with Jane Rowland and Tom Cantor and offered them chairs in his small office. Six-two, with reddish-brown skin, a square face, and thick black hair trimmed to a spiky mat, Mason's eyes were rimmed in red and hauled double loads of dark, weary bags. He was assistant field office director of Immigration and Customs Enforcement—ICE.

"I wouldn't want you Washington types to think all Texans are traitors," he said. "We're the most loyal citizens in the USA. Don't forget it—not while you're in this office."

Steel-barred windows, ubiquitous awards and service plaques, wall-mounted rack of service and Lynx spex, neat desk with empty in-and-out baskets, defined both Mason and his workspace.

"Never crossed my mind," Jane Rowland said.

Tom Cantor sat beside her and leaned forward to scratch his shoulder.

Mason watched them both, wrinkle lines making not quite a grin at the corners of his lips—sussing out their relationship.

Just being around Tom made Jane nervous. His big, child eyes gave no hint of either his intellect or his influence. Tom was utterly essential to dozens of clandestine operations. He had carte blanche entrance to so many agencies and yet never let on to anyone about his activities—even if those activities crossed paths.

Secret in one office, more secret still in another.

Not that he ever showed a hint of thinking he could lord it over her. No, ma'am. Ms. Jane Rowland—of the agency that had once split off from an agency that nobody officially acknowledged—was definitely the boss, and Tom Cantor was delighted to be in her employ.

Based on what she knew, that made her even more nervous.

"Airplanes," Tom said, as if that explained anything. His long, scraggly gray hair—wrapped around a high, balding forehead—made him look like a gentle-eyed Rasputin.

Mason finally allowed his smile to crack—and never was the word more apt. That expression looked as out of place as a wide split in an adobe pot. He waved one hand. "We've been sending warnings about Lion City and Talos for over a decade. Used to be no one in D.C. listened—too many oxen hitched to that particular wagon. Now some of these yokels have taken to plunking up our patrol vehicles—and of course they just love knocking down our birds, if they can see them. We've never tied incidents directly to Axel Price . . . but after a while, you'd be thick not to wonder."

Tom looked up, awaiting a useful point.

Mason took this bug-eyed presence with admirable tranquility. "We installed your transponder in one of our midsize, low-profile birds, with retrieval capability. We use them to pick up surveillance bots. She's out there following the county line, slow as a condor—transmitting to VRI right now."

Mason took down three spex, waved them over a small code plate, then handed two to Jane and Tom. The third set—curved dark lenses, very stylish—he slipped over his nose and ears with all the panache of an Elvis impersonator. "They've cut back half our personnel in the last six months. Our guys have families to support. I don't like to think some of them have gone over to Price, but it wouldn't shock me. We're down to about a quarter of the birds we flew two years ago. Still, if they're not too expensive, I'd love to put those snakes on our team . . ."

"Not a word," Jane reminded him.

"No, ma'am." Mason smiled. "But I hope you'll give us the next field test."

"Where's your pilot?"

"In Houston," Mason said. "We'll transfer to a local pilot shortly— one of our best. But I'm still wondering—why not just send in Hostage Rescue and pluck out your man?"

"Price would shoot him," Jane said.

Mason soberly absorbed this. "What are we heading for here—insurrection?"

Jane narrowed her eyes. "Your passengers will ping back to the code signal," she said. "That'll make them visible. They have to be picked up quickly."

"Curvalicious," Tom said.

Mason stretched out his arms, then grabbed his jaw with one hand and waggled it back and forth, working out tension. "Already in the program," he said. "Bird is turning over control . . . now. El Paso will fly the bird."

For the next three hours, Jane and Tom sat in Mason's office, watching the unmanned aerial vehicle's track of the west Texas landscape, drinking coffee.

Jane longed for white tea.

"We're covering their range," Mason said. "Unless they've run out of juice, they're still out there, squiggling around in the dirt and brush."

She pushed her spex down on her nose. "Discouraging," she said.

Mason was commendably patient, low-key—and good at politely keeping track of the one person in the room whose physical reactions seemed off.

Tom was fidgety. His face had worked its way through several phases of comic concentration, with occasional half-aware glances at Mason, at Jane—only to smile and relapse into his own world, somewhere out between the stars.

Jane took note of Mason's unease. She touched Tom's arm.

"Tired," Tom said. "Anyone have an Ibuprofen?"

"I'm full of coffee," Jane said, pushing up from her leather-cushioned chair arms. "How about a break?"

"Right," Tom said.

"Down the hall and to the left," Mason said. "Leave the spex here or alarms will go off."

In the restroom, Jane washed her hands—soaped and rinsed three times—then joined Tom in the hall. Tom had not been to the bathroom since their flight. He might indeed be from another planet.

"You're making Mason nervous," she said. "He's like a dog in a room with a quail—and you're the quail."

Tom shook his head. "Can't help it," he said. "I'm being twitched."

"What's that mean?"

"Ever since day before yesterday, somebody or something has been tracking everything I do. My work—my secure networks. Cameras. Traffic lights. I keep thinking Gene Hackman is going to jump out and yell boo."

Jane folded her arms and looked at him askance.

"I've put two and two together," Tom said. "It ain't you, right?"

"No."

"Because I'm a pro, you need me—you wouldn't fuck with me or try to scare me. Could be anybody, then. But the more I think about it, the more I ask myself, why isn't he looking at *you*, too? And then I realize, he is. He must be. You're the show runner, so he's more interested in you than in me. He's tracking me—because I'm helping *you*."

"I'm the only one you're helping?"

"Of course not," Tom said. "But it seems tied together."

Jane stepped over to the barred window at the end of the hall. Three cameras peered down from shiny dark covers in the drop ceiling. "Gene Hackman. That's good. What makes you think it's a he?"

"Well, we ceded our constitutional rights to any number of federal agencies, including yours, back in the bad old days. So I could easily enough picture a bunch of young hackers lined up in a dark room, tickling joysticks and taking control of every security system in the world, at the 24/7, caffeine-strumming command of, say, Laura Linney. They could aim satellites, take control of foreign CCTV, station millions of agents on every street corner, ready to pull out in black Suburbans or hop on Vespas . . . Cool. But that's not what's happening."

"How do you know?"

Tom gave her a quizzical glance. "Because I'd help design and install anything like that. I'd be Laura Linney's main man."

"Oh," Jane said.

"I love severe." He winked, not at all salaciously.

"We need to get back, Tom," Jane said, uneasy with the way this conversation was going.

Tom's demeanor switched to abject worry. He leaned in toward Jane to whisper, "He leaves an analog signature. A sound recording. Right?"

"Does he?" Jane said.

"I'm not going to violate any confidences if I tell you what that signature is. Because you already know."

"Do tell."

"A crying child. More specifically, a sobbing little boy."

"I see," Jane said, her arm hairs rising.

"He's smart, perfectly capable of breaking into this system, this fly-by-wire setup, and screwing us over. What if he's working out of Talos, or more scary still, out of MSARC? We gave up so many secrets to get those loans—"

Jane slapped her hand over Tom's mouth and pushed him to the wall. "Shut up," she said.

"Sorry," he said, muffled.

She let him go.

"Nothing has ever been able to track me that way before," Tom said, pulling down his shirt and trying to look dignified. "I'm good, I travel light. I'm mostly invisible. What if he means us harm? You should have told *me* what you knew eighteen hours ago."

Tom's hound-dog eyes turned critical.

Jane followed him back into Mason's office, feeling not just unease now but anger—because she no longer knew what was secure and what was not, and that meant she was vulnerable, and that meant all her colleagues—including Tom Cantor—*knew* she was vulnerable.

In their line of work, that perception was killer.

The Border Security drone flew over the southern extent of its range when it encountered Talos craft operating at the same altitude.

Mason spoke in a tense undertone to his remote pilot, then turned back to Jane and Tom. "We've been through this sort of standoff before. We've never taken direct fire from their birds—only from the ground, and only if we're near the Talos campus. Some of our pilots enjoy hot-dogging, but I just made sure we don't provoke a response. Don't want them thinking we're tracking any sort of unusual target. They can have armed vehicles out in that range within half an hour.

We're back on visual now."

Jane and Tom put on their spex and looked out over the dark early morning landscape. The cameras switched to FLIR—Forward Looking Infrared—then to infrared enhanced by computers and overlaid with satellite imagery.

Cross-hairs centered to a small circle.

The circle zoomed.

"Got something moving," Mason said. "Is that your snake?"

"Wow," Tom said.

"That's it. Only one," Jane said, disappointed.

The pilot dropped the drone quickly—too quickly, it seemed, as the black, green-speckled desert suddenly swooped up and the horizon shifted to a high line.

The display now changed to satellite side-scan radar, combined with the drone's IR perspective—additional overlays marking roll, pitch, and altitude.

The drone circled over the edge of the Talos campus.

"Maybe it got lost," Mason said.

The drone sideslipped into a steep helix.

Jane gripped the chair arm.

"Steady," Mason whispered.

The drone straightened as its descent smoothed and leveled at a hundred feet. One more veer east and it raised its nose and dropped spindly gear, then jounced and lofted twice before rolling to a stop.

The cross-hairs squared and the camera jogged left and right, then zoomed on a rounded W of shadowy curves—just a hint of motion in the detectors.

One snake.

"Send the signal," Jane said.

The drone lowered on its gear and somewhere behind them, in virtual sound, they heard whirring. The view shifted to the dropping ramp.

With a faint rustle, the snake maneuvered around a shrub, approached the ramp, and cautiously wormed into the craft's hold.

The ramp swung shut.

"Amazing," Mason said.

Jane settled back in her chair, chin almost on her chest. "No way of knowing whether it got what it came for," she said.

The pilot's voice announced takeoff. "I've got three Talos craft within a kilometer radius," he said. "Looks like they're taking an interest."

The drone was quickly airborne.

"Beeline home," Mason instructed. "Do not outmaneuver, do not engage."

"Up and away. Precious cargo—one, repeat, one snake," the pilot said. "We'll have it delivered in forty minutes."

"We always get our snake," Mason said, and glanced at Jane.

"Our team is bringing in the necessary equipment," Jane said. "We'll do the rest in the hangar—by ourselves, please. No observers, no assistance."

Tom took off his spex, shook his head with a sigh, and slumped in his chair. He was instantly asleep. His real duties began when the snake was returned.

If it carried what they were hoping for.

And failing that, if they couldn't save Fouad Al-Husam.

47

The Smoky

After the robot snakes, the night passed without further incident.

Fouad ate a small late snack of crackers and hummus and sardines, then turned on the television and watched a movie about young cowboys. Absorbing yet also disturbing that in a Western—so much about chivalry and honor—young men should be taught to kill and exact cruel vengeance as a necessary rite of passage.

Of course, he had no excuses before Allah. He had killed and likely would kill again.

He switched off the television, then spread his small threadbare rug and prayed *salatu'l isha'* but did not ask for advice or guidance, perhaps because it seemed his fate was already decided, and it was not polite to be pushy and impatient.

Fouad went to bed and slept soundly.

The soft noises of boots in his room brought him half awake, and a firm shove on his shoulder an instant later finished the job.

It was six in the morning, still dark outside.

Broad shoulders and a bullet head on a thick neck.

"Mr. Price requests your help," Schmitz said. "Fifteen minutes."

This time, they met in the office where Price received foreign guests. The room was palatial—a high-beamed ceiling arching over two thousand square feet of pearlescent slate tile, surrounding a circle of rustic wood floor on which Price's stainless steel desk sat, backed by great sliding windows that overlooked more acres of tallgrass prairie.

Price was signing papers as Fouad entered. The secretary lingered. Price waved her off.

"Thank you for coming, Fouad."

Fouad nodded but Price wasn't paying attention. The window drew his eyes out to peace and greenness: a controlled, secure domain, like the wilderness of myth.

"I'm embarrassed to have to talk about this," Price said. "A crack team of men has hijacked a high-profile prisoner from our Lion County lockup. So far, they've evaded capture, but we'll have them soon, and then I'm going to face a difficult dilemma." Price swung around. Fouad observed that he was genuinely angry but keeping himself in check. "Looks like the feds have come for Little Jamey Trues. Do you know anything about this?"

"No sir," Fouad said.

Price examined him closely, then glanced at his desktop, where a flat screen showed a schematic of a human figure—red, yellow, and blue blotches spread around limbs, face, hands. Price looked back at the windows. "I have four sons and three daughters. You?"

"No children," Fouad said.

"I can't imagine losing a son. You'd think FBI would teach its kids gun safety."

"A tragedy."

"Murder, actually." Price faced him, eyes mild but somehow, with that cold little smile, even more dangerous. "I also can't imagine having a son strapped down on a couch while a bunch of rednecks pump poison into his veins. I'd rather take him out and shoot him myself. *Patria potesta*, the Romans called it. Power of the patriarch. Isn't that what should have happened, Mr. Al-Husam? Taking care of our own messes?"

"It is not my place to comment, sir."

"Asymmetric warfare group has done excellent work getting our Haitian boys ready. No small thanks to you and your language courses. We'll be moving about two thousand of them to Arabia Deserta, into Jiddah and Riyadh, in three or four days. They'll join with crack team of Sunni officers . . . getting ready to subvert Shia guerrilla groups and pass power to a provisional Baathist government. Secular little fascists. Just love Adolf. Mind you, it's all with the covert blessing of key folks in the CIA and the State Department. How's that for irony?"

"Impressive," Fouad said.

"And for that, Talos will get a half percent of gross oil revenues coming out of the Persian Gulf for two years. A tidy bit of cash, even with oil futures dropping. Crazy old world, Fouad. In thirty years, the Middle East might not stack up to a hill of beans, but we'll have had our moment in the sun, we'll get out, and there'll be someplace else that needs fixing."

"No doubt," Fouad said.

"But this Little Jamey mess . . . I think the old FBI is looking for its own brand of justice. Don't you?"

Fouad said nothing. If Price was speaking the truth, then the complications could be almost too devious to imagine.

Price chuckled. "My God, Fouad, what an expression. You're shut tighter than a virgin's legs. Doesn't anything upset you or amuse you?"

"I am not paid to be amused," Fouad said.

"Well, if either of us were drinking men, I'd say we both need a snort of good Scotch. But we don't have that luxury, do we?"

"No sir."

"Ever thought of building some sort of foundation, having a family? I find strength in my wife and kids. Keeps me humble."

"Do you wish me to be humble?"

Price laughed. "No. But I won't be responsible to Allah for all your sins."

"Just the ones you are paying for," Fouad said.

Price chuckled, then assumed a somber cast, eyes glittering. "Tell Allah not to forget that."

"He is ever present and listens to the heart," Fouad said.

"I think him and my Jesus would actually get along pretty well," Price said. "Don't you?"

"I have no doubt, sir."

"This prisoner hijacking—it's a well-planned operation, as far as it's gone. Whoever carried it off certainly had help from inside the Texas DOC—and from Washington. You used to be FBI. You're the most prominent former agent on our payroll. Some of my security people are pointing fingers. They say you're the inside man.

"But my equipment—such as it is—shows you're telling me the truth. Still, if you have any insight—if you've heard anything, even rumors—I'd appreciate it if you'd pass it along. Could take some heat off the both of us. The mayor's screaming bloody murder, and Huntsville ain't happy, either."

Fouad stepped forward. "I know nothing of this, but I doubt that active-duty agents are involved."

"Well, that's not the sentiment around here." Price shook his head as if dismissing all that as beneath their notice. "We know they're using a truck with a falsified rancher RFID. We know they'll try to cross into New Mexico. They'll realize that route is blocked while they're still a little south of highway 62.

"If you have any way to contact these men—tell them we'll cut them some slack if they turn their prisoner over now. We'll ship them out of Texas, no rough stuff and no questions asked. But we keep Little Jamey, of course."

Another couple of seconds. The sound of grass whispering beneath the office windows.

"If this isn't why you're here, then I've got a real puzzle, my friend," Price said. "I've also got my instincts. I'm going to come down on one side or another, right here. Right now." He lifted his finger, dropped it to the left, then down. "One way or another, you're not being square with me. I just want to know why. I've had programmer trouble recently. Worse, I got some sort of gremlin burrowing into my infranet, but that might not be you—probably isn't, in fact, since a lot of it seems to come from outside. Very clever. Little boy sobbing. I'm thinking Spider/Argus—they do that sort of thing, don't they?"

Fouad lowered his gaze to the desk, the carpet.

Price looked over the display. "Bingo. No ice cups this time. Lots riding on our upcoming meeting. If you're after data—my experts aren't sure where you're hiding it. We've swept your quarters, it's not on your Talos body chips, and you don't have any others.

"You know I could kill you right here, but . . . you might have some other use, down the road a ways. Tomorrow, maybe. And I still might have something to learn from you. Maybe I can solve two problems at once. I like that approach."

Fouad knew better than to speak. Any protest or defense would be meaningless. It might be best if he just moved in and killed Price here and now. But he would get no closer than a few meters and then he would die, and there would be no point.

Price smiled, observing on his screen the play of Fouad's emotions. "Good boy. You're tensing in all the right places. You could be a bargaining chip if nothing else. Hell, even Little Jamey might have his use. Do we understand each other?"

"Not in the least," Fouad said.

"Get back to your bungalow."

Fouad was about to leave but Price held up his hand, an imperious gesture, accompanied by a dip of his chin and an undershot gaze.

His eyes were steely.

"Before you go, my technicians are going to strip out your chips. All of them. Won't take more than a few minutes. You can't go anywhere around here without them. As for the hijackers, if they don't hand themselves over to my people, the locals will find them. They have no love for federals."

48

Lion County

The Tahoe had come to a halt on the edge of an irrigation ditch with no water in it.

Water was scarce out here. The "tanks" were mostly empty and of course the cattle were long gone. This was a land of flyaway dirt and dusty, half-idled oil wells and gray scrub—and Mexicans flowing north, heading for anywhere but Mexico.

William was thinking about how those Mexicans could be useful.

"Something's jamming the grid," he said. "I'm not even getting GPS."

"That's illegal as hell," Curteze said.

"Let's sue Mr. Price, why don't we?" Kapp said. "What are they waiting for? We're sitting ducks. They know where we are, don't they?"

Curteze snorted. "What the hell was any of us thinking? We're out here upholding the honor of an agency that no longer exists, breaking every known law, in the middle of a state that's pretty much been abandoned by a government that's spent itself dry twice over. We're pissing off a guy who supplies decent paychecks to ninety thousand locals. Christ, you'd think we'd have better things to do."

"Shut it," Kapp said.

The boy was awake now and sitting up in the backseat, cradling his arm. William looked in the rearview mirror and saw his eyes gleaming like a trapped animal's—fright and trauma catching up.

None of them had eaten in many hours.

"Where are all the little birds?" Kapp asked, rubbing his nose, trying to keep from picking it. Their noses were dry and crusted, no matter that it was night and they were sucking down bottled water at every opportunity.

"They don't need them. They know right where we are," William said. "They're waiting to assemble a posse."

Curteze looked up at the headliner and made a face. "*Posse,*" he said.

"They're coming to take me back?" the boy asked, and his hand pinched the seat in front of him.

"Not if we have anything to say about it," William said.

He leaned back and closed his eyes. He was supposed to have been informed by now of the next step—another chance to locate and re- trieve Nabokov. But nothing had worked as planned.

Vengeance is mine, saith Axel Price and all of his rich cronies. *Do unto us—or let it be perceived that you do unto us—and we will give you a fair trial and then ship you to the Walls Unit in Huntsville.*

The boy's defense had been mounted by Justice Department attorneys—the very finest, but not used to playing criminal defense, and certainly not used to playing that game as currently allowed in the Lone Star state.

Little Jamey's attorneys had been threatened multiple times during the trial. One had his motel room firebombed by young men in pickup trucks, never identified, much less apprehended.

The judge had ruled against nearly all of the defense motions; she owed her seat to popular vote and the people owed their livelihoods to Axel Price, and she wasn't about to contradict his wishes, expressed or intuited.

The boy never had a chance.

Right now, Texas felt even more exotic than Mecca.

"Time for plan B," William said.

"Great," Kapp said "That's El Paso over there. We should have hit the state line hours ago. We should be having burgers and a beer in New Mexico."

"I can't go back," the boy said. "You guys know what that would mean." Suddenly he sounded very grown-up. "My father visited me a month ago. He said this was the worst thing he could possibly imagine—that they were going to execute his son for an accidental shooting. He said it was vengeance and not justice."

The agents in the truck watched the darkness. Low clouds had moved in and reflected some of the light from El Paso. Otherwise it was pitch-black. The truck still made a decent heat signature, of course. High-altitude birds could target them at any time.

Price had Hellfires on his drones, just like the military. Why were they still alive?

Because blasting federal agents to little bits—even agents whose agency didn't have a name any more—might look bad even for Price. No need to start a range war out here—or a new civil war. More precision action was called for—finesse, caution; hence, the delay.

Or Price was playing a crafty game of checkers, waiting to scoop them up when he could make two jumps at once.

Just as he had scheduled Little Jamey's execution to impress his gathering allies. And what did that reveal about his allies?

Calling them jackals might impugn the jackals.

"We're turning around," William said, gripping the wheel. "They know where we are, but they haven't got their act together yet. So let's drive back to Lion City."

Curteze shook his head low and wide like a cow. He groaned, then kicked at the door until the moment passed.

"That was good," Kapp said.

"Fuck you."

"There's a big meet under way," William said. "They're flying in politicians and bankers and oil sheikhs and corporate execs from around the world. They've hired hundreds of cars and trucks to transport all their guests from the airport to deluxe accommodations on the campus and at Price's ranch. The sooner we get lost in that crowd the better. They don't dare take us down in public—bad for business."

"You know too much, Agent Griffin," Kapp said, in a sinister Asiatic voice. "Who's playing who here?" He opened the door and got out. "I'm the speed demon on these rough roads. You drive like a pussy. Let's swap again and get the fuck out of here."

William swung down from the driver's seat. "Wait a sec." He went to the back and brought out a small bag.

"What the fuck is that?" Curteze asked, stretching.

"An earth-current transceiver," William said. "Interference won't block its signal—I think."

"That's not in our plan," Kapp said. "Where'd you get this shit? Who's out there listening?"

"There's a listening station outside Lion City, and supposedly there's another near El Paso. But we're way outside the normal range. Last chance." William kneeled and plunged the stake into the soil, using a small hammer to pound it deeper.

Then he hooked the battery to the amplifier and the telephone handset.

William's finger started clicking. After a couple of minutes, the answer came back in Morse. Tongue poking from between his dry lips, he penciled the words on a notepad from his shirt pocket, then read them back.

Surprise—Kunsler had been doing some last-minute thinking. Maybe the snakes hadn't made it to their target.

He kept the handset to his ear as he said to Curteze and Kapp, "I'm going back to the airport. But you're not. Your best chance is to walk. We're as close to El Paso as we're going to get. You'll just be a couple of heat blips—and the border is crawling with those. You'll blend in with the Mexicans."

"You're shitting me!" Curteze said.

William frowned—no more clicks but a tinny, scratchy voice. He waved his hand for silence.

"Highway too dangerous. Evade and hide. Ditch your vehicle. Wait outside Lion City airport. Then push through. I think you'll know when—still being arranged. That's the best chance. We're coming in. Be swift, be patient. And be there . . ."

The transmission faded into static, then the dots and dashes resumed, signaling an end to the message.

He barely recognized Kunsler's voice.

Nothing about Nabokov—nothing at all.

"We're out of options," William said.

Kapp was dismayed. "Jesus, you want us to walk in the dark?"

William flung up his hand at the sky glow. "There are the lights."

"That's nuts—"

His last words.

A bullet sang out with a melon-splitting thunk and the top of his head blew out over the truck. He dropped and piled up on the dirt, legs out, arms splayed, like a puppet with cut strings. He did not even jerk.

The boy cried out and Curteze held him down, out of the line of fire.

"Inside!" William shouted. He had already dropped the handset and climbed back into the truck to start the engine. As Curteze pushed Jamey into the backseat and then jumped on top of him, William notched the truck into grinding reverse, then spun the wheel, almost toppling the Tahoe as they bounced through a deep rut.

The cabin pitched and slammed right and left.

William continued the circle. Best to make a lot of dust. No looking back. Kapp was gone, the airport was miles off, and that likely meant they would still die—and then be erased from west Texas, the U.S. of A., this hard old world—never to be seen by anyone again.

Maybe Nabokov was already dead.

Goddamn, he had never thought Price would take it this far.

The war was on.

49

The White House

The president's chief of staff entered the room and sat at the long table across from Alicia Kunsler and beside Daniel Haze.

Rebecca had not met him before. He was a short, unimposing man with small, watchful eyes, pale skin, and a fleshy lower lip. He wore a toupee, she noticed—everyone noticed, it was a standing joke with the press corps. Nevertheless, he had a quiet confidence that showed he did not much care what people thought, or how he looked—though his suit was tailored and his soft reddish-brown loafers fit the current Beltway style—or established it.

Thalia Ripper stood by his side, laying out a series of zip pages. He looked down at them, then said, "Here's all that we've been given—all that's been presented. The president is listening to the Quinn sound file. Because Talos Corporation has been implicated in illegal and possibly treasonous activities, I've taken the precaution of removing their executive protection team and reinstating the Secret Service. Director Haze joins us for that and other reasons. Daniel, what can you tell us about Quinn's death?"

"Cumberland is keeping us out," Haze said. "Justice is pushing hard, but it's possible even some of their people don't want to know the truth. There's a lot of tendrils in law enforcement that lead straight back to Talos."

"Suicide?" the chief of staff asked.

Haze shook his head once, dubious. "He was supposed to be on suicide watch. It's a major cock-up. People all over are hiring counsel and updating their résumés."

The chief of staff allowed himself a tired grimace. "Poor bastard. What about Mr. Price?"

Kunsler removed her spex to concentrate on the people in the room. "We await the opportunity to give our report directly to the president," she said.

The chief of staff touched his earpiece and stood abruptly. "Yes, Madam President," he said. "All of us. I understand. We're on our way."

Ripper gathered up the zip pages and followed as he led them through the door. In the windowed hallway outside, Ripper spoke in low tones to the tightly assembled group. "What you're about to see must be kept strictly confidential. The president places her utmost trust in you."

Kunsler glanced at Rebecca, a peculiar look that was at once apprehensive and somehow relieved, as if she were about to share a huge burden.

"We'll be making an announcement in two days . . . if we have that long," Ripper concluded, before they entered the residence. She dropped her gaze to the floor and squared her shoulders as she opened the door to the president's bedroom.

From the opening wafted unmistakable smells of soap, antiseptic, medicine—a sickroom.

The heat struck them next—in the nineties and humid.

One by one, the chief of staff ushered them through the door, starting with Rebecca.

President Larsen looked up from a four-poster piled high with comforters and blankets. Her cheeks had sunk almost to the bone and the skin on her arms and clavicle appeared parchment-thin. Her veins and arteries stood out like a medical diagram.

"Sorry to put this off for so long," she said, and invited Rebecca closer. The president's labored breath was like a hot tropic breeze.

The change was startling—she looked more dead than alive.

50

Lion County

Little Jamey hadn't said a word since Kapp had been killed. The truck roared and bounced west along the old frontage road, followed by at least three surveillance birds—and probably soon to be tracked by larger craft, old Reapers or sleek new Condors, equipped with Hellfire missiles or worse.

William swung the truck hard left, then slammed it to a grinding halt in the middle of brush. Dust swirled.

He cleared his throat. "Best to get out here. Where I'm going, you don't want to follow."

Curteze had bitten his tongue on the last big bounce. Blood stained his lower lip. His voice was thick. "We need hostage rescue. They can't just abandon us out here. Someone has to stick their necks out and extract us."

"That isn't going to happen," William said. "We knew this was going to be tough going in."

Curteze glared out the window. "We were doing this for the old FBI. No joke. They *owe* us."

Dawn was five hours away. No extraction. No HRT. They both knew it.

"Thanks, guys," Jamey said from the backseat. His eyes were puffy, exhausted. "We still got some water, right? I can make El Paso easy."

"They'll track us down and blow us to bits!" Curteze shouted.

"The desert is full of targets—hundreds every day coming north— men, women, children," William said. "They can't track them all. Your best chance begins right here."

Jamey opened his door and got out, then walked around the Tahoe and tapped William's side window. William rolled it down.

"Hell of a ride," the boy said, and they shook hands.

Curteze looked between Jamey and William.

"You're going back to the airport?"

William nodded.

"Right now, the way this shit's going down, they don't care—they won't hesitate to blow you right off the road."

"You're probably right," William said.

Curteze swore and pushed open his door, half falling, half jumping out. He straightened and slammed the door shut. He still had some of Kapp's blood and brains on his sleeve and shoulder.

"Thanks for nothing," he said to William. "Come on, kid," he said to Jamey.

They slunk off through the brush, crouched low.

William swung the Tahoe back around, raising another big cloud of dust. That would look like panic, but also hide the pair in the brush for a few minutes, at least. Maybe the drone trackers would keep their focus on the truck.

Only idiots would jump out in the middle of nowhere.

On one deep bounce, William's head almost hit the roof of the cab. The headliner pressed his hair. Angrily, he swerved right and found the access road the GPS had said was there, back when it was still working: part gravel, part patched asphalt.

A single small car honked and veered into the shoulder as he nearly ran it down.

He roared through a dusty suburb, low flat houses on either side, parked Diesel semis surrounded by weeds. This was within a mile of where he had started. And here, it seemed a good time to talk to himself, just to keep up the illusion of company.

"I'll head to the airport and hope for the best. Planes coming in at all hours. Limos going 24/7," he said. "They won't take *that* risk."

To this, he answered, "Hell, they'd gladly blow me up in front of everybody, take me out with a pinpoint blast—call it a tactical *demonstration*.

"Two miles from the airport. There's the highway."

The highway was almost deserted. No line of cars blocked his path. Somehow, he had evaded Price's posse—or the posse had split up, pulled back, not to alarm the incoming guests. A bunch of good ol' boys in pickup trucks, standing up with assault rifles locked and loaded . . .

Through the dusty windshield, he saw a glint in the high sunlight of the coming dawn: a big drone at about a thousand feet, doing aerobatic loops.

"Fucking angel of death," he said.

William slowed and then gunned the truck up the frontage road. The road joined with an onramp to the highway. There were headlights ahead; at this hour, it had to be either ranch trucks or traffic from the Lion City airport.

A big black limo passed on his left.

He grunted. "An audience," he said, and wiped his mouth. Two more limos and a phalanx of eight or nine shiny black SUVs swooped by.

William could no longer see the high glint. He easily imagined the drone stooping like a hawk, then flinched and almost swerved off the road as a midsize jet roared overhead: a beautiful Citation making its final approach. It sported Arabic markings. The Texans and Saudis had always had a lot in common: deserts, guts, tribes, and oil.

Now he was passing pretty thick traffic on the other side of the four-lane road. Everyone arriving, no one leaving. If he stayed in the left hand lane, near the oncoming limos, someone would have to be very confident in their targeting skills—or very stupid—to try to take him out.

The truck or its debris—a flying tire or chunk of cab, even a body, William could see that clearly enough—could easily vault the divide and go through the windshield of a visiting prince in exile.

The Tahoe was much quieter on the highway. The smooth ride was unnerving. William could imagine all sorts of noises.

He turned his head left and stiffened up like a rail. "Well, looky who's here," he said. The drone was less than twenty feet to his right, flaps down, swinging like a huge seagull to keep pace. "Cannon, 20 mil, front turret mount," he added, as if admiring the features of a good-looking sports car. "And—yep—two Hellfires." He was half drunk with fear. "What idiot sold these cowboys tactical weapons?"

The highway up ahead was almost empty.

A lag in the airport traffic.

The drone dropped back, long wings wagging as if in warning.

William hunched over. He knew what was coming. These guys were happy to put on a show. He saw a spark in his rearview mirror, braked the Tahoe hard, skidding and fishtailing on the road, then threw open his door and jumped out—at thirty miles an hour. He tried to roll like a pro but got caught up in a painful rubber tangle of arms and legs.

He ended up on his back.

The Tahoe cruised on for a hundred feet, driver's door swinging, and was swiftly intersected by a brilliant streak corkscrewing from the rear.

The truck flew up a column of fire like some awful flaming insect, then fell back spinning and burning, lighting up the highway and the west Texas landscape.

51

The White House

"The bullets killed me after all," the president said, motioning for Rebecca to take the chair beside her heavily blanketed bed. "Have you ever heard of something called a synthobe?"

"I have," Rebecca said.

"Do tell."

The chief of staff and Thalia Ripper stared in undisguised shock at their president. Alicia Kunsler, Daniel Haze, an Air Force colonel, and several others Rebecca did not know waited at the back of the bedroom like guilty children, unable to decide what to do with themselves, other than numbly watch.

"Little factories," Rebecca said. "They were used in the soft drink canisters that blew up the Los Angeles Convention Center. Like bacteria, only more efficient at doing one thing."

"Well, in me, they're efficient at making a poison," Larsen said. "Synthobes were in the bullets that didn't quite kill me. They're destroying my connective tissue, strand by strand. First I'll freeze up like I'm made of stone. My lungs will seize. Then my heart will stop. I've got a day, maybe two. My doctors tell me there's nothing they can do. I've listened to Quinn's confession—'Two-step assassination,' he calls it. He knew about it more than a year ago." She looked up, still hoping it was all a nightmare. "Is it really Eddie on the file, Thalia?"

"That's been confirmed, Madam President," Ripper said.

"He wanted to be president—but my God, what would there be left to be president of? First blow—shooting me—knocks the markets down a peg. Second blow—timed with a series of other strikes . . . my unexpected death, after an apparent recovery. Like clockwork. And then everything will go to hell. All at the same hour, in the same news cycle—with MSARC looking over the world's shoulder. Do you know what else Price has arranged for?"

"We're receiving that data now," Alicia Kunsler said. "Jane Rowland is in Texas sending it back to us."

"And where is she getting it?"

"From the blood of an agent, smuggled out in a snake," Kunsler said.

Larsen's barking laugh turned into a fit of coughing. "Give me the fairy-tale stuff slowly, please, and warn me when it's coming," she said, half strangled. The chief of staff handed her the first of the zip pages. She read it with jerky motions. "We do get clever," she said, her chest still heaving, then took a puff from an inhaler and looked around the room. "One guess who's behind all this."

Her eyes had difficulty tracking both the zip paper and the people around her. Her vision was going.

"No need to guess," Kunsler said, and touched her earpiece. "MSARC has definitely been compromised."

"Devil's bargain from the beginning," the chief of staff said.

The president weakly waved her hand as if shooing flies.

Kunsler synopsized. "Price will in effect throw a switch from his office—and instantly control more than a third of America, through his proxies: non-nationals, banks, hedge funds in other countries."

"Is that all it takes?" Larsen asked.

"MSARC's judgment will be triggered by assassination and sabotage," Kunsler continued. "Compromised security, military personnel and police officers—"

An aide entered the room with a portable display pad and placed it delicately on the president's lap. "She can read it for herself," she said in a reverent whisper.

"Talk normal. I'm not dead, for Christ's sake—not yet," Larsen growled, and held the display closer. "Price has stationed snipers around key stations on the power grid, with deep-steel penetrating rounds, ready to take out custom-made transformer components that will require months to replace . . . Total power collapse across North America."

The president handed the display to her chief of staff. He took up the report as if joining in the family reading of a last will and testament.

"We'll be back in the dark ages. Then—the *coup de grâce*. MSARC will declare the U.S. financial situation dire and call back all our loans, the flexible bonds, cancel contingent purchase of bonds . . . all of it, America insolvent, incapable of paying its bills internally or externally, triggering a massive retreat from American investment—whatever's left by then. He'll declare most of the south financially and politically independent—from Kentucky and Tennessee down to Louisiana and Florida—whether the states agree or not. He's stockpiled the components necessary to repair the power grid—on a state-by-state basis. States that opt in get back their power sooner—days, not months— and become part of Price's governing coalition."

She controlled another fit of coughing, then took a glass of water from Ripper. "Singapore, Amman, Beijing, Dubai, Qatar, and the Saudis in exile will offer to extend financial aid and give Price the mandate to repair the situation. He'll have autonomy. And that will be the end of the United States of America. Pretty sweet, huh?"

The chief of staff balled his hands into fists. "They'll rejoice. They'll dance around a bonfire of civil rights and try Abe Lincoln for war crimes."

Rebecca listened in growing shock. The room seemed to be getting larger—more detail, harder to process. She blinked and wiped her eyes. Difficult to concentrate with so much to see. Her eyes hurt.

"My options are few and desperate," the president said, leaning forward. Ripper removed her pillows and plumped them. "We can't protect everything—we can't move that many troops fast enough, and in some states, the National Guard has already declared independence from federal rule. They answer only to sympathetic governors. Poor Governor Kinchley in Idaho—looks like she's first on their takedown list. The military will refuse to conduct any sort of preemptive strike within sovereign U.S. territory. Some of the joint chiefs sympathize with Price. All but one or two of the rest treat me with contempt. The generals know that a third of the troops would go over to Price. Maybe more. It doesn't help that we're months behind on payroll."

"What can we do, Madam President?" Kunsler asked.

"Tell us what's happening in Texas," Larsen said.

"They're gathering in Lion City," Kunsler said, "getting ready to throw one big party—all the would-be rulers of the world. The financiers, the politicians, the scientists and engineers . . . state's rights fanatics and amoral opportunists and every shade in between. Protected by Price's most loyal soldiers, as well as cadres of mercenaries from Haiti. They're practically daring us to drop a nuke on them."

The president crossed her arms over her knees for support, to relieve the pain in her stiffening back. "I refuse to be the first president to nuke Texas. I still have one or two friends down there. Options?"

Kunsler and Haze seemed to share something unknown to the others in the room. "Madam President," Kunsler said, "the Bureau has been working with loyal elements in the intelligence community and the military to keep track of the situation both in Texas and Geneva— a clandestine surveillance program centered on MSARC. We began contingency planning three years ago, when the loan documents were signed—by you—in secret."

"Congress and I had no choice," Larsen said. "We were heading over a deficit cliff."

"A general at Bolling Air Force base has offered a possible solution," the chief of staff said, "ready to deploy—on your express command, and upon a presidential finding of gross civilian insurrection. These officers are his representatives."

"What is this solution?"

The colonel stepped forward. "Generally speaking, less than lethal, but terribly inconvenient for any high-tech operation—and very clever."

"I really hate *clever*," the president murmured.

"Given the terrain and the technological savvy of Talos—and their fanatic devotion to surveillance and security—our device can incapacitate a high percentage of their personnel. And destroy virtually all electronic capability within the affected area."

"You'd shut down their computers," Kunsler said.

"Damned near everything that runs on chips and wires," the colonel said, and handed the chief of staff another zip page, which he passed to the president.

From her chair beside the bed, Rebecca caught a glimpse of what looked like flaming donuts.

"*Tesla bombs,*" the president murmured. "*Jerichos. Brights.* Where *do* they get these names?"

"Technically known as TEMPs, Tactical Electromagnetic Pulse," the colonel said.

The president nodded when she was finished. The colonel retrieved the zip pages and wiped them by breaking their corners.

"To complete our mission," Kunsler said, "I'm prepared to offer volunteers from the Bureau's Hostage Rescue Team to enter Talos and destroy their capacity to cause us more harm. Also, we have plans to secure all necessary evidence, in case this should ever become a matter of public controversy."

The colonel said, "On your express order the Air Force will authorize transfer—"

"I so command," the president said. "Colonel, if our good general needs a signed paper, hand me a pen. Screw the rest of the protocol. We're all way outside the law here. On my head be it—I'll be dead in a few hours, anyway."

The chief of staff summed it up. "Certain loyal officers in the Pentagon are arranging for the loan of a hardened and stealthy executive transport aircraft. Secret Service and Air Force will transfer two Brights from Air Force One to supplement our aircraft's current capabilities. Looks as if we have a hundred or so military and agency volunteers, happy to beg, borrow, or steal the necessary equipment and fly or drive it to Texas. Up against ten thousand of Price's best troops and security—his own private army."

"Nothing can save me," Larsen said. "But a few of you, working together, can save this country. How many in this room are ready to step up and put an end to this travesty?"

Kunsler counted around the bedroom. "You can't go, sir," she said to the chief of staff. "Nor you, Ms. Ripper. The president needs you, and very likely we're all going to get killed.

"Nor you, I regret to say, Madam President."

Everyone had raised their hands.

"Hell, I wanted to fly a fighter one last time," Larsen said. "Rebecca Rose. We've been here before, you and me, haven't we?"

"Yes ma'am."

"As much as possible, this needs to be a civilian operation—law enforcement, not military invasion."

"Pretty fine distinction," the colonel said.

The president ignored him.

"You and director Kunsler share operational command. Rebecca, you lead HRT into Talos and rescue our agents. And along the way, please convey my message to Axel Price. On occasion, the tree of freedom needs to be watered by the blood of arrogant bastards. Nobody can fucking *own* America."

She fell back onto the pillows and was beset by another fit of coughing. Flecks of pink appeared on Ripper's kerchief as she held it to the president's lips.

The White House physician pushed through and ordered them out of the room. "She's a human being, not a robot! She needs some rest. Give her peace, for God's sake."

Rebecca caught Larsen's eye just before leaving. The president gave her a trembling thumbs up, then was hidden from view by nurses and the closing door.

The chief of staff escorted them back into the hall. He wiped his eyes with the back of his hand. "Raphkind's probably going to be sworn in as president tomorrow morning. He hasn't been briefed. Knowing him, he wouldn't agree to any of this, anyway. He might even strike a deal with Price. If this team can't get itself organized and do the job, our nation is worse than dead. Alicia, Daniel—thanks. Rebecca, I know you by reputation—an amazing reputation, I must say. You've all put up with a trainload of grief on behalf of this country. Only true patriots . . ." He stopped for a moment, genuinely choked up, perhaps for the first time in his political career. In embarrassment, he lightly slapped his own face. "Excuse me. This is going to be a hard night."

Kunsler gripped Rebecca's arm as Haze led them to staff cars. "If I'd had a choice, I would have brought you in six months ago," she said under her breath. "You won't believe who's waiting for us down there. Like old times."

"Damn," Rebecca said. The whole world seemed huge—massive clouds in an impossibly vivid sky the size of six or seven ordinary lifetimes.

"We're going to be in Texas in less than four hours. Any messages I can send?"

"Not a one," Rebecca said, ducking her head as she sat in the limo.

"The Bureau's operation in Lion City . . . we're in this with Spider/ Argus, and there are two parts," Kunsler said, sliding in beside her. "One of the parts, Nabokov, delivered the information we needed, but the agent cannot withdraw. What—you know this already?" Kunsler looked prepared to be pissed off.

"Vladimir Nabokov loved butterflies," Rebecca said, shielding her eyes against the glare of headlights through the tinted windows.

"Right," Kunsler said, pulling back her irritation. "The other part is strictly hail Mary, and it's not going well. Let's join our HRT boys. I told them about Mecca, and they all want to meet you."

"Great," Rebecca said.

"I'll fill you in on the plane."

52

Over Arkansas

High in the air, leaning back in the white leather seat with eyes closed, keeping it together—

Not having a family or a kid is just another word for nothing left to lose. And now I'm losing that. Flying high, surrounded by brave men and women, duty bound—honor bound . . . Chosen by the president of the United States. Just like Mecca. Don't want to belong, don't need to belong. Gave it all up ages ago, just didn't know it.

"Rebecca."

She opened her eyes. Kunsler sat in the seat next to her.

"One hour," she said. "We've had a blip from William Griffin."

"He's still alive?"

"As of a few hours ago."

Rebecca glanced around the cramped cabin of the Air Force Lockheed C-99 Swanjet. Supersonic and bristling with countermeasures, designed to transport secretaries of defense or state or whoever else needed to fly into potentially hostile territory, on the brink of wartime—and fly back out again.

Stealthy, infrared diffuse—no more or less frigid than the air around it—and if pressed, capable of creating its own extreme difficulties for any and all attackers.

Haze walked down the narrow aisle and stooped beside them. "Thirty minutes until we're over Lion City," he said. "The president's slipped into a coma. Raphkind is being moved to the White House. He'll be briefed within the hour."

"We have to be finished before he's sworn in," Kunsler said, and laid out the battle plans on the polished maple tray table between her and Rebecca.

Haze looked down at the plans, then forward to the five agents of the Hostage Rescue Team, sitting in their black pants and T-shirts, going through their third equipment check of the flight—and brandishing recently bandaged arms. Haze pulled up his sleeve to display his own bandaged wrist. "We just bonded, me and your boys, slicing out our weapon chips. For me, one in each arm. Ambidextrous. Deep little buggers."

"I never had mine implanted," Kunsler said, and glanced at Rebecca.

"Belt," Rebecca said. "Skin current."

"Well, we were macho," Haze said. "According to our intel, every weapon within a hundred miles of Axel Price is ID'd to its owner. Won't fire without an implanted chip. You know what Lion City and environs is like. *Everyone* has a chip of one sort or another. More interesting, Lion County is littered with billions of the little buggers—for surveillance and tracking. Price is some kind of fanatic. And I'm just wondering—"

He looked again at Kunsler, tense and fragile as a china doll, and decided to rein in his enthusiasm.

"Sorry. Combat high. Ladies, time to buckle up. Talos has a lot of UAVs buzzing around. Not that this little marvel can't hold its own. But after our Brights are released, we'll be the only thing in the sky."

"You've flown on this airplane before," Kunsler said, peering with a squint through the tiny window.

"Oh, yes," Haze said. "Three years ago. Accompanying the SecDef and the vice president to Jordan. Probably part of that loan program thing, now that I think of it. Comes equipped with its own Bright. With the pair we borrowed from Air Force One, that gives us three. Should get the job done and then some." Haze grinned—in his element, ready for payback. He moved forward to be with the HRT.

Rebecca could hardly feel what he was feeling—or much of anything at all. How could she rely on instinct—when instinct was being rewritten?

Hell of a time to go into action.

Kunsler gripped her arm and tightened her fingers.

"You still with us?"

"Yes."

"You're the only one available to me with similar experience."

"Texas, Arabia . . . All the same?"

Kunsler grinned. "You know what I mean." The longer Rebecca knew her, the more the deputy director resembled a compact, vigilant falcon.

Rebecca pulled her chair forward and buckled up. "Saving one of my students is certainly important."

"Two, actually," Kunsler said. "Nabokov is Fouad Al-Husam."

Rebecca closed her eyes. Fouad, William, Jane Rowland—all had accompanied her to Mecca to find and eliminate a rogue former FBI agent with a plan to make the entire world forget its hatred, its religious bigotry—and all of its past.

To forget everything.

Peter Periglas had been executive officer aboard the USS *Heinlein*, which had taken them into the Red Sea, and from which they had flown to Mecca. Fouad and William saw the worst of the action and physically suffered the most—but got the job done.

And yet she was the one to come down with PTSD.

"Haze tells me you had another contact with Nathaniel Trace before we met with the president," Kunsler said. "What did he want?"

"He knows what your crying little boy is."

"And that would be?"

"Something called Jones. A high-powered problem solver, pattern recognizer. It's an integral part of MSARC. Modified in secret to follow the programmed orders of Axel Price. But Jones is acting pretty independent. Maybe he's had a change of . . . software. Motive. Heart."

"Interesting," Kunsler said. "Before she left for El Paso, Jane Rowland mentioned brilliant glitches. She says whatever it is might be better than Spider/Argus at surveilling the net. If we just left it all alone, does Trace think Jones would scuttle Price's plan?"

"He can't be certain."

Kunsler cleared her throat. "What's Trace going to do?"

"I can't tell you," Rebecca said, "because he wouldn't tell me. But he's heading for Texas, too. Farther south. Should be there by now."

"Do you know anything about him, really? Do you trust him?"

"Trust is not part of the calculation," Rebecca said.

"I hate this," Kunsler said. "I hate knowing shit like this. Better to be ignorant and focus."

Rebecca agreed the situation was less than ideal.

Aft of the VIP seats and the rudimentary galley, the two Air Force weapons officers pushed open an equipment hatch—access to luggage space on most of these jets—and wriggled their way back to prepare their equipment—the three Brights.

As they had been briefed before the flight, in very little technical detail, Brights consisted of thin concentric layers of high explosives and classified electronics wrapped around altitude-maintaining balloons—aerostats. They had never been tested in real-world situations—in combat.

Their effects were too widespread and drastic.

The jet began its final approach—a long curve to the south with a spiral loop at the end.

Rebecca unbuckled and moved forward to confer with the Hostage Rescue Team. They had placed all their communications equipment and electronics in a shielded and grounded plastic box. Their weapons were stored in another grounded enclosure, built into the forward luggage compartment. They would don their armor once the plane was on the ground—it presently filled a trunk strapped down in the small rest area.

The typical HRT Lynx-networked diagnostic undergarments had been dispensed with—too many wires and sensors.

Rebecca put her hand on the shoulder of the team commander, a hefty thirty-two-year-old from Montana named Calvin Forester. Forester had Sioux ancestry, his file proudly proclaimed.

"Any idea what we're going to run into down there, ma'am?" he asked Rebecca. His face was shiny but he looked confident.

"Hell on Earth for bad guys, I hope," Rebecca said. "A lot of pissed-off people, hopefully without much in the way of guns."

"What are the chances we'll locate our agents?"

"Tiny," Rebecca said.

"Director Haze seems to think he should be in charge," Forester said. The team members looked up with expressions that mixed hope and respect. They'd have all preferred Haze—and so would Rebecca, but—

"We have our orders," she said.

Forester knocked on another protected box in the seat beside him— their key to thieving a big ride, once they were on the ground. "These Brights—they'll crisp their machines, right? Just like fryers taking out bots?"

"Same idea, I think," Rebecca said. "But huge."

"And we do the rest?"

"Right."

Kunsler came forward.

"She's gone," she said, barely audible above the steady deep pulse of the jets. "President Eve Carol Larsen . . . 7:15 A.M., East Coast time. We're on our own now. We're orphans."

"To a brave lady," Forester said, slowly lifting his hand in salute. "To our president."

The team did the same, saluting as one.

Haze stood behind Kunsler with a bottle of water in one hand and a stack of cups in the other. He poured, his hand shaking ever so slightly, and they toasted their fallen leader.

"Bad day," he said. "Soon to get a whole lot better."

53

The Smoky

Schmitz's Torq-Vee and two others had remained parked in front of Fouad's bungalow, as if the game was reaching its inevitable conclusion—as if fate or death was in the air.

Fouad sat in the living room's shadows, feeling the adhesive tug of bandages on his wrists and a cold sting as the local anesthetic faded—one of Schmitz's small mercies.

Schmitz seemed to be according him the same respect he would a dog about to be put to sleep. He had cut out all three of Fouad's Talos ID chips with swift strokes of a scalpel. Now Fouad could not go anywhere on the Smoky or the campus—or in much of Lion City—without setting off alarms.

He was more than an outcast. Price had removed his mark. Fouad was no longer part of the tribe, and that meant, around here, he was no longer human.

He estimated there were at least twelve men positioned around the bungalow. They could easily sweep in and kill him without disturbing guests in the other bungalows—politicians, bankers and financiers, the Saudi prince in exile—gathering for Price's investiture.

Fouad maintained calm through controlled breathing and other exercises that both prepared and removed distractions—part of Sufi discipline. If possible, he would not be led off to execution without a fight. Perhaps he could take with him one or more of the guests . . .

But that was fantasy. Schmitz was too smart, too well trained.

He got up from the rattan chair at the sound of feet coming around under the bungalow's windows, up to the rear patio door—and then the front door.

The door opened. Two of Schmitz's Haitians entered first—lithe, with fine dark features under small green caps. They had been in Fouad's classes, receiving language instruction. They sported black shirts, holstered SIGs, yellow stripes on their sleeves, khaki pants, and high black boots, perfectly polished.

Fouad watched with languid eyes.

Schmitz came in behind them. He swung his chin and nodded to the door. "Mr. Al-Husam, time for the festivities," he said. "Mr. Price insists you stay close."

Fouad walked slowly between the Haitians. They prepared leg irons and wrist cuffs linked by chain—standard Smith and Wesson restraints, not the most up-to-date design, he thought.

He knew of ways . . .

Schmitz seemed to hear his thoughts. "I have respect," he said. "Show me some, too—no stupid heroics."

54

Corpus Christi, Texas

The Vertexion building rose thirty-five stories over the surrounding beachfront hotels and houses, flat islands and causeways, clusters of condos and light industrial development—an outrageous silver spire facing the troubled early morning ocean.

Right and left of the spire sat seven low concrete structures, arranged like Venetian blinds laid on end, behind which rose three strange horizontal horns like giant jai alai scoops.

"What's your name again, sir?" the uniformed guard asked. His name was Carlos, according to his brass name tag, and he stood behind a high steel podium, with a stool to sit on when things got slow.

"Sangstrom," Nathaniel said. "Robert Sangstrom."

Vertexion was a little-known but important point of entry for Mexican and South American IT traffic of all sorts—and thus an important node for MSARC's information-gathering network.

"I see you haven't visited in two years, Mr. Sangstrom," Carlos said, and spun around a small, palm-size wireless screen that mirrored some of the security display. Carlos always spoke with a broad smile. "Good to have you back. I have messages from five people on the fifteenth floor—they'll be happy to know you've arrived, and look forward to the meeting later this morning. Very early, sir."

Outside the wide wall of windows, beyond a pebbled flat walkway and a feathery low wall of saltbush, the Gulf of Mexico threw five-foot combers onto a dark-shrouded beach protected by riprap—mounded chunks of rebar-studded concrete.

The predawn sky had filled with wooly black mounds of wet cloud. Thick drops spat on the window glass with metallic tinks. Corpus Christi was getting a wet peck of a kiss—and nothing more. All that moisture would swing northeast over north Florida and into Georgia and dump itself there, making Atlanta once again as wet as Seattle—and stealing life from all but a northern wedge of Mexico.

"Pleasure is all mine," Nathaniel said. "I'd like to take a shower before the meeting."

"Certainly. Mr. Jones seems to have moved into his new office—he has opened it for your convenience. There's a full bathroom and a wet bar. The floor hostess will fill you in on the rest of the amenities, and direct you to the meeting room when the time comes."

"Thank you, Carlos," Nathaniel said. "Scan my chips here?"

"Mr. Jones indicates that won't be necessary," Carlos said, and switched off the gently humming security bar. "He confirms visual ID."

Nathaniel passed through the deactivated detectors, afforded the same treatment as a senior executive or a visiting dignitary. He carried no luggage.

Carlos had never met Mr. Jones. Such was the power of privilege—executive systems were almost always the favored point of entry for industrial espionage and sabotage. Executives hated to be bothered with fussy security—and hated worse being admonished by nerds.

"Fifteenth floor," Carlos reminded him, and stared with a puzzled sort of longing through the wide windows at Nathaniel's metallic blue Bentley. Rain beaded like clear glass game markers on the fresh wax.

Nathaniel hummed a Bee Gees tune as he rode the fast elevator to the seventeenth floor—not the fifteenth. He had thirty minutes. If Jones was with him—and so far, that seemed a solid supposition—the entire dataflow monitoring system for Latin America would soon require a maintenance technician's timely attention.

That lapse in the bitstream would ripple around the world, up the line to Geneva, and MSARC would enter a mode of vigilant relaxation.

The same type of unauthorized portal that Jane Rowland had exploited, but on a much larger scale. The Quiet Man would have been amused and perhaps chagrinned to learn that Spider / Argus had long been aware of his private backdoor into Talos.

For over an hour, in essence, MSARC would see and hear much, but would not render any important decisions.

Nathaniel had told Jones—who did not speak now, only listened—that the Quiet Man would have wanted it this way.

55

The Smoky

Schmitz and the Haitians led Fouad into another wing of Price's domicile, a seemingly endless labyrinth of hallways and rooms that could never be fully explored or resolved.

Against a backdrop of a wall covered with Western paintings—horses and cowboys settling their differences, with much dust—Price was conferring with two men in expensive and perfectly tailored suits—two distinctive, silken shades of twenty-first-century gray. One was Asian, probably Chinese, but the other was definitely of classic Yemeni Arab lineage, likely of the Banu Hanifa—a prominent member of the house of Saud, perhaps the Prince in Exile himself.

Fouad did not immediately recognize him, but pictures of the prince had been forbidden since the overthrow of the Hejaz and the subsequent founding of Arabia Deserta, administered by the six-nation Muslim Council. He had put on weight and grown a neatly trimmed goatee and mustache.

Relaxed, chatting and smiling, they turned as Fouad approached. The Chinese continued to smile, but the Saudi's face went stony.

"Who is this Egyptian?" he asked Price, who watched with some amusement.

"One of my instructors," Price said. "Excuse me, gentlemen. Just a couple of matters to resolve, then we'll continue." He gestured toward a plump black man in white livery. "Breakfast for our guests, Lionel?"

"This way, gentlemen," the servant said, and led the pair through a double door into an adjacent dining room.

"The prince didn't recognize you," Price said. "Odd—since he's put a rich price on your head—in secret, of course. I thought I'd bring you up to date on a number of matters we discussed earlier. It seems our kidnapping situation has resolved itself. Everyone's dead. Blown right off the airport road."

Schmitz and the Haitians walked beside and behind Fouad as Price led them down another hallway, yet another part of his maze. "Nobody's happy with the way that turned out, but the feds took the situation out of our hands."

Price opened the door to an interior room about ten feet square, richly paneled in dark wood, with a huge gleaming vault safe mounted in the rear wall. Antique prints of butterflies were illuminated by gently glowing ceiling spots—exquisite dabs of blue, green, and red. The room smelled of lemon oil and something Fouad couldn't quite identify—musty and repellent.

Price spun the combination, turned the vault wheel, and swung the steel door aside.

"My pride and joy—outside my family, of course. I do my best thinking here. Come on in."

The thick vault door wafted another sickly wave of odor—camphor laid over the ancient decay of myriads of tiny lives.

The vault was bigger than many houses, filled wall to ceiling with beautiful wooden cases fronted by nearly invisible glass. In the cases reposed tens of thousands of butterflies, arranged not in scientific order, but according to size and then color—dead but vibrant rows sweeping from duns and browns to one side, through reds, blues, and greens, to case after case of shining white.

Price chuckled at Fouad's wrinkled nose.

"Some of my contacts in Washington have penetrated your veil, if not your actual plan, Mr. Al-Husam. But I'm going to take one last swing at conversion. After all, my culture, your culture, we have a lot in common. My country has been occupied for a hundred and sixty years. Oh, we pretend we're used to it—we're polite to guests, and we're natural patriots. We even send our boys to die for the cause of the occupiers—because we share temporary needs and goals, not because we truly belong.

"Ask why all the fuss about the second amendment and a well-regulated militia—well, it was never about keeping arms to fight foreign invaders. It was about taking up arms against the government. That's our instinct. We hate government, any government, our own most of all. Our politics has always been guerrilla politics—fast and dirty. Best to lie low and always be ready to move. Maybe that's you, too.

"It was inevitable, after a few rocky decades, that the Islamic world and my people would find common ground and make alliances. We're both highly religious—both warrior cultures. We both kept slaves. It was our due. Then—the world changed. Now I'm going to help set it right.

"That's what's happening out there now. We're celebrating a new relationship, a new world. Your people—well, they'd like nothing better than to be rid of both the westerners and the Jews. Real thorns in their sides. So I will no longer support Israel—that's that. Your people—"

"My people are diverse," Fouad said.

Price leaned back into the far corner of the vault, and folded his arms. "Your daddy told his bosses over and over again they were screwing up. That's why he never advanced much in the CIA. Always a foot soldier. Have you been candid with *your* bosses?"

"On occasion," Fouad said.

"I doubt it," Price said. "You've never told them the truth. The *kafir* world itches your hide like a dug-in tick. Push out the West and you can find your own maturity—whether it's the Caliphate or something else entirely, I don't care. Once the Jews are out of Jerusalem and the Middle East, our dispute will be over. Your people will have enough on their plates to occupy them for generations to come."

"I am a citizen of this country," Fouad said. "My patriotism is not a shallow thing. Perhaps you can no more speak for your people than that Wahhabi can speak for all Muslims."

"That Wahhabi, as you call him—though I wouldn't use that slur to his face—that very fine Saudi gentleman doesn't know who you are. All he has is a few fuzzy pictures taken in Mecca, of all places. You, in the company of non-Muslims, killing the faithful by calling down fire from heaven. But if I put a name to those fuzzy pictures, you'll make a dandy gift, tied up with a nice big ribbon, for any would-be protector of the sacred cities. Unless . . ."

Fouad could no longer tolerate the smell in the vault. He stepped back, chains rustling, and bumped up against Schmitz, who stood with his pistol drawn—a formidable armored pillar. Fouad guessed the man's weight at 240, all muscle—but ten years older.

"Never," Fouad said.

Price shrugged. He followed Fouad out of the vault and swung the door shut with another cold sigh of insect decay. "Maybe real power is forever out of reach for a cultural half-breed like you. In which case . . . a rich reward. One hundred million euros. Truth to tell, I'd love to stick a pin through a true-blue federal morpho."

The vault locked and the combination reset.

"The next few hours are going to be impressive," Price said. "Pomp and circumstance."

Schmitz grabbed Fouad with two strong hands. The Haitians stood by in case Fouad struggled, but he was quiet, watchful, measuring with spread hands and rapid flicks of his eyes.

He slowly increased the tension on the chain.

Eighty centimeters from cuffs to leg irons.

A gift—for the right moment.

"From now on, sensible, moral people have little to fear," Price said, his blue eyes like hot little jewels masked in shadow. "Immoral people—that's a different story. They should run and hide. We're coming for them—and we've got the goods."

56

Over Lion County

Rebecca felt her ears pop.

The spiral grew tighter, until the plane banked almost on wingtip. The dry scrub and flat desert around Lion City spread below the little window beside her seat: grainy and tawny, too sharply detailed, like a mold-spotted pelt. Trails and road tracks cut long, skinny scars on the land. The boundaries of the window soothed her eyes—she did not have to look at everything all at once.

The weapons officer wedged and huffed his way forward in the tilted cabin. He carried a remote trigger—a small black wand with a square display. "Bright number one away at three thousand meters," he said. "It'll descend to a thousand, then inflate and maintain. Next two are on auto. Got any electronics you didn't declare back at the airport? I mean *anything*. This is going to be a wide-spectrum pulse."

Kunsler, across the narrow aisle, shook her head. Rebecca did the same. Haze did not dignify the question with an answer, simply held up his bandaged arms.

The pilot spoke over the intercom. "Blackouts starting in the northwest. Homeland Security is calling international code red. Not our work, of course—must be Price's snipers taking out their first power stations—but it fits our needs. Command is out to all military and civilian aviation—ground your planes.

"There's a Gulfstream G950 requesting clearance at JPB, last one in the air. I count twenty-three fancy birds already on the apron—maybe one is hard. The rest are about to become junk."

The weapons officer addressed the cabin. "Bright in five minutes. Sit inboard—fold your arms, don't lean against the cabin walls, and keep your feet on the rests provided."

He took his own seat and leaned over to look back at Kunsler and Rebecca. "The town east of us will suck up a pretty big dose," he said. "Anything within a hundred miles—cars, trucks, UAVs—is going to sizzle and stall. Discharge is minimal—like really bad static—not deadly unless you're holding a cable or standing on a rail line. But lots of people have MedAug these days—"

"Pacemakers for heart and brain, hearing aids, older model stents," the second officer said. "We've never worked a scenario where everyone stayed upright and healthy." He braced with his boots and shook his head in honest pity.

Then he dropped deftly into a seat, strapped in, and assumed the proper position.

57

The Smoky

Schmitz and his two Haitians hauled Fouad aside in the hallway beyond the butterfly vault room and with a fair degree of firmness, but no malice, positioned him against a concrete wall.

Schmitz took out a small syringe and swiftly injected it through the sleeve into Fouad's arm.

"Bring him down to the ballroom in five minutes," Price ordered, whisking by with two other guards.

Fouad guessed the drug, saw the size of the dose, and quickly estimated its effect on a man of his body mass and age. Not good—an hour of confusion and weakness, and no doubt they would then drug him again.

"I wish they'd keep me better informed," Schmitz muttered, his mouth close to Fouad's ear. "This whole Mecca thing—that's legendary. Nobody knew whether it actually happened that way or not—but here you are. You saved the whole damned city, didn't you? A man with those talents, a man who survives that sort of mission, is a man to be admired—not paraded around like a prize monkey. You deserve better, Mr. Al-Husam. But it ain't going to happen. Not today."

Fouad's vision fogged slightly and his legs almost collapsed. As he struggled to stay upright, the Haitians supported him by his elbows. Schmitz had cuffed his hands in front, another small mercy—and a potentially deadly softness.

His chains made dull music as they hauled him toward the ballroom.

* * *

The main ballroom of the Smoky was the size of a basketball arena
and sometimes doubled as one: prime red oak floor under gracefully arched cedar beams supporting a high curved roof, those
beams now richly festooned with banners in Chinese and Arabic
and Russian.

Long golden streamers dangled and twirled as the room quickly
filled with at least a hundred and fifty well-dressed men and about a
third as many women.

Schmitz escorted Fouad up a ramp and onto a gallery riser, several
feet above the floor, where a single red-draped table and four chairs
had hastily been arranged, illuminated by a single high spot.

They sat and a waiter promptly brought a pitcher of punch and four
glasses.

Fouad woozily surveyed the incongruities.

"I think these good people hoped they might sleep in this morning," Schmitz observed.

The Haitians nodded agreement. "It is very early," one observed,
his voice deep, mellifluous.

The ballroom crowd consisted of Middle Easterners, Europeans,
Russians, Asians, and a few Indonesians, all having just arrived or
been politely roused from their cabins in the last hour.

Ten white men in slacks and sports coats, who might have been
Russian or Middle European and who might have been more comfortable in uniform, kept to one side of the floor, watching with irritated
frowns. They did not like crowds or pageantry. Possibly they had not
reckoned on the scale of Axel Price's plans.

Serious men—men of might, international finance, and worldly
consequence—did not relish the prospect of all the rules changing
at once.

A slow waltz was piped into the ballroom and after a moment
of hesitation six couples started to dance halfheartedly to a steady
beat in the center of the floor. Fouad could hardly believe this specta-
cle. It almost made him doubt their sanity—or his. *So familiar—but
from where?*

Another group of older men—without women—entered from the reception area. These seemed contented with their present lot in life but more pleased still by the shining prospects.

Even in his present state, Fouad recognized a senator, a congressman, and an admiral—a member of the joint chiefs. He fought back against a muzzy tide of anger—not productive. Not efficient.

"Bastards," Schmitz grumbled as he pushed back his chair. "Whatever your loyalties, traitors always stink up a place."

Fouad could not entirely understand this man, but here was yet no opportunity—no weakness and no vacillation.

"Undignified," Schmitz added, and poured Fouad a glass of punch. "You'll want to keep drinking. Those drugs can do a job on your kidneys."

One of the new arrivals, the senator—an elderly man with pale blue eyes and a shock of brown hair that poked over his forehead—was escorted to their small table by a blond woman in a long, purple dress.

"Mr. Price has been telling us all about you. I just wanted to shake your hand, sir, on this fortuitous day," the senator said with a big grin, and held out his plump paw. He raised his eyebrows at the sound of the cuffs as Fouad thumped them on the tablecloth. "I see. A very dangerous man, but worth one hundred million on the hoof! Marvelous!"

Fouad struggled to fight the drug.

Others came flocking, standing beside the riser and gawking, as Price had obviously intended. Fouad turned away and clutched the table, feeling ill. Somehow, Schmitz shooed the crowd back. "Mr. Price is going to offer better distractions soon," he said. "Please move on and give us some space."

Across the ballroom, a huge screen began to unfurl, initiating a sequence of screens dropping around the room, lighting up with images and text feeds from news organizations around the world. The sound was not yet above the music of the waltz and the dancers continued to spin and step and spin again.

Fouad felt he might be hallucinating. This all reminded him of something from his youth, a frightening story . . .

Axel Price strolled onto the oak floor, wearing a tailored denim suit and pointed black boots, his handsome but undistinguished face angled to take in the nearest screen and the world's teeming details.

Six more of Colonel Sir's crack Haitians flanked him and kept close watch, all heavily armed, gimbal harnesses supporting computer-controlled assault rifles. Formidable—and a matter of concern to the ten men near the wall, who might have been Russians.

The music softened. The crowds gathered and began to reluctantly mingle—Arabs with Indonesians, Chinese with Russians, Eastern Europeans with members of congress and the military in mufti—and Price's assembly became one, with Price at the center and the world arrayed in glowing walls around them.

Schmitz poked Fouad and he sat up straight, groggily surveying the crowd, the floor, the swirl of video feeds.

"This is it," Schmitz said.

The two Haitians began to fidget in expectation. One broke a big, almost boyish grin at Fouad, his teacher, a man he had been raised by his mama to respect but now must stand guard over—then dropped the grin back into sober contemplation.

Price held up his arms. "Thanks for traveling so far on such short notice, and apologies for not letting a whole bunch of you get some sleep. We're all up and about early this morning for a good reason," he said, his voice amplified throughout the ballroom.

On two of the screens, his image came up and the room briefly filled with a feedback whine. Guests laughed and tapped their ears, and he laughed along with them, then waved at the dancers, who had, mercifully, stopped their gyrations.

"Sorry to interrupt such a pretty show, but the moment has arrived. Years of opportunity, years of planning, to correct centuries of injustice and incompetence—of cruelty, greed, and spite, visited upon us by those who are now about to—"

A sound interrupted him—a single high-pitched musical note, totally out of place. At first the guests cringed, thinking the feedback had returned.

But the high note resolved into a jerking, mournful cry—a child weeping.

A young boy.

Price looked puzzled, then waved his hand angrily. Two of his Haitians staggered off to investigate, their weapons wide and awkward as they pushed through the crowd.

The crowd laughed again, as if the weird weeping had been planned—the world's cry of pain only appropriate, considering their coming triumph

On the biggest screen, a net media news banner announced a breaking story—blackouts.

A wave of power outages sends much of the northwest and Canada back to the Stone Age—

Video pans of dark streets, black skylines silhouetted against the morning glow.

"Apocalypse *now*, by God!" the elderly congressman enthused in a booming voice.

The Saudi prince took this opportunity to push his way onto the riser, his own retinue glaring a challenge at Schmitz and the Haitians.

Schmitz did not intervene.

The prince's eyes fixed on Fouad. His face was stony but his hands quivered. He stepped close and leaned over. Fouad angled his head back, taking in this looming presence with doped nonchalance, then a twitch of his brows, a slight bow of his head, to a prince of the ancient blood.

Speechless with fury, the Saudi struck him hard across the face with the back of his hand, and was about to do so again.

Schmitz moved in this time to block the blow—

The air changed, turning suddenly crisp and terribly dry.

Schmitz cried out, grabbed his arm, and reeled back. His Haitians did the same, along with the prince's retinue—clutching the same spot on their right arms, as if branded by hot, invisible pokers.

The dance floor erupted in howls of pain.

The ballroom lights flared an intolerable white, then sizzled out in cascades of sparks.

58

Judah P. Benjamin International Airport (JPB)

Bruised and battered, blood streaming from his scalp down the back of his neck, William crept along the northern edge of the highway, sometimes crawling, sometimes marching in a low, awkward crouch, always aware of the traffic both on the ground and in the air.

Limos, Torq-Vees, a steady stream of light trucks . . .

Drones hugging the terrain along the highway, keeping low to avoid incoming flights.

He had come within a few dozen yards of the airport's northern boundary, protected by a high wire fence, when a Gulfstream sighed in for a landing to his left, catching the sunrise, its fuselage a gorgeous flow of gold and salmon pink.

Almost simultaneously, west of the airport, a big twinkle in the sky went nova. From the bright center, flares spread out to form a five-pointed star, each point expanding into a spherical front of purple plasma.

The plasma spheres warped, twisted, and merged, in turn provoking an atmospheric outrage unlike anything William had ever seen—a shower of spinning, darting puffs of intermittent light spreading out over the Texas landscape.

The air above the desert began to crackle.

59

Over Lion County

The sun rested on the horizon, cut in half, before its final heave toward day. The sky visible through the jet's opposite windows seemed to briefly flicker, like a passing torch flame. Fore and aft, Rebecca heard light mechanical clicking, like fingers randomly working keyboards.

Haze's face beaded with sweat.

"Bright number one," the first weapons officer announced. "Five-minute burn."

Something about the aircraft interior changed—something about Rebecca's own skull, as well. The air seemed dryer. Sharp pains wormed and twisted in her jaw, her mandible: the fillings in her teeth were getting hot.

Kunsler grimaced and covered her mouth.

Haze let out a whoop and bent over.

The weapons officer swore and produced mouth pieces from a bag. "Jeez, sorry! Most of my guys—here, use these—like a boxer," he said.

Rebecca inserted the guard between her teeth and sat back, feeling the pains subside.

"Range increasing." The weapons officer watched the lights on his remote trigger. He looked back at Rebecca and Kunsler, opened his mouth, and tapped his eyetooth with a fingernail. "Younger guys have ceramic caps, not amalgam. Double apologies—it'll pass. Keep those guards in."

"We're taking that first one well, ladies and gentlemen," the pilot announced. "Last plane into JPB has made it to the runway and is coasting. Engines puffing and throwing out sparks. That's quite a show down there."

"Second burn in three minutes," the weapons officer said, eyes bright. Totally into it. "Runway looks clear for a landing—if that's the plan."

Kunsler looked to Rebecca.

The HRT commander gave her a high-five—his team was ready.

60

JPB

William toppled from his crouch and lay on his back in the dirt, looking sideways. From this perspective, he saw a handful of metallic discs spark and dance on the pea gravel and sand.

Something was pumping the ubiquitous Talos surveillance chips full of energy. As if in rowdy applause, a number of nearby bushes snapped into smoky torches.

Under his legs, several of the chips burned his skin. William hastily kicked them away, then looked around for a place where there were no chips—nothing to absorb the pulse from the sky and catch his pants on fire.

A big drone came spinning down and augured into the dirt barely a hundred and fifty yards away. Its load of ammunition immediately began to cook off like a hideous popcorn machine, a continuous rolling snap-snap-*wow* followed by singing whines, much too close to his head.

Then its Hellfire missiles blew, knocking William several yards back into the scrub and poking small shrapnel holes in his legs.

He rolled and stayed low, waiting for his senses to return, then felt for injuries with filthy fingers, poking through torn pants legs and shirt. Eventually he realized that he wasn't much worse off than he had been before.

He had been tossed into a comparatively parched and empty patch of ground, no bushes, so he rolled over to watch the show.

Thousands of fist-size spheres of blue-green plasma bounced like elfin jewelry along the desert contours, following their own sense of magnetic destiny.

Without knowing precisely what was happening, William began to laugh like a maniac. This seemed to disturb a line of sizzling spook-gems. They backed off in sincere resentment, glimmering, studying his energy and static profile, and then accepted the new way of things. A few flowed around him. One touched his knee, and another an out-crop of boulder.

Both popped like tiny balloons.

Brush fires had broken out all over the desert. Smoke was already thick.

William realized he couldn't just stick around and play the stunned audience. He got up, brushed himself off, and walked toward the air-port's wire fence, looking for a gate, a culvert, a water drainage pipe, some sort of entrance.

Somehow he guessed there wouldn't be much left in the way of a security presence. Axel Price had just provoked a federal response William did not even know was in their arsenal—

Non-nuclear electromagnetic pulse.

Another drifting star went nova and it started all over again.

61

The Smoky

The unrolled screens went black as one. Throughout the ballroom, more fixtures exploded and threw sparks down on the crowd— already dancing to another tune, not a waltz but a frantic thrashing accompanied by swinish squeals of pain.

Three hanging banners had caught fire. In the weird glow, Fouad saw Price grab his mouth and bend over double. His Haitians had thrown aside their weapons, which crackled and sparked on the polished oak floor. Despite their pain, as the guards twitched and groaned, they tried to move him from beneath the banners and out of the ballroom.

Price jerked straight and resisted.

Some of the guests had already left but dozens more were bowing, cursing, and screaming, bouncing into each other—cutting spastic orange figures against the darkness.

Schmitz could not help but be distracted.

Fouad had no idea what was happening but did not much care. He saw his moment. He had tracked which of Schmitz's two Haitians held the key to his cuffs and leg irons. Lifting his legs, twisting his shoulders, he leaned and gave the other Haitian a wobbling, half strength slam of his elbow just below the nose. The blow was not what he had hoped, but still firm enough to shove the man's nasal bones into his brain—unseen by the others.

The man made a sudden *mimp* and fell back.

Fouad went under the table, grabbed the key-bearing Haitian's legs—the one who had smiled broadest, apologetic about showing his former teacher a lack of respect—and pulled him down from his chair. Slipping his cuffed hands over the man's head, he broke his neck with a swift reverse spin—then rolled him like a sack of potatoes to present the right pants pocket.

Now came the difficult part. Hunching along the corpse, Fouad reached into the pocket with cuffs still on, fumbling. After a moment, fingers poking the dead man's inner thigh, he looped through a steel ring, pulled it out, and grasped the key—

Schmitz pushed aside the red cloth and leaped under the table. He tried to knock the key loose. They fought for a long, difficult moment, but Fouad had the advantage. He was still feeling the effects of the drug, but not in searing pain.

With the cloth held back by Schmitz's torso, light from the burning banners flickered over his thrashing arms, which smoked through melted holes in the sleeves just above the wrists. The smell filled the air.

Fouad curled and grabbed Schmitz's right arm, squeezing the burned flesh over the ID chip.

"God *damn* you!" Schmitz yelled. His head thumped the bottom of the table.

Fouad let go, jammed the key into the leg irons, and twisted. Then he pulled away from Schmitz in the other direction and inserted the key into the cuffs. The irons dropped loose but the cuffs only partially opened, then jammed—they felt hot.

The fight under the table turned frantic.

Fouad's foot came up and caught Schmitz under the jaw, a kick that might have killed him outright had the drugs not dampened Fouad's strength. Schmitz grunted and wrenched his leg around. Fouad grabbed Schmitz above the elbow, pressing back and making the soldier roll in that direction to break loose—then grabbed his wrist, stretched the arm out, and with his heel pressed as hard as he could against the adjacent ribs, pumped like a tiger again and again, his kicks moving from ribs to stomach.

The arm gave with a pop.

Schmitz was making little puffing shrieks but still would not quit.

Fouad's cuffs finally came loose. He reached down for the long steel chain. Schmitz desperately warded off the chain with his one good arm, breath whistling in his nose, grunting, legs flailing against the dead Haitian—

Fouad came around on Schmitz's left and wrapped the chain around his neck and then, like a crocodile spinning in the water, twisted and twisted and looped and twisted again until they both emerged from beneath the table, pulling down the red cloth, and rolled off the riser, landing with a heavy thud on the oak floor.

Schmitz clutched and clawed at Fouad's hands, reached up and poked a thumb into one eye, then stuck it in one corner of Fouad's mouth and yanked.

Fouad bit down.

Schmit pulled out his fingers and grabbed feebly for Fouad's head. Everything was coated in sweat and blood—he could not find purchase.

In the flame-lit shadows of the ballroom, over the next few minutes— that awful interval of an adversary's final time in this world—Schmitz's arms fell.

He stopped struggling, stopped breathing.

His muscles relaxed.

Fouad regretfully twisted Schmitz's head on the limp neck until the vertebrae parted, just to be certain, then shoved himself to his feet and staggered to the middle of the dance floor. He was covered in blood and saliva, half blind from the thumb gouge in one eye—muscles stretched to their limits.

He knocked aside a staggering Chinese man and drew a welcome whoop of breath.

Still alive!

Allah would forgive all—he was still alive.

And now the time of Mr. Price was come.

62

Over Lion County

"Bright number three away," the first weapons officer announced. "Two-minute burn."

"Look at *that*," Daniel Haze said in awe as he stared through the window by his seat.

The ground around the Talos Campus—the landscape for at least twenty miles in all directions—was marked with the great, hashed brushstrokes of sooty fires—clearly revealing the criss-cross dispersal patterns of the aircraft that had years ago dropped Talos's ground-sensor chips.

Wherever the chips had fallen, they had absorbed energy from the expanding plasma pulse and conveyed it to the local flora.

At least ten thousand acres were ablaze. The fires were slowly merging into one great conflagration, with the Smoky, the Talos Campus, and the airport at three points of a triangle inside the burn.

"Looks like all the Talos drones are down," the pilot said. "I don't see anything flying."

Rebecca removed the mouth guard and felt her jaw, wondering if the heat had cracked a couple of molars. She should have had that amalgam drilled out years ago.

"We go down—what are the chances they'll shoot at us?" Kunsler asked.

"Their firearm ID chips are fried," the weapons officer said. "If what we were told about Talos armory rules is true, I don't think they'll be shooting at us for a while. The more high-tech they are, the harder they fall."

"They could keep unchipped guns for an emergency," Rebecca said, considering their options carefully—about to make her major decision.

"They're still feeling a world of hurt," the weapons officer said. "Our best-trained special ops take twenty or thirty minutes to recover from a Bright, if they're chipped. Burns like a sonofabitch. Some of the older model chips burn right through the skin and set clothes on fire."

"Tower systems are dead," the second officer said, coming back from the cockpit. "They have no way of knowing who we are, except by visual—and this plane is stealthy and can hide its markings. We disperse our heat. We should be ghosty even if they still have operational radar and IR—which they don't."

Haze and Kunsler looked at each other across the plane's narrow aisle, nervously awaiting Rebecca's decision.

Kunsler had never engaged in an actual combat landing before.

"If we land now," Haze said, "confusion and smoke will provide excellent cover. "We can't delay. Price's soldiers are disciplined. They'll regroup quickly, I think—and they'll find some way to arm themselves."

"I told William Griffin to get to the airport," Kunsler said. "If he's managed to connect with Nabokov—with Fouad—then they'll be looking for us. But that seems less and less likely."

"Last FLIR images show their escape vehicle blown off the road," Haze said. "One agent killed in the brush . . . Two released west of our strike zone. They're off in the desert somewhere by now, if they weren't captured or shot."

"One ejected," Kunsler said hopefully.

"That's a maybe. Could be flaming debris—or a burning body."

Rebecca felt the plane bank right. The pilot was preparing for a landing—or another pass. He had looked over the runways—two, in parallel, with taxiways and a third small plane strip arranged like a wobbly X in the desert, about two miles beyond the Talos campus.

The Smoky—where most of the guests and Price were likely to be located, as well as Fouad—lay northwest of the line between the campus and the airport.

Her own senses seemed sharp. Her visual field was still expanded, still intensely detailed, still showing weird patches of color—useful or not, who could tell?

Her ears sang sweetly. She felt a nervous jangle throughout her torso and legs, but that could have been nerves, excitement, anything.

All that she was, she was not *afraid*.

She felt strong.

To hell with spreading new wings. She could arrange for all that later, at her leisure. Life had not cut her any slack before now.

Maybe it was time to get her work done and force the issue in a better direction—

After all, she had always wanted to make the world a better place, and now she was being given a unique opportunity to do just that.

"Land this plane," she said. "Commander, gather up your weapons and alert the team."

63

The Smoky

Fouad maneuvered carefully between stumbling, disoriented guests, through the door taken by Price and his guards as they evacuated the ballroom—down a curving external hallway to the outdoors.

They all seemed to be living through an Edgar Allan Poe horror story—"The Masque of the Red Death." He had read Poe with guilty pleasure in grade school, in poor Arabic, better than nothing—but the vivid pictures remained, and now the mummers, the dancers, the guests, were in complete confusion, the world turned on its head, those who should be dead walking amongst them through darkness and smoke and pain . . .

Fouad picked up his pace after he left the ballroom and angled to the left, under drifting smoke, around the kitchens and dining areas. He avoided a few knots of wandering Haitian troops, who seemed to have lost all sense of cohesion and discipline.

They might have been well-trained, but the strike of a deadly invisible god reaching down and burning their flesh . . . Stopping their assault rifles and pistols from working (none carried guns now, and the ground was littered with expensive weapons—Fouad did not bother to pick them up)—

That had evoked an old, deep fear.

Three Torq-Vees squatted abandoned around the corner of the employee kitchen complex. Nearby, on the gravel employee lot, several small cars stood empty with doors open.

One old hybrid still had a driver, a young woman in cleaning staff whites who was stubbornly trying to switch on the electric motor, which did nothing—not even whir.

The volume of smoke increased. The air filled with whirls of ash. A foul wind began to rise, bitter with the corrosive stink of burning brush.

Fouad suspected there were no working aircraft or modern vehicles within many miles. The one place that might contain vehicles that could survive an electromagnetic pulse—that was what had happened, he was sure of it—would be old cars and trucks, cars without alarms or security systems or black boxes or complex electronics— cars with simple carburetors, where electricity only flowed if ignitions were switched on.

Cars that could recover well, if not completely, from a hot flash of radiated energy.

Classic cars.

Price kept a warehouse full of very expensive classic cars about a hundred yards from the ballroom, near the far end of the Smoky, where he sometimes took them out on a fenced oval track.

Price would no doubt gather up his family as quickly as possible and drive as far away as he could. Loyal staff would stay with them— they would use knives or whatever came to hand. Price could conceivably equip them with classic firearms.

Fouad needed to find Price before he had a full complement of guards effectively armed and in some sort of order—and before he reached his family.

He broke into a loose run, ignoring the shadowed vision in one eye, the spiking pain in one leg, and his ripped lips where Schmitz had thrust a forefinger to bring his head around—before Fouad had nearly bitten that finger off.

The crunch of the man's knuckle under his teeth remained fresh in his mind, an awfulness that would require much prayer to expunge.

He saw the garage, a long barn-like structure, the humped roof set on high concrete walls and studded with air conditioners and rotating steel vents.

Nearby, striding in that direction, a tight group of six men, two walking at a pace of protected if hurried dignity—in confident expectation of that nearby safety and security accorded only to the wealthy—and to royalty—

And four in black, two carrying long knives, two more carrying what might have been spears.

One of the four was Price.

Another was the Saudi prince who had slapped Fouad—him! Slapped a man worth a hundred million euros.

Fouad hung back for a moment—then looked into the open rear doors of an abandoned Torq-Vee. In the rear cabin, behind the parallel seats, four poleaxes were racked on metal loops—three on one side, one on the other. Each six-foot fiberglass shaft sported a razor-sharp ax and spear point on the business end and a steel point on the butt.

This was what two of the men accompanying Price had chosen for armament—sensibly enough. Fouad had no idea how they were ordinarily used—perhaps for cutting brush or as a particularly vicious form of crowd control. But he certainly knew how to use one. He had taught his Janissaries with similarly effective and simple weapons back at Incirlik airbase.

He yanked one down, hefted it, balanced it on a finger—found its center of gravity—then grabbed it in midair in both hands and followed the six toward the garage.

64

JPB

The swanjet landed with a series of bumps in the wind-blown haze, then braked and veered sharp left. Rebecca had moved forward to be with the HRT. They helped her don body armor, then prepared their weapons, reconnecting the team electronics and Lynx.

The last of her fashion accoutrements was the command-grade helmet, big and black and covered with cameras and visors and other stuff she had no idea how to use.

"Don't worry about it," Forester, said. "It's all pretty automatic. Just pull down whatever looks right and slip it over your eyes."

"Make sure it still works," his second in command warned, and they ran quick tests before the plane lurched nose-down to an abrupt stop.

"We're clear—no hostiles in range," the pilot said through the open cockpit door.

"*Currahee!*" Forester cried. "Me and my brothers and sister, we stand alone!"

Before she knew it, the plane's door had dropped and Rebecca was on the runway, following the five HRT agents at an ankle-jarring clip toward an abandoned Torq-Vee.

Pain did not matter.

Smoke covered much of the airport and the runway.

Forester pulled open the Torq-Vee's passenger-side door and hauled the black box inside, then sprung it open and pulled out a gray and black unit the size and shape of a toaster.

The youngest team member popped open the hood and rummaged in the engine compartment with yet another replacement component.

In three minutes, they had the Torq-Vee convinced it was operational. The engine roared to life. They all climbed in.

Forester showed her how to pull down and snick her combat gogs. Maps of the airport, the Talos campus, and the ranch popped up, downloaded from a satellite.

"What would we ever do without this shit?" the second-in-command marveled.

"Cavemen!" the team grunted as one and thrust their gloved fists in the air.

"Braves, you mean," Forester corrected. "Where to, ma'am?"

Rebecca pointed her gloved fist northeast. Fouad was last seen at the ranch. Who knew where William Griffin might be, if he was still alive?

"Jeez," one of the agents commented as they rolled. "They got pole-axes back here—wonder if they know how to use 'em?"

"I do," Forester said. "Back in medieval times, they taught peasants how to kill knights with those things."

65

The six men first noticed Fouad as the wind momentarily blew aside the smoke. The two with knives—not Haitians, Fouad saw, but beefy Middle Easterners, part of the prince's innermost protection team—broke left and right to flank him, while the others hung back.

The flanking pair assumed combat stance to test his revolve. They were going to do this the old-fashioned way and engage in hand-to-hand.

That was not his plan. He had neither the desire nor the patience.

Fouad came in spinning the poleax, dropping to one knee and swinging in a wide arc. The double-edged ax cut through the first man's boot and ankle and nearly severed his leg.

From his knee, Fouad lifted and thrust the ax blade past the man's throat, then pulled it back with a reverse cut. The man managed a breathy gurgle before he died.

The second guard fell over the body trying get out of the way. He did not fall fast enough to miss another series of thrusts and cuts—first from the side, incapacitating his knife hand, followed by a double-handed downswing splitting his skull.

Fouad jerked out the ax.

He looked up and sucked in smoky air.

Price and the Saudi prince were making a desperate dash for the garage. Their pace was no longer stately, privileged, or royal—they were in terror for their lives.

The last two guards, Americans attached to Price, moved in, brandishing their poleaxes like novices. Born of a gun culture, no doubt—in love with loud noises and gunpowder and not at all happy with blades.

Fouad was up again, jabbing and feinting.

The three formed a circle, poleaxes inward, almost tip to tip. The man on his right stepped forward and made his own jab, long and off-balance.

Fouad again leaped aside and brought his ax down. The first American's gripping hand flew off and his poleax dropped to the dirt and double-bounced, singing.

Fouad speared his upper leg, then sliced again as the guard dropped and rolled—his roll slowing and eyes glazing, lips turning blue, as he bled out from his femoral artery.

The second American leaped toward Fouad, eyes wild. This man handled his weapon better, keeping Fouad back with balanced, measured thrusts—then tried to hook his leg with the ax.

Fouad jumped left and brought his ax down. The man parried with an outward blow, hooked Fouad's shaft, twisted it, then grabbed and pulled it toward him until Fouad let go. This close, the poleax was of no use. Fouad seized the man's arm before he could again double-grip his weapon.

With a push of the guard's elbow Fouad shoved in face to face, caught the sweat slinging from the man's forehead—tasted its salt in his mouth—and used his two-inch height advantage to straighten, lift, and hard-jerk the arm up and sideways.

Not enough to break it, but Fouad's foot went behind him and the man tripped and landed on his back.

Fouad spun him on the ground and as he struggled, retrieved one of the crossed poleaxes and neatly removed his head.

A moment and no more to catch his breath.

The killing made him angrier and angrier, that he had to do such things because men were filled with arrogant greed, because some wished to rule with neither the wit nor the self-knowledge to see their inadequacies—and how many of their people would die.

Fouad followed the fleeing pair, poleax held before him, pacing himself: one-eyed, lip split wide, face swollen and smudged and dripping blood, an awful *ifrit* in pursuit.

He had to plan his moves carefully, not to be lost in fight-heat and regret it later.

They should not get away to regroup their wealth and power and try this again.

Killing them . . . perhaps necessary.

If there was no alternative.

66

The Smoky

The Torq-Vee took Rebecca's team down a short road to the ranch complex.

Forester pulled up in front of the main house. Staff dressed in white uniforms and a few older men in dirty, torn suits wandered down the steps and across a section of knee-high prairie grass, all half blind from smoke.

"Little people and a few humps, I think," Forester said.

"Humps?"

"Perps. Bad guys."

"Right. Forget them. Let's check out the ballroom," Rebecca said, consulting the map in her gogs.

She pointed and Forester turned the Torq-Vee about, making a counterclockwise circle.

"Along the way," she said, "We need to check out the bungalows and see if they have any of our people tied up or stashed."

Forester coasted the Torq-Vee along the guest roundabout. Three of the team worked in unison to search each of the bungalows. The three came back at the end of the circuit, shook their heads, and climbed aboard.

"Place is a mess," one said. "Two old dudes dead in their bathrooms. Looks like their heads exploded. What's that—brain chips or something?"

"Could be implants to control palsy. God forgive them," Forester said.

"I think one of them might be a congressman or something. He looked familiar."

"There's a garage up ahead," Rebecca said. "Could have vintage vehicles that still run."

"My thinking exactly," Forester said.

"Aston Martin! Ferrari! Jaguar XKE!" the youngest of the team enthused. "Spoils of war?"

"You wish," Forester said. "We can't afford the gas."

"For a day, I could."

To Rebecca, they all seemed little more than boys.

Rebecca watched the big garage grow close. Again, three of the team prepared to leap out and do reconnaissance.

"Squad on our right, waving," Forester said. "They seem to think we're with them."

"Colonel Sir's Haitians," the youngest guessed.

"Do we confront and subdue?" Forester asked.

"No," Rebecca said. "Go right, to the other end of the garage. I'll go in with you."

"Yes, ma'am," Forester said.

The wooden doors hung open, electronic locks sprung.

They climbed out of the Torq-Vee, leaving the youngest—against his wishes—to guard their ride.

Inside, three aisles passed between what might have been a truly beautiful selection of antique cars and trucks—but the lights were out and they saw little more than glimmers in deep shadow. Rebecca walked halfway down the garage's length, listening while the team ran down the aisles, then circled back.

"No gaps in the vintage parade, nothing obviously missing," Forester reported.

She gestured for a return to the Torq-Vee.

Just as she was about to shut the door, she glanced back and saw a woman standing in the dark at the far end, a diminutive, slender figure in white carrying a single candle. Three young children clutched her long dress. Rebecca thought there might two more farther back, standing in a doorway—outlined in faintly glowing pink.

She closed her eyes for a moment and the effect went away.

"You took my husband!" the woman shouted down the length of the building. "That awful man grabbed him from right in front of us! Where is he?"

The Haitians chose that moment to enter from the far end. They surrounded the woman and her children, carrying their own candles and boldly, loudly brandishing rifles and pistols.

All of them looked terrified, lost, desperate.

Rebecca let the door swing shut and climbed back into the Torq-Vee.

"Mrs. Price, I think," she said to Forester. "No sign of our people. One more circuit—avoid crowds. Then back to the airport."

67

JPB

Across the taxiway, two smudged, bloody figures limped through a hellish nightmare of crackling, burning luxury jets, crashed or rolled maintenance carts, abandoned fuel trucks—mercifully intact—and the last confused, wandering minions of Axel Price's empire.

These remaining few had used whatever they could find to cut out the source of their pain. All trailed blood and wove random tracks over the tarmac, like rabbits and deer after a brush fire. They presented no menace.

As if homing toward each other—recognizing friend amid dazed foes—the two men trekked across the main runway, William waving Fouad on, Fouad waving in turn, until they met under the orange-smudged sun.

Fouad laid down his poleax.

William lifted him off his feet and spun him around on the concrete.

"Mr. Nabokov, I presume?" he said, putting him down.

"Mr. Griff, it is excellent to see you, after all this time," Fouad said.

"That's my father's name," William said, hanging back from their hug.

"Yes," Fouad said. "The cub is now the lion. But tell me—how is it you come to be here, on this of all days?"

"Later. Let's find some water," William said.

"Absolutely. It is parched out here."

"What happened?" William asked as they walked back toward the airport buildings.

"I have only a small idea," Fouad said.

"Did you arrange for this?" William asked.

"No. Did you?"

A Torq-Vee came rolling through the smoke, around two disabled airport maintenance trucks.

The passenger door flung open and a woman in black body armor stood on the running board. She whipped off her combat helmet and waved vigorously.

"Who is that?" Fouad asked, wiping his one good eye to see more clearly.

"Rebecca Rose," William said. "I think she's offering us a ride."

"Our own Rebecca Rose? Will she have water?"

"Probably."

The Torq-Vee stopped ten yards from Fouad and William and four men in black armor jumped out to surround them, weapons ready.

"Stand down!" Rebecca called. "Is that you, William?"

"Yes, ma'am!" William called back.

Forester held up a gloved hand and called for a medical kit.

"Fouad? I hardly recognize you."

Fouad could not bring himself to speak.

"We're meeting Jane Rowland at Buckeye," Rebecca said. "Can you show us where that is?"

Fouad pointed in the general direction of the campus.

"Climb aboard, gentlemen," Rebecca said. "Buckeye apparently has a hardened server farm. We've been told to take it out, and then get the hell out of Texas."

William and Forester took hold of Fouad and guided him to the Torq-Vee, where the team offered bottled water and began to administer first aid.

68

Corpus Christi

Nathaniel pulled a chair into the focus of the projector and sat watching as MSARC went deaf, dumb, and blind. The lines of code and floating symbols announcing his success—or Jones's success, more appropriately—were suddenly interrupted by straight ASCII.

Is that you, Jones?

Nathaniel watched for a moment as the old-fashioned cursor blinked and another message wrote over the old one.

Who is this?

No harm in replying.

Not Jones. Who is this?

And then,

Tom Cantor. Do I know you?

Nathaniel responded,

We met at MIT ten years ago. How's tricks?

CANT> *Won't do any good to complain. You must be Nathaniel. Becky Thatcher says hi.*

NATH> *Hi back.*

CANT> *We're knocking out Talos business and bank records.*

NATH> *Me too.*

CANT> *Did you get the backups in Dubai and Iron Mountain?*

NATH> *They're wiped, all but the offline memory. That will go the next time somebody tries to access.*

CANT> *Mr. Price is going to have to start from scratch—wherever he is.*

NATH> *OK*

CANT> *You should vacate pronto.*

NATH> *You too.*

CANT> *30 on all bad guys. We'll be watching. That means* you, *genius boy. Say hi to Jones. Outta here.*

NATH> *Copy that.*

Nathaniel shut down the projector and sealed off his portals. He closed the heavy door behind him, cinched up his tie, and waited for the elevator.

Carlos was watching the news on his desk monitor and barely looked up as Nathaniel passed. Then he jumped and checked him out as if seeing him for the first time.

Nathaniel shook his head. "Lots of shit going down," he said.

"Sure as hell is," Carlos said. "What's it all about, do you think?"

"Some kind of weird weather," Nathaniel said.

He was in the Bentley and driving away when the Vertexion building's external alarms went off and steel shutters began to fall over the big windows.

Carlos was going to lose his job.

Nathaniel turned left and drove along the beach, studying the ragged front.

Definitely heading east.

69

El Paso

Jamey and Curteze walked like two ragged beggars along the lines of stalled cars and their puzzled, impatient passengers waiting to cross into Juarez.

The cars weren't going anywhere soon, perhaps ever; the offices and the security gates were dark, El Paso was quiet, and Juarez was equally quiet, but for sporadic gunfire and shouts.

The boy was no longer a boy, and Curteze had no idea who or what *he* was—only that their walk was almost over, the job almost done.

Jamey turned around between the lanes of cars and watched Curteze patiently as he caught up.

"Want to do this together?" Jamey asked.

"Turn ourselves in?" Curteze asked.

"Whatever it takes."

"Sure," Curteze said.

"I wanted to thank all of you," Jamey said. "Wish I could, now."

"We were idiots."

"Still . . ."

A few border security officers were trying to keep order in the lanes despite dead radios, fused spex, down Lynx networks, and no power anywhere.

"One of *them* should do," Curteze said, and prepared to flash his sparks—reveal that he was an agent, whatever that might mean in this part of the world.

"Am I your prisoner?" Jamey asked, staying close. "I mean, I don't want to get shot just because somebody's confused."

"You're nobody's fucking prisoner," Curteze said. "Once we're across, call your daddy and tell him to pick you up in New Mexico. And then—we're done. You're a free man. You don't ever want to see me again, right?"

Jamey wiped his eyes with the back of his hand, then agreed with a nod.

They both straightened at the approach of a tall officer with thick, spiky, black hair. The officer looked sure and confident, even in the chaos, as if he was the man in charge—and he was drawing a visual bead on Jamey and Curteze because they were filthy and bloody and did not look at all like tourists.

"Help you two with something?" he asked, then stopped dead and stared. "Jesus Christ," he said. "Jamey Trues. I got people searching all over the desert for you. Welcome home, boy. My name's Mason."

"Can we get across to New Mexico, Mr. Mason?" Jamey asked. "As soon as it's convenient."

"Right. Follow me. Are you Kapp or Curteze?" Mason asked the dusty man in the denims and work shirt, noting the tissue and blood on his shoulder.

"Curteze," came the muttered reply. He remembered to lift his credentials. "Special Agent Kapp is dead. They blew his head off, the bastards."

"Either of you know what the hell happened around here?" Mason asked.

The two shook their heads.

"Not a fucking clue," Curteze said. "You?"

One Year After

70

Pensacola Beach, Florida

Rebecca Rose picked a picture window seat in the long, flat, air-conditioned Fisherman's Shelter Inn, and started with a big stoneware bowl of thick, white clam chowder and seven bags of oyster crackers—twenty crackers per bag, one with twenty-two—plus a red plastic basket carrying seven slices of fresh baguette.

Then she moved on to a huge salad—crab Louie with avocado halves and six spears of steamed asparagus and two hard-boiled eggs.

Everything tasted unbelievably wonderful—as if she had never truly used her taste buds before now.

She had been stripped of all that she owned and faced at least half a dozen warrants for her arrest and detention. She was on the run, sought by state and federal authorities from Maryland to Texas, alleged by the Raphkind administration's newly appointed attorney general to be part of a vast domestic terrorist conspiracy to bring down the nation's power grid.

Life had never been better.

Wearing a purple two-piece swimsuit under a white net cover, canvas boat shoes printed with cartoon flowers—tanned, hair almost strawberry from sun and salt—Rebecca looked like a surfer girl who did not know how to grow up. That was what she wanted and needed right now.

She felt like a teenager and she had the broken arm to prove it—from surfing a big surge wave with far too much confidence in her not-so-young bones.

The flexible blue cast on her left arm was alive with shifting patterns and drawings—paisley curlicues, constellations, sunbursts, and smiling moons. She would be losing the cast in a week and thought she might miss it.

She did not resemble in the least the former FBI agent featured on news shows, the web, and plastered on wanted posters in every sheriff's office on the Gulf Coast—along with a handful of nefarious accomplices.

Alicia Kunsler was locked up in Cumberland, perhaps in the same cell once occupied by Edward Quinn. Daniel Haze, former director of the Secret Service, was rumored to be either dead—a suicide—or living in Chile.

Rebecca thought the latter was more likely.

Most of the cabinet members of the former administration were under house arrest. Their indictments and trial dates might never arrive. The whole story would likely collapse within a year—with unpredictable repercussions for President Raphkind, who was said to be neither a nice man nor a happy one.

Fouad Al-Husam and William Griffin were rumored to be in Singapore—perhaps following a trail. Whether or not they had remained in the Bureau and become witnesses for the government, no one could say.

Jane Rowland could have cleared them all. But of course Jane Rowland could not say a word. Her agency did not exist.

Tom Cantor also did not exist.

Little Jamey Trues met his family in New Mexico, which refused to extradite him back to Texas. Four months later, the governor of Texas was impeached and removed from office.

Half of the staff of the Texas Department of Corrections—along with the entire sheriff's department of Lion County—was relieved of duty.

Surprise, surprise—Axel Price and his large family had turned up six months ago in the Dominican Republic, to be warmly greeted by Colonel Sir John Yardley. Like the Saudi prince, Price reportedly sported two deep, unsightly scars, one on each cheek—and was said to be broken both physically and psychologically, perhaps because he had no idea where his fortune had gone, and so no idea what he was going to do next.

Fouad had never said a word about his actions at the Smoky. But to Rebecca he had murmured, on the flight back to Maryland, "Bad kings kill the land."

After several days of gray, wet weather, the Florida sun had this afternoon returned to its powerful conviction that the Earth was not nearly warm enough. Its brazen light was as extraordinary as the food. The parking lot reflected a hot metal glow on her face, but she barely squinted.

Rebecca dabbed the second half of a hard-boiled egg in the pinkish dressing—rich with chunks of green olive—and watched storm-driven combers roar up onto the beach, throwing golden spray almost as high as the fishing pier.

The long drought was over. One after another, powerful hurricanes were pushing up from the gulf into Texas and Mexico, bringing muddy floods to Lion County, El Paso, and Juarez.

Excellent surfing, the best the locals had ever seen.

The waitress approached and Rebecca lifted her dessert menu as if to block the glare, but in fact she was covering the woman's face. Faces were too intense even now—she read too much into them, did not know how to stop her infinitely detailed interpretation of the twists and tics of so many muscles.

She had as hard a time with faces as she did with utter darkness. Darkness terrified her—and that was only one reason why she loved it.

She took joy in being scared.

Rootless.

Nascent.

Still, she preferred daytime, wide white beaches, hot sun. And until yesterday, she had preferred to be alone.

Soon she would conquer both faces and darkness and society. She would come out of her cocoon and spread her wings, fully human again and stronger than ever.

Dr. Plover, the third time around, had finally gotten it mostly right—if you allowed for a long latency.

And some interesting new wrinkles.

The waitress asked her what she wanted for dessert.

"Key lime pie," Rebecca said. "And malt vinegar."

"For the pie?"

"Just bring it," Rebecca answered curtly.

"Sure thing, hon. Coffee with that?"

Rebecca smiled behind the menu, her eyes crinkling.

"No, thank you . . . hon," she said.

Vinegar acted on her much like coffee—which she could no longer drink. Vinegar was the new caffeine. Caffeine was the new cause of severe migraine headaches.

"Right." The waitress departed and Rebecca faced the sun again.

A man she did not know moved over from the bar, casually stopped by her table, and leaned in too close. "Waiting for someone?" he asked. In his thirties, sunburned, puffy from drink and worry, wearing a pink golf shirt and white slacks, he was from central Ohio, very likely on vacation from a recent divorce.

All this from the corner of her eye.

"Yes, I am," she said.

"Well, I'll be back if he doesn't show."

Rebecca forced herself to look the man full in the face. She lifted her upper lip, revealing eyeteeth, and blinked, eyes wide and green and pale, like a baby's.

Then she reached down for the black fiberglass cane with the shining steel head parked between her knees. Twirled it with two fingers.

The puffy, sunburned man backed away as if stung, bumping into a table. He quickly paid his check and left the restaurant, but not before muttering something to the waitress.

She brought Rebecca her Key lime pie and Heinz malt vinegar in a dribble-top bottle. "Man, I need what you got. Can you teach me that trick?"

Rebecca shook her head. "Comes with baggage," she said.

She paid her bill just as the metallic blue Bentley drove into the parking lot, top down.

The waitress gawped. "Jesus, what's that kind of car cost? Where does he drive it, to the grocery—to the beach?"

To Brazil, Rebecca thought.

Nathaniel came into the restaurant and stood by the antique brass cash register. With a big grin, he hoisted a cardboard sign with three words lettered in thick black marker: "Jones Motor Tours."

Rebecca picked up her cloth sling bag—all she had in the world, plus the cane—and walked over to take his arm.

They had not seen each other in a year.

They hardly knew each other.

The waitress gawped some more, lost in her dreams, then smiled broadly and silently applauded Rebecca.

Nathaniel led Rebecca to the parking lot and opened the Bentley's door.

"She's going to remember this," Rebecca said as he pushed the starter button and the Bentley purred to powerful life. "Can we be a little less obvious from now on?"

"Of course," Nathaniel said. "How's the cosmic mind?"

"Coming along," Rebecca said. "Killed anybody yet?"

"No," Nathaniel said. "Well, actually—I found Jerry Lee in New Mexico."

"Oh," Rebecca said.

"He was in a bad way. Not really a human being any more. I did him a mercy. There's still a couple of hundred of us out there . . . Could go either way, I guess. Not much I can do about them."

"What did Jones think?"

"Jones doesn't communicate with me anymore."

"Still working?"

"Who knows?" Nathaniel said. "Let's just say he was feeling generous. Mr. Price's money has been placed at your disposal."

"My disposal? Not yours?"

"I'm not sure Jones trusts me. We're too much alike."

The Bentley's warm, cream leather heated her skin as they drove northwest along the Bayfront Parkway toward Pensacola.

"How long do we have, really?" Rebecca asked Nathaniel.

"What, until we can't stand each other, or we find something useful to do—or until we run out of money?"

"Any of those," she said.

"A day, a week, a thousand years."

"Which shall it be—good or evil?"

"More good would be interesting," Nathaniel said. "But it's really up to you."

"Jones trusts me?"

"He trusts you to keep things lively."

Lightly, cautiously, like a shy adolescent, Nathaniel touched her arm. Rebecca withdrew it, then relaxed. Creamy leather everywhere and rich wood and the wind rushing by, hardly touching her hair. It was okay. The bad stuff was over.

This time, it hardly left a mark.

She reached out and grasped his hand, squeezing it tight.

The sun vanished below the horizon with tropical haste. There was no green flash.

There should have been.

The world was that new.